# RECORDS OF THE ORDERS

I

# The Omens of War

LIVIA J. ELLIOT

*To C. because the love you gave me was larger than life.*

# Contents

Before you read, please note that my **flavour** of English is Australian. I **apologise** to everyone in advance. Please don't be concerned if you **realise** something is wrong, or think I've committed an **offence**. Who knows, you may even get used to it while **travelling** through the pages.

"Oh, no!" Someone may exclaim, but rest assured, the quotes remain **double**… at least when someone speaks aloud.

*"There are many secrets in these pages…"* Someone may hand-signal or gesture (using double quotes), and then think without quotes: *Just thinking, hopefully in privacy.*

Finally, alchemists mind-whisper with single-quotes, *'Speaking directly into someone's mind.'*

Also, shall frontiers and places seem unreachable, you may enquire the **Map** disclosed after Chapters 1 (Global) and 3 (Regional).

That said, I'm **honoured** that you're interested in my work, and hope you'll enjoy it.

*Livia, a writer with Aussie grammar.*

This is a dark and psychological book. The violence is thematic, not exploitative; the horror is existential, not voyeuristic.

You will find scenes of physical and verbal violence against children, depictions of cPTSD and PTSD flashbacks (fire related), descriptions of blood, gore, severe burns, strokes, wound suturing. There are discussions implying autopsies and their findings, but these are neither graphic nor explicit.

You WILL **NOT** FIND mentions of gender or racial discrimination, and neither of sexual abuse—not on the page, and neither implied. That boundary is deliberate.

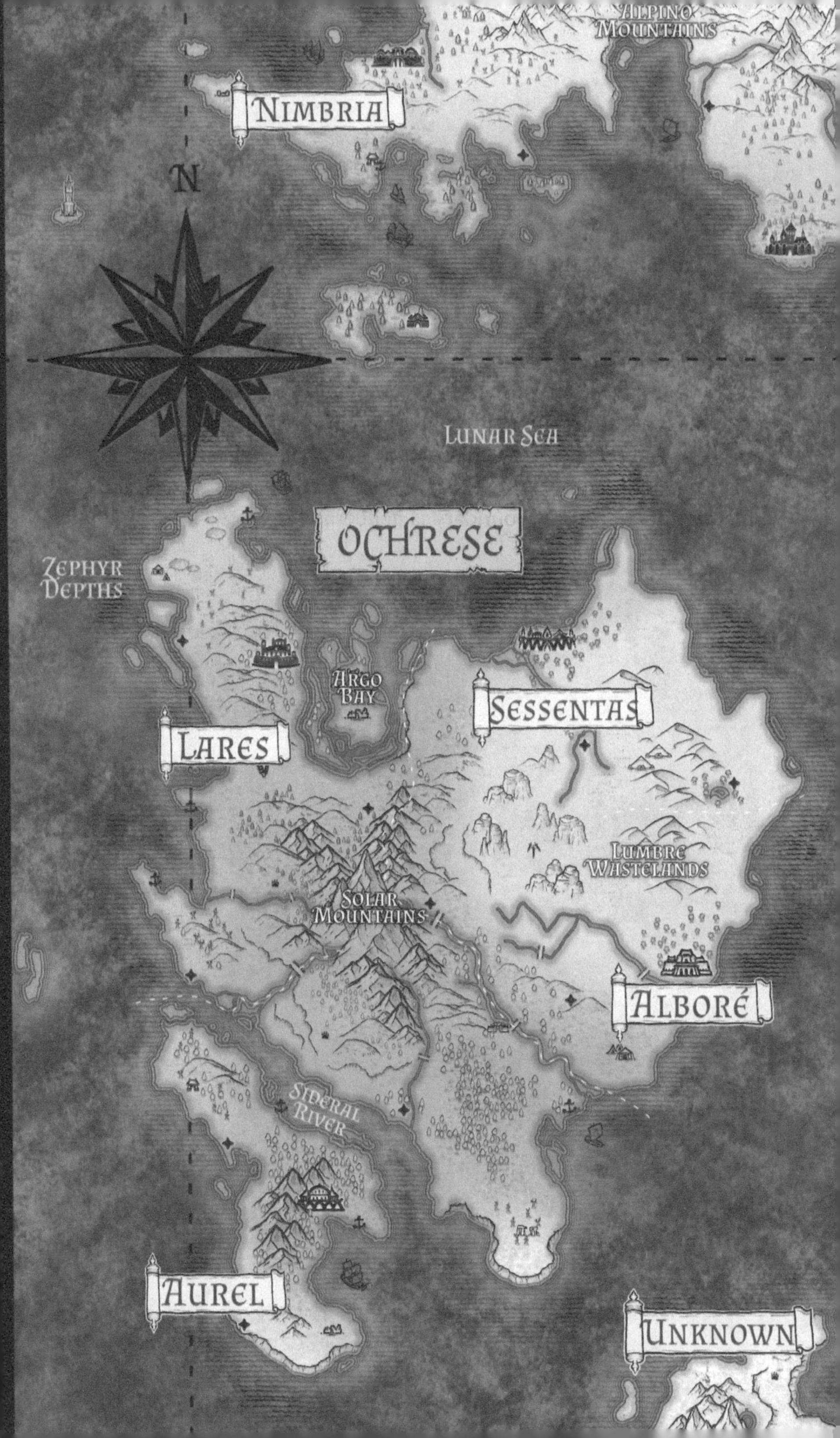

ALPINO MOUNTAINS
NIMBRIA
N
LUNAR SEA
ZEPHYR DEPTHS
OCHRESE
ARGO BAY
SESSENTAS
LARES
LUMBRE WASTELANDS
SOLAR MOUNTAINS
ALBORÉ
SIDERAL RIVER
AUREL
UNKNOWN

Vesperia
Verdant
Orenos
Sestel
Volátil Sea
Zafiro Gulf
Firard
Umbra
Peaks of Nadir
Ferro Keep
Arborum
Egon Hold
Sanguine Sea
Efímero Sea
Presya

# The Towers

## Somewhere, Somewhen

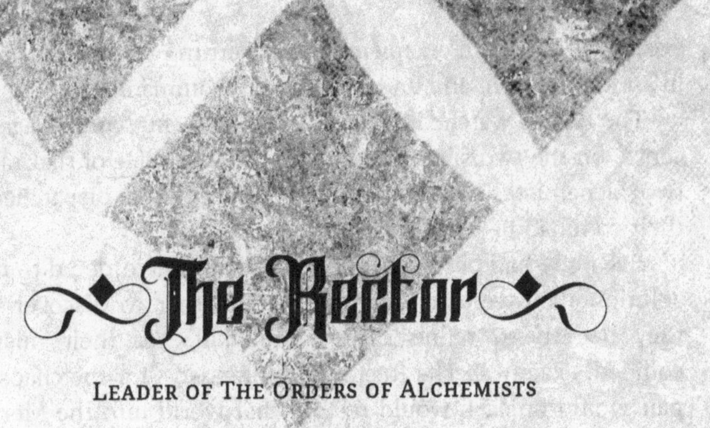

# The Rector

The future was the vast unknown—an elusive mirage, an unreachable destination, a pathway that reshaped itself while being traced. It existed beyond the horizon of certainty, teasing the rim of knowledge to demand more, more, *more*. More wisdom to grasp its shifting form, more wonder to bridge the gap between possibility and reality, more will to step forward despite the unknown.

To any alchemist, the future was a state of the universe itself.

To The Rector, the only alchemist with the four transfigurations—Soul, Matter, Protean, Machina—the future was but a simple concept. A state to be crafted through the curation of events, purposefully guiding individuals to converge, collide, coalesce and thus enable the pursuit of knowledge.

Amidst nowhere and nowhen, they raised an arm, and the scimitar hovering alongside it pierced the threshold of reality.

It rippled, silent, spirals twisting like rings, the abyssal nothingness beneath whirling alongside the clouds to hurry a morning zephyr. The wisps hushed, translucent at the dawn of two silver suns, mere blurs amidst a mistwoven lilac firmament. As The Rector moved that living image, a mountain range dawned into view, its peaks slashing into the sky, its shadows sinking in the ravine that halved it so purposefully. A fortress guarded its western entrance, its enclosure suffocated with an excess of troops; an enemy army was settling on its eastern exit, in another nation, and under a different command.

The Rector watched the scene, spinning the scimitar again to centre on the two silhouettes perched at the edge of that ravine: two alchemists, glamoured to invisibility, and dispatched on their command.

Each one had been sent for a purpose—one ordered to find a solution they weren't looking for, the other to discover what they needed to refine a new soul-skill. Yet their missions collided, exactly as The Rector had intended—for the chaos that pair would unleash would restore that world into the Meridian of Existence, ushering in a new era to enable the future so outlined by the leader of all alchemists.

Yet the path leading to that future was one of conflict and struggle, of turmoil and unrest. It mattered not. The omens of war were now inevitable.

# Chapter 2

# Furia Gorge

Zaro 10th, 17002
Reclamation Era (RE)

# Dante



LEGATE OF EGON HOLD, EASTERN LEGIONS OF FIRARD

*I warned them, again and again… but the Legions crave a spectacle more than peace.* Legate Dante Praeto hurried across the ramparts, pressing his lips to avoid a grimace—one could not afford such an emotional outburst in front of as many legionnaires as those plaguing the area. *All here to witness the War Game, their presence a threat to Firard's stability. A detail they most certainly ignore.* He hastened down the bricked path, his confident footfalls muted by the noise of the surrounding soldiers.

Half of them were useful; archers taking position, messengers and Watchers with veilwings perched on their shoulders, Prefects ready to relay commands in case of emergency. The other half were pockets of high-ranking officials obstructing the way with the sole purpose of watching the War Game between Firard's Northern and Eastern Legions. *All baggage. Unnecessary, and impossible to please.*

That thought elicited a frown, yet Dante eased it as he crossed under the shadow of a tower, following the curvy rampart alongside the cliff's shape. Egon Hold was strategically built from the range itself, guarding the Firardian entrance to Furia Gorge. *And thus it's the unwilling host of the War Games. Again.* The scowl returned when the bright morning twin suns bathed him anew. *The Marshals and their power plays will doom us all.*

A few more steps delivered him onto the rampart's last stretch, extending about two hundred paces along the Gorge's southernmost cliff wall—and his shoulders eased as the familiar silhouette of Imperial Elixane Ritz shaped in the distance. The tall, thin woman was leaning over the crenellations, a spyglass held tightly in her hand and away from her face. She was dressed in the strategist's field outfit, with a white linen camisia tucked in emerald trousers, a closed boots. A cool breeze whistled between the merlons, loosening a few strands of black hair from her braid—and when she looked over her shoulder, her slate grey eyes met Dante's.

"As usual," she whispered, careful.

Dante glanced down the mountain, confirming what he'd assumed would happen. Centurion Sittia's Legion was assembling on the plains before the Gorge, while Decanus Ler's Legion had moved first as part of the Game's rules. *Of course, Sittia will bait him out; that's what she does, no matter the cost. Even in a simulation, she measures victory in terms of human sacrifices.* The Legate observed the opposite side of the Gorge—devoid of vegetation and streaked in the reddish hues of iron-rich ground. *Ler won't attack from above; there are no ridges to use, and no path to climb to the top.* Dante's gaze trailed down the opposite cliff wall. *His troops will likely spring from the caverns. He'll—*

"Centurion Petra is on the Hold, supervising Ler. He's her Decanus," Elixane interrupted, casual and flat. "She arrived earlier in the morning, and so did Centurion Juçe." The Imperial gestured covertly with the spyglass—not to the plains or mountains, but to a lower-level rampart. "He's there, tailed by the Prefect I assigned."

Dante nodded to his Imperial, one part grateful for her prompt response—exactly as he'd commanded—one part wary of the Centurion. He didn't care about Petra, her presence was just another contingency to mitigate; her ruthless campaigns deep into the Five Vaults may have been more savage than needed, but she was known to be more politically savvy than the average Centurion. Instead, Juçe was a liability. *As if dealing with Sittia weren't enough, my father had to arrive as well.*

Yet despite his reluctance, Dante glanced down, instinct guiding him until he found the broad-shouldered figure on a lower rampart.

Juçe stood at parade rest amidst a pocket of other officials, his knee-length boots planted firmly on the stone. His one-shoulder emerald cloak shifted in the wind over a steely cuirass, its elaborate plated pauldrons a testament to his rank. He could have been a statue, unbothered by the heat, the wind, or the Prefect standing one step behind him.

Yet almost on cue, Centurion Juçe glanced over his shoulder and up the ramparts' levels, his gaze finding Dante's like an arrow shot to kill. *Even his silence carries judgement.* The Legate held that gaze, raising his chin because being a level above and having power over the Centurion's Legion was not enough. *Nothing is enough. No matter how far I've climbed, how quickly I did it, nor the victories I claimed for the Emerald Legions. To him, I'm an embarrassment to the family.*

The Centurion snarled after a tense moment, almost as if he'd read Dante's thoughts. It was a minimal gesture—just a curl on his upper lip and a tightening on his sun-kissed, aged forehead—but enough to defy the Legate. He met that gaze, then rolled his hand, dismissing Juçe. *His defiance is undue pride; nothing else.* Dante watched his father scowl before returning his attention to the other officials. *If it offends me, it's by my judgement.*

Dante's hands clenched atop the crenelations but he forced them to relax, instead glancing at the legionnaires—the useful half—preparing across the ramparts. They were under his own command, to protect Firard's territory in case their neighbouring nation, Sestel, chose to attack. *If that happens, the War Games escalated the tensions between our nations. As I anticipated.* He pressed his lips to swallow a sigh. *Promoting Ler and feeding Sittia's ego is not worth the risk of warring Sestel.*

"I imagine the Sestelii are already guarding their side of the ravine." Dante's statement was a question for Elixane even though his gaze had now wandered westwards and towards the Legion on the plains—mere shapes barely recognisable. "Do we know who leads them? Lord Aurri?"

The Imperial dipped her eyes, stepping back from the crenellations. "I was informed of four armies, equivalent to our Legions in size; their vanguard is roughly two-or-three hours into the ravine, thus remaining on their side of the frontier." She paused, lowering her voice. "I also have word Lady Seve herself is leading them," she confirmed, enunciating one missing word —the information's source—with a delicate flick of her slender fingers: "*Spy*."

*Thus, the Lady wanted me to know her exact formation. Otherwise, the leaked information wouldn't be so precise.* The Legate reasoned, focusing on that looming threat he couldn't ignore. *Undesired, but not unexpected.* He gritted his teeth, his prior frustrations returning tenfold. *The Legions could've fought someplace else. The geography is not worth the risk it poses to our feeble peace with Sestel.*

Since their inception, Firard's Emerald Legions and Sestel's Forces—the Seve armies and the Zuria navies—had taunted each other with subtle moves and mindful politics, with strategic alliances and military connections. *And it drove us into a fragile equilibrium.*

Dante glanced down at the Gorge, pondering whether he should descend to ground level. Were anything to happen, his presence there should be enough to fulfil his role—taking over the Legions in the area, stopping the War Game, and preventing any action from escalating into a geopolitical debacle. *The War Games shouldn't happen here; if the Sestelii misread the simulation, the ensuing war…* Collecting himself, he discarded his echoing worry —*Focus on what comes next*—and all possibilities of visiting the ground level. Given his role, staying near the Legions could be seen as a threat—and neither nation could afford such a misunderstanding.

"Do you think Lady Seve may attack us?" Elixane asked, eyes narrowed in pointless defence against the twin suns—two silvery discs now rising above the mountains. "Should we read her presence as a threat?"

*Not quite.* Dante observed, shaking his head; a minute gesture, but enough to release a few strands of black hair from his half tail. They tickled him on the cheeks, spurn by the breeze.

"A warning, not a threat," the Legate corrected, facing Elixane. "In case our War Games are just a façade. It'd be naïve of Sestel to leave Furia Gorge unprotected." *Another reason the Marshals deemed too trivial when I presented it.* He exhaled, refocusing. "What would you do if you were in charge of the Sestelii ground forces?"

"I wouldn't assume the War Games to be such." Elixane stated, crossing her arms.

Confident, but not enough to be arrogant. *A good balance.*

"I'd spread my forces high above in the mountains and at ground level, both at the entrance and slightly into the cliff walls. The formation should be defensive in appearance but easily adjustable." She glanced at the Gorge's Firardian entrance, gaze darting to the places where she'd assemble her hypothetical armies. "Pretending to watch us without actually revealing my plans... but I wouldn't attack. We all know our armies and navies are matched in power."

Dante nodded at his Imperial. "Yet even then, you can't deny how this looks..." He paused, jutting his chin towards the pockets of high-ranking officials cluttering the ramparts and the excess legionnaires clogging the plains—Sittia's presence in any Game would always attract obscene amounts of observers. "It wouldn't be unreasonable to assume that Lady Seve has stationed a reserve a few hours away from the Gorge, perhaps towards the Claw. Close enough to recall them if needed, but not so much as to be perceived as a threat." *Just a careful balance of perception to tweak reality without denying it. An excellent play.*

The Imperial frowned, worry waning her features. "My... contact confirmed no such placement," she confessed, the concern lingering on her features; her pruned brows flattened into a line as she understood the command disguised as a lesson. "I'll send a veilwing and report back."

She vanished before Dante could respond, leaving the Legate to bask under the morning heat and mull over his frustrations—and he did, narrowing his eyes towards the ravine while pretending to ignore the excess legionnaires behind him.

It wasn't passivity that had led him to accept the Marshal's arguments and host the War Games—it was politics. *It is always politics. This time it was Marshal-Strategos Gora Rachen vying for more power within the Emerald Council, and the next time it'll be another Marshal.* He stalled, pocketing his hands into his deep emerald trousers. The breeze now slipping through his camisia chilled his skin. *At ease. The Marshals have their reasons, and I have mine.*

Dante remembered it then, that old and shabby book he'd found in the library of Arborum City when he was barely six years old. He recalled the theory written in its pages, and the challenge to find another pathway towards the elusive Meridian of Existence—the ideal midpoint where societies balance struggle with stability and reach their zenith. *Philosophy, if I'm generous; delusion, if I'm not.* His fists tensed inside his pockets. *Yet it shaped my career as a strategist of the Eastern Legion.* He remembered, just like he did on the eve of any conflict, because finding that Meridian was his goal. The problem for which the solution continued to elude him, the challenge he couldn't solve. *Not yet, at least.*

Footsteps approached rapidly from behind, too purposeful and directed to be ignored, too familiar to be wary of them. Moments later, Elixane's silhouette shadowed him.

"The message is sent. The Games are about to begin," she whispered as the crowd in the lower ramparts quieted. "Anything else?"

"Keep the Watchers and messengers at hand, and the Prefects near the Centurions that shouldn't be here. If anything happens, we must ensure they do not engage," the Legate murmured, pausing for the cornua resonating down below, then glared at his Imperial. "We are only the safeguard. Let us hope we aren't needed, but be prepared in case we are."

The call echoed through Egon Hold, muting her response while duty eased the concern on her face. Dante knew that reaction—the one triggered by the noises prefacing war, even a simulated one. It was an enforced tranquillity, a calmness of the mind that enhanced all senses and trapped all worries somewhere unreachable. *No time to dwell.* The cornua strengthened. *The outcome won't be mine, but the bearing will.* Birds scattered into the sky, rumours circulated like murmurs through the ramparts, caligae shuffling over the bricked floors in restless anticipation of the simulation to come.

Dante glanced at the Peaks of Nadir and the clean sky above them, then into the plains. Sittia's Legion was splitting, the cavalry hurrying north—*Likely to patrol the caverns' entrances*—while a third of the legionnaires marched into the Gorge.

The War Games had begun.

# Calya



HEAD OF THE SEVE HOUSE, SESTEL

*Simulated wars. Ah, the things nations do for political order.* Lady Calya Seve toyed with the reins on her gloved left hand, patting the horse's neck to calm it—the War Games had upset her mare as much as they had rattled the armies posted on the entrance. *Four cohorts stationed in make-pretend observation, three stratoi a few hours away, a dozen Nobles rattled, an Exarch upset.* She recounted, tucking a strand of her caramel hair behind an ear; a few paler gold locks tickled her cheeks as her gaze assessed the armies ahead—those she'd carefully arranged as a warning to whoever was guarding Egon Hold on Firard's side. It was a decent formation, defensive in appearance but easy to command into a choke force if needed. *I wonder for how many months I'll be dealing with the fallout of this nonsense. The Firardians should know better than Game on—*

A few voices yelled amidst the Sestelii armies ahead; strident, but with a confidence that indicated her Generals were shepherding restless troops rather than reacting to an enemy. *At least they know their trade… something they may forget later on.* Calya patted her mare again—a sleek chestnut with a white blaze— while glancing north towards the outline of Ferro Keep; a dark, multi-level fortress built into the northern, iron-rich Peaks of Nadir as a statement of the Sestelii power in the region. *But*

*power built in stone is no power at all; it doesn't command but endures…
and endurance alone has never won a war.*

A flock of birds streamed from the Peaks, their dark shapes
barely spotting the shine of the twin suns—two silvery discs
moving towards the cliffs and casting sharp, geometrical
shadows into the land where she waited. The armies quieted in
its wake, their small shapes taut with anticipation. *Four months;
that's how much. The last Firardian War Game sunk me into a full-month
political upheaval, and it happened further north. But now? In the Gorge?*
Lady Calya eased her mare leftwards and into the shadows to
earn a temporary respite. *Four months. At the least.* Her field
clothes—a protective leather tunic with riding trousers and
closed boots—were unforgiving on the eve of summer. *Yet they're
still more bearable than what's to come. My mother will, for sure,
leverage this encounter on her move against Exarch Luxa.* She exhaled,
raising her chin as if to look ahead. *This charade of monitoring the
Firardians is… tiring. I'd rather return to thwarting Teoda's plans.*

Battle noises grew far ahead, distorted by the sinuous length
of Furia Gorge. *The Firardians are marching. Half a cohort, perhaps?*
Calya tilted her head, imagining the neighbours' formation. *They
couldn't fit more than two hundred—*

People shouted behind her, outlining a horse's gallop. She
glanced over her shoulder—grateful she'd lifted her long hair
into a bun—and nodded at the rider heading towards her.

Lord Asier Aurri cut an impressive figure, tall and bulkier
atop his blue-roan gelding, often passing for a bodyguard when
he was a politically savvy ally. *A cousin, an asset, a risk.* He slowed
upon noticing her stare, sliding a leather-gloved hand through
his rowdy shoulder-length auburn hair.

"What did you find?" Calya demanded as soon as he
stopped, running her eyes through Asier's features. *Too expres-
sionless.* She glanced past him, scanning the scattered officers. *Do
we have more eyes here than I'm aware of? Interesting.* "It must be
valuable enough to justify your delay. The Games have already
begun." Then, with a flick of a finger, she hand-signalled, *"New
spies?"*

Asier assented before jutting his strong, squared chin towards the northern side. "One of the Firardian contestants is Decanus Ler Halde from the Northern Legion. I understand this is another test on Ler's path towards a Centurion rank." He moved his gelding closer before whispering, "The ground forces seem to belong to Centurion Sittia Praeto from the Eastern Legion."

"Why am I not surprised a Praeto is here?" Calya retorted, aware of the tiny, ironic smile creeping on Asier's lips—similar to her own. The Praeto family was a known nuisance plaguing the Eastern Legions. *Family issues and politics should never be combined. Alas, they seem inseparable.* "Did you confirm whether Legate Praeto remains in charge of Egon Hold?" *I rather this doesn't become an issue. My mother's meddling is enough.*

Asier remained unfazed, but his horse neighed as if to convey the Lord's annoyance. "Centurion Juçe Praeto is there, but I understand he's only watching." He lingered as if mulling the next words into existence. They dragged coarsely when he spoke. "The Legate is in charge of Egon Hold, but not of the Games."

*Of course he would.* Calya smirked—tiny, barely pressing the centre of her plush lips and tightening the outer corners of her eyes. *A worthy challenge, then. I wonder if he guessed my formation's goal.* She'd always been curious about facing him directly; Legate Praeto was a trailblazer within the ranks of Firardian Strategists.

Yet her eagerness was smothered by a more relevant concern. "What about the younger Praetos?"

"The Decanii? Not here… to my knowledge," Asier confirmed, the tension in his jaw easing. *He looks relieved. As I am.* He waited stoically as the War Games' noises subsided before adding, "I was given a few more names and clues. The number of Centurions and Decanii observing the Games is… unusually high."

"What do you make of it?" Calya wondered, gaze etched on the armies ahead—the Sestellii archers were switching their positions on the Peaks. *Tracking the incoming cohorts?* Her gaze fell to the nearest messenger; when he noticed, she glanced at the archers and hand-signalled, *"Status?"* with her right hand.

"Sittia's reputation is something," Asier offered, conveniently patting his horse as if to earn time. "But it's an oversight too large to be just that. Do you think this is an alibi? For an invasion?"

*A sensible observation but ultimately incorrect.*

On cue, the messenger she'd sent to check the archers looked back and smiled with relief, gesturing, *"Regaining visibility."*

Calya nodded before dismissing the youth and returning to the conversation with her cousin. "The Sestelii Houses seem to think so..." she grieved, switching the reins and rearranging herself into the seat. *But then again, they're not the brightest either. Except Lord Zuria.* "We cannot discard it. The tensions between our nations have risen considerably." *Another reason to continue my private conversations with Sessentas' Minister, dear enemy. If his nation breaks its alliance with Firard...*

The Lordling stifled, his bushy auburn brows knitting into a line. "They may need Ler's promotion." Pressing his lips, Asier dallied again, chewing saliva as if translating thoughts into answers required careful consideration. "I understand the Northern Legion has... a demand for more Centurions."

"A quest for internal power balance?" The Lady wondered, glancing briefly at her cousin. "Do you have word of the Northern Legion's Marshal? Is she still embroiled in a political manoeuvre against Marshal-Strategos Gora Rachen?"

"To my knowledge..." Asier agreed, barely audible under the noise echoing from within the ravine. It had increased in volume with each passing moment.

*Delightful. As if dealing with the Sestelii Nobles' inner bickering weren't enough.* Her fingers, still resting on the leather reins, tightened slightly. *Balance...* That word was a perennial mark on everything she did; a fundamental goal.

Calya remembered it then: that lanky, ageless librarian she'd met in Umbra City when she was barely eight years old. She recalled the theory that woman had shared, the challenge to find a pathway towards the elusive Meridian of Existence—a balancing act between war and peace, suffering and fulfilment—to reach a societal thriving zone that was closer to a utopia than reality. *Yet it has shaped my career leading the Seve House.* Her features tightened as she looked at the entrance to Furia Gorge, her mind lost in that past encounter.

That librarian had asked one question—how to reach the Meridian—and little-Calya had given an answer too theoretical to be applicable. *I was naïve.* She remembered, just like she did when the stakes were high, when the threat of her work dismantling due to others' ineptitude loomed over. *Balancing the power of the nations. What a foolish, child-like answer!*

"My Lady?" Asier. Concerned.

Enough to dispel her memories and return to the present.

Calya tightened her hold on the reins, waving Asier into silence while half-listening to the clamour of the simulated battle inside Furia Gorge. *She was right, that librarian. It wasn't the only way... and neither the only reason.* The Lady's gaze sifted through the fields before her, seeking the same messenger from before.

He noticed her immediately. *"Ler will ambush Sittia,"* he hand-signalled, admiration glowing in his youthful face. *"Through the caverns."*

Asier blinked, absentminded and clearly lost in thought. After a moment, as if the implications of the Firardian strategy had sunk in, his broad shoulders tensed. *Understandable but unnecessary.* Calya had taken precautions to place patrols on the caverns leading towards Ferro Keep and the Sestelii valley, but they weren't many, and most were unworkable for anything larger than rats.

"If word of that strategy gets out..." Asier muttered, barely enunciating the words.

Lady Calya hummed in sour agreement. *But why are they doing this?* She wondered, refusing to acknowledge how many more months of political distress she'd need to overcome just because of that strategy; executing such a manoeuvre so close to Sestel was dangerous. *Is it a warning? A demonstration of what they can do? A new tactic to be applied against Orenos?* She stored the last thought for future consideration. Orenos, their mutual northern neighbour, had remained quiet since their botched attempt at an invasion over three years ago... but not considering them could very well mean an oversight on her part. Something she couldn't truly afford. *Five months, then.*

Yet the political upheaval—sure to come but still distant—enticed her enough that she smirked, eager for another opportunity to leverage in her favour.

Until she noticed something.

Careful, Calya glanced askance at Asier, but her cousin was as impassive as before, frowning at the Gorge's entrance while clearly immersed in his thoughts. *I must have imagined it.* The thrums of war rumbled from within the ravine, small compared to the chaos they could unleash.

Yet whatever she'd imagined was now undeniable.

A pressure in the air. A distant, quiet rumble.

# Berserk

Soul & Matter Transmuter. The Dragon One.

The wind howled high-above the mountains, whistling while slithering through the crags then coiling in gusts as if to dislodge the petty archers perched on the ravine's crevices. Glamoured to invisibility, Berserk spread their wings to enjoy the zephyr—colder than Omega's—and studied the humans around Furia Gorge.

As usual, there was nothing unique about them.

No ingenuity, no deviating thoughts, no nuances to discover. They believed themselves masters of their era, always living in the age of progress and illumination when, in actuality, they had always produced similar alive elements—variants of the same thoughts, the same attitudes, the same identities. Across ages, across worlds, across myriads of millennia.

Humans built and destroyed, struggled or stagnated... yet died nonetheless.

So transient. So fleeting.

So utterly unsurprising.

Berserk narrowed their ruby eyes, their infinite gaze finding the figure they'd been observing from afar. Legate Dante Praeto. Leaning on the crenellations of Egon Hold. There was no need to soul-link him, he was just another ordinary man, occupied with ordinary concerns that the alchemist easily inferred—the egos he'd need to appease, the expectations he'd need to meet, the tensions between nations he'd need to control. Nations that were but fleeting events amidst the universal history he was unaware of.

There was nothing surprising about Legate Dante Praeto, nothing that Berserk hadn't witnessed before in others. Nothing, except that The Rector had gone as far as to indicate this human—this time-framed, insubstantial, ephemeral human—could provide a solution Berserk was not looking for.

The Rector. The four-transfigured alchemist who seldom interested themselves in the ordinary. The one who existed beyond dimensions and comprehended the universe like no other could. The leader who, since time immemorial, had crafted a convoluted labyrinth of untraceable decisions for unfathomable purposes.

This mission was a confounding statement meant to hide The Rector's true intentions while suggesting enough to tease Berserk—and it would unfold as intended, with consequences yet unforeseen. More than a mission, this was an omen of disruption, of discovery, of change as they had craved for almost two-hundred millennia.

Berserk could not wait. To unleash the inevitable chaos, to bring forth the destruction of these transient human settlements, to enable a scheme grand enough it demanded that them —Berserk, the discoverer of the Meridian of Existence, the founder of Omega, the alchemist who single-handedly had solved a myriads-old alchemical mystery—set in motion a scheme whose results would likely remain hidden for ages.

Insanity, except it had been proposed by The Rector.

The Rector. The leader of The Orders. The one who saw across time and dimensions, the one who manipulated existence.

Eager, Berserk glanced back, confirming their schemes with Amok. The younger Soul Transmuter hovered forth, their cloak of ink leaking glyphs from its frayed edges as they crossed into the ridge before the ravine—and their triangular, cerulean eyes of infinite refractions narrowed in approval.

That was all the agreement Berserk needed.

They sought the pressure building within the mountain

range—deep within, rippling and shaping, coursing through the plates that built the world. It was a mild rumble, a complaint posited by the non-alive elements that composed it—metals, fossils, remains left to rot—and one Berserk incensed with masterful control. They pressured segments of the cliffs, tearing them apart by knowledge and will until the land roared, dust raising like crimson clouds from the ravine's flanks.

The humans below yelled futilely while Berserk ignored them, instead heating the stone with careful precision. It weakened the ravine until it rained pebbles on the armies, each rolling larger and larger as the cliffs bellowed and moaned, so deafening and all-encompassing their clamour swallowed the alchemists.

'*Careful,*' Amok warned, mind-whispering directly to Berserk —perhaps to avoid the chaos below, or to warn the older alchemist in an ineffectual way. '*It must look Natural.*'

Berserk did not answer, instead commanding the air to split and reshape, extracting its useful non-alive compounds, coercing reactions, willing missing components to exist, to vaporise, to transmute and leak into the ravine. The humans breathed them in mouthfuls, so foolish they were, so powerless, so defenceless.

'*Enough!*' Amok called, their cerulean eyes aiming for Berserk. '*More will destroy them. Look!*'

Thoroughly aware of what they'd aimed for, Berserk leant into the ravine with one foot planted in solid rock. Within an iota of time, they intertwined the humans down below— hundreds of them, Firardian and Sestelii yet all equal regardless of the colours they wore—and revelled on the alive elements they produced.

Confusion, restless and growing. Fear, incipient and all-encompassing. Terror, for everyone around, allies or enemies, the former quickly disappearing. Resentment, revulsion, hatred, horror—mingling, brewing, exploding nonsensical and maddening as their minds crumbled in pieces. Chaos unfolded. It screamed, mutilated as the humans that yelled for it, chasing enemies that did not exist, mauling monsters that could not be and would soon fade.

To Berserk, those emotions—those alive elements—surged like strands of smoke chasing the sun, soaring into the sky and scattering like lies. Distorted like the human minds that had produced them, now clogged by their alchemical mix.

'*The gas will eventually dissolve,*' the Dragon One chuckled, mind-whispering to Amok. '*But the chaos? For it, this is just an omen.*'

# Furia Gorge

## Zaro 10th, 17002
## Reclamation Era (RE)

# Dante



LEGATE OF EGON HOLD, EASTERN LEGIONS OF FIRARD

Hours after the games had started, the ravine rumbled and fractured, spilling dust and threatening the War Games. *Ler's tactic? The Northern Legion has destroyed caverns before, when facing the Orenians.* Legate Dante Praeto frowned, narrowing his eyes to shield them from the dust. A dozen fissures sneaked through the cliff-walls, close to the entrance and as far ahead as he could see. When the land quaked slightly, the Gorge groaned again. *No. He should've disclosed it to me before the Games. Unless…*

"Stand by," Dante commanded between gritted teeth, barely glancing at Imperial Elixane—already relaying his request to the Hold's Prefects.

*Could this be an accident?* After all, the War Games leveraged natural conditions to train the Legions; quakes and floods had already interfered in prior simulations. He could not intervene without a solid reason. *Not unless we're attacked, at risk of losing too many, or about to cause a war.* Acting too soon could undermine his position, while reacting too late could damage Firard.

Dante lifted a hand, demanding the spyglass. Elixane pressed it into his open palm, and he expanded the barrels to search for the distant silhouettes; the ravine's sinuous walls hindered his sight, but he searched nonetheless. *Could this be a Sestelii attack? Lady Seve has sacrificed troops before…* His tongue clicked, rejecting that last thought. *No; she's not that reckless.* He noticed some shapes before a turn in the cliffs' walls, barely distinguishable under the dust raining from the mountains. They seemed to disregard the quake, continuing the War Games. *The Orenians, then? Trying to ignite a war between Sestel and Firard?*

The ground bellowed again, its cry distorted by the ravine into a deep, resonant wail. *Could it be a coup? Or something to weaken Strategos Gora's standing?* Dante's frown secured the spyglass to his face while he observed the fissures sneaking upwards like capricious veins tracing the cliff's iron markings. *No; it seems… unworkable.* Far ahead, a slab of stone sheared free from high above, plunging to the ground and blocking his mangled view of the rearguard. Its destruction echoed loudly, drowning the remote clash of metal. *Whatever it is, Sittia will risk her Legion for a simulation. She should ret—*

Fog. Dense.

Spilling from between the cliffsides' fractures, deepening the dust and debris from the shattering Gorge. It cascaded to the ground, blurring the shapes already diffused by the distance, then pooled to fill the ravine, expanding like an opalescent, silver-edged river so thick it swallowed everything on its wake.

*That's not natural. It can't be.* That smothered clash of steel rebounded, warped into disfigured echoes. Voices surged, commands slashed into meaningless twists that barely resembled human speech. Dante frowned at the fog, watching it curl along the jagged stone like a mindful predator, pooling in the cracks and crevices with a sluggish weight.

"That's enough," Dante gritted, lowering the spyglass to lean over the crenellations. The fog was now reaching the Gorge's entrance, crawling higher and clinging to the ramparts' walls. "Break off and fall back!" He shouted to the Prefects on the lower, more receded levels. "Recall the Legions! Halt the War Game! Everybody away from that fog!"

The Prefects snapped to attention, commanding the nearby Centurions while two cornua blared timidly to deliver the command.

Amidst those calls, Dante heard Juçe's refusal—demanding explanations, barking his arguments, demeaning as usual—but ignored him. *Rash and thoughtless. As always.* The Strategists' colder voices grew louder, stomping on that refusal, on the generalised shock, on the chaos Dante needed to control. Juçe's voice faded beneath them. *I'll deal with him soon.* Archers trotted through the bricked ramparts, the movement partly impeded by the unyielding quake.

For a moment, Dante and Elixane scowled down at the ravine; she frowned while he narrowed his eyes at the fog to coerce it to spread and fade away. It was futile; it had flooded Furia Gorge and remained, strangely, caged within its boundaries.

"I've never seen something like this," Elixane. Shocked, although it did not reflect in her impassive countenance. "That's not... normal fog."

The breeze picked up, whistling yet barely upsetting it.

Dante sniffed—once, worried; twice, concerned—and grimaced at the faint, sweet scent emanating from the ravine. He stepped back on reflex, arm bent to cover his mouth with his loose sleeve, gaze etching on the foggy tendrils now sluggishly creeping onto the crenellations.

He raised an arm, palm facing inward for a moment before pulling it back to his chest to signal a retreat. On cue, the nearby archers withdrew immediately, bows trained on the ever-approaching fog as though an enemy may spring from it. *Spooked; on edge. I must be cautious.* He dallied for another moment, studying those silvery tendrils before finally moving back.

"Agree," Dante confirmed to Elixane, gaze etched in the fog. *But what is it? Where does it come from?* "Despatch veilwings, at least three. We must know what the Sestelii are doing."

"Understood," Elixane whispered, nose and mouth hidden in the crook of her elbow. "Do you think this is... their doing? Or Orenos'?"

*A question without an answer,* Dante pressed his lips, holding his breath while Elixane gestured at the nearby Watchers, dispatching orders with rapid hand-signals. A handful of them squared in acknowledgement, readying the blue, raven-like veilwings on their shoulders before releasing them into the sky; those birds were trained to fly over battlefields and report the troops' positions using their flight pattern. Dante traced their ascension with his gaze, half-blinded by the twin silver suns. *It's too easy to blame the Sestelii, but… even if they somehow released the fog, we can't engage them under these conditions.*

The cliffs bellowed again, but a perverse hue coloured its twisted echo—as if thousands of wails rimmed its edges, pained voices coiling in a cacophony of misery and shearing stone. *What's—?* Another slab shattered, a rain of pebbles drumming relentlessly before deteriorating into faint, sibilant hisses.

Mutters and curses rumbled between the gritted teeth of the archers withdrawing alongside the Strategists.

"We must be prepared to face any assailant, but we can't assume it's the Sestelii." Dante finally stated, glancing at his Imperial while picking up the pace. "A baseless accusation will reignite old tensions, and we cannot afford—"

Silence; sudden. It devoured the ravine, so absurd and deafening it muted Egon Hold, imprisoning it in absolute stillness.

Dante halted his retreat, lips pressed into a line—but his jaw fell when the howling began.

Pruned like the remnants of panic and terror, buckling between histrionic laughter and fearful crying, hammered by the distorted clatter of metal, by the shrieking of a dreadful frenzy, by the erratic rush of a stampede. The fog swallowed it all, murdering the frantic chaos into irrational silence and spilling it again, louder, louder, louder.

The Hold lingered, suspended in shocked silence.

Coldness washed over Dante's shoulders, his heartbeat rushing into madness, desperate and powerless until rationality cleared his mind. *I command the Legions, but not their fear,* he reminded himself, fists clenched at his sides, arms taut with resolve. *Strategos Gora may have enabled this, but it's my problem to solve.*

"Control Egon Hold, Elixane. Blast two dozen cornua to call for a retreat. Those inside won't hear us otherwise." *I need Lady Seve to hear my call as well.* He hushed the Imperial's retort with a curt glance. "I will ensure the entrance is guarded." *It's a wager, but one I must take; my options are limited.*

He didn't wait for her response, instead turning to sprint

through the ramparts, undoing his prior path to veer into the closest stairway. *Control Juçe, extract our Legions, prevent an escalation.* He leapt through the stone guardrail and landed on the steps, descending on a run although these were polished after centuries of use. *Mitigate the damage, find the cause. Learn; solve another challenge.* The first section ended on the middle ramparts, where Juçe had been until moments before. Two Prefects halted upon encountering Egon's seniormost Strategist.

"Something is attacking them!" One said, beckoning at Furia Gorge. All colour had left his face.

"We couldn't hold the Centurions," the other clarified, jutting her chin to the lower ramparts. "Juçe went down. He wanted to march in!"

The Legate fisted one hand, hissing, "Watch the entrance and shoot anyone who moves in!" He walked backwards not to waste any more time. "Avoid breathing that fog!"

Dante rushed through the sloped ramparts, the Prefects' ensuing commands fading behind. A few legionnaires parted, clearing the path for him to leap onto the next stairway—narrower and without guardrails, built to hinder any assailants climbing up. Dante leaped down the steps, precise and controlled. *Mitigate Juçe first; his disobedience is a risk.*

The lower ramparts had cleared of the high-ranking officials, and only archers remained; their bows were trained on the Gorge's entrance, their faces contorted in alarm. Dante started towards the final stairway but stalled, scowling at the fog—thinning and receding with sluggish reluctance. When he inhaled, he barely detected its sweet scent.

Relief teased him for a few heartbeats before he noticed the silent cornua. *Why aren't they blasting a call as I've—?*

Silence. Anew.

Abnormal in its overwhelming quiescence, aberrant by its sheer impossibility. It omitted existence, ceasing the rustling of life and lurking in the depths of the fog-flooded ravine to augur only one outcome.

Mayhem.

Recklessly chaotic, laughing and wailing and crying and screaming. With frantic elation, with abject terror, with devastating fright, with primal agony. It shifted between tones like a tide swayed by a storm, taken aback and reinstated in a sweep of emotions not even legends could capture.

It lingered. Distorting time with a horror that smothered the Emerald Legions into absolute stillness.

Dante squandered his shock, marching towards the next stairway, jaw clenched, brows knitting tighter with every fragmented howl, with every fissured bellow reaching the Hold. *Too panicked, too primal.* It was unbecoming of legionnaires trained since childhood to breathe and live war. *It sounds... impossible. That fog must be distorting all sounds.* That cacophony continued, disorganised and confused, chaotic as nothing he'd heard before. *And it's terrifying my Legions into inaction.*

"Call a retreat!" Dante shouted to the Triarii commanding the archers, subduing his disapproval—of the inaction, of the pointless fidgeting. "Blast every cornua you have!" *Instead of sharpening themselves through this, they just—*

The young woman looked at him with concern, squaring in agreement but flinching when a wail—*A howl? Human?*—reached them with uncanny clarity. *It matters not. I must act. Now.* Speeding, Dante leapt onto the last stairway, taking the steps at a sprint, breath ragged, heart pounding as he reached the ground level.

Centurion Juçe was not far away from the landing, holding the reins of a black-bay stallion while hissing orders to a handful of Decanii. *Against my orders.* The Centurion pointed a callused forefinger towards a woman's chin, lips curling into an all too familiar snarl. He hissed, unintelligible, before squaring and moving the horse as if about to mount. *Reckless as always, father. But not on my watch.*

"Centurion Juçe!" The Legate called, approaching the official with a measured gait—neither fast nor slow, but enough to set the pace of the conversation. "I trust you have heard the orders."

The surrounding Decanii retreated a few steps, squaring at attention—formal although they hesitated. Juçe spared them a glance before watching the approaching Legate like a predator measuring his prey. *Anger? Hatred? Both, most likely. It's always been both.* He slid a hand through his grey-streaked black hair and snarled minutely, thin lips stretching with contempt. Under the light of the twin silver suns, his pale grey eyes shone like polished blades.

"That feeble call for a retreat? Clearly a mistake," the Centurion observed, voice hoarse from age and decades of barking orders on the battlefield. He flung the reins towards the nearest Decanus. "Only cowards would retreat after the Sestelii attacked us so shamelessly."

Dante's features steeled. "Do you have any evidence to support your claims, Centurion?"

"You think they wouldn't strike the moment we showed weakness?" Juçe snorted, smoothing his well-groomed beard with a gauntleted hand. "I see you remain an unobservant child."

The stallion neighed as a Decanus tried to ease it while the others stared at the exchange with utmost attention. Beyond them, that undefinable turmoil raged in the Gorge, a single cornua blasting a timid retreat.

Between father and son, a different war raged. *One that began when I enrolled in the Strategists' trials against his wishes.* Juçe held his ground in defiance, straightening until the leather straps of his cuirass rustled when his hands fisted.

Legate Dante Praeto took on the Centurion's stance, barely sparing a glance at the stubborn Decanii. "So you have no evidence, Centurion. Is this a repeat of Orenos' botched invasion?" *Your pride is your greatest weakness.*

Juçe's cheek twitched at the mention of his single tactical failure in over five decades of service. "My experience is evidence enough. That fog—that poison—can only be a Sestelii weapon."

"And you want to lead your Legion into it." Dante held his father's gaze. *Albeit I wouldn't mind your death, I can't afford its political cost.* From the corner of his eye, he noticed the Decannii shuffling restlessly. "Your recklessness could deal a fatal blow to our Legions, while caution can lead us to victory."

Juçe chuckled, relaxing with the demeanour of those who've wrongly assumed to have won the battle. "Of course you'd call it caution. That's all you've ever done in your life; avoid, hesitate," the Centurion hissed, looking down at the Legate—he was taller, bulkier, instilling fear in others with a single stare. "You only lead from afar, from safety. Are you afraid to engage, son?"

*Never the paragon he claims to be.* Dante hummed only once, feigning curiosity and waving a hand towards the Gorge's chaos. "What do you want to engage, Centurion? The fog? That poison, as you called it?" He stretched the silence—alive only between father and son, but murdered by mayhem anywhere else—to its breaking point. "What you are proposing is not engagement but suicide, and as the Legate of Egon—commanding the Eastern Legions in this region—I will not allow it." Another pause, deathly like the sheen of an enemy's pugio. *The Legions are no place for pride.* "You will stand down, Centurion, or you will be detained for insubordination."

Dante shifted his gaze from his father's enraged frown to the Decanii around them—and arched a brow back to Juçe, demanding compliance. His subordinates stood firm, gazes trained on their Centurion but ready to subdue him if needed.

Juçe swallowed so hard his reddened, taut neck stretched as if passing a rock—then uttered, "As you command, Legate."

Lingering for another moment, Dante dismissed the Centurion to command the three Decanii. "Prepare your cohorts and set a ring around the Gorge's entrance. Three lines only." He paused for emphasis, barely sparing a glance at his father. "Hold your ground, and attack only if an enemy emerges from the ravine. Am I clear?"

The Decanii squared to attention, departing to carry their orders while the howls raging from within the Gorge continued without end. *I must know what is happening inside that fog. Until then, I can't engage.* Dante backtracked, hurrying towards the central door. *Whatever happens, we cannot attack blindly. But Juçe's view… he's not the only Centurion too eager to fight.* A group of cornicen was assembling there, a handful departing towards the plains, another group ready to climb into the ramparts. *Two-dozen cornua, and a wager to stall war.*

Dante halted to watch the skies for the veilwings he'd commanded not long ago. Far into the distance but above the ravine, the birds were still flying in circles, signalling nothing. *Blind, just like us.* The Legate bit his lip, counting them. *Seven veil-wings. Who sent the rest?* Realisation eased his countenance; unexpected, but certainly compelling. *Are you blind as well, Lady Seve?* His eyes narrowed at the sky. *Or are you also sending me a message?*

# Calya



HEAD OF THE SEVE HOUSE, SESTEL

It wasn't the rhythm of a war, Lady Calya Seve had heard its variants before. The grind of steel scattered through the hills of Sombra Forest, the distorted racket of battles fought in the Vast Expanse, and the subdued rage across Tormenta Plains— howling with both the wails of sinking vessels and the uproar of large-scale, tri-nation melees. *No, this is sheer terror. Unrestrained and primal.*

On the Gorge's entrance, the outermost Sestelii forces held their ground while the archers had retreated after the cliffs sheared, shattered stone raining down. *But where is the vanguard? They should have sent a rider back!* The Lady pressed her lips, gaze trained on the troops guarding the entrance. She considered the vanguard inside the ravine and groaned minimally when reaching the only feasible conclusion. *The fog. How far does it expand? I thought it was just at the edges! Should I use tubas to signal a retreat?* Calya exhaled harshly, rejecting that last thought. *I need at least two dozen to be heard above that… mayhem. The Firardians will hear them, and I need to know what they are doing first.*

Blocking the late-morning light with her leather-gloved hand, she swiped her gaze past the rattled troops and through the Gorge's entrance—then frowned at the dense, silvery fog still flooding the ravine. It oozed densely, halting paces away from the edge and without spilling outside. *That's not fog.* Whatever was happening inside—whatever caused that absurd, impossible blend of noises that continued still—remained an invisible, latent threat. *If that is Ler's doing… was the War Game a façade, then? A coup? Or just an accident?*

Keeping her hand to the brow, Calya looked up to the sky and scowled at the veilwings circling the ravine. *A circular pattern. No visibility; unable to report.* She translated mentally, averting her gaze for a moment before tracking the birds again.

"Seven veilwings," Calya observed, patting her chestnut to soothe it; the mare was restless. *Like the troops.* "We sent only three. Who sent the other four?"

Realisation dawned on Asier's stoic face, tightening his bushy auburn brows. "Our Watchers may have seen their origin." He paused, skimming the landscape for someone to interrogate. "Could Legate Praeto have sent them? Or someone else?"

*The latter would be terrible; especially if it's the Orenians trying to ignite a war between Sestel and Firard.* Lady Calya hummed neutrally, skimming the Gorge's entrance, the restless troops, the shuffling messengers. "If those are the Legate's veilwings, then whatever happened also took him by surprise." *This couldn't have been part of Ler's tactic, unless—* She stalled her thinking, displeased by the possibilities that augured nothing short of a geopolitical debacle. Lifting her chin, Calya sifted through the area until her gaze fell onto the field-messenger she'd used before. When he noticed her, she hand-signalled, *"Why hasn't our vanguard retreated?"*

The young messenger shuffled, signalling with quivering hands. *"Not responding to our calls. T-t—"* Grimacing, he continued with slower, mindful motions. *"They may have engaged an enemy."*

Lady Calya restrained a snarl, instead glancing at the Gorge and counting the veilwings again—still seven, and still circling the ravine. *This cannot be a covert Firardian attack.* She concluded, drumming her gloved fingers over a thigh—a steady rhythm compared to the chaos emanating from the Gorge. *The Emerald Legions also hold War Games on allied soil; overseas, on Alboré and Sessentas. Attacking us during one would likely shatter their diplomatic relations.* Her tapping quickened for a moment, tensing her arms until her leather tunic protested. She exhaled, forcing the rhythm back to its prior pace. *Whatever the cause, the political fallout could be extensive. Sestel cannot afford it. I cannot.*

"The veilwings are likely Firardian," Asier growled, interrupting her thoughts.

*Likely?* Calya arched a brow at the belated—and worse, inconclusive—information, the gesture a silent demand. A drop of sweat tickled down her cousin's forehead, but he held her gaze with a steely demeanour. *I'll deal with that later.*

In that impasse, his countenance darkened, lips barely moving as he uttered. "Could this be a natural disaster?"

"That would be the worst-case scenario," Calya gritted, dismissing the other's confusion with a wave of her hand. "A natural disaster would mean that nobody is to blame, and neither the Sestelii Nobles nor the Firardian Legions would accept that as an answer."

Asier groaned, nostrils flaring minimally. Calya allowed herself a small grimace while holding her reins with both hands. Her gaze was now fixed on the troops near the ravine's entrance —they had stalled for long, and there was a pressing need to act. *Any delay would breed disaster. Any misjudgment will be fatal. Whatever this is, I must resolve it quickly.* Whatever happened in Furia Gorge could shatter the fragile equilibrium, upsetting the power balance within Sestel and across the world.

"Go back to the reserves," she commanded after a moment of silence, beckoning towards the rearguard stationed hours away. "They cannot approach the Peaks of Nadir, and no messages should depart further inland." Lingering, Calya fidgeted with the mare's pommel-bag, producing her long, hand-painted headscarf; once the fabric was tangled in her hands, she hand-signalled, *"At any cost, Asier. Do what you must."*

The Lord's eyes read her instructions with the same impassivity he'd carried since arriving, providing no other acknowledgement than a curt nod. He spurred his blue-roan gelding into a gallop, riding further inland.

Lady Calya watched him vanish while wrapping the hand-painted fabric around her mouth and nose. *Now, to deal with the Firardians.* She kicked the mare's flanks, coaxing it into a gallop towards the ravine's entrance while assessing the formations. Her external forces were holding position, but the vanguard hadn't returned yet. *Are the Generals limiting themselves to verbal orders? Are they afraid of—?*

Horns blared above the distorted, undefinable mayhem of the ravine—just echoes, yet clear enough as if many were blasting at once.

*Those... aren't ours.* Calya frowned beneath the guise of her headscarf, redirecting her mare further left where two Generals now looked at the sky in obvious confusion. *Firardian cornua, then?* Still watching them, Calya slowed her mare to a canter—finally recognising the cornua's pattern. *A retreat call?* She gestured to the nearest official, walking the horse toward her. *Furia Gorge is... wide. About six or seven hours of marching. How many are they blaring?*

"When did that begin?" Lady Calya demanded as she stopped to a halt, lowering her scarf to let the other recognise her. "How many do you estimate?"

The General—a grey-haired, squat woman with a scar across her nose—hesitated. "Bare moments ago, my Lady." Her voice was roughed by decades of service in the Seve armies. "Cornua are meant to be loud, but given this... mayhem?" She paused, tilting her head as if the motion were the scale of measure. "I'd estimate two dozen. Maybe more."

*Only a Firardian Legate or Strategos can halt a War Game and call a retreat like that.* Calya dipped her head in silent acknowledgement, letting the scarf fall away from her nose—it wouldn't do to hide her face when giving orders to a General, even if protectively. *What are you facing, Legate Praeto? A coup or an accident?* She pursed her lips, listening as another retreat call blasted over the ravine's distorted echoes. *Should I assume this call is... more than a command? A message to me, perhaps?* As it echoed, she gauged the fog emanating from it—thinning enough that the edges were now a silvery, translucent haze. *I couldn't expect anything else of you, especially after our last encounter... but cannot assume you understand why we should both retreat now.*

Stretching her silence—one interrupted by the twisting cacophony surging from the ravine—Calya looked up to the sky.

The seven veilwings were still flying in circles, reporting nothing. *But I can give them something to report.* She smiled, assessing the troops stationed in the entrance—flinching at the noises, but holding that flexible stance she'd commanded when they settled here. *Give me evidence of your purpose, Legate Praeto, and I'll leverage it like no other would.*

"Change to a half-circle formation, General." Calya beckoned with a hand towards the troops not far away. "Four lines, slightly open, shields interlocked. Keep two lines of archers behind them and retreat a further twenty paces east."

Nose-scar scrunched her face. "That… is a purely defensive formation, my Lady."

*The absence of foresight in my army is staggering.* "Precisely," she confirmed, colder than the steel blade sheathed on the General's hip. *It's preferable nonetheless; their lack of grand ideas makes them easier to manipulate.* "While you are at it, set twenty tubas to blast a retreat call for the vanguard still inside the Gorge. They haven't heard your verbal orders."

"My Lady!" The General snapped to attention. "As you command!"

Calya watched nose-scar trot ahead, gesturing with a muscular arm to summon a few messengers. *I must bring this episode to a close. Immediately.* When they approached, the General barked her commands, gesturing sharply to convey the new formation.

Satisfied, the Lady patted her mare while perusing the field for the scout-master—a younger man with hair so pale it shimmered white. *I cannot give the Firardian grounds to believe we released that fog.* She found him moments later and ushered her mare in that direction. *Legate Praeto may be sensible enough not to engage us over this, but the Emerald Council could turn against him—just like our Exarch would turn against me were the public opinion to demand it.*

"Scout-master," Calya called as she approached, again halting her mare near. She looked down at the leather-armoured man, already standing at the ready. "Our vanguard hasn't retreated. I need them to return."

He hesitated for a moment, gaze darting between the nearest troops—repositioning as Calya had commanded—and the thinned fog; its edges were nothing else than a deep haze, translucent and lighter than it had been before. The man's cheek twitched as the tubas blasted the first, deafening call for retreat.

"My scouts stationed on the cliffs have already descended," white-hair finally observed, tilting his head towards the north-ernmost cliff. "We have no visibility for now, my Lady."

*As if I hadn't noticed.* "Then send four of your scouts into the Gorge and recall the vanguard." Calya stated, gauging the man while his already pale skin lost all colour. *Four more lives. A menial expense compared to how costly it could be if the Exarch chose war.* "Cover your faces with wet clothes if you must, but the vanguard must exit Furia Gorge."

The scout-leader saluted, lips pressed into a grim line. His countenance was already mourning the soldiers he would likely send to their deaths.

*From now on, everything I do must ensure I remain in power. There is no other outcome.* Calya looked up, pressing her lips into a demure, satisfied smirk—the four Firardian veilwings were now arching over her defensive formation. *Your move, Legate Praeto.*

# Dante

The tubas' metallic blast reached Egon Hold as a faint echo, shrieking like metal on stone while it ricocheted across the ravine. Legate Dante Praeto closed his eyes, tilting his head to focus on the sharp tune of the Sestelii tubas. *It must be more than a handful, or they wouldn't echo this loudly from so far away.* The sounds clashed against the cliffs, distorted but clear. *Is that Lady Seve's answer, then? Retreat?*

Deep in thought, Dante ambled toward the crenellations lining the lowest rampart. The noon twin suns cast sharp shadows, and he scowled tightly when staring at the cliff walls to assess the hazy remains of the dying fog. Hours had passed since it'd swallowed Furia Gorge, and although the mayhem had subsided, the Legions had yet to retreat. The blaring cornua—which hadn't stopped their call—now pounded at the rhythm of Dante's headache.

He groaned, massaging his forehead with both hands. His movement became firmer against his head, in tandem with his thoughts. *Does this mean the fog swallowed most of the Gorge? Could it have spilled onto Sestel? Why wouldn't our spies report it?* Slowly pocketing both hands, the Legate focused on remembering the maps etched into his memory.

The ravine connecting Firard and Sestel was sinuous, walled by iron-rich mountains and often requiring six to seven hours of march to cross from side to side; the Games had been scheduled to happen no further than two hours from Egon Hold, located precisely on the Firardian entrance.

*We could assume Ler and Sittia continued their fight, but the screams...* Dante's cheeks twitched when recalling those laughing howls, and he retrieved the spyglass hanging from his belt to trace its length with a fingertip; in his mind, he was drawing the ravine's path. *The Gorge amplifies sounds as it is doing with the cornua and tubas... which means our armies could've engaged closer to the frontier.* The spyglass protested when his grip tightened, metal and leather straining in defiance. There were too many scenarios, none favourable, all politically complex—and Dante pressed his lips at the thought, gaze etched on the lines of immovable cohorts protecting the entrance. *Lady Seve could have used verbal orders first, only resorting to the tubas after she heard my call and its covert proposal.*

The Legions' cornua blared again, two dozen screeching to reinforce his prior command—to retreat to the Hold. Something those deep within the Gorge had yet to acknowledge. After a sensible delay, the Sestelii tubas answered with another blast, their sluggish, distorted wail echoing the same order before unravelling into a grating cacophony. Dante's grip on the spyglass eased, the tension in his arms releasing. *But what if Sittia and Ler engaged the Sestelii? What if this is not a confirmation but—?*

His thoughts stalled as a new sound emerged from the ravine—bootfalls reverberating on the narrow space, metal chafing over stone and trailed by the moans of the wounded.

Leaning over the crenellations, Dante scowled as the uneven rhythm of a retreat became clear. *Not an ordered march. Unusual. Our Legions' discipline is renown.* Boots dragged, weapons clattered, painful moans and howls echoed closer. Hushed voices carried across, some heated, others sore and exhausted, but most sobbing and panting like terrified children. Somewhere in the distance, the wind caught the last dying echoes of the Sestelii tubas.

A familiar, stocky figure was the first to trudge out of the haze, a muscular arm pulling at the scarf covering a short-haired head. *Sittia?* The fabric swirled in the wind when the Centurion disposed of it, refusing to land on the ground. *Of course my mother survived; I wonder how many she doomed to ensure such an outcome.* Soured, the Legate raised his spyglass and focused it on the old soldier, immediately noticing her missing shield and the empty scabbard on her hips. *Even if it pleased me, her death would've stirred enough Centurions to make war with Sestel inevitable.* Sittia stopped after a few paces, swiping a hand through her short, greying hair before half-turning towards the Gorge—and Dante swiped the spyglass over the newly emerged legionnaires.

Coughing, rattled; trudging forward while dragging others, some falling to their knees as if depleted. They retched, vomiting violently before crawling further west or simply passing out in their filth. Dante's jaw fell slightly as he perused figure after figure from afar—then stepped back, lowering the spyglass while scouring the ramparts for a cornicen.

"Call for Medicii support! Prepare to receive the wounded!" He shouted to the closest one—a lad so young the cornus hung loosely around his body, oversized for his thin frame. "Now!"

The boy jolted, acknowledging the order before blasting the requested command. After he repeated it, the other cornua joined, and the Hold's ground floor erupted into motion. Medici rushed to clear space, the stable-hands scrambled to ready carts for the wounded, and runners dashed to fetch supplies. Moments later, archers marched across the highest ramparts, repositioning themselves into the crenellations veering over the Gorge's entrance—clearly intended to shoot any chasing enemies. *Imperial Elixane's call, most likely… but I doubt there are any enemies left. The survivors didn't seem concerned.*

Dubious, Dante aimed his spyglass at the Gorge's entrance, finally targeting the seemingly unperturbed figure of Decanus Ler Halde. Just like Sittia, he walked straight although a scarf draped loosely around his neck and shoulders, his shield clearly missing; most of his blonde hair and sun-burnt face were covered in dust and debris, obscuring his features. *Was he trapped inside the caverns?* Dante's grip softened around the spyglass while he thought, idly locking it back into his belt. Behind him, more legionnaires continued to spill out, tumbling forwards, some dragging passed out fellows, others barely staying upright. *Are these* all *the survivors?*

"Legate!" A woman's voice. Aged and sore, but not rough.

Half-turning—and expecting a messenger from the cohorts he'd posted in the plains—Dante glanced over his shoulder to scowl at the woman approaching him. Tall, aged, and dressed in the lightweight, dark uniform of the Watchers. *She must be coming at Elixane's command.* Given the marks on her vest, she was a Peritus—a rank equivalent to an Imperial but belonging to the Support stream.

"Imperial Elixane sent me." The Watcher bowed before him, right arm across her chest—wrapped in the deerskin protector common of her trade.

"Report," Dante demanded, impatience sharpening his tone.

The woman straightened, looking at him with amber eyes. "We spotted a defensive position outside the Sestelii entrance. Four arched rows, Legate, slightly spread open." She explained, arching both hands to enact the formation with a simplified gesture. "Two rows of archers further back, also ground level. It must be somewhat recent."

*A purely holding position?* Dante hummed in acknowledgement, narrowing his eyes while quickly skimming the Gorge's entrance —now spilling more legionnaires, each one more ragged than the previous one. *Unreasonable given the prior formation allowed rapid changes... does that mean this fog also surprised you, Lady Seve?*

"How long ago was this?" He beckoned with his eyes towards the Peritus' hands—still demonstrating the formation.

The woman frowned with non-existent brows, lowering her hands. "Given the Peaks' height, the veilwings have to fly back to report. It's faster than a soldiers' march, but... there is a delay." She lingered, clearly considering her words before adding, "About one or two hours ago."

Dante nodded. *The change in formation must have happened as the tubas began blasting. This could be part of her hypothetical response to my disengagement proposal.* "Had the Sestelii vanguard exited the Gorge when they assumed this formation?"

"We received no such information, Legate." Amber-eyes shook her head, the noon's unforgiving light reflecting on her white-grey hair. "So far, the veilwings have only reported this formation."

*Therefore, Lady Seve was likely still blinded by the fog when she ordered this.* He glanced at the Peritus—a spot of peace amidst the noisy, fast-paced madness that now coursed through the Hold. *Clearly experienced, or she wouldn't hold this rank.* Relaxing his posture, Dante tilted his head, softening his features before asking, "Any thoughts, Peritus?"

Amber-eyes chewed her already-mauled bottom lip, upsetting the scar near the left corner. "The veilwings were inconclusive, Legate, but the Seve formation... may have retreated further away from the entrance." Pausing again, she glanced up at the sky—blotted into a pale blue. "I'd hazard a guess the Sestelii are blind. They sent three veilwings first, three more moments ago." Raising her left palm up, she began tracing circles over it with her right forefinger. "The birds were flying in a common observation pattern over Furia Gorge but never moving past the centre."

*Never invading territory, then. A careful move that compounds with the new formation and the retreat call, and one only Lady Seve would dare.* A smirk tugged at Dante's lips, but he restrained it. *Were I facing any other strategist, I'd gauge this was just a coincidence. Coming from her, I must assume this is a disengagement confirmation.*

"Understood," he finally answered, returning to his usual, commanding stance. *I'll need the Sestelii informers for my next move.* "Before you return to your post, find Imperial Elixane. Request she directs the... ears towards me." *They'll need to eavesdrop and report my intention not to engage.*

Amber-eyes nodded, unfazed at the unusual request. "Will do, Legate."

As she retreated, five archers marched back into their posts on the crenellations, respectfully nodding to the Legate when their paths crossed. Dante acknowledged them as he walked to the narrow, descending stairway leading to the ground floor. *I need to interrogate Sittia and Ler; those legionnaires... looked sick.* He hurried down the steps, his gaze already scanning the floor for a mount. *The orders I'll give—to hold, to understand what happened—should confirm my intentions to Lady Seve.*

Dante landed on the ground floor a moment later, aiming directly towards the open doors; a few messengers were stationed there, and he could fetch one of their horses. *A simple plan. Find Juçe, control Sittia, wait for the Sestelii spies, and send a response to Lady Seve.* That smirk tugged at his lips again, and Dante let it flourish while beckoning towards the nearest messenger. *Hold to the method: chaos teaches, challenge tempers.*

### LEGATE OF EGON HOLD, EASTERN LEGIONS OF FIRARD

The palomino's gallop faltered into a rough canter, neighing nervously as Dante crossed the plains surrounding Furia Gorge's entrance—barely half an hour ride from Egon Hold. The surviving legionnaires scattered about, some staring emptily while seated in half-packed carts, while others wandered aimlessly before collapsing to vomit bile. *This isn't exhaustion. This is something else.* Dante steadied his mare into a walk, leading it away from a group of survivors—clutching their heads with panic in their eyes. *Are those… wails?* He veered in time to avoid a handful of meandering legionnaires tailed by medici apprentices. *They move as if waking from a nightmare, except it still clings to them.*

Patting the mare's neck to soothe it, Dante assessed the cohorts guarding the Gorge's entrance. They hadn't moved since he'd stationed them there earlier that morning, but the formation had now broadened into a larger half-circle. Several Triarii had dispersed to patrol alongside the medici, a trio of well-armed legionnaires protecting the latter. *What happened here? Have the survivors… attacked our healers?*

Blinking to scatter his stupefaction, Dante frowned at the single well-assembled tent in the fields—low and rectangular, with stained leather and open flaps—and hurried his mare towards it. It'd been settled for the War Games only to be repurposed in the quake's aftermath.

A flurry of people swirled around it, each pretending to be busy but clearly attempting to eavesdrop on the conversation inside. *The Sestelii ears must be here already. Useful now, but problematic in the future.* He recounted two medici assistants unloading supplies, Watchers and runners ready to depart, three Prefects—precisely those assigned to tail the Centurions—a handful of Triarii standing guard, and a few stable-hands; one was soothing a black-bay stallion. *That is Juçe's.*

Dante reined the palomino near the stable-hands, tossing the reins to one as he dismounted in one fluid motion. *As planned: hold and understand first. Then, decide.* The surrounding crowd hurried to salute, but the Legate strode straight through the tent's open flaps. He halted a few steps in, acknowledging the legionnaires that had snapped to attention—all except two.

Centurion Sittia Praeto sat on a stool in the centre, her cuirass half-disassembled while the medicus sitting near washed her wounds with a cloth. Her sword arm was bleeding from several cuts, a bruise mottled the left side of her neck, and a fresh gash split her right cheek to run down along her jawline. She blinked twice—as if trying to focus her eyes—before sitting straighter. *How much blood did she lose? Her burns after the Nadir erupted were worse… and she kept leading from the front.*

Behind her, Decanus Ler Halde sat on another stool, stoically allowing another medicus to wash him clear of the debris; grimy water dropped across his face, slowly revealing his fawn hair and the sharp dip of his gaze—a makeshift salute the Legate acknowledged in kind. *Curiously unscathed.* Centurions Petra and Juçe completed the group, each tailed by a pair of Decanii, all still squared at attention.

"At ease," Dante dismissed them with a hand. Glancing over his shoulders, he beckoned the Prefects into the tent—they would need to execute his orders. "Keep the flaps open," he clarified, turning back to the group, gaze etched in Sittia. "What happened?"

She inhaled sharply, sucking saliva and spitting clotted

blood. Her medicus watched the carmine clout, blinked, and fetched another wet cloth to press into her bleeding cheek.

"That fog…" Sittia coughed, swallowing hard. Her voice was roughed after five decades of shouting in battlefields. *But it's… harsher now. Did inhaling the fog cause this?* "—that can only be a weapon. Sestelii, undoubtedly."

*If it were a weapon, why would Lady Seve have called for a retreat instead of pressing the attack?* The Legate breathed calmly, schooling his countenance and pocketing one hand. *Could it'd been an attempt against Lady Seve?* Taking his time to answer, he glanced askance at the other Centurions, noticing Juçe's tight scowl and Petra's curiosity. *If so… from who? The Seve matriarch?* He turned back to Sittia, now grimacing as the medicus replaced the cloth for a clean one. *Remaining open-minded is essential; there is a lesson in this.*

"The fog only spread after the earthquake," Dante observed, intent on understanding what Sittia and the Legions had experienced. *I have only baseless conjectures. I need something concrete.* "Where did it come from, and why did you stay?"

"It wasn't fog at first; it felt like moisture in the air. Just humidity." She licked the blood trailing into the corner of her mouth, swiping her left hand over her iron hair—sticky and clammed into thick strands. "It started after the cliff sheared… but impossible to know when."

*That's not what I asked.* Dante narrowed his eyes, thoughtful. "Air moisture doesn't turn into fog, and this region is too dry for haze that deep." *We aren't precisely close to the Nadir, but the air here is still crisp and dry. Was that fog, then, induced?* He pointed down with a finger. "And why did you stay, Centurion?"

Sittia snarled, the gesture upsetting her wound. Blood bubbled from it, dripping onto her wounded arm—tense, fisted hand resting atop her knee.

"The quake was no reason to halt the Games. We had already engaged Ler's first… ambush wave and were winning. We—" She gritted her teeth as the medicus looped a strap around her upper biceps, cinching it. "—we've faced worse; in The Sweep, in the Siege of Ílun Fort, when the Nadir erupted above us during the Orenian invasion. A mere mist wouldn't stop us."

Her eyes shut when the medicus washed her wound with a spirit, beginning the sutures. "When the soldiers began stumbling and... garbling nonsense, I understood it as..." Another pause, another stitch. "—as the cowardly bouts of untrained legionnaires stricken by a decent ambush strategy."

*And thus, the reason she overstayed was her legendary stubbornness.* Dante clicked his tongue, choosing to convey his exasperation at the uncharacteristically haphazard report. "How come the soldiers were 'garbling nonsense'?" He pressed, raising his voice and hissing, "Report, Centurion!"

For the first time since his arrival, Sittia glared at him, unfazed even as the medicus stitched her cheek. Dante lifted his chin and held her gaze.

"After the fog thickened... we heard the Sestellii approaching. Running straight to us." She lingered, lips so tightly pressed that her lower face contorted in a hundred furrows. "Some had hidden within our ranks, while others rushed at us. They were everywhere."

*The... Sestelii?* Dante's frown eased as surprise washed over him—and then he finally studied Sittia's features. Her sweat-slicked forehead, the sickly hue of her olive skin, the dilated pupils of her brown eyes. *Blood loss? No, she's been through worse.* His frown returned, fuelled by concern before meeting the medicus' knowing gaze. He nodded grimly, continuing with the sutures. *Sittia is feverish at the least. Not as bad as the others outside, but enough that I cannot trust her words.*

Displeased, Dante stared at Ler—now cleaner than before—to demand, "But how did *this*—" He flung an arm towards the tent flap, indicating the fields cluttered with weeping soldiers who easily bounced into histrionic laughter. "—happened? *When* did it happen?"

The ensuing silence was cut short when a group of meandering legionnaires collapsed paces outside the tent's placement. The chasing medici yelled for assistance, and three guards rushed to help.

"I cannot provide too many details, Legate," Ler finally answered, swiping his mouth with the back of his hand—clear of the gauntlet and wrapped in bandages. "We heard enough of our vanguard's first ambush to know it was time to move. Shortly after my main unit exited the caverns, the landslide trapped my rearguard inside. After it quelled…" His features disclosed a hundred doubts in tiny gestures. A parted, speechless mouth, narrowed eyes that widened in confusion, a loose hand that tried to grasp for words, and an intake of breath to muster courage. "We heard weapons, erratic. Distorted voices, shouting, laughter, crying. We… kept marching through the caverns that hadn't collapsed." Pausing, he glanced briefly at Petra—as if seeking approval—before continuing. "We exited near the midpoint of the Gorge, yet still within Firardian territory. The fog was thick, and we saw the Seve army fighting far onto their side, but… the fog was too dense to determine against whom or what."

*So he survived through a convenient misfortune.* Dante nodded, his prior tension now returning redoubled, a tight fist shaking within his pocket. *But why were the Sestelii fighting on their own side? Did our troops march that far east? Or did they engage someone else?* Pressing his lips, he rolled his free hand to demand more information out of the Decanus—but Ler simply shook his head, mouthing an apology. *This… contradicts Sittia. And he has nothing to gain by doing so.*

"You saw the Seve army…" Dante stated, continuing without waiting for a confirmation. "How many? And where did they come from?"

Sittia blinked, barely noticing the medicus stitching her jawline. "Hard to say. Half… our numbers." She paused when the man cut the sinew. "I gauged… the Sestelii were lurking close to our side of Furia Gorge. They caused the quake and attacked. They l-likely knew… where Ler was."

*But if so, Ler should've seen the Sestelii corpses upon returning.* Subtly, Dante arched a brow at him—questioning, demanding. *I must confirm this when the medici attempt to retrieve the fallen.* "What happened after you saw the Sestelii? What happened to your vanguard and main unit, Ler?" He angled his head to indicate the survivors outside. "It seems that at least half of each Legion perished."

The Decanus dropped his gaze. "We crossed plenty of fallen

legionnaires. All those I saw…" He glanced at Sittia before clenching his hands over his knees. "—were Firardians; I assumed they had collapsed due to the fog. It was sharp when inhaling, and after minutes of marching under it, our vision blurred and advancing became strenuous." Pausing again, he swiped his mouth. "We dragged only those who seemed to move, but even that was difficult. There was almost no visibility."

*If Ler only saw Firardians… were Sittia's forces fighting each other? Why?* He exhaled loudly, pinching his nose while a group of medici assistants hurried inside, bringing clean water and removing the bloodied clothes. *What happened inside the Gorge?*

"Why didn't you retreat when the cornua began calling?" Dante demanded again, halting when the survivors outside howled again. He waited until they dissolved into wailing before adding, "They blared for hours."

Just like before, Ler pressed his lips into a line. Meanwhile, Sittia gaped, licking her lips and swallowing hard. *Thirsty? Her lips… look cracked. Dry.* She snapped into her usual, brutal glimmer of anger, her gaze finally focusing on Dante's.

"We disengaged soon after hearing them." Sittia seethed, saliva dripping from the corner of her lips. "The legionnaires… they were too untrained and green. They wouldn't march back."

*Untrained? Only fewer than a quarter were fresh!* Dante rolled a hand to dismiss her. *I'd hazard a guess they didn't recognise the cornua's command… if they heard it at all. Whatever happened under that fog… I won't unveil that mystery now.* Half-turning, he glanced over his shoulder to find the three Prefects he'd requested— standing at attention, and ready to receive their orders. *Just as decided: hold and understand. Given what I just heard, attacking now would be madness.*

"After the survivors have calmed, organise a report. Everyone conscious enough to speak will be called." He stated, searching the trio for whom to task. His gaze landed on the blonde woman he'd found earlier that morning on the middle ramparts. "Partner with medici to do so; Viators or Peritus ranks or above; nobody less experienced. We'll need to understand when we can retrieve the fallen. Report to me once you are done."

She snapped to attention, acknowledging his command—but from the corner of his eyes, Dante caught Juçe unfolding his arms, eyes narrowed in contempt. *Concerned for Sittia? Impossible; your marriage has always been an alliance.*

Dante pretended not to see him, instead returning towards the Prefects to beckon at the second one. "Reinforce the guard around Gorge's entrance; but use only defensive positions. We are not preparing an assault." The Legate stated, beckoning the man towards the tent's flap and into the plains beyond, then gestured to the last Prefect. "Send Watchers south to Tormenta Plains, and request Imperial Loren to survey the area. He must remain in a defensive stance. Do you know where—?"

"We should attack now, not retreat!" Centurion Juçe clicked his tongue, anger roughening his voice into a hiss. "That Sestelii noblewoman has always been a coward! We must leverage her weakness!"

*Of course.* The Legate glanced over his shoulder, his gaze locking onto Juçe's. After a long moment, he turned to face the Centurion while raising a deliberate brow—a taunting gesture perfected over years of outranking his father. *This... can be useful. Lady Seve will understand my stance once she learns of this.*

"The Sestelii struck first, and with a weapon we don't understand. Then they fled. Like cowards." Juçe pointed one quivering finger down, then slowly directed it to the entrance. "We must strike now before they deploy that fog again."

"You already proposed such an argument, Centurion. There is no evidence that this was a Sestelii weapon; and if it was, we cannot counter it. Not without understanding what caused *that* —" Dante jutted his chin towards the outside, where the echoes of weeping and puking continued. "You forget the Seve army retreated. We would be attacking with no grounds except guesswork." *There is a reason why both our nations have endured for almost thirty-four centuries.*

"What you propose, Legate, is doing nothing but licking our wounds," Juçe countered, gritting his teeth. "We cannot hesitate now. We must strike before they refine that weapon and finally overpower the Emerald Legions."

*And what you propose, father, is acting out of fear and wounded pride; neither would ensure the survival of our nation.* Instead of answering, Dante remained quiet, bobbing his head in idle acknowledgement to taunt the Centurion. *Discipline after. For now, only control.*

As the silence stretched, he swiped his gaze to Petra and Ler, Sittia and her medicus, and then to the Prefects and Decanii surrounding the group—each fixed on him, waiting for his word, for his command.

"Lady Seve has already retreated. She tested that fog on us and withdrew to save face." Juçe redoubled, taking a step forward and pointing to the Gorge's entrance. "She is testing how we react and, for now, we keep falling into her trap!"

"What you are proposing is to wage war over a hunch and, according to your view, when at a disadvantage. We have no evidence of whether that fog was a natural occurrence or a weapon." Dante finally rebuked, beckoning eastwards as if he could point to the other continent across the world. "Do you think our Ochrese allies would sit idle?" He let the question linger, rolling a hand to demand an answer and only continuing when none was provided. "Lares and Aurel would either attack us to cement their alliance with Sestel, or revive their old quarrels with our allies, Sessentas and Alboré." *And what do you think Orenos and Presya would do? Sit idle as we weaken each other?*

Juçe pressed his lips, looking around as if to gather support —but Sittia's gaze was unfocused and unseeing, and both Petra and Ler stared, purposefully, at the Legate. Beyond them, every other Decanii stood at attention, staring away from Juçe.

When Juçe inhaled, the sharp slash of air hissed like a reluctant retreat. "Then at least let me send a force to test their defences."

"No. We hold," Dante commanded, loud enough that the surrounding legionnaires squared as if the order had been issued to them. *I'm not here to salvage your ego, father. I just need Lady Seve to be informed of this conversation.* "My order is final, Centurion."

Juçe nodded—a curt tilt of his head he disguised in a half-turn towards Sittia. Her bleeding was finally contained, and the medicus was now wrapping her sword arm with deft motions.

*Yet she has remained awake. Perhaps her intoxication is not as terrible as the others...* She stared at him with a lazy gesture, and Dante ignored her, instead assessing those surrounding them. *If she recovers, she'll push her view as the sole truth. She's the Ash-Walker, the Invicta; she has the standing for it.*

Dante studied the scene for a moment before turning on his heels and striding towards the tent's entrance. As he stepped into the daylight—with the Prefects filtering out behind him to carry his orders—his eyes flicked to the familiar figure waiting for him.

*Legate Ilia Larya? When did she arrive? How much did she listen?* He strode towards his Northern Legion peer. She was slightly older than him, darker than the night, and wore the strategists' uniform—a simple white camisia tucked into emerald trousers —with an elegance any Sestelii Noble would envy.

"I admire your patience, Legate Praeto." She stated as he slowed to a stop, smiling with a roguish hint in her onyx eyes. "Not many could look beyond the immediate chaos and see what's at stake long term." Dipping her eyes, she proffered a stretched arm, palm open—then relaxed, whispering, "Some things never change, Dante."

*So she's been here long enough to listen. Even better.* Dante smiled openly at her, taking her proffered arm to grip her forearm. "You haven't lost your timing, Ilia. We find ourselves involved in quite a complex situation." He beckoned to the surrounding mayhem with his eyes. "We can't provoke Sestel before understanding what happened."

"Indeed." The Northern Legate released his hand, gesturing to the stable-hands to approach. One was holding his palomino, another Ilia's bay. She picked her reins but leant closer to enunciate, "I understand two of the five Marshals may be on their way to us. Likely Gora and Nagore."

"Understood." He exhaled, retrieving the reins of his palomino. *The Marshals enabled this chaos. It matters not; I'll manage it.* Pulling the horse, he mounted in a swift motion. "Ride with me, Ilia. There is much to discuss."

"I can imagine," she grinned, displaying a row of perfect

white teeth. "This is already more complex than the Orenian invasion."

Dante grimaced; that former clash had been the most difficult of his career until now. *Yet the challenge was worth it. It taught me... even if I still cannot find a path towards the Meridian.* Pulling the reins, he guided the mare southeast towards Egon Hold; it neighed before springing into a gallop. As they travelled, Dante spared a single glance eastwards. *Now, answer me, Lady Seve. One way or another. But if this was your doing... I won't stand still.*

# Calya

The sleek chestnut flicked its ears, so exhausted it barely swished its tail. Sitting stiffly in the saddle, Lady Calya Seve switched the reins into her gloved left and rolled her aching right shoulder. As she did so, she scrunched the minute paper roll—a veilwing's letter signed by Lord Asier Aurri—between her fingers. *So he did as requested; intercepting the reserve's messages headed further inland. It serves as contention, but...* The clatter in the fields swallowed the papery noises as she stuffed the missive into her pommel bag. *Why hasn't the Legate answered me? Should I assume Firard will blame us?* Her eyes watered, and she massaged her forehead while blinking the moisture away. *It matters not. Whatever Firard does, my next move is to control public opinion by presenting us as the victims of an unprovoked assault.*

Sighing, Calya gazed into the afternoon sky—a muted, metallic grey, tinged with lavender above the mountains. The fog had lifted, but dust still shimmered in the air, catching the light like pearlescent specks. Furia Gorge had been quiet for hours, with neither the Sestelii tubas nor the Firardian cornua blasting their retreat calls.

*That fog... it must have affected the Firardians as well. The archers reported the landslide to be slightly west of the Gorge's midpoint.* Calya chewed on her bottom lip, scowling at the formation still posted around the entrance. They had retreated a further twenty paces, giving room for the smaller units marching into the ravine to recover the dead—knots of healers and stretcher-bearers flanked by soldiers, all breathing from behind wet scarves. *But what truly happened? We have only mumbled, drooled confessions from half-conscious soldiers! What poison was in that fog? Who released it?* Calya's cheek twitched as a unit emerged, dragging their stretchers, two corpses piled on each. *I need actionable information. Now. What are you doing, Legate Praeto? Did you kill my spies?*

Still chewing her lips, Lady Seve assessed the area before her —cluttered with stretchers and occupied by healers tending to the remains of her vanguard. It'd been over two hundred soldiers, but it had sustained heavy casualties—and the few survivors were collapsing at an unforgiving rate. Most were drooling or breathing harshly, often panicking at the air itself. *It looks like the aftermath of a collective hallucination. Disastrous, were it a weapon.* The mare neighed when a painful wail cut through the eerie quietude, and Calya patted it on the neck while searching for a runner. *I need Lady Varre. If anyone can uncover something convincing enough for me to sway the Nobles and redirect public opinion, it's her.*

Finding a messenger—a boy with sharp features and a focused frown—Calya beckoned him to approach while steering the mare to round on the youngster.

"Fetch Lady Hori Varre. Immediately," she commanded upon arrival, barely glancing north for directions. "Inform her we will meet shortly at the encampment outside Ferro Keep. Go."

The boy sprang to attention, muttering his acknowledgement before dashing northwards and out of view. Calya watched him for a moment, subtly massaging her thighs—they ached with every shift in the saddle, a dull burn threading through each muscle. Her hips had stiffened hours ago, and her back had long since abandoned any pretence of comfort. A groan hovered on her lips, but she pressed them shut, steeling her features. *I need to understand what the fog—*

"My Lady!" A familiar voice called from afar; bright and youthful, yet slowly melding into a mature tone. "My Lady!"

*Ruria! She must bring news from the Firardian spies!* Suppressing a blossoming, pleased smile, Calya ushered her chestnut mare forward. Every hoofbeat echoed on her tired back, but receiving the promised news outweighed her discomfort.

Ruria Laxalt, slight in her scout's dark leathers, rode like a shadow against the washed-out landscape. Her small perlino gelding obeyed with crisp precision, halting neatly as she met Calya halfway. She bowed while repositioning side by side, discreetly proffering two rolls of paper.

Lady Seve retrieved them in a swift motion, studying the paper—thin and translucent, classic veilwing note. She traced a finger along the torn edges before carefully unfolding it, noting the smeared ink. *Written and folded in a hurry? Did Legate Praeto catch my spies?* Tilting her head in consideration, she pressed her lips while reading it.

> *Centurion Sittia survived. Legions sustained heavy losses. Centurion Juce requested to attack. Legate Praeto enforced a standby. Argued against warring Sestel. Requested investigation of the fog's symptoms.*

*Too detailed. Deliberate or poor planning?* Impassive, Lady Calya unfolded the second note with as much care as a battlefield afforded. *Deliberate,* she concluded while skimming through a detailed list of symptoms experienced by the surviving Firardians—then arched a brow at a particular note. *Fighting each other? What happened there?* She stared at the words as if to coerce them to explain themselves. *An attempt to induce war? A failed weapon test?* Exhaling, she ignored the for-now unsolvable conundrum to focus on what mattered. *Regardless of the reason, Legate Praeto chose to make his stance—peaceful, for now—clear to me.* A smirk unfurled on her lips, fuelled by the zeal of possibly reforging the thin peace balancing Sestel and Firard—ever wary, but never quite fearful of each other. Whatever happened then was another chance to steer both nations into a delicate balance. *Another opportunity to leverage.*

Calya refolded the notes, carefully stowing the first on her pommel bag, but keeping the other on her fist. *Lady Varre could use this to produce the evidence I need; she'd also appreciate the insights.* "Did these come together?"

"Same veilwing. One on each leg..." Ruria focused on the Lady, lingering until the silence became an implicit allowance to whisper a question. "Do you think the fog... was a Firardian weapon?"

"What do *you* think?" The Lady countered, tilting her head enough to taunt the youngster. *Think, little one. I need my aides to understand the basics of politics.* After all, and for the plan to work, there was an opinion to leak to Firard, and another to feed into the Sestelii masses.

The redhead brightened with delight. "If this was their doing, they could destroy us." Ruria glanced at the stretchers laid methodically on the fields, then sucked her bottom lip. "I doubt Firard would taint the War Games like so. They are fundamental in rising through the ranks of the Emerald Legions to become a Firardian citizen. Given their strategists are anything but fools..." She paused, pinching her chin with slender fingers, emerald eyes narrowed in thought. "—it was either a natural accident, or the mistake of a dissident faction. Non-citizens, perhaps."

*Sharp; quicker than anyone else.* Calya nodded with deliberate slowness, darkening her voice until only the youngster heard. "Or it could've been an Orenian attack. One meant to pitch Sestel and Firard against each other."

"Retaliation from the invasion? To force us into a war, then attack us?" Ruria whispered, the mere idea waning her already pale skin. She blinked rapidly for a moment, prolonging the silence until a realisation slackened her features. Restraining herself, she toyed with her reins while hand-signalling, *"Regardless of what you think, my Lady, Firard must understand this is your stance."*

*An excellent yet dangerous observation.* The Lady hummed in acknowledgement, approving the response and the implied path forward. *Foreign or domestic, it changes nothing; public opinion is meant to be shaped, not followed.*

Ruria straightened at the subtle approval, the tiniest,

proudest joy reflecting on her countenance. Her reins were already tightly held when she hand-signalled, *"I'll inform our contact, my Lady."*

*She sees the game… or part of it.* "Come back to me afterwards," Calya requested, adjusting her seat—both to ease the grind of leather and bone, and stir her mare to attention. *But seeing is not enough; I need her to play my way.* "Go!"

Without waiting, she ushered the chestnut into a trot, let it stretch into a canter, then pushed it into a gallop toward the nearest encampment. *Ruria's message to Imperial Elixane should be enough of a confirmation for the Legate.* Leaning forward, she stole a glance over her shoulder, barely catching sight of Ruria's red hair—retreating to act as ordered—before the wind whipped her focus forward again. *Now, Exarch Luxa must read my truth… and so make it* the *truth.*

Lady Hori Varre cut a striking figure amidst the frantic movement of the encampment. Lean and dark-skinned, she wore her long black braids twisted into an elaborate ponytail. *Beautiful and capable, a deadly combination.* Her onyx eyes flickered from those clustered around her—all wearing worn field clothes and grim resolve—onto Calya's. Without waiting for further instructions, she offered a few quiet words to the group before sending them away.

Appreciative, Lady Seve slowed her mare to a walk, then halted near Hori. Her boots hit the ground with relief, and although her knees threatened to buckle, she held herself up while a stable-hand took the chestnut away.

"My Lady." Calya steered her peer further away from that spot and into a small clearing amidst the busy encampment. "I trust you'd been briefed on the day's events?"

Hori dipped her head, a slight scrunch on her button nose. "I have, although the descriptions of symptoms seem… conflicting. Likewise, the earth-scholars I brought are confused about the fog." Her deep, fruity voice dragged the words to highlight their inaccuracy. "It seems similar to what we've seen in the mines of the Petricor Mountains, yet not quite so." Hori lingered, frowning delicately before lowering her voice to a bare hint. "May I ask what you are considering, my Lady?"

Calya hummed in acknowledgement, appreciating the subtlety. *A whisper in this encampment is the loudest message I could send.* "We know the fog sickened our soldiers, but the details of the events are inconclusive at best," she lingered, offering a pensive frown. "Now for the source of it... I have my reservations, yet cannot discard the Orenians to be this far south—perhaps searching for revenge after their disastrous invasion."

Hori's eyes widened enough that the afternoon light reflected like silver discs on her onyx eyes—then she controlled her expression, clasping her hands near her navel. "I will focus on unveiling whatever that fog was. Perhaps understanding its nature will guide us towards its source."

*As I said, beautiful and clever.* Calya dipped her head, shifting close enough as to pretend to confide on the taller woman while pressing the second note—the list of symptoms—onto Hori's hands. She curled her fingers, enclosing the note while lifting a delicate, questioning brow.

"Information. From a source," Lady Seve clarified, taking a step back to raise her voice—just enough for the breeze to carry it. "Do inform me of your findings, Lady Varre. I trust we will speak again soon."

"Of course." Hori slid her hand, still clutching the note, into her hip pocket—an almost invisible opening on her tight trousers. "I'll send a veilwing to you."

With a polite nod, Calya turned on her heels, striding towards the Watchers—a cluster of three, guarding an ensemble of cages occupied by birds that shone cobalt. *One more message, then I can finally return to Ferro Keep.* As her gaze fell on the nearest one, she quickened her pace, the faint sting in her legs urging her forward. *After that, it'll be a matter of finding an acceptable culprit for this event. One that stirs us away from a war with Firard.*

# Dante

Dante's gaze drifted away from the note in his hand and onto the inner patio outside the window—an enclosed garden built centuries ago yet maintained to perfection. The dusk had begun, washing out the teal of the plants and layering the sky with cool twilight hues that blended into the ghostly silver lingering from the afternoon. It contrasted with the warm lanternlight emanating from within the room, mirroring the edge of his countenance on the window's glass.

Sharp and precise, outlined with the strands of his now loose hair, but missing his grin—edged with hunger, lit by thought. Ravenous to solve the political puzzle before him. *I'm there again; teetering on the edge between peace and war. Toying with lives, yet fixated on the challenge.* It was a feral feeling, bright with curiosity, eager to uncover the knowledge to prove the Meridian was either unachievable, or real and within reach. *This is what guides me forward. Can I hold Firard over that edge?*

He chuckled bitterly, hanging his head, raven strands falling into view before he swiped them back with one hand. *Or perhaps it's just a vestige of the thrill I felt when young; the one that guided me to disobey my father and join the Strategists.* That memory soured him, and Dante strode away from the window, reaching for the marble desk and quickly opening the lantern atop it. The thin paper of the veilwing note crackled as the fire ate it.

"She must have fed us the information," Elixane hissed from across the room, chin jutting towards the lantern.

She was standing near the closed wooden door, one hand pocketed on her emerald trousers, the other fisted at her side. For a moment, her slate-grey eyes seemed to reflect the fire, almost in fear of the letter burning there. Her emotions were flourishing on her features—parting her mouth with a tremor of concern, narrowing her eyes with reluctant weariness, and squaring her shoulders in preparation. It was the moment of truthfulness every Strategist allowed themselves when in private.

"But even if my contact wasn't compromised..." The Imperial's whisper hung unfinished as anger and confusion warred on her gestures. She waved them away with her free hand. "No; it's too detailed. Could it'd been... an impostor? If so, my backup contact could also be compromised!"

Still enthralled by the populated bookshelves lining the room's walls, Legate Ilia Larya barely acknowledged the concern. She retrieved a book, swiping through its pages.

Dante didn't reply either, absorbed by the flickering flame. It hissed, devouring the paper, tongues orange and red like flowing blood, like burning wounds. It snapped as it tore one edge, growing larger and louder, popping and crackling until Elixane's voice was lost in the screams.

They were so loud. So terrifyingly loud.

He blinked, and ashfall rained again, sticking to his uniform, burning even though the fire was surging far away in the Nadir. It spat molten stone to the sky, pouring it upon the Legions a moment later, mud-flows sweeping down and obliterating paths of retreat. From afar, the Peaks were hills of flames—yet he'd used it to Firard's advantage. From his vantage point, with the cold-headedness only distance could afford, with his sight set on the victory because duty called for it.

The fire flickered, wailing, consuming, growing and growing—

"Dante?" Ilia's voice. Too real, too present.

The Legate snapped his gaze away from the lantern's flame, clenching his jaw—there was no time for memory. That was then. This was now. *And it demands answers just like Lady Seve does.* He waved an apologetic hand before sliding it through his hair—both to tame some strands, but also to swipe away the sweat dotting his forehead. *It didn't bother me when Sittia mentioned it... but now? In privacy?* The stench of burnt flesh lingered in memory, yet it forced him to swallow hard. *After my focus is gone, the memories... they always come back. Always.*

Closing his eyes, he forced himself to remember the spy's letter, letting the thrill of the problem ahead reignite his mind.

"I wouldn't put it past Lady Seve to feed us information..." Dante stated after a while, savouring each word to ground himself in the present. When he faced Elixane again, that ravenous smirk again tugged at his lips. "—but one has to admire her nonetheless."

Forcing his focus, he met Elixane's eyes—frowning, piercing, confused. A question dangling unasked.

Dante arched a brow. "Can't you see? That letter, those few lines of half-coded words, is a prime example of strategic positioning." *I'm back; I'm here. After the fog, after the quake.* He raised a finger, counting the implications. "By leaking her public interpretation of the events, Lady Seve informed us of Sestel's position. We all know the Exarch will not openly contradict her simply not to make himself the target of the Seve armies—armies that will outmatch the Luxa enforcers in numbers and expertise." Assessing the Imperial's waning countenance, Dante raised another finger. "Given prior events, we can assume Lady Varre and Lord Zuria will also align with Seve's view, thus combining the support of four out of six Sestelii Noble Houses." He pointed towards the map on the leftmost wall—a rich, hand-painted outline of Firard's and Sestel' territories outlining regions, cities, and trade routes. "That is Luxa, Varre, Zuria and, of course, Seve itself. After that, their Ochrese allies—Lares and Aurel—will also accept this view."

Silence pressed in. Taut, breathless, and thick with the implications now hovering above them. Imperial Elixane half-stumbled towards the wall, resting her weight as if the stone-made bookshelf would support her standing; she shifted her weight, shielding her waning features with both hands. On the other side of the room, Ilia continued to skim the pages of a thick tome—a volume on the Grand Conclave—with the concern one afforded to messy handwriting.

"By making that stance public, Lady Seve forced our hand." Dante breathed sharply, the echoes of the past now replaced by the challenge of facing a political move that outplayed him. *For now. Only for now.* "If we attack now, our actions would be an unjustified breach of an unspoken understanding of non-aggression with Sestel. Besides plunging us into a war with a rival that matches us in resources, technology, education, military, and navies... such an attack would shock our allies, shattering their trust in us." He lingered, watching the marble desk and tracing the Ochrese continent on its veins. "Enough, perhaps, to request we remove our Legions from their land and our fleets from their ports."

Ilia snapped the tome closed, the sound echoing in the room. "And losing our Ochrese allies would mean also losing resources during wartime. Sestel may destroy us." She chuckled, her lips curling in a grin as savage as Dante's—half awe, half dread; the kind born of minds who acted for the long-term even when the price was blood. "One has to admire that woman."

*It is a risky, clever threat veiled as a move for peace.* "But Lady Seve gave us something more interesting still." Dante continued, rubbing his hands as if savouring the moment. "She gave us a public stance strong enough to corner the Centurions: Juçe, Sittia, and the handful vying for war. They worship honour above everything else, and we can use this view—of suspecting an Orenian attack—to temporarily restrain them."

Elixane frowned, tilting her head; her long, black braid tumbled from her shoulder and onto her back. "Why do you think she's doing this?" She waved a hand towards the map, struggling for words. "Lady Seve is anything but a pacifist. The way she subdued Aurel... even a decade after we keep studying that political throttle."

*A keen observation.* Dante's gaze steered back to the bookshelves as a feeble reminder to reread his notes of the Sideral Accords in search of clues. *I learnt much from that strategy.*

"Yet after she did so, she spent five years rebuilding the relationship with Aurel until they became one of Sestel's stronger supporters. A move that also put Lord Zuria on her side," Ilia interjected, pocketing both hands with a calmness seemingly misplaced after the day's events. "Therefore... we must ask ourselves what her underlying reasons are. What motivates her?"

Dante nodded in agreement—but when he looked up, his gaze fell on the open lantern. He strode back to the desk, closing the contraption to hide the flame from view.

Elixane grunted, moving away from the wall to hiss, "I could request the spies to be killed... but that itself would be a message we may not want to send." The exhaustion of the day was setting on her features, purple half-moons embracing her eyes. "What should we do?"

*Face the challenge, find the answers.* "I'll write to the Emerald Council, while you share the same view with our Centurions. That should be enough for Lady Seve to confirm our stance." Dante commanded, tucking a few strands of hair behind his ear. He looked at Ilia, holding her gaze. "I believe our focus should be to understand that fog and, through that, its source. Without that knowledge, we have nothing but conjectures."

ORENOS
ZAFIRO GULF
SESTEL
VENTUS HARBOUR
SOMBRA FOREST
IZURE ABYSS
COBALTO RIVERS
VEGA FORTRESS
UMBRA
PETRICOR MOUNTAINS
THE DEADLANDS
NORTHERN LEGION
ILUN FORT
BRUMA PASS
VAST EXPANSE
IRON STRETCH
WESTERN LEGION
PEAKS OF NADIR
TERRO KEEP
CLAW'S FOLD
CENTRAL LEGION
TURIN GORGE
EGON HOLD
FIRARD
ARBORUM
SILENTE VALE
SANGUINE SEA
PRESYA
QUINTET RIVER
EASTERN LEGION
TORMENTA PLAINS
SOUTHERN LEGION
LIMINAL HARBOUR
N

# Amok



Soul Transmuter Alchemist. The Untamed One

Darkness coated the region, the twin-suns long hidden under the horizon to bring true night. The sky had blurred into cooler, plum and cobalt hues that washed the world in a spectral haze; it flickered on the pearlescent specks remaining from the quake Berserk had induced, each spark contrasting the rich warmth emanating from the torchlight scattered throughout Ferro Keep. Rising at its centre, the Central Residence glistened in the abyssal light, its marble exterior a sharp contrast to the rough-hewn ironstone of the outer walls.

Amok recognised what it was. A display of opulence and power seldom merited, a trait of humankind that would always exist. They built structures that would endure ages because their ephemeral lives were so fleeting, so easily forgettable, so fluctuating and irrelevant nothing else would leave a mark. No matter the world, no matter the age, no matter the beliefs and creeds, humans would always lean towards the same—discord, destruction, and delusions of grandeur.

Amok understood what it was. Humanity's perennial quest to be remembered, to build legacies, to carve a place in a history that would never allow them to be anything else but sources of alive elements.

Yet on that night—glamoured to invisibility, cloak swaying in the zephyr—Amok turned their focus to the woman leaning against the decorative, marble rail of that private terrace. Lady Calya Seve. Dressed in a gossamer gown that draped from her shoulders to fall in fluid lines, loose hair blending caramel and citrine strands to match the gold-threaded sash with artful beauty.

Amok appreciated what she represented. A curated façade meant to bias the observers and craft a narrative that needed no words but appearances only—one that other humans would eagerly, unknowingly approve because they had never learnt not to be swayed by aesthetics. A perfect exploitation of a never-ending human weakness.

Curious, the Untamed One hovered down until their feet grazed the marble, their footfalls silenced by the glamour that hid them in plain sight. They toed that edge, six-fingered hands clasped tightly on their back, their cobalt, infinite gaze etched on Calya as they halted so close their cloak leaked glyphs near their target.

The one selected by The Rector themselves.

The Rector. The leader of The Orders. The commander who, since time immemorial, had achieved what no other had—the four alchemical transfigurations, and thus the understanding of a universe few fathomed. The one who manipulated existence and crafted schemes that subsisted beyond Amok's compre-hension.

An opportunity like no other, to be yet again involved in such plans.

Amok raved, and their cerulean eyes arched in half-moons to fixate in Calya. Without soul-linking her, the alchemist's assess-ment was impaired—but they welcomed the limitation, the slowness it induced, the flavours that lingered from that almost limited perspective. Regardless, her alive elements—the thoughts and attitudes emanating from her mind—were enthralling.

She was looking at the troops encamped outside the city, three thought-lines surging like strands of smoke, each weaving action paths.

One, factual. *Liabilities, all of them.* Two, swirling as her gaze decanted into the healer's tents. *I must give them an answer, smother their fear into trust*. Three, scheming as she stared into the troops at the edge of the Gorge. *A noble cause. That's what they need; what I must provide.*

To the Untamed One, Calya's mind—even without a soul-link—was a fascinating spectacle. A window to a truth nobody else but her was aware of; a phenomenon meant to be gradually understood with a method so purposefully deliberate it wouldn't alter her *self* but reveal it to Amok.

A true Naturalist approach.

*—mitigate the Praetos. The Centurions—* Unconsciously, she retraced Firard's five Emerald Legions, reviewing the ranks of service, noting key individuals, forecasting the impact of her message. Amok's glyphs shivered when another thought danced across. *Let them chase honour; I will chase outcomes.* She smiled, not from joy, but from the shape her next move was taking. *I will bring stability from the ashes of their pride.* Her nails drummed a muffled rhythm on the marble rail, thoughts embittering as they deviated. *Yet a problem remains: who did this and why?*

Anticipating a discovery, the alchemist crouched low on their perch, knees splayed wide, elbows pressed on the thighs, hands hanging loosely. The glyphs leaking from their cloak swirled with the breeze as Amok tilted their head—almost to extract some hidden truth from the angle alone.

It teased them soon enough, when a hazy recollection slithered through her mind—a mere hint of a memory, a feeling, a desire, a truth barely considered yet thoroughly known, a quest so deeply ingrained Amok only grasped its surface.

Forgetting themselves, the Untamed One finally soul-liked Calya.

Calya's alive elements burst like colourful motes, materialising thought-patterns that swirled under the night sky, dancing in the wind and layering her identity for the alchemist to peruse. Theoretical worlds waltzed around decisions, long-term schemes deconstructed into moves so subtle, so shrouded, so meticulously strategic they crafted outcomes from the shadows themselves. Networks of ideas spread before them—all known, all assessed, all continuously considered in a way so instinctual, so inherent and natural she never thought of them although she knew them.

Amok basked on those alive elements, peeling the layers of Calya's plans, flaying the current memories, stripping her cold-headedness and diving beyond her awareness, and into the unaware—the past that clung to her like a disease, the baseline corroding her future, the secrets that ate her dreams and twisted them into atemporal nightmares.

Each memory was tied to a lesson. Each lesson was now a creed.

One memory. Calya's hands—so small, so pale, so wet with the tears that dripped into them. She was kneeling, shaking, howling—and each scream was a blade tearing reality until nothing but the blood before her existed. It pooled around her knees; it reflected those lifeless green eyes staring back at her. It rippled when Teoda's knife fell.

One lesson. *Every friend is a blind spot, every emotion a liability.*

Another memory. Calya's fear—so overwhelming, so all-encompassing, so muffled by the hand strangling her throat yet scattered with every slap across her face. Teoda was yelling, her face contorted with anger, her features blurred by Calya's tears. Her words were but fragments: smiling, clueing Lady Motza, ruining the scheme.

Another lesson. *Gestures speak louder than treaties.*

A last memory. Calya's reflection—on the mirror, so curated, so perfectly crafted, so methodically constructed it was empty, a void of nothing, a façade held together because it was needed, demanded, safer. There was chatter around, gazes seeking hers, people needing her. There was loneliness in that crowd. She didn't need more.

A last lesson. *No one close, no one to betray me.*

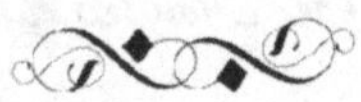

When Amok ended the soul-link the world dulled, those unconscious lessons entombed again on Calya's memories.

Another moment passed, unbeknownst to her as the zephyr whistled, but heavy enough the alchemist grinned—*grinned*— and the gesture sliced their featureless mask, splitting their non-face and revealing the abyss within.

It craved knowledge. It sought to disrupt conformity.

There were so many emotions to extricate, to incarnate out of her—if only that soul-skill were fine-tuned enough, if only Amok knew how to help her survive it. After all, it'd be a shame to lose a mind like this, so instinctively alchemical it warranted nothing else but to be trained as an alchemist.

Exactly as instructed by The Rector themselves.

Amok's grin vanished, restoring their featureless mask albeit their ecstasy glimmered on those narrow, cerulean eyes—fixed on Calya, on her irrevocable, profound need to adapt, to evolve, to survive. To—

"Calya?" A man's voice; a sharp mind, but dull compared to hers. Exhaustion clung to him like the grime in his leathers.

Amok assessed him from afar, slightly amused by Calya's reaction. She offered him a gentle smile, then walked towards him with measured steps, her features melting into feigned concern. When she was close, Lord Asier Aurri proffered his hand, a tiny veilwing note held under his thumb.

*The Exarch's seal!* Calya's surprise remained tucked away, visible to the alchemist but foreign to her features. As she unfurled it, her interest sparked like stars, swirling so fast Amok stood up on their perch—and from that vantage point, the letter became readable.

*...war ill-serves us now, when the balance tilts with each breath and not a sword drawn. Yet the words among people remain too quick to shift, too eager to follow unseen hands. Were they to favour function over unity, the Houses would forget their purpose.*

Calya hummed, glancing at her cousin. "He agrees. For now."

She offered a smirk, but the Untamed One revelled on the secrets it held—visible to them, even without a soul-link. She was crafting scenarios, pondering possibilities, and already tuning the long-term to her desires. *A veiled request or an honest fear?* Calya stared at the letter; Amok tilted their head, the hood shadowing the starlight. *Most likely a fear-induced suggestion.* They followed that thought, amused as it twirled around another. *Concerned about the Houses? Did my mother take her plans too far?*

Asier shuffled his feet, resting a hand on the hilt of the sheathed sword at his hip. "Ruria also sent the other messages. To the Nobles and beyond," he lingered, tapping a finger against the metal, lips curling as if to coerce the words to form. "Should I tail Teoda? She may... see an opportunity." A whisper; barely audible to the humans, shouted to Amok—surrounded in concern, in dismay, in weariness groomed after decades of enduring the matriarch. He gaped, then hand-signalled, *"We cannot afford her splitting the Seve armies."*

*She will not take that away from me.* "She won't," Calya stated, carefully rolling the note again, the paper's texture an anchor to the present. "Never again."

A grunt. That was all Asier answered, albeit his concern was —to the invisible alchemist—a towering, looming mass shrouding his thoughts.

"Lady Varre... does she have anything useful?" Loyalty sparked around him, its trails curling like rivulets that reached for Calya.

"Enough for now," she whispered, offering a shy grin— methodical, rehearsed—then hand-signalled, *"Mass hallucinations. Unreliable reports."* Her thoughts sparked alive. *All the better; fear or interest, whichever is needed, this will support.* "Let us meet tomorrow, cousin. I trust you must rest."

At first, Asier straightened—solemn, disappointed, yet hiding it with polite understanding. He lingered for a moment too long, eventually turning on his heels—yet he stopped after crossing the portico, hesitating for another second before sighing and finally departing.

When he vanished inside the Keep, Calya fisted both hands, setting her face as she turned around. Her gaze—azure yet sharp, dark yet alive—pierced through Amok's. Curiosity leaked through the frayed edges of the alchemist's hood, a hundred possibilities refracting on their eyes—but she looked past, scowling at the Peaks far behind.

The Untamed One revelled in the mission ahead of them. The pursuit of knowledge was subtle, the prey held the answers, and Calya was a curious target, indeed.

# Berserk

SOUL & MATTER TRANSMUTER. THE DRAGON ONE.

Humans. In all flavours and colours, in all shapes and states. Some strewn in stretchers, drooling and dreaming in nightmares, their alive elements erratic and half-lost. Some more walked around, scowling and frowning, silencing their doubts although those surged like tendrils of smoke—coiling with fear, but suppressed by training. Others were grimly quiet, directing the rest, collecting information, plotting and scheming for their petty, trivial interests.

Berserk slithered through them like a rivulet of liquid copper, glamoured to invisibility. They crept through the fields under the night sky, harbouring piles of corpses, then climbed the battlements of iron-stone to sneak through staircases populated by restless Watchers and tired archers.

There was nothing surprising about the humans, nothing to spark Berserk's interest as they slipped into the Citadel—the central, heavily fortified residence within Egon Hold. A summit for Strategists, a residence of sweeping views, a monument to humanity's necessity to establish boundaries and classes, defining power through structures meant to intimidate and divide. Unamused—yet pleased by the reduced number of humans—Berserk crawled through walls of stone decorated with gold-made lanterns, skidded over patterned rugs, and finally slipped under a heavy wooden door.

The room inside was a private library—lined with marble-made bookshelves, outfitted with cushioned lectii, and dominated by a marble desk. Unfazed by the architecture, the Dragon One crawled through the door and rested on its handle.

"—least some Marshals in the Emerald Council support our view," Imperial Elixane Ritz whispered, pacing the room's leftmost side while chewing on her knuckle.

A bright woman ripe with potential. Nothing out of the ordinary.

Legate Ilia Larya hummed in response, departing from the table to plunge into the rightmost lectus. "Our renewed stability with Sestel is feeble. For it to last, we must resolve the fog's mystery. The Marshals need answers as much as the Legions do."

A clever woman with keen eyes and a mind sharper than average. Nothing but an echo of past occurrences.

Still at the desk, Legate Dante Praeto poured over the note stretched on its surface, idly tucking a strand of black hair behind an ear. "The Marshals suggested Orenos and Sestel as possible culprits." He pressed a finger into the paper. "Even going as far as to mention that the intention to begin talks with Sestel is split among them. However, they carefully omitted any consideration of the Legions themselves."

A brilliant man. Just like many others across myriads of civilisations.

Ilia chuckled sourly, elbows pressing onto her knees, hands dangling between. "Which means that, behind closed doors, they're blaming each other for a possible internal, failed coup." She jutted her nose towards the map framed in the opposite wall. "Likely the Northern Legion, given Ler's unfortunate choice of strategy."

Berserk dropped onto the floor, sneaking through the carpet —a fine, hand-painted rug—to climb into the desk and observe their target.

There was nothing new about the Legate, nothing that hadn't appeared before in history, nothing that counted as novel, unique, or surprising. Nothing remotely close to the purveyor of a solution Berserk was not looking for.

Yet The Rector had selected this target themselves.

"Our peace with Sestel is now even more fragile," Dante sighed, each whispered word leaden with concern. "Regardless of my call to retreat, the subsequent standby, and Lady Seve's move... there is now a dubious precedent of escalation. One exacerbated by the half-conscious soldiers claiming they fought hordes of Sestelii."

"That has to be a mass hallucination," Elixane observed, accurately enough that Berserk's liquid metal flickered, fire and chaos shining within—yet she remained ordinary. "Ler confirmed it. The Sestelii never crossed the Gorge's midpoint; they never left Sestel's territory."

The Legate drummed his fingers on the table. "Which is why we'll need him to share the truth in due time."

What was the solution he was due to provide? And to what dilemma exactly?

Neither question would be answered at that moment, and so the alchemist rolled through the ground, slipping beneath the door to crawl through the hallways' gilded walls. As they moved, they transfigured into a dragonlet—four-legged, winged, and shaped from liquid copper. They leapt and flew, meandering through one hallway and another, circling each room, and eaves-dropping on petty conversations in search of *another* target.

One who'll make their mission more involved, since The Rector had encumbered them with no other than Amok—the founder of the Naturalism: a limiting school of thought. A target close to the Centurions, but not too far removed from the Strategists; someone keen, but also savage. One to study, discard, and wear as a façade.

Unable to find that elusive second target, Berserk spread their wings of molten metal, hastening their flight to slip as a door closed for the night. Once outside, they soared along the currents, inspecting the ramparts, the parapets, the guard towers and training grounds. Failing to find a fine target, the alchemist surged again then dived, invisible, past the archers, past the Watchers, past the Prefects and Imperials and—

Her.

Centurion Petra Arvina was a sturdy, bodily powerful woman

with copper hair adorned with a few white strands. She wore it short, buzzed on the left side and swept over to the right—enough for her populated brows to be free for scowling at the menial legionnaires snapping to attention on her approach.

Berserk revelled upon finding their target, gliding around the human before flying behind, through the ramparts, across a gate, down a guard tower and into another hallway—a broad corridor scented like metal and sweat.

Within a fraction of a heartbeat, they soul-linked the human, skimming through the shards of her alive elements until they found the only one needed—her goal to find the medici tent, to meet Decanus Ler. Before that heartbeat ended, the alchemist soul-shaped that shard, willing the goal to change—a minor shift, just enough to coerce her to stop in the nearest door to find an armoury.

Petra hummed at the new idea, blinking in confusion as the soul-shaped need settled in, then reviewed the sheathed sword hanging from her cingulum. She brushed the hilt with her fingertips, tracing the swordbelt as her frown deepened, then looked around for a door. One ajar teased her from afar, and she half-trotted towards it to slip inside.

The door locked with a hollow clunk. She scowled, half-turning—but Berserk dived into her chest like a thrown spear, glamour vanishing, claws of molten metal shrieking across her cuirass. It clattered when she hit the stone floor, a grunt torn from her throat as her body arched. The dragonlet landed hard atop her, wings flared, maws open although no sounds echoed around.

She didn't scream, and they didn't roar.

But when the amalgamation began, her mahogany eyes widened in terror.

Petra's identity opened like a starfield of alive elements, each flicker of light an essential component of her *self*. Thoughts, attitudes, beliefs, creeds—all shining in hues, colliding and colluding, blending to shape her emotions, her perceptions, her senses, her identity. There were suns of values she'd carried for decades, wormholes of pain, nebulas of memories with blurred boundaries because the battlefield allowed for nothing else than the primal need to survive.

Berserk perused that realm, tracing starcharts of alive elements, scouring for whatever was useful yet disregarding the rest because—after the amalgamation ended—there would be no Petra at all.

Beneath the dragonlet the woman wrestled, grunting and groaning, muscles twitching, arms tautening in defiance while her armour screeched—but Berserk took away her bodily control, vanishing her will to move because it was useless to the alchemist.

Instead, he found the recollections of her training, the echoes of those practised movements and reactions, the instinct perfected over decades of training and swordplay. They learnt them all—how to walk like her, how to stand like her, how to run, how to fight, how to seat, how to laugh, how to frown with intentions, how to look down upon her subordinates, how smirk sharper than a blade. Gestures, stances, reactions. They absorbed it all, consuming the alive elements they extracted while the muscles of her chest tore open, ripping, bleeding, stretching, contorting.

She gurgled blood, and it leaked from the corners of her mouth, hatred and revulsion flaring on those deep, warm brown eyes. She uttered something, a remnant of will spent in twisted words—but Berserk wrenched her senses away.

They shredded her speech to pieces, assessing it to absorb it all—how to chuckle and slur the words like her, how to cuss, how to flirt, how to raise her voice until the legionnaires scrambled to do as she commanded.

Yet she still tried to fight—so little that was left, so maimed, so mutilated. It was worth admiring and so Berserk did, flaring the dragonlet's wings, watching her intently as her oozing blood crafted a carmine, liquid mirror that carpeted the floor. There was defiance in her eyes—blind and almost gone, but still rimmed by a scowl. There was rebellion on her grimace—peeled and without lips, so thoroughly flayed it was almost unrecognisable.

But there was more to learn, and so Berserk plucked the remaining alive elements—still bright like suns, still charting a starfield—and reached her knowledge. Of the Legions and the Council, of the Centurions and Legates, of the Firardian history, creed, factions, memories. Of her childhood, lovers, miseries, sorrows. Of the fear she refused to feel, even then.

Bone shattered, consuming itself, each crack remarking Berserk's search as it grazed its end. There was little of her left, yet the alchemist scoured through those lingering alive elements until they found what was needed—that unyielding, ruthless yet pragmatic, shrewd and fierce demeanour everyone within the Legions recognised. An attitude so formative and foundational, its extraction led to her demise.

When the amalgamation finished, the silence was deafening.

Berserk soared, landing on the nearest rack to look down upon the remains.

The blood had sipped into the joints of the bricked stone-floor, crafting carmine rivers that threatened to approach the door—and so they coerced that non-alive element to change, anchoring on the iron it contained and oxidising the rest to air, willing to nothingness the compounds that didn't serve them, and staining the air with a rich, metallic tang.

The armour came after, non-alive alloys and mixtures disassembled as they saw fit, specks merging into the blades stored in the room, into the armours, into the walls. The alchemist flicked their tail, assessing the fragmented body, the shattered bone, and the tendrils of sinew and veins—then dehydrated the first, willing the moisture to scamper away, breaking the carbon and reassembling the air. The bone calcified on Berserk's command, eagerly reshaping into limestone, reforming the stonework and adding a layer of dust no soldier would notice.

When the alchemist battered the wings to fly again, the

armoury was as clean as before, and they used the space to cast a glamour.

It shaped from strands, weaving into the form they'd just learnt, adding hues and shimmers, inducing sounds and scents, mimicking voice and movement as glamour-Petra rolled her shoulders, grinning when Berserk willed it.

A perfect illusion of a boring human.

# Corvera Peninsula

## 5082 Concordia Era (CE)

# Élan

The storm howled in the night, roaring in pain and colliding with the world beneath; an imperfect, chaotic moment where Élan tempted the air to change, soaring through the currents it so induced. They coiled between the strands of smoke, some scented like clean summer air, others so pungent and charred the alchemist grinned—a gesture that slashed their shadows into four wings, a mirage of nightmares and electricity transforming into a metal-made armour gloom as night. When they swirled again, their hair rustled with the wind, silver eyes narrowing with zeal as the clouds thinned over Pantera Bay.

Panic burst down below—from the feeble vessels shrieking as fire devoured them, from the dying humans that vanished alongside their alive elements, but always about the alchemist down there basking in that mayhem. Vim, a Protean Reshaper, a maker of chaos, a fleeting existence doomed from its inception. Élan's target.

The one selected by The Rector themselves.

The Rector. The leader of The Orders. The four-transfigured commander who, since the dawn of history, had enabled the pursuit of knowledge, guiding evolution and redefining alchemy. The one so old their existence was shrouded in legends and myths, never too certain nor uncertain, yet enough to shroud the truth. The one who had discovered what nobody else had.

A fifth alchemical transfiguration, and a blend of elements so far impossible to achieve.

A way to progress, to evolve, to capture the flavour of all knowledge. A secret purposefully kept not to ignite an alchemical war.

An absurdity, except—five years ago—Élan had confirmed its existence.

On The Rector as a glimmer of what would come. On their mentee as a secret truth. On themselves, but as a possibility—verging on unreality, tethering the edge of the impossible, yet all too achievable to be disregarded. How could they, when the outcome was new knowledge, when beyond it lay evolution? How could they, when the mean was just to doom Vim?

An absurdity, not to pursue the genesis of change when the key awaited within reach, when the truth it offered only demanded a most desirable path: transformation.

Élan could not wait. To amalgamate another alchemist in a practice banned for myriads of millennia yet suggested by The Rector. To devour the knowledge that soul-skill could offer. To pioneer the promised path in a scheme it demanded that them—Élan, the Raven One, the Chaos Tamer, the most powerful Full Transmuter, the only alchemist unconstrained by affinities—tore themselves apart again and again and again to emerge reforged, reshaped, redefined.

Lightning discharged at that moment, blinding the moonlight and murdering its light.

Amidst that darkness Élan plunged, fearless, four ravenshade wings spreading open and trailing wisps of nightfall. Their silver gaze set on Vim, and they glided through the sinking, screeching vessels, flying past curtains of flames, above the rampaging waters and towards the last galley—swarmed by a living heat, timber screaming as the sea claimed what the blaze could not.

The air choked, and a few surviving humans hurled themselves over the rail and into the void—yet the alchemist hovering above that galley chuckled, their amusement sparking on the liquid embers dripping from their bladed wings. Fire burst from their feet, chasing another handful of escaping humans while a savage smirk curled their onyx lips—the only feature visible beneath their horned helmet. Élan hastened, approaching, then flared open their four wings, halting airborne with so much violence the surrounding embers twitched back in fear.

Vim soured. "Raven One," they greeted, a mere formality, their epicene voice twisting through the smoke like ribbons of burning light. "To what do I owe the displeasure? Did I misguide your little mentee? That tot alchemist upending Strezia?"

Élan did not answer, instead tilting their head to assess the younger alchemist. Vim was *just* a Protean Reshaper; powerful to some extent, yet vulnerable to soul-skills.

"I'm here for you, Vim. To tame your chaos. This—" The Raven One flared a wing towards the pyres of burning vessels. "—is out of control. You'll drive this world out of the Meridian, and we cannot afford it."

Vim lifted their chin, defiance reflecting on their armour. "Liar. You and Verve tore this world apart. You are worse than me." They lingered, blazing rivulets surging and reaching for the sky in a hollow threat. "I will not submit. Not to you, nor to anyone. I will exist."

To Élan, that observation was irrelevant—their lie would be a truth, for The Orders and every other alchemist unless The Rector demanded the contrary. To Élan, that threat was nothing but a futile attempt to disguise the emotions now sparkling within Vim's façade of metal and blades.

Certainty, that death was before them, armoured in a mirage of nightmares and electricity. Anger, to be targeted and denied existence for a ploy that exceeded them. Terror, of the most absolute quality, so deep it enraged the Protean's fire into a senseless need to fight and survive.

The Raven One grinned, still hovering about the sinking vessel. "Existence is not yours to decide. The Rector's requested your demise, and I shall obey."

Fire leaked from Vim's bladed wings, swallowing the vessels and clamouring as it breathed, tongues of orange and red flowing like a burning penance that blasted the night. Élan laughed—at the resistance, at the key, at what soon would be theirs—and commanded the air to extract its non-alive compounds and feed them to the vessel's wood—suffocating the fire, but also oxidising the planks. The hull dried in hues of silver and iron, Vim's flames snapping and mewling as the Protean Reshaper willed the air to fuel the fire again. It surged, renewed, but Élan reforged the wood, adding minerals until veins of pale crystal slithered across the hull, fossilising what was left.

"I will not submit!" Vim's was a fractured bellow, a howl locked in the moment it first formed, dredged from the bottom of the self, where time had stopped, where no growth was permitted, only repetition.

It was history, unyielding and unmoved.

It held knowledge unreachable otherwise—and so within a sliver of the infinite Élan amalgamated Vim.

The amalgamation revealed an infinity of alive elements crafting the network of Vim's self. A core identity, a prime attitude, a conjunction of thoughts, a half-forgotten past as a human, a blend of knowledge rimming half-alive elements encircled by an affinity—a preference, a bias. A limitation foreign to Élan but applicable to everyone else.

*'I will not break! I will carry my name through the fire!'* Vim, mind-whispering, clawing to existence.

Élan ignored them, diving into that network. There was pain underneath; the misery derived from an undeniable powerlessness, the struggle empowering every fight for and against identity, the will creating a consciousness.

*'I will echo past this moment!'* Vim, Vim, Vim, clinging to everything, avoiding nothing. *'I will not vanish!'*

There was fire underneath; a blazing will fighting to survive, an inferno of hatred craving to subsist, to feed, to twist.

The Chaos Tamer tore the other apart, smothering that will

and suffocating that inferno to lay open every one of Vim's thought patterns and emotions—and they hurled them into destruction, discarding those too dangerous to be absorbed. Their penchant for destruction, their preference for chaos, the past that no longer mattered, the pain oozing from the remnants melting down below, over the Bay, suspended in time.

Élan disposed of attitudes, demoting Vim's identity while detaching the only value they could offer—their comprehension of half-alive elements and Protean alchemy. The understanding that would enable the impossible. The unachievable made achievable, as The Rector had promised: the key to the genesis of change.

"Why!?" That howl. A remnant of Vim, an echo carried through the fire. "Why me!?"

It was worth answering before they carved out the rest of Vim. It was worth indulging because the zeal for knowledge was imprudent, shameless.

*'For your half-alive elements! For the change you will enable!!'* That truth, bouncing across the amalgamation.

Élan found them—amidst the remnants of molten metal, between the screams Vim could no longer bellow—and consumed them all. Fragments of theorems, shards of alchemy, concepts long ago foreign but now familiar. The gaps in their knowledge bridged with every intuition, every ability, every theory now within their reach.

While time held its breath, Élan watched the universe unfold and understood it, so thorough it was, so orderly, so perfectly attuned. Yet amidst the shimmer where *now* became *then*, chaos unfurled—destructive, voracious, defying the foundations. Antipodean to their *self*. Averse to all they had been.

It was an omen of war for and against identity.

"Élan!" Another voice, silvery and polished like jewels. "That is enough!" Hellion, the herald of nightmares, the first Soul-Protean. "You'll lose yourself!"

Élan. That name. So familiar, so anchoring. So *own*.

The amalgamation ended abruptly as the Raven One looked up, jaws parted and gasping, liquid metal leaking between their fangs. Hellion stood before them, uncannily slender, moth-like wings fluttering as they splintered the remnants of no-longer-Vim.

Only silence remained, lingering in the void of a peace that would not return.

# Verve

SOUL & PROTEAN ALCHEMIST. SECOND-IN-COMMAND

Lightning lashed from the storm, enraging the currents and bleeding into the darkened clouds; an imperfect, deafening moment where Verve emerged from the storm, dashing across the firmament like coils of smoke and death. They ignited the charges all around, leashing the light into The Towers and forcing its doors open—on its cusp, above the world, where only few could reach it.

The alchemist clashed inside like a barrage of destruction, smoke transmuting into their true alchemical body—a humanoid figure with a tight and seamless armour of iridescent white foil, ringlets of sooty hair framing a featureless non-face. Amethyst sparks blasted from Verve's back while tendrils of lightning shaped their feathered wings. The Towers rattled upon their landing, the corridor's onyx floors rippling as the alchemist stood, wings folding, four ruby eyes slicing their mask before etching on the ceiling—a living map of glyphs trailing a path towards the Library.

'*Where is The Rector?*' Verve mind-whispered to The Towers themselves, as bold and demanding as no one else. '*Sententia! Answer me!*'

An impervious silence mingled in the hallway, creeping around the alchemist like a predator taunting another—

unmoved, unmarked, unchanged. It lingered at the seam of becoming, reshaping the corridor into an ascending spiral that hastened with every breath.

'*Somewhere. Somewhen,*' The Towers finally mind-whispered, amidst the countless echoes of untold voices. '*Beyond the Mirrors Room.*' ·

The lightning in Verve's wings twitched with displeasure. The Beyond was unreachable, even for them. '*And Élan?*'

Silence renewed, tense as the corridor twisted, soaring with a purpose yet unshared, thus unknown.

'*Fractured, but still existing,*' The Towers mind-whispered, unknown voices joining the cacophony. '*Hellion is with them.*'

Amidst the quietude that unfolded, a single truth apprehended Verve's thoughts. The Rector was anything but haphazard in their decision making, and so they would not spend a mind like Élan's in a purposeless experiment—a mind shaped for meaning and devoid of affinities, a limitation plaguing two of the four transfigurations. One impairing even Verve, the second-in-command.

'*They wait for you on Delta.*' Sententia again, hastening the corridor's transformation, onyx floors blending into nightmares and consuming the space. '*Go, Verve.*'

The hallway opened into a column of light—woven from all alchemical elements, each strand blending a hundred hues, a myriad of voices, and links to a time yet to come or long gone. On a whim, each string took a shade of cobalt, each endpoint folding the universe as needed to open a pathway.

Verve's wings unfurled, lightning discharging as they vaulted into the portal.

The portal opened amidst a thunderstorm, lightning lashing as Verve plunged into the supercharged clouds before hurtling across the indigo firmament. Pulses of brightness swallowed the alchemist, diffusing the cloud-filtered twilight and parting in their wake. The thunder struggled to follow, each roar razor-sharp and pungent although the mountains rimming the horizon shimmered with a static halo.

Basking in Delta's electric chaos, Verve pierced the stormwall, slicing through the raging gale and plunging into the forest below—a blend of squat trees and tall, hollow ones with fractal branches to harvest electricity and recharge their canopies. They shimmered mauve and cerulean with unspent static, the air around humming and zapping while the alchemist tore through them, emerging into a clearance.

Hellion stood in its centre, tall and slender, moth-like wings spread open. The leaf-like faulds of their armour swung back, contorting when they gazed into the sky—and their spiralling mask vanished into the hood, revealing a featureless, eyeless face of crystallised stonewood.

On cue, Verve dropped from high above, coercing the recharged air to settle down with measured slowness. They exchanged a glance with Hellion—an unspoken demand cavorting between them—until the latter pointed to the cradle of vines and leaves before them. Shadows pooled at its centre, ill-shaped tendrils coiling and twisting yet barely assembling a single, dishevelled raven wing. The spark of nightmares and electricity rippled within it, shady ringlets barely twitching in response.

"Élan?" Verve's modulated voice flattened into a threat as they stared at the pool of shadows. "What happened? And where is Vim?"

Hellion shrugged, and the vines sprouting from their armour snapped into fractal shapes before the thunderstorm roared again. Their eyeless face turned towards the cradle of leaves and branches, tilting as if weighted by the answer they'll never surrender.

"Vim does not exist anymore..." Hellion finally confirmed, sharp as a diamond blade. "Albeit I expected Élan to splinter the young Protean, not to amalgamate them." A pause; meaningful, expectant, but ultimately reluctant. The Soul-Protean faced their peer, chin lifting as if to gaze at the sky. "Vim's actions were far from stirring Lambda away from its Meridian of Existence. Their destruction may have been extremist, and thus its purpose… concerns me."

In the blink between the blinding lightning and its deafening blast, Verve stared at Hellion, unflinching—then strengthened their Integrity Shield, barricading their *self* and banning access to plans they would not reveal—thoughts and ideas rimmed by desires and fears, yet otherwise accessible through a soul-link. After all, the concept of a fifth transfiguration was too ground-breaking to be left unprotected; it could prematurely ignite an alchemical war.

Even if that meant—perhaps, for now—hiding it from Hellion.

In the echoes of that blast, Verve's four ruby eyes arched in feigned amusement. "Are you challenging The Rector, Hellion?"

The vines surrounding the Soul-Protean crackled. "No more than you do."

"Are you a Naturalist, perhaps?" Verve pressed on, towering over the other, eyes narrowed. It was a lie, blatant yet misdirecting enough.

Hellion laughed, granting nonsense the reverence only irony could afford.

"Far from it, yet…" They soured, facing Élan's shadows then Verve again. "That amalgamation was different. The Raven One tore Vim's foundational core while absorbing their fundamental knowledge of half-alive elements. It wasn't purposeless destruction; there was a premeditated hue in their actions, one which I barely glimpsed when their Integrity Shield flickered."

A stillness, thick as the thunder raging through Delta, yet unravelling the threads of the past as Verve looked at Élan—into the sparks of electricity, into the tendrils of nightmares, into that dishevelled wing—and sighed. A minute exhalation, a breeze that blended into the world's, a sound that didn't exist because the second-in-command forbade it.

Hellion's opinions, subtle as they were, yielded a clear view. Élan had been cautious during the amalgamation, avoiding the alive elements—attitudes, thought patterns, beliefs—that could have fundamentally altered their self. Instead, they'd focused on absorbing the knowledge of Protean alchemy missing from their original composition.

Yet as a doubt teased the edges of Verve's understanding, Hellion rustled their wings, folding them into a velvety white cloak.

"I splintered the remnants of no-longer-Vim before Élan lost themselves." They shrugged, the vines aiding a gesture that was far from nonchalant. "They transfigured after, returning to their raven-form before melting like so." They pointed a thorny finger into the pool of shadows. "I must assume The Rector foresaw this, Verve. They tasked me with assisting Élan, explicitly detailing I should bring them to Delta in the aftermath." One last pause, a smirk hinted on the curves of that blind stonewood face. "Madness, except it was the leader who commanded it."

Verve hummed in acknowledgement, and the soundwaves hovered around them before blending into the never-ending electric murmur of that world. "Not madness, but a scheme. As usual," they acknowledged, a feigned grin slashing their non-face. "I will take it from here, Hellion. You may go."

"As you say," the other agreed, moth-wings fluttering open as they hovered above the ground. "Shall you need me, I'll be in the Corvera Peninsula. My mission hasn't ended yet."

Hellion left shortly after, soaring into the storm and hurtling southwards towards The Towers' portal—yet Verve barely noticed their lack, so focused they were on staring at Élan's shadows. There was something there—in the flicker of those elements, in the span of their existence, in the struggle of those tendrils that kept leaking, curling, contorting yet failing to reform.

Struggle.

Lightning rippled on the alchemist's wings, sparked by that single word and unleashing a hundred memories of the most confounding mission Verve had ever undertaken. A mere observation that had been anything but simple, a study in patience and bias, a saga that had ended in a conversation with a human too unusual to be allowed to live.

Verve remembered what they'd said to that human five years ago, lifting a hand while regenerating the soundwaves of those echoes; they grew into a small circle, bumping and twisting with each recovered word. "Struggle exists because *identity* exists. *Someone* struggles because external wills affect their identity, and everything it implies."

Verve fisted that hand, vanishing those words. The genesis of change had been a portent of chaos, and Élan's was the first glimmer of it.

# Egon Hold

## Zaro 11ᵀᴴ, 17002 RE

# Berserk

Paces. Rhythmical, measured, remarked by the metal bootfalls of Decanus Ler Halde over the polished marble floor. "I cannot say the truth, even if Legate Praeto entertains it." He exhaled through his nose, hand swiping his blonde hair, nose scrunching as he hissed, "My words would be deemed lies, blurred by the fog and my need to recover from a War Game that has now stalled my progress through the ranks." He stopped abruptly, fist slamming over the back of a lectus before spinning around. "I cannot—" Ler swallowed, a grimace tugging at his mouth, a myriad of confusing thoughts cloaking his shape. "I ought to be careful not to contradict Centurion Sittia. Her version of events will have priority."

An astute man, enraged by a context he couldn't change, yet mindful enough to understand his limitations. Nothing but a mirror of past instances, doomed to be forgotten by those unshackled from their morals.

Unfurling their wings of molten metal, Berserk's dragonlet-form soared through the room, glamoured to invisibility, and alighted on a nearby bookshelf—then turned to watch glamour-Petra. The illusion was crafted to perfection, and her plated cuirass chafed as her arms folded across it.

When Berserk commanded her to shift her weight, her boots squeaked over the polished marble floor—recalling Ler's attention before the illusion arched a demanding brow. The gesture, identical to what the original woman would've intended, had the desired effect. Ler flinched, pressing his lips and vanishing the futile shimmer of hope—for answers, for solutions, for pathways out of his conundrum—from his eyes.

A myriad of alive elements—thoughts, gloomy as his features, emotions, mixed as his gestures—swarmed around him, coercing his nose to scrunch, teasing his feet to tap the floor, and commanding his arm to snap open to signify the plains around Egon Hold.

"All the high-ranking officials here, all the Centurions, all the Imperials… they came to see *her*, not me." His voice roughened, biting like a string pulled too tight. "Centurion Sittia Praeto. The Ash-Walker, the Invicta, the only one who—besides Juçe Praeto—became a Centurion before her third decade." Venom leaked, unspoken and voiceless, yet layering meaning to what he left unsaid. "I cannot confess her Legion was fighting against each other like madmen! Using their dulled swords from the War Game as clubs before resorting to their pugios! I heard—! I saw—!"

Howls; panicked but laughing. Hands with fingers spread, clawing, mauling, lynching the shadows. Blood, poison, saliva dripping from open, gurgling mouths that could not scream, could not speak, could not find the logic to cry for help.

Berserk's tail lashed in the air, proud of the results. They hadn't aimed to spare anyone within the ravine, but Ler's timely misfortune was useful. Such unforeseen consequences were always intriguing; humanity's only ingenuity was to imagine innovative ways to bring chaos into the stability they so craved. The alchemist could only approve.

"I saw horrors unlike any other battle. Incomparable even with the Siege of Ílun Fort." Defeat clung to Ler like a death sentence, dragging his gaze to the painting hung on the wall—aged and fading, yet clear enough. Centurion Sittia, in gleaming armour, in golden hues pattered with the carmine remains of her victims, a sword raised to command her Legion. "To think I celebrated with my peers after discovering my next War Game would be against her."

Sittia. Sittia. Sittia. Juçe. Juçe. Juçe. Sittia. Juçe. Sittia. Juçe.

It seemed Firard was built upon two legends, their names and images clinging to every soldier, every Strategist, every human to ever walk those lands. It was a nuisance, a shadow coating every memory, a fleeting tale stretched to the might of myths. It was infuriating, irrelevant, yet all-encompassing as humans could believe it was.

Within a heartbeat, Berserk spread their wings, summoning the memories they'd amalgamated from Petra to lore-weave them into a network so detailed it'd unravel the mystery. Knowledge was perennial, and before that heartbeat exhaled into oblivion, Berserk scoured that grid, searching for the so-called legends.

Berserk found them shortly after. Through the eyes of a young Triarus Petra, charging behind Centurion Sittia across the Peaks of Nadir to chase the Orenian amidst a snowstorm never to repeat. Through the mind of Decanus Petra, during The Sweep of Tormenta Plains, with Juçe's cavalry flanking the west and Sittia's vanguard charging the Presyan. Through the rain and the dirt, through gales and ashfalls, through the darkness of the Five Vaults, and through the fires of the Siege of Ílun Fort. Through the eyes of Centurion Petra, under the might of the Nadir, spilling fire while Dante repositioned the Legions in a move that would make history.

Berserk found them. Human and mortal, yet powerful because perception was the basis of authority and after five decades of victories and impossible feats, all grievances and coarseness had been glossed by fame and polished by time.

Berserk discarded them, unamused, thus halting the lore-weaving before the heartbeat expired.

A gold statuette clanked atop a round marble table, screeching as Legate Ilia Larya held it. She released it shortly after, tapping the figure's head before pinching her chin. Her countenance was impassive, a painting more perennial that Sittia's, but Berserk briefly soul-linked her to peruse her truth—thought-patterns swirling with plans, ideas woven by names, by places, by theories, by interests. All small, all ephemeral, all irrelevant for the universe they remained unaware of. Those thoughts—those alive elements—hammered over her until she sighed, onyx gaze steeling.

"Your information, Ler, is crucial to Firard's future. You cannot—" She stalled, worrying about undue reputation, about certain retaliation. It blurred her shape enough for Berserk to tilt their head in fleeting curiosity. "The Emerald Legions are founded in honour and courage; to fight our enemies and protect our people both on the battlefield and beyond. It is how we built an empire that has endured over three-thousand years, what Firard lives for. Honour and courage, Ler; that is what it's demanded of you."

A keen woman with a masterful control of her gestures, and a rhetoric capable of commanding masses. Just like many others across worlds, often succumbing to the weight of history and its distortion of the truth.

Berserk grinned, the dragonlet's fangs leaking molten metal while their tail lashed to command glamour-Petra to nod in agreement. After all, Ilia's was a clever move: one that appealed to values and morals as tools, one that worked on any age and civilisation that had and would come. One that, if needed, could become yet another source of chaos.

It prompted the expected response. Ler gaped as ill-shaped words tumbled between his lips, each sound murdered by the dichotomy of doing what was safer or what he ought. His chaos emerged as a grunt, rimmed by a click of his tongue and the squeaking of his leather vambraces. As his fists clenched, rivulets of pain—carmine and electric—sparkled from his body.

"Your knowledge, Decanus Ler, bears on our future; it must be brought to light. The Marshals *must* hear it." Ilia's words, remarked by an onyx gaze as monumental as the Citadel in which they stood.

Ler listened, but slouched after. His fists unclenched, and a snarl contorted his mouth—his morals struggled, leashing his reason, his pride, his self-preservation.

Berserk observed him, willing glamour-Petra to sigh. "It is your duty, Ler."

She watched the Decanus—nodding with reluctant agreement—yet before he could answer, someone knocked at the door in a martial cadence. It opened after the Legate allowed it, the non-alive wood screeching as it dragged through old hinges. The young messenger flinched apologetically, saluting the glamour-Centurion.

"Legate Larya, a veilwing arrived for you." His gaze darted around the room, chased by the urgency of information that couldn't be withheld. "From the Northern Legion."

"Understood." Ilia dallied for a moment, glancing at Ler—then shook her head, departing without another word.

As the door groaned towards shutting, Berserk crouched—wings quivering, leaking metal—then leapt, flying through the narrowing gap. They left glamour-Petra in the room with the Decanus, controlling the illusion with a fragment of their mind. In the hallway, they rode the currents, hurtling past the walking Legate and towards the Hold outside.

Research was due.

# Dante



LEGATE OF EGON HOLD, EASTERN LEGIONS OF FIRARD

*I warned them, again and again…*

A child, so small. Running barefoot, trudging and tumbling, escaping away, escaping from them, always from them. Through the darker and darker, on and on and on. He looks back, and they are there. Two figures, larger than life, tall and towering, looming and lurking.

*No matter how far I've climbed, I'm an embarrassment to the family.*

One crosses his arms, snarls, chin up. The other raises her fists, scowls, lashes out. A gasp, so small like the child. He scampers and runs, away from the danger, away from the lack, blinder and blinder yet on and on. He shuts his eyes, amidst that silence. It chases him.

Like icy tendrils tingling his shoulders. Like howls curling and caressing him. Like pressure taking all breaths away.

*Even their silence carries judgement. Even to this day.*

The darkness endures, all around, all about. With the watching, so intense, so aware of what it waits for. A flaw, a fault, a blunder to remember, a reason to punish. In silence. Always in silence, in stares, in the impasse before the searing storm.

*Anger. Hatred. It has always been both.*

It howls then, deafening, dreadful, deadly. Even when the child stumbles, his strides longer, heavier, guiltier. Running still, running all along. From them but also towards them, still tall and towering, still looming and lurking. Always, always, on and on and on.

Even when others raise in the hundreds, in the thousands. From now, and from before. Some burnt yet floating adrift. Some more ablaze and melt, empty eyes staring and staring and staring.

Others. Others! In the shadows, so many. Like statues, so sculpted, so stable. They clap, they bow, they approve, they smile.

But never those the non-child runs towards. Never those.

Rage. It rises in a wail so full of hope.

*I wouldn't mind your death. What a lie.*

Hands. Ahead. A single pair, fingers stretched, arms spread open. Towards him, for him. Expectant. An embrace, an offer of protection, of absolution. The fiction of forgiveness, the falsehood of fondness. The unyielding yearning as he runs, runs, runs—towards the lie, towards the myth, towards the fable he can never reach.

*It's your fault. It's my fault. Always.*

The hands vanish. Translucent and tortuous, feigned and faked. The abyss opens afterwards and he falls, down and down, smaller and smaller, on and on and on and on.

Dante jerked to a sit, gasping for air, palms spread open before him. Sweat tickled down his forehead, strands of raven hair sticking to his cheek. He blinked—once, twice, thrice—assessing the twilight coating the room in moonlight lavender hues.

*A nightmare; just that.* He breathed, parting his mouth and feeling the air pass through. It grounded him just enough to recognise the silky sheets slipping through his bare legs. Pulled leftward as the woman beside him stirred, mumbling a complaint with the eloquence of slumber. In that dusk, Ilia's naked back—slender, toned—shimmered with the remnants of sweat. *Still asleep.* She groaned again, pulling the sheets enough to compel Dante to slide off the bed.

His bare feet touched the rug under the bed, and he pattered across the room towards the round marble table. He stared at the empty cups over its surface, making no move to cover himself; only when the summer breeze caressed his back, did Dante pour wine into the nearest cup, downing it at once. He replaced it without refilling, mindful of the clatter as his gaze decanted onto the discarded veilwing letter. *The Northern Legion's.*

The worn out paper was splotched with ink, so thin the dusk's silver light passed through as he picked it up. It rustled when he angled it to reread in the dimness.

*The Five Vaults are so far clear; the inspection continues. Olun Fort remains unbreached. No sign of Orenos; no fog detected.*

Dante dropped it, uncaring as he snatched a linen to wrap around his navel. *This complicates everything. Firard needs an enemy, and I need—* He scowled, fingers trembling as he knotted the fabric, mouth parted and gasping again.

That nightmare had stripped him bare, recalling everything he'd so carefully buried under layers of logic. *Nothing would be enough; not even producing an enemy to quell the Centurions' fear.* A rueful snarl-smile curled his lips, and he meandered around the table, across an archway, and onto the private balcony.

The air was cold, but not as cold as the shame slithering under his skin. It tugged at the past he couldn't change, echoing with the screams he'd never forget. *I wasn't meant to be in the Forces.* He gazed into the starry firmament before leaning over the guardrail—and his gaze landed on the warm, flickering torchlight scattered through Egon Hold and into the plains.

A sigh escaped him; heavy, and weighed down as he lowered his gaze, pinching his nose. When the breeze picked up, he stared at his hands as if they had never belonged to him. *Still reaching. Always reaching.* His jaw tensed at the thought, eyes narrowing under a frown—aimed at the Citadel, at Egon Hold, at Furia Gorge, at everyone else. *It matters not. The past is what it is.* The corner of his mouth tightened in a smirk. *Firard could collapse. I won't allow it.*

# Berserk

The Peaks loomed over Egon Hold, sharp shapes carved into the starlit canvas of the night and rimmed with the darkening plum of the dying dusk. It'd sent the fortress into a slumber, its ramparts dotted with flickering torchlight, its silence never permeated by the noises down below. Amidst that quiet, Berserk alighted on the marble guardrail of a terrace, wings folding over the dragonlet's back to craft a mantle of molten metal; they lingered a moment, peering down at the fortress below before meandering through that edge to sit one pace away from the Legate.

He was leaning on the guardrail, hands dangling above the abyss, loose hair waltzing in the breeze. He remained oblivious to its coldness and ignorant of the invisible alchemist beside him, his obsidian gaze lost where logic couldn't reach him and sense had no reason to be.

An influential man, afflicted by the same malady most in his position endured: an image fragmented into as many façades as people inhabited the Hold, each too biased to be reliable and seldom holding more than a semblance of veracity. In a few hours, Berserk had soul-linked them all, scavenging for details only to find mere reflections of the truth.

To his fellow Strategists, Dante was just his achievements—the eloquence of his strategies, the unexpected quality of his solutions, the surreal calmness not even the Strategos had mastered. To the legionnaires, he was just a source of achievements—admired for the victories he brought, but feared for the cost some had. To the so-called legends, he was an inconvenient nuisance, and to the woman on his bed, he was the impossible.

To the Dragon One, Dante was an echo of past occurrences, displaying the same brilliance they'd seen in many others across the ages, and aware of his transient lifetime although too eager to waste it in idle remembrance. To them, there was nothing surprising about Legate Dante Praeto. Nothing, except The Rector had declared him the bearer of a solution Berserk hadn't asked for, and a candidate to alchemist they did not need.

The Rector. The one alchemist old enough to be surrounded by legends. The only one yet to be proven wrong. The mystery aggravated Berserk; the secrecy enthralled them.

Insanity, thus, not to further evaluate this target only because the knowledge he carried remained unthought of.

Yet as the breeze coiled through the terrace, chilling and sibilant, Dante lifted his hands. His fingers stretched, his palms faced him, and emptiness cleared his features. A nightmare clung to him like a residue of the unaware, staining the edges of his reality with a shadow of his self—and it teased the Dragon One, promising darkness, auguring chaos.

Berserk could not wait—and so they quelled the breeze, silencing that terrace before soul-linking Dante.

The world perished into abyssal darkness, clogged with the shadows of alive elements. Each was an inky gust, swirling chaotically to shape a windstorm of unstoppable currents, all whirling in tandem with Dante's thought-patterns. Plans, hypotheses, curated reasons, lessons learnt, past evidence, fragments of history—all known, all assessed, all continuously considered while the man on the terrace leaned against its guardrail, a mere heartbeat after the soul-link had begun.

Yet those alive elements swirled far away, creating a hollow of stability—pierced by the sharpened edge of a steel blade. It balanced, precariously, the Legate's self: unfazed by the storm because each flurry of shadows was a strand weaving the shield protecting him. Muffling the chaos of the emotions he denied to live amidst the feeble prison of apparent calmness.

Berserk abhorred that enforced peace, and so they soared from that blade's edge to plunge into the bottomless pit of that hollowness. Beyond the layers of Dante's awareness and into his unaware—the past from which that windstorm streamed, the one rippling with the emotions now muffled, the baseline of chaos slowly engulfing his present.

The currents beneath were labyrinths of past lessons still driving his present actions. Each current had carved a wound in his mind; each wound still bled unattended.

One maze, walled with bloodied books, crimson raining on the corridor, rooms spinning and falling. Dazzled like little-Dante, clinging to the table, fingers curling atop the wood, blood dripping, dripping, dripping. He looked up at the thick volume on Decanus Sittia's hands, at the blood dripping, dripping, dripping from its spine. *Mine.* She was young, angry, pregnant with a little brother—but she snarled as always, brutal, book up, up, down. He cowered, shoulder creeping towards his ears, so futile, so—

Berserk swerved into another labyrinth.

Another maze, a floorless hallway, held over an abyss and beneath a splotched darkness. Enduring like Dante—held by the collar of his camisia, the shimmer of a ring rushing down, down, down into his temple, into his jaw, his cheekbone. In between, fragments of Decanus Juçe; black-haired and angry because Dante had just mastered the Strategists' trials. Each puzzle, each test, each question of history, of logic, of maths, all solved, all perfect. Still an embarrassment to Juçe. Temple, jaw, shoulder, chest. Dante grinned, spitting blood; angry but proud, resentful but hopeful. *This way, one day, I'll show them—*

Berserk soared into another pathway, departing from that ludicrous desire.

Many mazes, woven like branches walled with mirrors because it was always the same, always the same. Hopeful like young-Dante—standing tall because the War Games were his. A crushing victory, an unseen strategy, the youngest Tribune in history now crowned in laurel by Legate Gora Rachen himself. People, applauding in a performance of honour and approval, of admiration and respect; Ilia, young, grinning at him. It ought to be enough.

Wrong, so wrong. Wrong success, wrong recognition. Wrong because Centurion Juçe was displeased, that crown of laurel crushed under his boot. Wrong, but perhaps if he learnt, if he improved, if the challenge was greater, perhaps... perhaps... *But what if it's never—?*

Berserk hurried into a future past, away from that latent fear.

A last maze, made of smoke and debris, blazing stones raining upon a harbour city, vessels burning on the sea beyond. Raging, furious, hurrying through a siege to emerge into an aftermath of rubble and smoke, the scent of scorched corpses and burnt hair acrid in Imperial Dante's nose. He looked down, to the saliva dripping from his boots, dripping contempt; Juçe's, always Juçe's.

Strategos Rachen stood beside him, pleased. "You saved Liminal Harbour, Dante. Be proud." That smile; the weight of that hand on his shoulder. Support, approval.

Wrong success, wrong recognition. Insufficient challenge. *No matter; learn. Improve.*

The Dragon One soared, higher, higher. Through the burning air of that memory, through the clouds of child-like hopes, through the twisted ambitious and beyond the threshold that refused them all. They were an unwavering burden, but as the alchemist reemerged into that hollowness within the storm— amidst that void of denial—their pressure subdued again, muffled by the gusts of shadowy winds.

The night was quiet when Berserk ended the soul-link, starlight above, shimmering torchlight below. That storm of shadowy gusts had once again become Dante's measured calmness—the one every other human in the Hold recalled so perfectly, and the alchemist now understood as sheer denial. Only four heartbeats had passed, yet the Dragon One unfurled their wings to release the nightmarish tendrils still clinging to the present. They curled, fading, albeit their shadows never left the Legate, instead wrapping his neck like a noose too eager to be tightened.

A brilliant yet perturbed man, haunted by a past that would never leave him, and chasing a goal so deeply buried on his unawareness he refused to acknowledge it. A typical archetype overflowing every society, for whom composure wasn't serenity and neither peace, but an armour forged from denial and the dread of what intangible wounds he'd sustain without it.

Berserk watched him from their perch on that marble guardrail, paws pressed together and shielded by their curled tail. The dross coursing through them crackled with intrigue, while the heat haze emanating from their molten metal curled in aggravation.

Legate Dante Praeto. Still frowning at his open palms, unable to provide any solution while armoured in dread and denial.

"Dante?" Ilia's voice. Coated in slumber. Distracting the alchemist.

The Legate blinked after hearing her, exhaling with measured precision to relax his hands—then turned towards her. Grinning. Raking her naked body with his eyes, leaning back on the guardrail to tease, "Did I wake you?"

She grinned just like in that memory, but two decades older. "Come. You can apologise for it."

Dante strode towards her, rivulets of lust swirling in his wake. They coiled in the breeze, burning against the cold—but the alchemist flicked them away with a wing, eyes narrowed at the lovers. His lust was just a semblance of a connection; a rudimentary and unfulfilling pretence of emotions that would never be more because the Legate's armour would not allow it.

A curious target, the Strategist. Brilliant and full of potential, but unable to leverage it *because* of his dread and denial.

It was a truth of alchemy, Berserk knew, the bane and boon of alive elements—thoughts, rationality, emotions, attitudes, identity. They could not exist in isolation nor in ignorance of each other, since rational thought may have given form to ideas and theories, but emotions had driven humans—and alchemist alike—to venture into the unknown for a sole purpose: to expand their knowledge through innovation and, thus, evolve.

Yet innovation demanded the emotional intensity that guided reason through risk and uncertainty, and the Dragon One knew—having pursued it for almost two hundred millennia —that Dante's solution was, for now, unreachable. Only his unique combination of alive elements could think of it... and only if that armour, that hollow in the storm of his emotions, collapsed to guide him to it.

Insanity, not to assist him in such an endeavour... but how?

When the lovers tumbled further into Dante's chambers, Berserk peered over the terrace's edge and into the torchlight-dotted ramparts of Egon Hold. Those fiery droplets moved alongside their lethargic patrols, guiding the alchemist to a conclusion.

One incision—personal to Dante, and aimed at his private dread—would begin his unravelling; a second one would prepare him. How the rest unfolded for him would depend on the shift in his alive elements... yet the war it would trigger was inevitable. The only path through which history would progress, the only outcome that wouldn't lead to humanity's extinction. The Rector had decided it, indicted it so, and it would happen as commanded.

The dragonlet's maws stretched in a grin that dripped molten metal, then plunged from the terrace and into Egon Hold, traversing ramparts, slipping through doors, hurrying through hallways and turning in corners.

Berserk found their target sitting in her leathers within a lavish room, greying hair wet and dripping, murder darkening her inky eyes. She raised her right arm, tensing the roll of clean bandages held between gritted teeth before wrapping it deftly.

The Ash-Walker. The Invicta. Centurion Sittia Praeto.

A pitiful woman. Forged by resentment, fuelled by pride, and fated to die while only experiencing the most limited range of alive elements—fear and rage. A prime example of the vast majority of humanity ever to live.

Berserk alighted on the nearest armrest and soul-linked her.

That connection was a journey to the past, leashed perennially to the present because her rancour knew no bounds, met no peace. *A spineless coward; a disgrace to our name.* Her thoughts boomed through the soul-link, while her unyielding hatred coated every action, directing every other thought. *He never learnt; unlike his siblings.* It was an endless war focused on the Legate because his betrayal—enlisting in the Strategist Trails instead of the Forces'—was unforgivable. *A retreat? Pathetic. A mockery of the Legions.* Yet her mind occasionally wandered—to the Nadir's eruption and the strategy that'd granted her a title— and the echoes of that event she refused to acknowledge embittered her further.

Soul-shaping her was trivial. A tweak just so, a spark, a need... and she rushed under the guise of the night.

# Egon & Ferro

## Zaro 12ᵗʰ, 17002 RE

# Calya

"As you saw, the survivors remain... dazed although their breaths are no longer sweetly scented." Standing before the closed door, Lady Hori Varre squared her shoulders while her robes—healer's white, neatly pressed—wavered with the soft breeze. "Their aggression is now inconsistent, blending between dozing off and jolting in sudden anger." Her forehead creased with the barest of considerations. "Feeding them has been challenging. Their shaking prevents them from eating on their own, and they vomit more than what they keep."

*Intoxication? Permanent or temporary?* Lady Calya Seve hummed with concern. "Will they survive?"

"Possibly, but unknown." Hori exhaled, her deep eyes framed by deep half-moons. "I have discovered symptoms, but no clues to reveal what caused them."

The ghost of displeasure—*Frustration? Intrigue?*—creased Lady Varre's brows as she meandered towards the rugged desk; a central piece in the barely furnished stone-built office, attended by a sole chair set with its back towards the narrow window. She rounded it carefully, scowling gently at the ink-stained paperwork scattered over the table—as if whatever was written there fell short of her expectations.

Calya glimpsed at them discreetly—lists, descriptions, the edges of a sketch—then averted her gaze, considering the night swallowing the world outside of the window. Quiet; like the healer. *I need Hori's findings. Now. Before my mother arrives later today.* A patrol's bootfalls resonated outside, their shadows marching past the windows; their silhouettes obscured the starlight for a breath. *Before she tampers with this investigation.*

"Have you inspected the fallen?" Lady Seve's voice teetered between curiosity and grief. *Hori's knowledge is invaluable. An asset to negotiate, a tool to scheme—with and against.*

Lady Varre blinked out of her thoughts. "Indeed. From our external inspections, most deceased had blue lips. Half had..." She trailed off, sweeping through the paperwork to produce a sketch—a human contour with shaded areas. "Half had reddened eyes and dilated pupils, while only a dozen had a blue hue on these regions." Three taps—mouths, hands, toes—and a pause too long to be consideration. "I conducted only two open postmortems and found their lungs to be drowned."

Calya hummed in approval. *The open postmortem; only Hori dares, and only she knows how—although it cost her whispers that now follow her as a shadow.* "Have you seen that before? Drowned lungs?"

"Twice. It explains the colouring, but not the hallucinations." Lady Varre's frown was not of concern but of concentration. "Regardless, I have two hypotheses." Her palm curled up, fore-finger subtly unfurled. "One, the Peaks' iron deposits may have influenced the groundwater for a long time, altering its compo-sition. The landslide could've unfortunately exposed an inner pool, thus releasing the fog." Her eyes narrowed as if chasing an explanation. "It could be volcanic gases. After all, we ignore how far the Nadir's roots stretch."

*A workable hypothesis. Sensible enough to appease the masses if prop-erly distributed.* "How likely could this be?" Calya prompted, her interest as real as her need for information.

"I... don't know," Hori shrugged with the weight of past concerns. "But it's not unseen. Five years ago, Lord Eneko's mining operation struck something deep within the Petricor Mountains, and the air became unbreathable. Most Varre earth-scholars gathered there..." She pressed both hands into the table, the paper protesting underneath her curled fingers.

"There was no fog at that time, but the miners choked to death. I still have the reports, since my scholars failed to reproduce the deadly combination."

*A useful connection; most Nobles remember that event.* Calya dipped her head as she sifted her gaze through the paperwork, assessing its risk—it was crucial information, left open out of naïve trust, its dangers all but disregarded. *Especially when my mother is due to arrive.*

"You mentioned two hypotheses..." A tease, apprehensive yet curious. *Something perturbs Hori. Little does.*

When Lady Varre looked up, her scowl didn't hide the fear in her eyes. "It could be human made."

Calya's mouth parted, dragged by shock. She allowed a frown to crease her brows, taking a step around the table. "How likely... would that be?" *This could upset the Exarch and the Nobles. Induce mass panic.*

Silence. Alarming like the hurried march outside, like the budding calls of patrols. *It matters not; Asier can handle it.* Calya tightened her frown, but the healer shrugged, palms up as if to cradle her theories.

"A decade ago, I visited Master Izar in Lares. They were searching for mixtures to cleanse steel tools for healing interventions." Hori tapped the table, marking a rhythm, breathing in tandem. "An apprentice mixed salt and sulphuric acid, releasing a pungent cloud. Those too near choked to death, and when we recovered them, their lips and hands were blue." She reached for the drawing atop the table, tapping the same areas—then hesitated. "Those who survived also had shaking limbs, but I cannot tell whether the cause was fear or the cloud."

Calya's fingertips dug into her leather belt, and a pulse jumped at her jaw. *A possibility I didn't consider. Lares is Sestel's strongest supporter.* She allowed her concern to show, warning the healer of what could happen if notes of the ill-fated experiment spread untamed. *Lares could've tested it on us. Firard could use it as an excuse to attack us, and my mother will leverage this in her play against the Exarch.* Her teeth grated together again, rimmed with anger, rustling with demands. *How didn't I consider this!?*

Restraint. Tensing Calya's hands. Sinking her nails into the belt. Restraint. Shushing as she smoothed her black trousers.

"Do you think that ill-fated experiment... could relate to this?" Lady Seve prodded, her quivery whisper lost under the turmoil budding outside. *Asier will handle it. This is more important.*

Hori braced herself, dark hands clinging like shadows to her healer's robes. "To my knowledge, all attempts at containing vapours of any sort have so far failed. And... to think Izar could've transported the salt and the sulphuric acid to mix it here? In such an outrageous quantity?"

She lingered; nervous, rattled. *Unlike herself.* Flinching when soldiers shouted outside, hurrying away.

"I don't think it is plausible. Besides, we found no flasks or containers in the Gorge, although we can't access the caverns from our side." The healer jolted, paced to the desk's edge and back. When she spoke, only her enunciation mattered. "Our survivors confirmed having seen monsters in the shadows and attacked each other. Izar's accident... it only caused choking, breathing issues, and severe shaking. Not mass delusions."

*A detail easily forgettable. Especially if rumours abound.* Calya scowled, taking a step forth, breaching propriety. "Hori, if this spreads..." She paused, leaden with warning. *Fear would proliferate. Lares would become a target.* Her scowl tightened, a hundred worrying scenarios known but left unsaid. *They'd request support. Firard would attack us.* Her next whisper was muffled by the tubas blaring a defence call. "This cannot surface. Not now. Not until I choose the moment."

Torchlight beamed through the windows, horses neighing and breaking into a gallop. Calya raised her chin, impassive. Hori's lips parted then pressed into a dot. *I need your knowledge. I can't—*

The tubas called for an attack. *Hurry!*

"I must have your word." Lady Seve. Commanding. Gauging the woman before her, ready for all. *Even with her knowledge, I cannot risk—*

Lady Varre's gaze flickered to the sketches, to the notes, to the woman before her. "You have my silence. I trust you."

The door slammed open, and the mayhem outside burst into

the office. Calya's posture eased, breathing tempered, gaze sweeping towards the figure under the archway—Lord Asier Aurri. *Concerned. Deeply so.* One hand held onto the handle; the other clasped tightly around his sheathed sword. His auburn hair was tousled, sticky with sweat, gaze burning in worry as he searched for Calya's.

He breathed, just once. "We are under attack. Firardian cavalry."

# Dante

Two knocks on the door. Two more, three more.

"Dante!" Imperial Elixane. Knocking again, again, again. "Dante!"

*Chaos. Move!* He jerked out of the bed, snatched a linen to cover himself, traipsed forth—around the table, across an archway, glimpsing at the midnight sky outside the window, and reaching the chamber's doors. It clicked open just enough for the Legate to frown at Imperial Elixane. *She's pale. Too pale.*

"Sittia is gone. She vanished." A whisper, bare like her pale eyes. "She took all her cavalry. A hundred-fifty legionnaires."

Dante scowled, clenching the door's edge. "How? Where?"

"Nobody knows!" Elixane hissed. "Not even Juçe!"

A snarl arched Juçe's lips, upsetting his groomed beard. He leant forth, menacing and measured, the restraint of his movements enhanced by the night beyond the glazed casements' light— flickering with frantic torchlight. It outlined his broad-shouldered figure, casting a pale glow around his greyed hair, and darkening his countenance with the shadows of his wrath.

It quivered in his rough, threatening tone. "Am I a prisoner now, Legate?"

*Just a liability.* "Careful, Centurion," Dante warned, meeting him eye-to-eye. He flicked a wrist, and eight legionnaires surrounded the older man. "You were requested to stay put, but were found fetching your stallion." The corner of his eyes twitched. *What I cannot afford is not to be careful.* "You will stay here until I command it so."

Silence lumbered between them, unquenchable like an unmet need for retribution.

Juçe fisted his hands; slowly, measuredly. That gesture was an unsheathed blade, sharp like his whisper. "I will not forget this, son."

*Threats? How unusual.* Legate Dante Praeto angled his head to watch the other with a calmness that augured a sentence. "My orders are final, Centurion."

*I should've posted a guard… but I thought she was too weak.* Legate Dante Praeto scowled at the horizon—shimmering, opalescent, a rim of pale amethyst blurring into the darkness above. It slashed the ramparts with streaks of twilight hues colliding with honey torchlight. Sittia's insubordination was more than disobedience of the Emerald Legions; it was the pinnacle of her grievances against Dante. *No. This is not the time to make it personal.*

"The Watchers discovered two trails." Imperial Elixane was calm embodied. She pressed two fingers onto the map spread atop a merlon. "One north, one south."

"Decoys only," Dante rebuked, staring at the map—*Sittia defied the Legions, not me*—then glanced up to count five dark motes circling above the ravine. "Sestelii veilwings," he observed, aware he'd sent none. "Sittia must have crossed the Gorge already with a third group. Lady Seve always keeps it guarded."

The Imperial looked down, hesitating for a heartbeat. "Shouldn't we send a patrol? Follow her?"

"No." Dante toyed with the spyglass between his hands; it creaked when he clenched it. "Sittia left without orders. Against orders. Sending a patrol would only reveal our inner turmoil. Any word from the spies?"

She hummed a negative. "Should I write?"

"Not yet. We should hear soon enough from them." Dante frowned at the Gorge, squaring his shoulders with resolve. *Lessons, not feelings. That's all I have time for.*

## HEAD OF THE SEVE HOUSE, SESTEL

Death. In the breeze. Chilling and biting, whistling in the predawn, slipping from the north. The horizon shimmered opalescent, a rim of pale amethyst blurring into the darkness above. *Wars have begun for less.*

The chestnut whinnied as Lady Calya Seve hauled back the reins, curbing the gallop and skittering to a halt. The mare's ears flicked back in protest, its restless snort cut short as she steered it rightwards to watch the healers—tending to the wounded, foreign and own. *Terrified of a legend, surprised by the night.*

She pulled the reins to her left, gaze trained in the distance. The Firardian warhorses were lashing out, rearing violently as a handful of footsoldiers rounded them in. *How many did they bring?* A few were pulling at lead ropes, kicking up mud. A few more were already tethered together, eased by the handlers patting their noses. *Three, four dozen, maybe?* Calya clicked her tongue, easing the chestnut forward. *It matters not. If we warre, it'll be on my terms.*

At the Gorge's entrance, the formation lay in disarray, its defensive arcs reassembling while one General barked his orders. Her gaze trained on the southern cliff wall, tracking the archers resuming their position before looking at the sky. Five veilwings circled the ravine, reporting nothing. *No reinforcements, then. They came alone? Why?*

"Ours only?" Calya shot a questioning glance at Asier.

The Lord nodded, mounted beside her. His blue-roan gelding moved restlessly as his chin jutted towards a cluster of soldiers ahead.

"The captives are still here. Some there." A pause, looking at the prisoners being hauled away, then back to the circle. "We haven't moved *her*. Not safe yet."

The Lady didn't answer, instead scowling at the defensive circle—their backs toward her, shields held high, spears aimed at the centre. *A dozen? Not unexpected, but still...*

She kicked her feet free of the stirrups, dropping in a heartbeat and tossing the reins over the saddle. Behind her, Asier's boots hit the ground with precision. Someone moved their mounts. Orders echoed near the Gorge.

"Clear a path." The Lady demanded of those ahead.

They obeyed. Quietly, effectively. Plated armours chafed as they parted. Boots pattered over grass, opening a way. *This is an opportunity like no other.* Whispers ran amok, the zephyr whistling through—scented metallic, blended with poultices, soured with sweat. *For power, for control.* Calya walked, shoulders straight, chin lifted. A smirk curled her lips; diplomatic for others, feral for her. *Firard would owe me. The Exarch would owe me. Teoda...* The soldiers parted, the dawn shimmering between their shields. *Teoda is doomed.*

She halted at the edge. Looked down at the captive.

Her eyes, first; abyssal like death, brimming with revenge. The scowl, next; so vicious, so vengeful. Her cheek, oozing blood and fluids between old sutures. Her mouth; snarling, a corner twitching, hatred leaking. Her arms, so tense under the ropes; right bandaged, left scarred with old burns. Her legs, kneeling on the grass. Her cuirass and warkilt, soiled with blood and gore.

Calya smiled. Proper; polite. *I will use her.* Rejoicing privately. *To leash Firard to my whims, to gain power so far unseen.*

Centurion Sittia Praeto. Firard's finest. The Invicta no longer.

"We finally meet, Centurion," Lady Seve teased, tilting her

head at the woman kneeling before her. "Who knew it'd be like this."

Looking down, the old warrior spat a clot of blood—and iron hair shielded her grin. Her ropes fell. Her arms spread free.

Soldiers jerked, shouting.

A pugio—thin, sharp—beamed in the dawn. Aimed at Calya's neck.

Lord Asier Aurri hurried left then right again, halting to scowl at nothing, returning to peer through tent's flaps, then exhaling with a sharpness unusual for him. His auburn hair was tousled, brows dishevelled after rubbing them too much, his camisia half open.

"She could've killed you," he gritted, still pacing. His sheathed sword clattered with each footfall. "Standing so close was reckless."

*Always worrying; since we were children.* Lady Calya Seve allowed herself a smile within the privacy of that tent. "The soldiers handled it. Is Lady Varre with her?"

He groaned, his words mauled and throttled before dying in a sigh. "She is. I also assigned twenty of the highest-ranking to guard our guest, and thirty more spread across two decoy locations." He paced forth, reaching the table and moving a stool away before scowling at the paper in Calya's hands. "Should you be writing now?"

The Lady remained silent, rummaging through the wooden case spread open atop the table—a field writing kit, harbouring paper sheets, rolls for veilwings, a few reed pens and ink bottles. She extracted one, fingertips rubbing against the glass.

"Expedite action is foremost," she stated at last, uncorking the ink bottle to place it near the blank paper. *But even if the decision is mine, the Exarch must know. If he knows, he'll trust me.* "If we keep the captive too long, she becomes a prisoner of war, the threat to her life increases, and Firard will grow restless. If we release her without further action, every other nation will see us as weaklings." *And my mother will either kill Sittia, or use my handling of this against me.* She brushed all pens, inspecting their nibs. "Have we heard from our spies?"

Asier growled a negative, pacing back and reopening the tent's flaps. "I sent Ruria. I also gave her my seal to bring the clockjays."

"Good. And the message to Lord Zuria?" Calya pressed on, fetching the reed pen with the narrowest nib. *If he repositions the navy on the Sanguine Sea, as I requested, our stance will be clear.* Then, with the reed pen still between her fingers, she hand-signalled, *"We must act before Teoda arrives. She may harm Sittia."*

Asier grimaced, standing near the tent's flap, the incoming light blurring his broad-shouldered figure. Hand on sword hilt, he signalled, *"Teoda should arrive in five hours… and I set decoy locations precisely to deter her,"* then stated, "I sent a veilwing to Lord Zuria."

"Excellent," Calya smirked—a mere pressure at the centre of her lips. *Soon, all pieces will be in place, and new alliances will be forged.*

Dipping the nib into the ink, the Lady hovered it atop the paper for a single heartbeat—selecting words, remembering the Exarch's preferences, decorating her intentions. *A reminder first. In his own words.*

*As you said, my Exarch, war ill-serves us now, when balance can be achieved through conversation.*

Light blasted into the tent, flickering with the half-open flap —but Calya simply refilled her reed pen, tapping it on the pot's edge while footfalls trudged inside. The next warning had to be precise. *Without asking for permission I do not need. After all, who controls the Seve House controls foreign relations.*

*A treaty with the right conditions shall bind Firard tighter than any chain.*

Calya smiled when two heavy objects plunged into the dirt, lifting a small cloud of dust. Shielding her letter with her left, she refilled the pen yet again while pondering the last few words —a gentle reminder to strengthen her own position as the lead of the Seve House and, thus, its armies. *Sestel's blurred lines of succession and ascension to power do, after all, have benefits.* The reed scratched the paper as she wrote.

*I'll act on your honour, as I have done for two decades now, bringing you a stability so far unachieved. After this, the people's words will praise your wisdom.*

"My Lady?" Ruria Laxalt. Bright, yet chased by hurry.

Holding the fresh letter from its edges, Lady Seve assessed the young woman—in her scout's leathers, Ruria was a slender stretch of darkness eclipsing the light incoming through the tent's open flap. She bowed, gently, hand-signalling, *"No news from the spies,"* before beckoning to the floor—where two engraved wooden coffers now waited to be opened. "I had them brought in a hurry."

Calya allowed her pleased smile to be the answer. *Ten in all the world. Five in Sestel. Two under my control.* She stared at the coffers, waving the paper to dry it faster. *Nothing conveys urgency like using the unfathomable as messenger.* Quietly, the Lady beckoned Ruria to close the tent's flap while retrieving the wax from the writer's kit. As she gently warmed the rim with the lantern's flame, she checked the coffers again. *One to the Exarch, another to Legate Praeto.* Rolling the paper, she held it still with one hand, dropping wax on its fold, and pressing her ring into it.

She rounded the table while tugging at the chain around her neck, resurfacing three keys—one steel-made, two silver and delicate. The former unlocked the nearest coffer with a click, and Calya waited for Asier to pull the lid open, revealing its steel-lined inside. *At last.*

As she bent closer, her gaze fell on the clockjay inside—a

raven-like bird made of an unknown, iridescent metal. *As beautiful as shrouded in mystery.* It lay on its side with eyes closed, wings and tarsi folded into themselves and pressed to the body.

"It looks dead," Ruria observed, stretching to peer into the coffer, red locks framing her features.

"It's not dead," Asier countered, his repeated exposure to the unusual having dulled his astonishment. "It's not alive either. It… works."

*A sensible explanation of what we do not understand.* Still smiling, Calya slipped her free hand under the metal-made bird before sweeping to a stand, the weightless clockjay secured against her chest. She placed it on the table, caressed its smooth metal crown with a fingertip, and inserted one of the silver keys into the keyhole on its nape.

Its eyes snapped open, shining silver from the inside. The tarsi clicked loose as it leapt to its feet, shoulders rustling on the flanks, feathers parting like blades opening to shape wings. They rustled twice before falling back into a more natural shape, tail spreading as it skipped atop the crude table. *Surprisingly lifelike.* It chirped, glancing askance at Calya as if to pose a silent question.

"Welcome back," the Lady stated, proffering the note between two fingers. "From Lady Calya Seve, to Exarch Elor Luxa in Umbra City."

The clockjay crooned, seized the note, and swallowed it down. Its wings fluttered open again, each blade repositioning as it perked, tail fanning open. It hovered above the table, then hurtled out like a gust of wind, a chorus of startled shouts rising in its wake.

"H-how?" Ruria whispered, startled. "How can it fly so fast?"

*Exactly what we've all pondered for centuries.* "Nobody knows," Calya answered, rounding the table and selecting another roll of paper from the writing kit. "Clockjays are remnants of another era. Casually discovered, and treasured like nothing else." She found a suitable piece and stretched it over the grisly table. "It should reach Umbra City in less than a quarter hour. Nothing moves that fast."

"Nations have warred for them." Asier scowled at the closed coffer. "And you'll send another one to Firard."

*Symbols are just too useful.* "Precisely," Calya confirmed, her tone colder than the clockjay she'd just dispatched. Retrieving her reed pen, she cleaned the remnants of ink on the table, then refilled it again. "Clockjays do not obey without the key, and Firard is in no position to start a war over a device useless to them."

He grunted in response, lips pressed into a line as flat as his scowl. He sighed a moment later, dipping his head in acknowledgement before resuming his pace across the tent.

Tapping the pen between her fingers, Lady Seve bent to write again. Her eyes narrowed at the paper, head tilting to force her thoughts to fall in order. *Firm; without room to dissent. Gentle but threatening. Revealing just so.* When the pen scratched the paper, each word tugged the corner of her lips into a satisfied smile.

She was waving the note in the air when hooves skittered to a halt outside the tent, boots hitting the ground as horses whinnied. Moments later, light blasted into the tent, outlining the figure of Lady Varre—long braids still knotted, although she'd changed into field clothes. *At last.*

"Lady Seve. I come from—" Hori gasped, eyes widening at the open coffer. She blinked, assessing the other before straightening with the slowness of one who understands the stakes. "I was tending to... our... *guest*," she resumed, as clean and sharp as her healing knives. "The gash on her cheek needed to be cleansed and sutured again, but she had no other wounds."

Calya cleaned the reed pen, stashing it. "Yet there is something else..."

"I am afraid so. Her lips tremble, and her pupils are dilated, unfocused." Lady Varre paused, taking one step forward. "Her limbs quiver as well."

"She must survive." *Healthily, lest Firard defends her actions as another delusion caused by the fog.* Calya restrained a snarl, flicking the letter to dry it. "She's too valuable a guest."

"I have grounds to believe she will. But—" Hori hesitated, approaching the desk before hand-signalling, *"Those are mild fog symptoms. We have... little experience dealing with it. Too many unknowns.*" Then, whispered. "She seemed calm, but exhausted. Has refused to eat."

*No hallucinations, then? Useful.* "That can be problematic. We cannot mistreat our guest." Calya waited, allowing the weight of her voice to carry the implications. *Sittia wants to be a martyr to recover her honour. But martyrs are too dangerous for politics.*

"I requested soup and ale to be brought, prepared in the Firardian style," Lady Varre confirmed, glancing over her shoulder. "I have reassigned the healers tending to the survivors to stay with our guest."

Lady Seve dipped her head, rolling the note and warming the wax again. "Select a few healers to stay with our guest—permanently, of course. We cannot risk her health." *And they'll likely follow me into the ravine.* Sealing the new letter, she pressed her ring into the wax, waved it in the air, and rounded the table to unlock the second coffer. "You must stay here and continue your investigation."

A slight scrunch twisted Hori's button nose—*She understands, clearly*—but it smoothed as she bowed. "Will do."

She left as Calya retrieved the second clockjay, placing it on the table and unlocking it with the last key. Just like the other, it flickered to life, bladed wings spreading open, tail fanning out while it chirped in excitement. It was larger than the first, with lilac eyes and a few dishevelled metal feathers on its crown.

"From Lady Calya Seve, to the Legate of Egon Hold, Dante Praeto," she commanded, holding the closed note between two fingers. "To be opened by nobody else, and to return with a response within two hours." *I must return Sittia quickly.*

Just like before, the clockjay snapped the note, gulping it down before opening its wings. It chirped again, almost melodious, then lashed out of the room like lightning about to strike. The horses outside whinnied, adding to the startled remarks of the soldiers standing on guard.

"What now?" Asier groaned, nostrils flaring. "That one should reach Egon Hold within minutes."

*As intended.* "Assemble a guard; you will stay here, Asier. Ruria will come with me to the Gorge," the Lady commanded, lifting her chin to slip the chain and keys inside her leathers. *If*

*Ruria stays, my mother may poison her... and I'll need an aide.* "Set a watch for Teoda, cousin. She—"

Soldiers shouted outside, not startled but rallied, armours rattling as they leapt to attention, horses skittering to a halt.

*Could it be?* Calya's eyes widened before she could control them, the chaos of an arrival swirling beyond the tent. The zephyr whistled, stained with the stench of sweat, leather, and fragrances too misplaced to belong in the field. *Not now. It's too early.* A coldness tickled under her leather vest, scratching her skin while her heartbeat skipped nervously—one, twice, thrice as Calya struggled to collect herself.

Around her, Asier rushed to lock the empty coffers, whisking Ruria away through the back of the tent. She did as told, sliding near the ground and scampering away, footfalls muffled by the impending racket.

*I can do this. I can face her.* Lady Seve squared, prodded her bun with a hand, smoothed her leathers with another, and strode outside the tent with half-closed eyes. When the morning brightness subsided, a silhouette was already waiting for her— thin, shorter than remembered, and dressed for the court rather than the field.

"Child," Teoda greeted, her smile as biting as her aged voice. "It's been a while."

# Dante

*Sittia's insubordination is a risk I must deal with; not a betrayal.* Legate Dante Praeto descended the steps in pairs, landing on the ramparts outside of the Citadel to hurry down the bricked path. His scowl was tense, but he disguised it as an attempt to temper the harsh morning light. It cast sharp shadows across Egon Hold, each peak on the cliffs tracing lines of darkness every legionnaire seemed to secretly covet—even as they patrolled, saluting the Legate that moved past them. *They protect the Hold. I guard the Legions... and I failed.* As he turned a corner, Dante pressed his lips to subdue a grimace. *The legionnaires may feel the doubt, the wound; as a Strategist, I cannot.*

A few more steps delivered him to another curve, and he nodded at the nearest officials before sliding into a tower—packed with weapons, scented to rust and sweat, but offering a staircase with guardrails. Dante paused in the penumbra, shimmering with the light that slipped through the open doors.

*Strategos Gora...* He clicked his tongue, flinching at the echo. His latest message—regal, but hastily scribbled in a veilwing letter—had been of support. *If one reads only the written words.* Dante smoothed his camisia, descending the spiralling steps with more care than was due. That message had been a warning he didn't need a reminder of. *Gora only supports what's useful to him.* His boots hit the last step, and he exited through the open door, barely minding the legionnaires snapping to a salute. *But two more days of travel?* The silver sunlight stabbed down from above, and Dante shielded his eyes, kept walking, and did not look down. *Either Gora is bringing troops, or something else delayed him. Neither is preferable.*

The familiar silhouette of Imperial Elixane Ritz shaped in the distance. She stood tall amidst a nook, hands clasped behind her back while talking to a Peritus Watcher—the same woman Dante had spoken to, two days ago. Their lips barely moved, silhouettes washed out by the incandescent morning light. *Something happened.*

"Report," Dante commanded upon arrival, impatience sharpening his tone.

"We've been observing the Sestelii veilwings, but they haven't moved past the frontier." The Watcher's amber eyes were rimmed with dark circles, yet her demeanour remained matter-of-fact. "I believe... they may be patrolling only the ravine, but not beyond."

*A careful, deliberate message. Lady Seve's, then?* Dante exhaled, assenting to the information but gesturing towards the winding path ahead. It was a dismissal, and the Watcher clicked her boots, departing with strides swifter than expected—as if eager to outrun the silence her news had left behind. A silence he knew too well. *No room for indulgence. Keep steady.*

Only when alone did Dante stare at Elixane, a question lingering unspoken.

"There is more..." The Imperial prefaced, barely moving her lips. "Our veilwings found Sittia's cavalry stationed four hours of march from here." She paused, glance hopping north and south in the Legions' directions—then stretched two fingers, a crumpled veilwing note pinched between them. "From the northern group. The southern replied similarly."

Dante glanced down at the ink-stained paper, unfurling it carefully and reading through the scribbles.

*Camping four hours north of Egon Hold. Cavern entrance nearby; Centurion Sittia ordered to hold and guard. Current orders: march back at dusk. Confirm?*

*Deliberate instructions.* Dante allowed himself a frown, haphazardly folding the paper before returning it. *Which implies an intention… but which?* He nodded to his Imperial, letting his gaze sink into the vastness north of Egon Hold—a green, hilly expanse that ended near the Quintet River, far beyond sight. *Did they know why they were being sent?* The veilwing's note crumpled again as Elixane pocketed it.

"I ordered them to return immediately, and will interrogate them upon arrival," she interrupted, flat.

The Legate hummed, approving her actions—exactly as he'd commanded—yet focused on the distance. Those Decanii were just decoys, unaware of their part in Sittia's ploy and only guilty of following their Centurion's orders. Punishing them would set a terrible precedent for the Emerald Legions, while ignoring their actions would encourage any other high-ranking official to disobey the Strategists. *I'll deal with that later; understanding Sittia's goal is a priority.*

Pocketing his right, he ambled along the ramparts, drifting closer to the crenellations. His fingertips grazed the stone; rough, as Sittia's manners and actions. *She clearly expected this to be over soon, or wouldn't have ordered them to march back at dusk.* Some legionnaires shuffled away as he stalled near the edge overlooking the plains. Once there, only his thumb moved, tracing the stone's rim in a slow, precise loop. *Perhaps she wasn't expecting to return, meaning—*

His jawline tensed, drawn taut by the force of realisation—and his idle movements stalled so suddenly Elixane hurried to his side.

"What did you discover?" She whispered once near, the concern implied and never marring her features.

*A betrayal—no, a risk—greater than expected.* Dante swallowed, drumming his fingers over the stone before taking a step back.

"Sittia's intent was clear: to undo the Retreat and ignite a war. Her method... there are two possibilities," he whispered, muffled by the Hold's noises—then lifted two fingers he later pocketed. "One was likely to kill Lady Seve; it's known the Exarch owes her Sestel's expansion overseas, their trade routes, and the state of the army. Her loss would threaten his standing." Rolling both fingers, he arched a questioning brow. *Can you see the other problem?*

Elixane blinked twice, her breath catching before she controlled it. She looked down, and when her fingers grazed her belt, she hand-signalled, *"Two. To be a martyr? Regardless of whether she reached Lady Seve?"*

*Indeed.* The Legate's fingers curled into a fist, the tension noticeable as his knuckles whitened, veins sneaking through his sun-kissed skin. *I underestimated Sittia.*

"The first coerces Sestel into war, the second motivates Firard," he observed, struggling to release the tension. *War awaits on either path.* His cheek twitched as he forced his fingers to open, the tension easing just enough. *Emotions aside, the danger is greater than I estimated.* Fisting that hand again, he pressed it to his mouth before finally relaxing it. "In either case, Centurion Juçe could be a problem."

"I can assure you he's restrained, but—" The Imperial paused, glancing over her shoulder and scowling at the nearby archers; they hurried further away, gazes etched on whatever they ought to ward. Looking back, she crossed her arms and hand-signalled, *"Revenge? For Sittia?"*

Dante tilted his chin up, readying himself for his father's petty defiance. *Just more risks to account for.* Juçe's rudimentary deviances, even his failed attempt to fetch his stallion, were not-so-subtle skirmishes for revenge, meant to be exacted when the opportunity arose. *And he's searched for it my whole life.* The Legate clenched his jaw again.

"We must be careful," he finally whispered to Elixane. *I must, or war will be certain... and perhaps not favourable.* "If something happened to Sittia..." He held back the words, swallowed, then added, "The Marshals will be upset, and the Centurions' need to mourn a legend would ignite—"

"Legate!" Ilia's voice. Firm, loud, impersonal enough to augur concern.

He blinked, relaxing his features before glancing over his shoulder. His peer was approaching with swift strides, long braids lashing behind with each step. Her scowl was so fierce the legionnaires hastened to give way.

"I received word of the Northern Legions," Legate Ilia Larya informed as she halted close, tilting her head so none of the archers could read her lips. "They continue to inspect the Five Vaults, and report no signs of Orenos..." Ilia exhaled, slender fingers tracing the curvy path of her nose—as if the motion grounded her. "It seems Sittia did not approach *any* of the other Legions here in Egon Hold; not even the Centurions or Decanii that had come to the Games for her, or those with long-standing relationships."

*Resorting to loyalty, or abusing the chain of command?* Dante rolled his shoulders; only once, a controlled movement that settled his tension. *Friends could've denied her request, while subordinates could only obey.* "Which means she sought to minimise her risks."

"Or, perchance, her influence was limited." Ilia's smile sharpened with old ironies. "Albeit I wouldn't count on being so lucky."

A chuckle bubbled from Dante, ricocheting with the sourness accumulated after a lifetime of grievances. He shook his head, the smile playing on his lips rapidly embittering. *I can't make this personal. Not now.*

He'd been through delicate situations before—treaties on the verge of collapse, trade-routes turned into theatres of war, Marshals that only cared about their own prestige. He couldn't forget when Vesperia engaged Sessentas on the edges of the Lunar Sea and he sailed upon request of the Central Legion, nor when Presya almost burnt down Liminal Harbour, or the Nadir erupted, unpredictable, amidst an invasion. Yet somehow, none of those events carried the same instability, the same lumbering, impending portent of destruction. *No, this is just one more challenge. Emotions can wait. Lessons cannot.*

Dante looked down, finally coerced by the blasting silver

sunlight. "The way we manage our relations with Sestel…" He scrunched his nose, fulminating a grimace; he couldn't allow that—not for the legionnaires surrounding them, but neither for himself. *Focus on reality. Contain the damage.* "Are Centurion Ciro's units settled outside the Gorge—?"

Silver slashed the air, plunging from above with brutal intent. It chaffed like metal slashing the wind, reflecting the sunlight, shrieking a warning—a request, an order—and blinding the trio.

Elixane gasped as a legionnaire pulled her behind his shield, archers tensing their bows to aim at the air itself. Ilia swore out loud when a shield was lifted before her, raising a hand to stall more soldiers from rushing to the rampart's nook.

"Hold," Legate Dante Praeto didn't raise his voice, but the group stilled with the gravity in his tone. "Make way."

Two soldiers parted, boots shuffling over the bricked floor, shields still held high as if to defend themselves from the tiny, iridescent danger awaiting them. *Impossible.* It'd perched on the nearest merlon, hopping back and forth with metal wings half-open as if ready to take off. The dishevelled feathers of its crown refracted the light, tracing patterns on the ramparts. *A clockjay?* It halted when Dante emerged from behind the shields, enthralled by the lilac eyes staring askance, their pupils drawing smaller as if narrowing on him.

The silence was absolute. Pressured by the legionnaires' stares, by their harsh breathing, by Dante's footsteps and the scrape of the clockjay's talons on stone.

It chirped when he was close enough. "From Lady Calya Seve, to the Legate of Egon Hold, Dante Praeto." Its voice was impossible to define and devoid of intonation. "To be opened by nobody else, and to return with a response within two hours."

Whispers threaded around, but Imperial Elixane quieted them while Ilia ushered the archers away—yet nobody approached, keeping their distance as if that strange contraption could attack them. *Not a physical attack, no…* Dante reasoned as he offered his left arm, palm open. *Just a political statement nobody will forget.* The clockjay leapt onto his forearm, weightless as its talons locked around him before spitting a sizeable roll into his open palm. Dante rolled it with his thumb.

"The Seve Seal," he observed, gaze fixed on the crest imprinted in the blue wax.

"Two hours left," the clockjay stated, as impersonal as before.

# Amok



SOUL TRANSMUTER ALCHEMIST. THE UNTAMED ONE

Silver light blotted the encampment—a pocket of tents and stables assembled near a thicket at the foot of the mountains. It refracted on their leaves, on the grimy whiteness of the shelter's leather, on the steel of armours and weapons. Soldiers patrolled around with menial purpose, under transient orders, with short-sighted intent. Horses whinnied, exhausted and sweaty, yet nothing else than tools. Messengers abounded, running errands, carrying messages, distributing orders and adding to the overall confusion that disguised the moment's truth.

On that noon, on the eve of summer—and glamoured to invisibility—Amok awaited outside the central tent, their attention focused on the newly arrived matriarch.

Lady Teoda Seve.

Descending from her mount, dressed for the court yet wrapped on a gilded leather vest, her carmine one-shouldered cloak folded over a forearm. To the alchemist, she was an anchor to the reality of humans, standing with the preternatural calm of a raging storm that neither lashes nor subsides. A façade hiding the clamour of refined brutality with a mantle of nobility and age, translucent yet taunting because her embellished clothing and pristine manners were just a carefully crafted lure.

Almost to welcome her, the breeze picked up, slithering with the horror of the recent skirmish. Teoda smiled, clasping her hands near the navel and taking on her surroundings with veiled disapproval—then turned towards the makeshift command tent. Lifting her chin, she narrowed her eyes to watch her daughter emerge into the fields.

To others, there was nothing but pleasantry in Teoda's pale blue eyes. To Amok, there was destruction in her mind. Soaring like strands of ploys and schemes, plucking filaments as she coveted the deaths of her adversaries, and entwining into pathways she aimed to create, each thread assembled by the lies she ought to weave. To the Untamed One, those alive elements were remarkably clear—even without a soul-link.

*All that promise, and this is what she's become.* A snake formed around Teoda; woven from her disillusionment, humming with misfortune. It snarled at Calya—walking, approaching—but bit the matriarch's cheek. *I pushed too hard; shaped her in my image.* That thought scattered with the snake's buzzing, slashing the thudding of incoming footsteps. *Should've moulded her more like her brother, predictable and useful.* Gestures, recalled; so many of them, so blurred, so ill-remembered, so overlapped above the younger noblewoman's face. *My fault; for creating Calya. My task, to remove the danger I sowed.* That snake again, just a rivulet of smoke—suffocated with fear and brimming with destructive intent.

Amok understood what it was. Humans' imperishable quest to exert power, to dominate, to carve an unforgettable imprint on others and become immortal through their suffering, through their uncontrollable behaviour, through those thoughts that would forever haunt the victims, lurking amidst their unawareness.

Within a heartbeat, those strands of ploys flared from Teoda as if to attack her daughter. Another footstep thudded, their gazes crossed, and clouds of smoke blasted from Calya to swallow the noon into the darkest, lightlest night.

Her mind became a void of abyssal darkness, chaotic and convoluted, yet brought into the present by the mere sight of the matriarch. It was an enticing, unexpected private reaction—and so it teased Amok's curiosity enough they soul-linked Calya.

Within the soul-link, Calya's alive elements burst like shadowy tendrils lurching towards respite, aiming to leash it with logic, to beget it with actions, to preserve it around her. It was nowhere to be found—not then nor now—and so the thunder howled with emotions long discarded yet lurking beneath it all.

Terror, like a distorted cry ululating all around. Anger, blasting and self-destructing because it blinded reasoning. Detachment, echoing in the aftermath since that lingering rumble was the only path forward.

In the abyssal darkness, faces soared like black streams that stretched Calya's mind into the past and brought them to the present like embodied shadows. To the alchemist, these countenances were alive, and reenacted versions of Calya she had long dominated because none ensured survival, just suffering.

Each shadow resembled one of those lurking feelings, each feeling an obstacle she had overcome.

One shadow, little-Calya. So small and pale, so smothered under knitted brows and puffed cheeks, framed by opalescent streams of dried tears and broken lips. Her hands, also small and pale except for tender splotches of purple, clutching a toy and then bracing herself. She stood, hair pulled up, her bodily marks—swollen, maroon—covered with a silky dress purposefully draped, shoulders slouched and curled inwards to be smaller, subtler.

One feeling, abject terror. *She'll hurt me again.* Haunted by a horror so certain, vulnerable to bursting anger, exposed and betrayed, strangled, screaming, suffocated. *Help me! Help me!* Punished by hands so soft and refined, spat at by lips always rouged, scratched by nails so perfectly manicured—then put down by a voice so harsh, so uncaring, so un-motherly.

Teoda's; always Teoda's.

Another shadow, young-Calya. Slender and taller but not fully grown, cheeks sunken in enforced austerity, glossed lips pressed not to scream a promise of destruction. Her scowl was a weak contention to the rage storming her azure eyes—staring ahead as her hands clasped tightly on her navel. They seemed gentle—like everything else in her—but her oval nails sunk into her palms, their sharpness an anchor to reality.

Another feeling, raging wrath. *I'll take everything from you, mother.* Fuelled by a resentment so deeply ingrained, bursting irascible after any gesture, boiling impatient yet repressed because she knew nothing would change—not the unfairness, the misunderstandings, or the invalidation. *The world is rotten, but I'll survive it.* It had a target, that spite, that wrath. A middle-aged woman, with eyes so clear yet so murderous, with words so carefully crafted to demean, to destroy, to disregard and dismiss.

Teoda; always Teoda.

A last shadow, precursor-Calya. Dressed for the field, blonde hair knotted up, azure eyes set on the armies ahead. Beautiful in everyone's eyes, a strategist like Sestel had never known so far, a newly discovered asset to the Exarch, a politician the world would soon respect. An empty husk—too barren to need, too blank to feel, too hollow to harbour anything else than strategies crafted for a purpose hidden to everyone but herself.

A last feeling, calm stillness. *Feel nothing, show nothing; survive.* Subdued by experiences so harrowing, so repeated. Sliced apart and reshaped from the remains, keeping what served and discarding everything else. *Feelings lead somewhere I cannot return from.* Yet within that abyss, blossoming from that inner wasteland, was one need. The only one she allowed, the sole purpose she'd chase.

Power.

Above all, and for none other than herself.

When Amok resurfaced from the soul-link and into the present, barely a heartbeat had passed. Teoda still awaited with eyes narrowed in feigned pleasantry towards the incoming threat. Calya still approached in her curated gait, a polite glimmer in her eyes, not a trace of anything else leaking away.

Yet to the Untamed One, Calya's mind—thanks to the ongoing soul-link—was the result of a past so haunting it now allowed the three shadows to resurface. Not as fragments of her *self*, but as echoes long-ignored yet impossible to scatter.

Little-Calya was pouting and shivering, trailing behind and not eager to face the monster she feared. Young-Calya—her excessive thinness more glaring under the noon's light—stomped with shaking fists, hatred leaking from her like fire spilling from a furnace. Precursor-Calya walked straight, not quite nonchalant but mentally reciting her litany of calmness.

To Amok, the leading thinker of the Naturalists, such a scene was a remarkable unfolding—likely hinting at why The Rector had selected Calya. After all, the Untamed One knew, those shadow-versions were a perfect subject to one day incarnate.

At that moment, the matriarch smoothed her gilded leather vest.

"Child. It's been a while." Hers was a measured voice, not derisive and neither incriminating, yet sharp and fatal like a blade piercing a heart. Three intentions weighed it down—upsetting the other, appearing in control, finding a weakness—visible to the alchemist yet easy-to-guess for all Calyas.

"Go away! You shouldn't be here!" Little-Calya howled. Slouched and half-hidden behind another's leg, squinting from beneath a swollen eye.

"I'm digging your grave! If only you knew!" Young-Calya, seething between gritted teeth, pointing a bony finger at the other.

"How timely of you to arrive now, mother, when the danger has passed," Precursor-Calya, a statue of perfection, a rising talent offering nothing but a sly smirk.

*Always a joy to be demoted by bloodline.* "Mother, I trust your journey was safe," actual-Calya dipped her head, a polite and welcoming smile curling her lips. Her veneer was collected, her mind a network of calculations and possibilities nobody but Amok perceived. "We were expecting you past noon. Your messengers have clearly miscalculated." *Yet to your displeasure, you did not interrupt my plans.*

Teoda chuckled demurely, choosing her words like a general would choose a formation. "I heard what happened during the War Games and thought you may need my advice." She waved her hand, the twin-sun's silver light refracting on her many rings. "I was already close when news of the Veiled Retreat arrived…" Her tone lowered at that name, dipping like her gaze as she scrutinised her daughter's updo. "I knew you may need my help, so I hurried to meet you."

"But I did nothing wrong!" Little-Calya bellowed, bracing herself and quivering. "I can do this! I'll show you!"

"Advice? Help?" Young-Calya chortled, quivering with ill-restrained wrath while reacting to the present as a shadow of the past. *I've led the Seve House for eighteen years! I don't need you!* "Liar! Don't you dare touch what's mine!"

Precursor-Calya nodded once, a minimal gesture nobody would notice. *The Veiled Retreat?* She'd heard that name scribbled on the notes sent by Ruria's connections. *So Teoda has spies in Egon Hold or our messages were intercepted.* Delight ignited within; muffled like a spark shielded between both hands. *I need more details.*

"Of course. There's always room for perspective after the outcome is secure," actual-Calya commented, nonchalant although her gaze was already scouting for reactions—and she found a tiny clench on the elder's jaw. *Do you think I'm lying, mother? Or else?* She gestured towards the nearest trees and the copious shadows underneath their canopies. "Let us find some respite from the suns' light. They are unforgiving."

For a moment, Teoda did not waver—but a hundred questions exploded from her, the trails of unspoken sentences clear to the invisible alchemist. *Am I late?* An agreeable dip of her head. *What does Calya know? What did she do?* Pinching her dress and lifting it enough to reveal riding boots. *Are my secrets known to her? Have I been betrayed?* A few steps forward, following the other towards the canopy's shelter. *Or is she just taunting?*

Amok followed close behind, cloak curling in the breeze and leaking glyphs that recorded every pertinent alive element. It was a most enthralling conversation, and one key to their mission.

"It is a quaint situation, child. Especially after the last War Game irritated the Nobles just so," Teoda whispered as they walked, artfully stepping on firmer ground. "I am afraid Sestel may not endure another upheaval."

Little-Calya cowered at those words, traipsing, rolling in the grass, lifting up in shame. *Four months! Five months!* "Don't hurt me! I tried! I calmed it!"

Young-Calya's breath caught, rattling her clenched teeth, anger blending with fear. "Don't you dare accuse me, since you spurned the last debacle." *It lasted a month because of you.*

The Untamed One's ink rippled at those comments. What Calya's shadows said were atemporal reactions—depending on current knowledge, yet unleashing past emotions never quelled.

Precursor-Calya kept walking, gaze etched on the tree ahead. *Let her words echo in vain.* Her lips pressed tight, her countenance calm albeit her mind pounded alongside her galloping heart. *She cannot affect me if I do not allow it.*

*A shared concern, although for different reasons.* "I see your interest in the well-being of Sestel remains as strong as always." Actual-Calya spoke with a shimmer of awe, her intonation receding into a hint of foreboding. "Are you aware of the latest developments?"

Teoda dipped her gaze, paused beneath the canopy, and with practiced care, tucked a pale strand back into place. Her bun, tight and perfect, seemed impervious to the breeze. "The earthquake? A most unfortunate coincidence." She looked up, as if enthralled by the tree leaves and the splotches of light coming through. "I brought a few units with me, and I'd be delighted to lend you my Generals if needed. As a gesture of support."

Terror flared from little-Calya, rolling like ill-formed stutters. "I can do this, mother! I promise!"

Hatred burst from young-Calya, hissing each word. "You snake..." Her tongue clicked. "Are you threatening me with an army? Are you so eager to retake Ferro Keep?" She cocked her head, chortled savagely. "It's mine! Since the Exarch named me Head of Seve!"

*That... must be deliberate.* Precursor-Calya reasoned, mindful of the tightness of her lips. *She's not threatening me; not directly.* She guessed the size of Teoda's units, compared them to Ferro's forces, found the former at sheer disadvantage, deemed them a decoy, and worried about unseen subtleties. *You're aiming for something else, but what?*

"A gesture, indeed." Actual-Calya lingered, rearranging her camisia. *A careful gesture meant to upset Firard—especially after Sittia's impromptu attack.*

Amok circled them, crouching under the canopy to be close —not to the matriarch nor to the shadows, but to actual-Calya herself. Amidst that atemporal crowd, and within two heartbeats, four thought-lines surged from her like tendrils of shadows offering paths of action.

One, implied. *Legate Praeto could read her presence as a threat... and even doubt my intentions.* Two, cavorting as her gaze sifted the tents far ahead, realisation dawning. *That's what she's after; to upset our feeble equilibrium.* Three, scheming as she nodded at the nearest patrol, dallying as if mindful of being overhead. *I can use this. To reveal her intentions, to upend her allies.* Four, a decision, a truth enabling action. *My silence unnerves her.*

To the Untamed One, actual-Calya's control was amusing— and so they watched, glyphs swirling around them while the women below embattled in a silent, formal brawl. Calya lingered, angling her head just so, watching her mother, blinking twice in expectation.

Teoda held that gaze, pressed her lips, sighed. "My dear, I am concerned about the events, about..." The sorrow on her face was so well rehearsed that, hadn't Amok seen her true intentions, they'd believe her. "This does not look well for Sestel nor for you. The rumours..." She moved closer, counting her heartbeat to measure how long to dally. *Now.* She whispered, "Let me help you."

"Mama?" Little-Calya; naïve, foolish. Stepping around the others, hands spread open, reaching out. She didn't tremble, her need for love overriding her sense. "Mama? Help me?"

"No... no, no, no..." Young-Calya backtracked like a prey, grimacing, hands clenching around her chest. *Please, please, please.* "You're lying, you're lying. It's a trap." *But— but— but—*

Precursor-Calya swallowed her words, minding her breathing, stalling her feelings.

*That trick again? Why are you so desperate?* Actual-Calya, as unfazed as her precursor yet far gentler in demeanour. "I appreciate your concern, mother..." *But you can't deceive me.* She paused, clasping her hands behind her back. "Yet it's known we measure reputation differently, and as I did with the Sideral Accords, I'd rather shape events before they're seen."

Teoda didn't react—not outwardly at least. She toyed with the gemstones of her many rings, grazing the minute metalwork, then adjusted her signet, dallying with the fingertip atop its ruby. Inwardly, the alchemist saw the thoughts throttling her; worries about measures already taken, spirals of long-prepared ploys, negotiations failed simply because Calya had planned for it. They melted into wisps of smoke, suffocating the woman until she parted her mouth, holding her façade to—

The wind buzzed savagely, slashed with unnatural speed and shearing the conversation. Teoda startled, taking a step back as an iridescent raven-like bird circled actual-Calya, each round scattering her shadows until only *she* remained, amused by the contraption now perching on her forearm.

An automaton, the craft of a Machina Reshaper alchemist. An alchemical construct developed from the combination of half-alive and non-alive elements. A remnant of an era gone by, having inhabited this world long ago, but not anymore. A curious encounter, intriguing enough that the Untamed One severed the soul-link, instead wondering why such devices had been allowed to remain even after The Reclamation.

Another moment passed, unbeknownst to the women below —the mother, stunned, the daughter, pleased—until the alchemist grinned, enthused. It was, indeed, an opportunity like no other, to be yet again involved in The Rector's missions.

"I see... the Exarch has reached out to you," Teoda dared, so distant, so irrelevant. So focused on the royal seal atop the note the automaton had just spat.

"A response," Calya corrected, patting the device's head and pocketing the note. "Duty calls me, mother. I'll ask Lord Aurri to ready your accommodations."

SOUL & MATTER TRANSMUTER. THE DRAGON ONE.

To the Dragon One, the private library was an interesting room with tall marble ceilings engraved with alchemical truths the humans beneath didn't notice. The bookshelves—built from the walls—were filled with tomes documenting their limited history, while the door's relief outlined events nobody remembered correctly. To its side, a framed map established human frontiers, while the wooden lectii and the imposing desk silently endured those lies.

"We cannot wait for the Marshals." Legate Ilia Larya sat on the rightmost lectus, elbows on her knees, fingers laced beneath her chin. "They won't make it in time, yet... this requires more than us."

"We have discussed that already," Imperial Elixane Ritz countered for the third time.

Only humans, so short-lived and transitory, would waste so much of their scant time in frivolous debate. Enough to have circled across all arguments while reaching no conclusion. Enough to have wasted their precious minutes amidst circular reasonings, veiled indecision, and pointless considerations. Enough for Berserk to have nested atop the marble table, glamoured to invisibility yet curled so tightly their chin rested atop the tail, wings spread high to enjoy the breeze.

On their left, Legate Dante Praeto pressed his palms into the table, strands of black hair framing his countenance. He scowled at the note unfurled atop it, pretending to read while his every thought transformed into another shadowy gust swarming the edges of the active soul-link.

*Sittia's choice was her sheer recklessness, not an insult to me.* It rushed, so abyssal yet real it projected that hollow of denial into reality. *The insult lies in my own reading of it, and nowhere else.* Within a few heartbeats, each gust transformed into shadow-made plates that added to the Legate's armour, swirling alongside the windstorm Berserk saw at the edges of the room. *The fallout is mine to resolve, and it's an opportunity like no other.* Dante's eagerness for knowledge sharpened each plate, the shadows within swirling in the abyssal hues of everything he butchered through cold logic. It guided him, even if impaired—and so he grunted, squinting and reading the letter again. *No; this is my problem to solve.*

Berserk followed the strategist's gaze with lethargic intent. The paper was thicker than regular veilwing messages, and inked delicately.

A curious oddity arrived through Furia Gorge into Sestel's territory alongside a remarkable cavalry. The Ash-Walker, of all. They are all in my custody, unharmed and fed.

I presume their presence was not sanctioned by you, the Legate of Egon Hold, or Marshal-Strategos Gora Rachen, the leader of the Eastern Legions. In the interest of preserving the balance between our nations, I would welcome the opportunity to return these misplaced legionnaires, along with their warhorses.

Let us meet on the frontier, within Furia Gorge, on Zaro 13th, two hours before noon.

"One hour left," the automaton informed, chirping once before its beak clicked closed. It hopped alongside the table's edge, restating, "One hour left."

A most foul contraption, crafted out of alchemical combination and not creation—as only Machina Reshapers alchemists did. Berserk curled their right wing forward, shielding their sight from the automaton's presence.

Ilia chuckled, jutting her chin towards the desk, gaze etched on the note. "As I said two days ago, one has to admire that woman."

Dante offered a rueful smile. "This is Seve's style: pragmatic statecraft." His jaw tensed as he beckoned to the note, lifting three fingers to count facts. "Her wording is careful. Clearly outlining she doesn't equate Sittia's actions with Firard's position, clarifying her preference for balance, and even revealing she'll return the warhorses, aware of the economic loss it could be for the Eastern Legion."

"She's trying to preserve Firard's dignity," Ilia stated, straightening and tracing circling patterns into her emerald trousers. "Power not exercised is power retained... or so it seems to be Lady Seve's preferred path."

An incomplete understanding of power, yet bordering on being correct. It amused Berserk, and so they studied the Northern Legate—only to be distracted when Elixane approached the table, looking past the invisible alchemist to read the letter yet again.

"Could Lady Seve betray us?" She whispered a moment later, carefully grazing the note. "Perhaps, set the expectation for a peaceful encounter, then ambush us?"

Dante's thought echoed through the soul-link, recalling the Dragon One's attention: *A sensible worry, if this weren't Lady Seve.* He was now standing still, fingertips tracing circles along the table's edge.

"Lady Seve knows she ought to be careful. If she humiliates Firard, whatever arrangement we reach will be an open wound... and it will fester, becoming a myth of betrayal, victimhood, and righteous anger." He tucked a strand of inky hair behind an ear, and four gusts of shadows swirled to harden the armour he was so unknowingly reinforcing. "I estimate she wants to prevent our shame from fermenting into a future conflict. That is what her Sideral Accords achieved for Aurel."

To the alchemist, the Legate's interpretation augured a clever but unwieldy proposal that could stall the chaos they were aiming to create—yet it mattered not. Humans had a predilection for crafting their own downfall and, eventually, would charge again towards the horizon of chaos.

To the Strategists, that interpretation had unleashed a variety of inner opinions Berserk briefly assessed. Agreement and disagreement, strategic considerations based on prior experience, on old documents, on legends, on loyalty to the flawed political system they served. The same that preached honour and courage yet cowered in disarray when faced with the reckless actions of one so-called legend—one Berserk had not created but merely nudged through a soul-shape to prepare for the first incision.

"Dante..." Ilia's voice, so grim it recalled Berserk's attention; her countenance was as cold as the winds grazing Omega's nights. "What are you planning?"

He didn't answer immediately, and the Dragon One folded back their wings, concentrating on the soul-link they'd ignored for too long.

It was a hollow of stability amidst a unanimous and restless abyss, serene, yet surrounded by that silent windstorm of shadowy gusts. They soared ravenous, chaotic, like inky brush-strokes interlaced with others to deaden every alive element beyond that violent barrier. Those gusts remained far away, the serene nest within still pierced by the edge of a steel blade— emerging from the shadows behind to traverse that darkness into the shadows ahead. It shimmered silver, sharp, a perennial threat to that hollow yet balancing the Legate's self. The windstorm did not perturb him, and neither did those brush-strokes. He was unfazed, unaware of the alchemist hovering before him on that edge, each flurry of shadows weaving into the plates that armoured him with denial shaping his prison of apparent calmness.

Yet to the alchemist, that soul-link had changed since the night before. The hollowness within was not just the restless, dense quietude of a ruminating mind, but the dynamic haste of logical thought curving and coiling to solve one meaningless, human conundrum: how to answer Seve's request.

There were hundreds of pathways enabled by Dante's knowledge, by his experience, his character, his values, his reasons—and they emerged from the abyssal below like obsidian doors. Sealed and locked, each inkier and blacker than the gusts yet rearranging to circle Dante's self. Far from him and the alchemist, but neither close to the hollow's edge.

Berserk could not wait to unlock them, for each door opened into the unknown, thus enabling an innovative strategy to deal with Lady Seve—and each door could harbour the solution they'd been sent to acquire. Yet these pathways—those hallways hidden behind each door—were, for now, unthought of. Just potential opportunities Dante could pursue, none real until he considered them fully.

A mildly intriguing man, brilliant and logic yet shackled by—

The lantern crackled in the real world.

Dante's attention snapped to the flame, twisting the soul-link until visions of past battles emerged between the shadowy gusts like fleeting glimpses relieved as they were present again.

Vessels, aflame in the sea, burnt corpses floating adrift; couldn't breathe, couldn't see. *Another test. Another step forward.* The gusts thickened, denser, covering that fragment.

Boulders and jars, the latter raining ablaze into the harbour, soldiers on fire. Howling. Suffocated by destruction, stone raining and crumbling, people mewling and wailing. *Mistake made. Now learn and move.* Shadowy brush-strokes, blackening, blurring.

Lava, molten, soaring in frenzied pain, in furious agony. Tightening his throat, blurring his vision. The Nadir; eating the legionnaires down below, coughing a fiery avalanche of ash and gas. The howling, the agony, far away but own. *Duty first. I'll mourn them after we survive.* Brush-strokes, blacker, blacker, darker, desperate. The truth, between them, for Berserk to see. A slender, four-armed marble figure, directing that orchestra of alchemical fire—unbeknownst to the human, even though that presence had been seared in his memories.

*Focus!* Dante, leashing himself, recalling his mind with violent intent. Ink and shadows, swirling, swirling in that silent windstorm. *Focus. On Sestel, on Lady Seve!*

The gusts hastened, violent, soaring, surging—surrounding the alchemist and the human, swallowing doors, blocking thoughts, morphing, reshaping, reforming into a woman's silhouette. Emerging from under the ashfall, left arm twisted in burns, left pauldron melted, left leg lynched by the fire. Spite in her eyes, slander on her mouth. One thought. *Personal or not, the burden is mine to carry.*

The shadows smeared the image, swallowed another door.

Berserk snarled, grieving the lost knowledge—but the gale grew, vertiginous yet silent, the spaces in between its inky brush-strokes distorting the echoes of the past with the thoughts of the present. Another image. Sittia, snarling, spitting at Dante's feet, threatening disobedience amidst a tri-nation melee. *Feel nothing. This isn't about me. It never is.*

More doors gone; gone!

The windstorm shook the soul-link, darkening, darkening amidst a third flicker. Juçe, laughing at him, laughing within a crowd. A third thought, thickening the brush-strokes, muffling Dante. *At ease; steady, steady. War has no room for emotions.*

Three more doors, all gone, all gone!

Insanity, to waste so much knowledge, to squander innovation!

Berserk unfurled their wings as the windstorm hastened, vertiginous yet restrained like a threat lurking in the night—known, treacherous, latent. It flickered between the gusts, impressions of Sittia blending her snarls, her hatred, her violence with sheer imagination—of her rushing in the night, of her dying like a martyr, of her causing a war.

Dante's denial became intuition, disregarding his resentment, neglecting his aggravation, burying his distress, maiming his logic, his innovation, his uniqueness until only a few doors remained, fissuring under the windstorm, quivering as the Legate struggled to think, to focus, to strategise amidst that restless quietude.

When another heartbeat passed—the third after the soul-link had deepened—golden threads emerged from the Legate's frustration. A dozen, all faint and sparse, all swirling erratically as if guided by a gale of their own. The Dragon One beheld them, eager, craving for Dante to hold on to one and recall the past, for memories could only be soul-weaved the moment they were remembered—and if those echoes teased him now then, perchance, the solution Berserk was now intrigued about lived in Dante's past.

Yet those thin echoes were just semblances of threads, mere golden sparkles. Just memories teasing the edge of Dante's awareness, yet weaving towards a door—one at the left, fissured, but still unthought of, still potential, still—

"Three-quarters of an hour left." The automaton.

In the real-world, Dante and Berserk snapped towards the bird.

In the soul-link, the simmering gold of those threads brushed a door—and it opened to smear the windstorm with the clarity of logic.

When Berserk emerged from the depths of that soul-link, the gusts had thickened to reinforce Dante's armour, clearing his eyes. He was still leaning over the table, that perfect calmness easing his features, the others' attention centred on him.

A curious human, eager for knowledge, resolved to stabilise Firard, and determined to armour himself in denial at the cost of his novel thinking. An intriguing case, to access one novel idea thanks to a memory he hadn't fully recalled.

The alchemist stretched, ruby eyes narrowed at the Legate— still struggling with the idea behind that mind-door—then severed the soul-link.

What Dante had done was an oddity but not an impossibility, unusual enough to sow intrigue about whatever had happened in the past. His reinforced armour was a problem, but Berserk's schemes remained untouched since the consequences of Sittia's disobedience—the first incision—had not begun to fully unfold. However, the Legate's plan was a human solution to a human dilemma, and Berserk needed a human solution to an alchemical question... whatever the question was.

Thus, Dante's armour would soon have to be melted down.

# Dante

Dante scowled at the letter stretched atop the table. "As I see it, the danger of Lady Seve's proposal lies within Firard..." He pressed two fingers onto the paper as if to hold on to the idea that had emerged amidst his frustration. *Solve the challenge; first and foremost.* "This will not be just an exchange, since whatever agreement we reach tomorrow may stabilise the relationships between both nations, and reshape Firard's internal politics." He paused, angling his head. "We *must* consider this in a response to Sestel. After all, Centurion Sittia should be trialled for her insubordination, but doing so will incense Juçe and her supporters. Likewise, doing nothing will foster disobedience." He lifted a hand, stalling an interruption before rolling it forth alongside his thoughts. "Thus, disagreements will resurface, divisions will surge, and the tensions between the Emerald Legion inner branches—the Forces, the Strategists, and the many trades of Support—will become evident."

Ilia grimaced, pinching her chin. "It is *plausible*... but the effects will not be immediate."

"Indeed," Dante confirmed, mulling over his next words. "In the long path, we may slowly become aware of the Legions' inefficiencies, the military shortcomings, and how their short-sightedness led us into this conundrum." Pausing, he gestured to the trio while meaning something greater. "Although Firard's political power lies with the Strategists, it's always been the Centurions and Magisters who shape public opinion; on their own, they command the largest group of Firardian citizens."

"Support is the largest... in numbers, at least. But they're split into their many trades, each with different preferences. Most care little about politics," Elixane corrected, brushing the edge of her sleeve but smoothing nothing. "We, the Strategists, are less than a quarter of the Forces; few pass our Trials."

Legate Ilia Larya grunted, ignoring the Imperial and staring at Dante. "Regardless, we should focus on retrieving Sittia first. Marshal-Strategos Gora can decide what to do with her later."

*As he certainly will.* "Agree," Dante nodded curtly, drumming his fingers over the table to steady himself. "If Sestel determines all the terms of the exchange, Juçe and many Centurions will equate it to a moral defeat. Therefore, it must be perceived—at least within Firard—as a negotiation in equal terms."

The pause was deliberate, the weight of the matter acknowledged in it. They withheld speech, yet as the Imperial steepled her fingers under her chin, Ilia rose with the slowness of motion impeded by thought. Dante followed her with his gaze, expectation stalling his own reasoning. *No time for it,* he chided himself, instead opening the elaborate box atop the desk to retrieve an ink pot.

"Are you suggesting we make demands of Sestel just to appease Firard's internal factions?" Ilia asked at last, a small crease marking the space between her brows. "Even when Sittia's recklessness caused this?"

"Not demands, but an offer..." He corrected, uncorking the pot to release a pungent scent. *After all, honour demands an enemy. No enemy means no retribution. No retribution breeds unrest.* He dallied, rummaging for paper. "Presented as a token of gratitude for returning our misplaced legionnaires, but aimed to shape our internal narrative about the consequences of Sittia's recklessness."

The conversation lapsed again, laden with unspoken considerations. The silence crackled as Dante stretched a piece of paper, the noises enough for Elixane to sigh and turn towards the many tomes gathering dust on the opposing wall. Ilia didn't answer, instead watching him with hands clenched on her hips. Dante teased her with an arched brow.

*The Centurions will return to deeming the fog a weapon, likely ruling this agreement as Lady Seve's attempt to disguise her guilt through a treaty.* Easing the gesture, he smoothed the paper before him, then retrieved a writing plume from the box; white, with an ink-stained nib and a gold decoration. *The consequences could be fear of the weapon, shame about the agreement, or both.* He rolled the plume between his fingers, revelling in the silence while his ideas developed. *I need to give Firard enough time to resolve this instability… by causing unrest in Sestel and forcing the Emerald Council into an agree—*

"Half an hour left." The clockjay chirped loudly.

Ilia swore between gritted teeth, then rounded the table to glance at the empty paper, at the box, at Dante. "What are you thinking of?"

*The basics: fear, honour, interest.* He met her eyes, pointing with the unused plume at the empty paper. "Let us meet with Lady Seve; the War Games and the earthquake are bound to be discussed. Once there, if she claims the fog was a natural disaster, or continues to argue it was an Orenian weapon… then she should have no issues with conducting a joint investigation." Dante lifted the plume to silence the Imperial's ill-timed retort, then stretched the moment into a silent remark. "Especially if I offer Lady Varre access to both our survivors and tunnels."

"But…" Elixane scowled, dallying as if her reasoning had scattered without her permission. "The earth-scholars could be enticed to come, but Sestel's medicine is more advanced than ours. The Varre healers are responsible for much of our current knowledge. How would—?"

Ilia's laughter interrupted her. Amused and shocked. *Like when I proposed that strategy during the Siege of Ílun Fort.* Dante saw the recognition in her features, the glimmer of awe in her eyes— it was validating, and so he dipped his head, pleased.

She waved an apologetic hand to Imperial Elixane, then pinched her nose to collect herself. "If that works, you'll leash the Emerald Council into an agreement they wouldn't be able to deny lest they risk dishonour... and you'd answer Lady Seve's threats in kind. She may not forgive you."

*Always keen.* "She will see me as an equal, and that will give me power of negotiation," Dante rebuked, finally uncorking the inkpot and dipping his pen. *I'll limit Sestel's perception, just as she does with us.*

As he wrote, the plume scratched the paper with consistent strokes, each trace methodical.

> Your letter concerning the detainment of the Ash-Walker has been received with relief. I commend your propriety in this matter, Lady Seve, one befitting your record of peaceful alliances.
>
> While the reasons for Centurion Sittia's journey remain unclear, I appreciate your offer to return these wanderers, grateful that their misplacement has renewed the correspondence between our nations. Let this be a reaffirmation of our mutual commitment to preserve the balance.
>
> I shall meet you at the frontier.

"Interesting wording, saying just enough." Ilia commented, tracing a few lines with a finger as if to guide a reread. "I should come with you. The Strategos may require a witness."

"Do, please." Dante tapped the plume atop the inkpot, then met his Imperial's gaze. "Egon Hold will be yours, Elixane. We march at dawn."

# Chapter 6

# Furia Gorge

## Zaro 13th, 17002 RE

# Dante



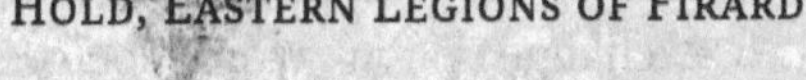

The incipient daylight died above the ravine, reflecting on the lighter stone and sinking the sinuous paths in ominous shadows. From below, the cliffs' rusty iron streaks darkened like trails of dried blood. *Don't show weakness; stay composed.* Legate Dante Praeto pulled the reins, pressing his heels into the gelding's side. It snorted in acknowledgement, keeping the pace while he glanced over his shoulders; his armour—slenderer than a Centurion's—shrieked.

The Firardian delegation marched behind him, the footfalls of two dozen legionnaires and stable-hands raising a cloud of reddish dust. Behind them, four carriages trailed in a column, wooden frames shuddering as they advanced through the rocky path. They were prepared to harbour the recovered soldiers, with additional space for the wounded.

*I'd be foolish to allow Sittia's cavalry to ride back with us.* Yet the mere sight forced Dante to press his lips and murder a grimace. *She never lived by her own rules.* Her hypocrisy was legendary; that famous stubbornness the Forces praised even though it'd always toed insubordination. Dante's grip tightened over the reins, the leather rough against the uncovered sections of his palm. *She never deserved the respect she demanded.* That thought tightened his scowl—a shield to the hovering dust—yet he soon eased it away. *No, her hypocrisy proves she's the one at fault, not me.*

He looked ahead for a moment, then to the sky—pale lilac and marred with a few cirrus. Eight dark dots flew over Furia Gorge, clear in their message. *The Sestelii are marching towards us.*

Horses neighed, and Dante glanced over his shoulder again, catching sight of Centurion Petra Arvina—riding a stallion as bloody-looking as her hair, her deep scowl shadowing her eyes. She'd been selected at Dante's request because he needed loyal Eastern Centurions—*Like Ciro and Rhea*—to stay in Egon Hold to counter Juçe's potential impulsivity. *Just as prevention.*

As he thought, Centurion Petra nodded at him, turning back to Ilia to exchange a few words before the Northern Legate spurn her palomino.

They had a few more hours of marching left.

Minutes passed, delimited by the legionnaires' march, by the carts' groaning and the horses' snorts. That repetition brought something else—a tension, a memory of the cornua before the Game. He blinked twice; the air shimmered, silver light catching the dust that never settled. *Not the time to worry, but to demonstrate mastery.*

"It shouldn't be long," Ilia noted, catching up with him and jutting her chin eastwards. Toying with the reins between her fingers, she hand-signalled, *"If not you, then no one."*

There was truth in her onyx eyes, a flicker of warmth that reached Dante—but he cut short his incipient smile. *Just work; just duty.* Instead, he nodded curtly, weighed down by his awareness of the stakes. *There is no room for doubt. Only the next step.*

Dante swung down from the saddle, boots hitting the rocks beneath with a precise clack. He flung the reins over the dark-bay's saddle, rolling his shoulder, and the plated pauldrons chafed. He prodded his cingulum, testing its hold and catching Ilia's gaze as a stable-hand moved both horses away.

From where he stood, the Sestelii delegation seemed larger

than expected—protected by a wall of footsoldiers, their shields catching the light. Behind them loomed mounted cavalry, two Generals set apart by their unmistakable bearing. Farther back, rooftops of carriages peeked over the formation, but the misplaced Firardians were nowhere in sight. *They must be in the carriages.*

"Stay close, but not too close," the Legate whispered to Ilia, lips stiff not to be read, gaze set up ahead—then he gestured to the legionnaires. "Four with us. Two scribes." As the soldiers jogged to his side, he stared at Centurion Petra, hand-signalling, *"Hold."*

Her acknowledgement was a curt dip of her gaze while she steered her stallion just enough to mutter a few indistinct orders. Dante observed her, squaring his shoulders before turning towards the Sestelii delegation.

When he marched, each step was deliberate. Weighed not to look rushed, measured not to seem inflexible. The distance closed slowly, and he noticed two silhouettes emerging from between the line of shields—hooded and slender, the reflection of steel cuirasses visible through the folds of their cloaks. The pair stood still, the thinner one two steps behind yet flanked by two scribes—unmasked, old, and too pale to have travelled much.

The breeze hastened as Dante halted to a close, the silence between the delegations muddled by the myriad of noises the ravine enhanced. Leather over rocks, hooves on dry soil, horses snorting, metal chafing. He breathed, focusing on his own sounds, gaze etched on the hooded pair.

"I'm Dante Praeto, Legate of Egon Hold, acting on behalf of Marshal-Strategos Gora Rachen for the Emerald Legions." His voice rumbled between the cliff walls, projecting as he intended. While its echoes were still alive, Dante lifted the Sestelii note, raising it enough to showcase the broken Seve Seal.

The shorter hooded figure nodded, long porcelain fingers pulling the cloak back to reveal a bun of caramel hair streaked golden. A few strands framed a striking countenance, and her eyes—azure and deep like the Abyss separating Ochrese from Verdant—etched in him; scanning, judging, revealing no verdict.

She was stunning. Elegant and poised—but it was her bearing that stalled the soldiers from following, ushering them into stillness with a tilt of her head.

"Lady Calya Seve, Head of the Seve House. Acting on behalf of Exarch Elor Luxa of Sestel." She stated, her smoky voice akin to a knife hidden beneath silk. Slowly, she raised a hand, showcasing Dante's letter for all to see. "It was due time we met, Legate Praeto."

# Calya & Dante

He looked exactly as she'd expected—handsome, sharp, detached. They had crossed before in a handful of battlefields, luckily never facing each other, yet somehow she'd never imagined him wearing a Centurion's armour; it fitted him, aesthetically, but his presence loomed larger. Legate Praeto was composed, every motion and tone practised to assess, appraise, decide. His eyes—darker than ink—held her gaze, unflinching, his black hair grazing his shoulders in tandem with the breeze. *Longer than Firardian regulations. Defiance? To whom?*

Lady Calya Seve pocketed his note, studying the armoured woman nearby. Composed, and with soft features arranged in practised ease; her black braid, resting over a shoulder, was woven from thinner ones. *Legate Larya, most likely. From the Northern Legions.* Looking past the Strategists, she noticed the stocky Centurion awaiting alongside their cavalry; the redhead scowled, lips pressed into something akin to a snarl. A detail struck clear: Centurion Juçe had not come to the exchange. *An expected development.*

She allowed another heartbeat to pass, then extended her right, palm angled slightly to beckon those around her.

"Varre scribes. They shall document whatever we discuss." Calya introduced, lingering as the two clerks she'd brought snapped to attention. "I trust you'll confirm their written accounts before we conclude, Legate Praeto."

He didn't flinch, his gaze steady on hers as he looped both thumbs through his cingulum—then inclined his head a fraction, as if beckoning the scribes behind his legionnaires. The pair raised their writing tablets like shields.

"I trust you'll confirm our accounts as well, Lady Seve." His voice was neither subtle nor harsh—just tuned to neutrality, as if waiting for a move.

*He doesn't have enough margin to act, so he waits for me...* Calya assessed the Firardian scribes, lifting her chin as she did so. *He's no fool.* It wasn't their presence that bothered her—it was expected if not routinary—but Praeto's restraint. Neither asking for Sittia nor extending any further courtesies; waiting, impassive, as if a hundred counter-tactics had already been considered. *Careful, then; he must have a plan.*

Lingering just so, she half-turned enough to meet Ruria—waiting a step behind, hood down, gaze expectant—then blinked once, as per prior instructions. She relayed her commands and the Sestelii wall moved, boots thumping on the rocks, shields clinging as they parted to reveal the guest. Centurion Sittia Praeto, not tied or restrained and neither humiliated; she may have lacked her weapons, but her armour was polished, her arm neatly bandaged, and her cheek recently cleaned. *Hori's healers never disappoint.*

In the distance, the Legate's stance shifted minutely—boots adjusting on the dust, arms folding behind his back. His eyes lingered on the Centurion a beat too long before flicking back to Calya. *Not what he was expecting?* She rolled two fingers, and the soldiers reshaped their wall, the matter of their exchange now hidden from sight—and given the footfalls, they were marching back to the carriage.

"Unexpected as Centurion Sittia's arrival was, we extended only our best courtesies," Calya prefaced, holding the Legate's inky gaze. Unflinching, unyielding. *What is he hiding?* "We were fortunate that Lady Hori Varre was visiting Ferro Keep; she tended to our guest herself. Thanks to her advice, we recognised some of the fog's lingering symptoms on Centurion Sittia; we believe she is still under its effects." A premeditated pause, waiting for an acknowledgement, receiving none. *He'll break when he understands.* "Because of this, I'd be keen on not escalating this matter any further, if Firard is willing not to seek retribution."

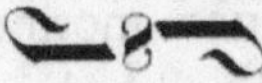

Legate Dante Praeto kept his expression neutral, but his mind was a battlefield. *That... is worse than I expected.* His fingers twitched behind his back, curling into a tense fist—yet he relaxed it before the leather straps creaked. *My fault. I considered the consequences of Sittia's return... but not Lady Seve's excuses for it.*

From afar, Sittia had looked well, living up to the promise he'd received—but two days ago his own medicus had also implied that the fog had affected her. *Juçe heard it as well. He'll argue Sittia wasn't in her right mind.* Worse, Lady Seve was using this unfortunate yet plausible reason to justify returning the misplaced legionnaires without escalation. *A carefully presented trap. Denying Sittia's sickness would be equally dangerous for Firard's internal stability.* Dante allowed himself to glimpse at the scribes —their plumes had stopped scratching their papers, having documented her words.

He nodded curtly, jaw flexing in acknowledgement as he glimpsed at Ilia—meeting his gaze, all too aware—then etched on Lady Seve's eyes again.

"I appreciate your courtesy, Lady Seve." He paused. One heartbeat. Two.

She didn't so much as gesture in response.

Dante continued as if nothing had changed. "As I indicated in my letter, while the circumstances of the Centurion's journey remain unclear, we'll investigate this matter with due respect." *We could argue she's no longer fit.* His breath caught, drawn taut by the future conflict, by the pointless arguments. *Not now. I have a trap to set.*

Lady Seve dipped her gaze; graceful, practised. Utterly ambiguous. "I trust you will, Legate."

She waited; purposeful, like a predator gauging when to

lunge. Unwavering as gusts of wind wailed through the ravine, sudden and ill-timed. It seemed to howl in pain, horses whinnying as their riders restrained them. A carriage groaned in the distance, a few blurred orders repositioning the rearguards.

*As I thought, she wants to cause unrest within Firard.* Dante gave her nothing; not voice, not motion—nothing as the gusts quelled. Softly she tilted her head, chin raising just barely to taunt him—but he stayed still, gaze fixed, letting the moment stretch. *I will not allow that. Not now, not ever.* That calculated pause seemed to unnerve the scribes; the shuffling of their caligae on rock interspersed with their nervous breathing. *Now, onto my plan…*

"We appreciate you returning the misplaced legionnaires. As a show of good faith, I wanted to extend an offer." Dante unlocked his hands to place them at his sides, then studied her.

She was as composed as a sculpture, the most polished façade Dante had ever seen. He found no curiosity, no anger, no interest, no distress, not even the pacing of her breathing. Perhaps there was acknowledgement in the careful, methodical way she kept her azure eyes on his. *Did she foresee this?* The Legate prolonged the wait, ignoring the bellowing wind. *Have I made a mist—?*

Lady Seve rolled two fingers, lacquered nails reflecting the sunlight. The scribes recorded the gesture in brittle silence, their scratching harsh and taut.

*Not shock, but careful curiosity.* Dante lifted his chin, gesturing north with a tilt of his wrist. "Our current concern, which I believe is mutual, is that the earthquake and the subsequent fog may not have been an entirely natural disaster…" He held the silence, waiting—for a confirmation, for a rebuttal. Nothing came. *Won't commit? Or won't agree?* "It could be of use to both Sestel and Firard, and a signal of our mutual commitment, to preserve the balance between our nations by conducting a joint investigation."

One heartbeat. Another gust. Two more heartbeats.

Lady Seve blinked, a hint of curiosity brightening her features. "An interesting proposal, Legate. How do you see such an investigation developing?"

*She's deferring.* He exhaled; keeping his face blank. *Earning herself time to think.* Dante hummed—appreciative of her response, and showing his willingness to cooperate. *Did I catch her unprepared? Possibly.*

"During the War Game, Firard had almost four-hundred legionnaires within the ravine. Most, if not all, were affected by the fog." It was a casual observation, and he delivered it neutrally, the tension—real and poignant—barely tautening his jaw. *Can she see where I'm going?* "Given the landslide and the subsequent fog affected both our nations, I would like to offer access to our medical records and our survivors to the Varre healers. If needed, perhaps safe passage for their earth-scholars to investigate the Gorge's cavern systems—only accessible through Firard."

Calya didn't breathe, didn't blink, didn't allow one thought to steer her into the avalanche of chaos he'd unleashed with such an innocent-looking proposal. The wind howled again, gusts slashing at random, upsetting the horses—whinnying, nervous, refusing to stay put—yet she simply tucked a devious blonde curl behind an ear.

There was one feeling she'd allow: curiosity about him and the thorns he'd just nonchalantly sown on her path. She clung to it. *He's a worthy opponent.* It was the simplicity of his offer that she admired and loathed at the same time.

Externally, it leveraged the stance she'd so carefully spread to manipulate public opinion—that a mutual enemy, Orenos, could've caused the landslide—and thus force him into the Veiled Retreat. *Thus, declining his offer would undermine my public position...* To the pedestrian observer, her refusal could be seen as a lack of cooperation, thus weakening Sestel's position in the eyes of their allies. *Which are always so feeble.*

Internally, the Legate's proposal played at the core of Sestelii politics and what its Grand Conclave had established thirty-four centuries ago. The Noble Houses may have had a stronger presence in some cities, even maintaining specific strongholds—but none owned territory. Instead, they owned a function across all of Sestel. While whoever led Seve controlled the frontier armies and the foreign politics, Varre reigned over education, research, and medicine. *And Lady Hori Varre is a fundamental ally.*

Calya parted her lips—just a thread—releasing a whisper of a sigh. Enough to ground herself, the warmth of her breath warring the suddenly cold gusts.

Refusing the Legate's offer was unreasonable. *Limiting Hori's access to knowledge could cause undue friction… and I need her to leash the other Houses.* After all, having her loyalty ensured that Lord Zuria—owner of the Sestelii navy and merchant fleets—stayed on her side. The sum pressured Luxa—the Exarch's House, controlling domestic politics, civilian enforcement, and infrastructure maintenance. *Yet agreeing to this will give a new angle to my mother, while losing Hori would weaken me enough to encourage Teoda to move.*

Her lips twitched, the smirk—partly awed, partly aggravated by being caught in her own play—held back by will alone. *Such a simple, yet powerful move.* Calya had misjudged Legate Praeto; critically so—and if not done properly, deflecting again could land her in an even worse, yet perhaps more graceful, trap. *I must close this in my terms, then deal with my mother's meddling. She will attempt to leverage this.*

"This could certainly benefit both of our nations, Legate." Calya paused, stretching that impasse as she tilted her head—delicate, measured. *I must pressure him into committing a mistake.* When she spoke, curiosity leaked purposefully into her tone. "However, while Sestel would welcome this knowledge, especially to support Varre in their research… it is Firard that would benefit the most from it. Our healers are the best in the world." She held his gaze, assessing his countenance—sharp, impassive. *Only for now.* "So tell me, Legate, what would you do in my place?"

# Amok



SOUL TRANSMUTER ALCHEMIST. THE UNTAMED ONE

Sunlight skidded over the ravine, rays bouncing on the stones, shade cascading upon the delegations now stationed down below—each feet away from the imaginary frontier, each organised with footsoldiers ahead, cavalry at the centre, and a column of carriages at the rearguard. There were no sounds sans the sparks of metal and the groans of leather, voices suppressed not to echo, relentless, across Furia Gorge. The wind was subdued that morning, the air shimmering as dust swirled lazily on its path.

From high above—where Amok hovered airborne, glamoured to invisibility—Lady Calya Seve was little more than a hooded smear, her shadow sliding behind her as she drifted past a motionless line of soldiers. Behind, near the centre of the formation, four guards manoeuvred the Firardian prisoner down from a carriage.

Centurion Sittia Praeto.

To the Untamed One, her actions represented both a personal failure, and a betrayal. A failure because they had been so absorbed by Calya's shadows, they hadn't spared a shard of time to even soul-link this Ash-Walker—at least not until early that very same morning, when they'd discovered what Berserk had done to her. A betrayal, because in soul-shaping her, the Dragon One had jeopardised the mission.

Annoyance rippled through Amok, threads of jet ink weaving their hooded cloak, the edges fraying into glyphs—sparkling cobalt, flickering cerulean as they soared, their cloak filling with the starless abyss that shaped a humanoid figure from the folds of the universe. They hovered well above the ground, wrapped within the ravine's shadows, yet far enough that the humans below were just motes of colour.

Upon stopping, the alchemist's glyphs burst forth like liquid light amidst the darkness of inky tendrils, enveloping them in a protective, pulsating aura—an Integrity Shield. It shifted in sapphire, teal-like hues, sparkling with splotches of ideas, flickering like a constellation of knowledge that barricaded their ipseity—their experience, their existence, the core encompassing *them*—from what was to come. It brought the perennial continuity of stability established by a barrier that pushed all struggle away, all threats into a place that couldn't be breached—at least not while that aura, that Integrity Shield, endured.

At that moment, Amok glanced down.

Lady Calya was lowering her hood, speaking out loud, while the Legate—the other target—watched her intently. Beyond the pair, mounted in a blood-bay stallion, awaited a glamour-Centurion—red-haired and deceiving every observer with looks, sounds, and scents so masterfully imitated the Untamed One could reach a single conclusion. Berserk had amalgamated the original, assimilating her alive elements to craft an imitation so close to what had been, that no human would even doubt her.

Wrath slithered from between the folds of Amok's cloak, leaking into the inky tendrils and shimmering across the glyphs holding their Integrity Shield. Berserk's actions were against the principles of Naturalism—and thus, an interference of incalculable consequences, a taint that couldn't be contained.

'*Reveal yourself, Dragon One. The fault is yours, and I'm not ignorant of it,*' Amok mind-whispered to the glamour down below.

The Centurion remained unperturbed, leaning to mutter orders to the cavalry under her command—the alchemist soared into the sky.

First like a rivulet of liquid copper, then a four-legged,

horned dragonlet. Their wings fluttered, luminous tides stretching its surface until it melded into a viscous gleam, glowing, growing, dross shattering atop to enable another transfiguration.

A humanoid shape, encased in an armour of scales, each row oozing and spilling, blotches of dross reforming as the sharp edges of high-plated greaves braced their tights—forged in jagged spirals, locked with straps of liquid copper. Their forearms bore the weight of bracers radiating oppressive heat, their cracked crust hiding burning gold and sinking into pauldrons of layered scales. Wings reshaped—wider, looming, raising high above with membranes of ever-flowing copper. The tail lashed after, waving softly like a pendulum outside of time.

When Berserk lifted their chin, a shimmer of recognition coated their shape—an Integrity Shield unlike any other Amok had seen.

It mattered not.

*'You soul-shaped that Centurion, and amalgamated another,'* Amok mid-whispered, the accusation sharp like the clawed finger stabbing down—to Sittia, a mere slab of anger walking back to a prison-carriage. *'I did not agree to such interfering manipulation of alive elements.'*

The Dragon One tilted the head—and sunlight bounced on the four horns curling upwards from their head. Their jaws spread, fangs bared as blinding amber dripped down; sluggish, savage. *'I merely encouraged what was already there.'* Mocking. Like the mind-whisper that existed in the ravine's silence. *'The Rector asked for chaos. I delivered.'*

Silence. On their minds, on the world, on the humans down below.

Berserk's was a lie, an excuse, an outrageous disregard for the sanity of their mission and of their targets—those that, after providing knowledge, could morph into source-beings for future alchemists.

Silence. On everything around.

Amok's silhouette gleamed with the glyphs surrounding them, a fragment of their mind scanning the other alchemist.

For a lapse in their ipseity, for a contradiction in the narrative that held them together, for a fissure in that Integrity Shield. For a breach that would allow them to cripple Berserk enough to remove them from their mission and thus safeguard Amok's target—the one that could, potentially, assist the Untamed One in perfecting the nascent incarnate soul-skill.

*'You disregarded The Rector's instructions. But this—?'* Amok's pause hushed at the hinge of nothingness. *'This is worse. You have compromised our mission, our go—'*

Laughter. Roaring, rolling, drumming like the inevitable chaos that would always preface all wars. It swelled, furious, and the wind ululated in mockery, demeaning yet pulsing. When it bellowed, gusts slashed upwards through the ravine, subservient to the Dragon One's Matter alchemy—the second oldest Soul-Matter Transmuter.

*'Naturalism, naturalism...'* Berserk mind-chanted, rolling a hand—and the gusts surged with the strains from down below, echoing with the gritted orders of upset humans. *'There is no basis to your proposal, young one, save the folly you inherited from your source-being. That brittle penchant for inconsistent principles.'* They laughed again, their wings splotching carmine as if human blood spilled over them. *'One would think that after seventy-seven millennia you'd finally dispose of it, but it seems you cannot.'*

Displeasure bellowed across Amok's figure, the echoes held back by their own Integrity Shield. It lingered in the impasse of non-existence, pulling back as the Untamed One surveyed those lies, dismantling the insights it offered and the plans it enabled. After all, they couldn't soul-link the older alchemist, not while that Integrity Shield held taut.

Yet they could wait, as long as needed, until an existing fissure allowed an exploit.

*'You have tainted this process by soul-shaping that Centurion and amalgamating another.'* A curt mind-whisper. Offering no edge. *'Our targets will not interact with the originals, and so their reactions may not be Nat—'*

*'Tainted? Natural reactions?'* Berserk's tail snapped. The air swerved, gusts coiling like blades drawn to kill—yet their ruby eyes curled into jeering arcs. *'I see you are more than afflicted with*

*foolish principles. You're so bound and blind you can't even acknowledge reality,'* They soured, wings spreading, beaming gold and copper swirling within its shattering crusts. *'I only manipulated those around our targets, Amok. Their reactions remain truthful because alive elements always are—regardless of what caused them.'* Anger. It blasted like sunfire coiling from the edge of those wings, sucking the wind's warmth as it bellowed brutally. *'That's why your Naturalism is flawed. It is inconsistent with—'*

Amok found it. Through those words, within Berserk's alchemical composition. A flaw, a fissure. A need untilled, unaddressed, unforgiven and thus whirling through their Integrity Shield like an unspoken plague. Desire—for freedom, for control. Fear—of weakness, of memory.

It lingered, half-split, within the Dragon One, even when rimming two-hundred millennia of existence. It coruscated as Amok willed it closer, aiming to link it, to leash it, to—

It vanished, scattered like a mirage.

*'Oh?'* Berserk lashed their tail, an incandescent glow surging from within. Their mind-whisper thickened, dense and dangerous like the molten metal composing them. *'Are you trying to mind-yoke me, Amok? Isn't that against your Naturalist principles?'*

Laughter, gleeful, amused.

So foolishly irreverent. So fatally erroneous.

The wind clamoured with feigned solemnity; more violent, more zealous.

*'You won't win against me,'* Berserk mind-hissed, all traces of folly merry evanescing as they pointed a jagged finger towards the silence below—where Calya's thoughts burst like networks of ideas grounded in the past. The Dragon One remained indifferent; their mind-threat a truthful warning. *'Try that again, and I will suffocate them.'*

The Untamed One stilled, their glyphs burning brighter, beaming, weaving the network that protected them. It coated their form, barricaded their being—and from within its protection, they quavered at the truth gleaming from Berserk's intentions, the impending destruction that'd named them the Harbinger of Annihilation.

It teetered on the brink of realness.

*'If you kill these humans, you will disavow The Rector's orders...'* Amok warned, a threat veiled in that mind-whisper.

The wind chilled, slowing, sluggish. Like Berserk's response. *'Will I? Or did our mighty four-transfigured commander foresee this as well?'*

# Dante



LEGATE OF EGON HOLD, EASTERN LEGIONS OF FIRARD

She held his gaze, her countenance a shield of curious calmness. "So tell me, Legate, what would you do in my place?"

*Exactly what you just did, Lady Seve. Shift the burden.* Dante's silence lingered, excused by the gusts howling furiously through the ravine. Her words, so reasonable to anyone listening, were just a calculated feint. With a single question, she'd unveiled the advantage he aimed to secure, remarking its impracticality, and outlining the problems Dante needed to solve—on her behalf, and publicly for all to hear—before she'd considered accepting. *She merits her renown. I respect that.*

His goals were transparent to Lady Seve—since Sittia's return would sow chaos within Firard, he needed Sestel to also be in a feeble situation to prevent it from hoarding more power than due. His token of gratitude was exactly what he'd planned it to be: a threat to Seve's domestic power and, through that, to Sestel's unity. *And we both know that… just like we know she cannot refuse my offer. Doing so would have consequences for her.*

Yet the problem remained. While a wrong answer would label Dante as a reckless risk-taker, one too careful would under-mine his position—and the Centurions, especially Juçe, would leverage that. *Which she also knows.* After all, a wrong word, a wrong gesture, a wrong insinuation was all it'd take for her to refuse his offer.

The thrill of the challenge awoke on the Legate, his grin of excitement held back only because of the stakes. *Let her act. I've already accounted for it.* The wind whistled, so chilling each gust felt like blades on his skin.

"If I were in your place, Lady Seve, I would ask myself why the Emerald Legions—who could lose so much—would make such an offer at all." Dante spoke low and unhurried while dismantling her next argument. "Then, I would realise that neither Firard nor Sestel can afford not to know what, or who, released the fog."

*Refocus on what matters, Lady Seve.* He breathed, looping both thumbs through his cingulum, boots planted on the floor. She'd given him this leverage three days ago, through letters and rumours that clarified her stance about Orenos. *She cannot undo her words now. She should—*

Calya nodded, nonchalant, as if noting an oddity that had landed, maybe too casually, on her lap. "You say neither of us cannot afford to not know the cause, and you could perhaps argue Sestel is reticent to accept your token of gratitude..." Her voice held an undeniable authority, carrying weight without being loud. "Perchance, that would be a correct assessment, Legate." The corner of her lip pulled up—a hint, nothing more. Spreading her fingers, she calmly beckoned at Furia Gorge. "After all... we are here, discussing this, only because of the Eastern legionnaires misplaced in Sestelii territory."

The plumes; scratching, screeching. The wind; whistling, colder and chilling. The horses, the legionnaires, the cavalry; increasingly restless, shuffling in place, pretending not to do so. The ravine; groaning and howling as if warning of impending doom.

Lady Seve, expectant, impassive; fencing with her words as if she knew exactly what he'd planned. She had not missed a single opportunity to parry his arguments—and neither had Dante. *Cunning and dangerous; we're at an impasse, which I cannot ignore.* They were both waiting for the other to slip, dancing around the same point, each word precisely selected to reveal nothing while making everything clear—but only to each other.

In that moment, while the scribes were still inking their

words, Dante mirrored her nod. *She's stating her narrative, and that's the only path to an agreement.*

"A fair read," he admitted, only because it was convenient. "However, our real concern remains the same. While everything may have escalated from an ill-timed natural disaster, we cannot deny—not now, at least, without proper research—that it wasn't someone else's design. Perhaps a mutual enemy."

One heartbeat passed; the wind bellowed. Another heartbeat; the cliffs shrieked.

Beneath it all was that underlying need to challenge himself, to dismantle the complexity of that negotiation, and stabilise Firard again. It was duty, but also a quest that'd begun long ago, within a library, through an old and shabby book and a few words so easy to write yet so difficult to achieve. *The elusive Meridian of Existence. A precarious balancing act.*

A third heartbeat—and the wind halted abruptly, the sudden silence deafening.

"That is one plausible read, however..." Lady Seve smoothed her leather vambraces with the nonchalance of a predator that didn't need to strike to be feared. "Given this misplacement , how am I supposed to allow our Varre healers and scholars , valued for their skills, to travel safely into Firard?"

*Implying we're untrustworthy. Not false, but not fit to speak of, either.* Dante nodded, rubbing his thumb into the inside of his cingulum to anchor himself amidst that ear-splitting, windless silence. *She won't concede, and won't propose a solution either.* He blinked slowly, acknowledging her with the sombreness that was due; there was no perfect outcome, no true balance—just an edge less tilted, less sharp, less deadly for only one nation. *Few choices remain.*

"A reasonable take, considering we cannot bring our survivors to be tended here at the frontier," Dante pretended to sigh, conceding what he knew wouldn't be enough for Sestel, but had to be recorded for Firard. *Or Juçe will see betrayal where there is none.* "I can offer you faithful copies of the survivors' accounts and our medici's reports in a show of good faith. Once the Varre healers deem it sensible, the Eastern Legions will invite a delegation, sending another to Sestel."

Lady Seve tilted her chin, arching a brow. "It sounds to me that, given the impracticality of your original proposal, you are now offering less..." She let her words settle like the shimmering dust within the Gorge. "Nonetheless, given the events three years ago during Orenos' invasion and the Nadir's ill-timed eruption, this joint investigation could be useful... if only approached correctly."

Dante tensed his jaw, softening his shoulders and releasing his hands from the cingulum while her azure gaze trained on him. Etched with unspoken demands, expectant as if a truce were acceptable only after the right conditions were proposed. After all, Lady Seve's statement was a covert clue. *She'll agree only if I shift the balance in her favour... at least externally.*

The Legate dipped his head. "Most certainly. Which is why Firard will ensure Sestel's efforts are remembered and answered in kind... at a time, and not to excess."

# Berserk



SOUL & MATTER TRANSMUTER. THE DRAGON ONE.

The noon light slashed over the ravine like blades of steel piercing the cirrus. They seemed to contort, upset by Berserk's manipulation of the air's components, the wind above stilling while the one below wailed. Beneath them all, shadows clung to the Gorge's jagged cliff-walls, unmoved by the shifting air, yet murmuring with the annoyance leaking from the alchemist's scales. It poured from their molten metal, the dross shattering and fracturing like their patience.

That annoyance—that prosaic alive element—was caused, solely, by the alchemist before them.

Amok. The Untamed One, the leader of the Naturalists. Clothed with midnight draped as if each fold charted a galaxy. Their cloak swirled behind them, starless, the hood kept in place over their featureless non-face by sheer will alone. That countenance—that blank mask of the palest marble—shimmered with droplets of iridescent ink, cerulean eyes darkening into pitch-black slits.

Amok. A nuisance of the maximum calibre. An inconvenience that had seen through that flaw still haunting the older alchemist after two-hundred millennia. An irreverent, noxious Soul Transmuter with ideas dangerous enough to taint The Orders with what they'd been free of since their inception—inconsistent principles.

A pestilence Berserk had bequeathed at the mission's outset.

Glamoured to invisibility, the Dragon One spread their wings, clawed fingers pointing down in threat. The air wailed at their command, the gusts lacerating with their coldness.

'*Do you think I'm not capable of this?*' They mind-whispered, the unspoken echoes of their threat sneaking like the gusts beneath. Brutal, chilling, and hazardous.

The young one didn't answer, their ever-darkening glyphs weaving a tighter network, gleaming with intention, strengthening that Integrity Shield. Berserk observed them, motionless yet hovering in that glamour; they could splinter the Untamed One and thus eradicate that flawed, inconsistent school of thought Amok had ideated.

A most apt solution. One that only required patience to find fissures in the other's Integrity Shield, and exploit its weaknesses.

'*Threats, then silence. How predictable, Amok,*' the Dragon One taunted, the air's components waiting for their command to shift, to split, to suffocate those colourful motes beneath them. '*Inconsistent, just like your Naturalism…*'

No answer was offered, the Untamed One's concentration was a gesture on its own. Their darkened eyes remained narrow, the abyss within their cloak curling on itself like strands aiming to weave reality, yet managing nothing more than empty threats.

A thread of concern slithered between the burning gold leaking from the Dragon One. That negotiation below was likely strengthening the Legate's armour, closing more doors towards novel thoughts—something they'd wouldn't be able to deal with while enduring Amok.

Within an iota of time, they soul-linked their target, and a fragment of Berserk's mind flooded with frivolous, densely-packed yet narrow-sighted human's concerns. Favours to exchange, appearances to keep, debts to indulge in. The Centurions' response, the Marshals soon to arrive, the so-called legends and the rumours they'd spread. The standing that could be gained, the position that could be lost. The woman before him; her gestures, her voice, her words, her actions and ploys and schemes and knowledge and guesses. Amidst those irrelevant murmurs, one thought. *She's stating her narrative, and that's the only path to an agreement.*

'*Leave the mission, Berserk,*' Amok mind-whispered above those murmurs, finally raising one finger as if to threaten the other. '*You'll only compromise it further.*'

The Dragon One laughed. Slowly, deliberately, making no secret of their disdain. The air sharpened at their command.

'*Or what? Will you try another mind-yoke? A splinter perhaps?*' Their annoyance transmuted, melting into anger, brimming within the molten metal that so composed them. '*Are you so dependent on humans to develop your theoretical incarnate soul-skill?*' They teased, remembering The Rector's promise to Amok—a pathway to unravel what remained a mystery. '*How long have you been failing to develop it? A thousand years?*'

Liquid light blasted from Amok's glyphs, despise leaking from its shimmer. '*You understand nothing of what an incarnate may reveal to Soul Transmuters.*' That mind-whisper slithered like the inky tendrils coiling from Amok, shielding, protective. Impervious and flawless. '*It could enable an active study of alive elements—*'

'*In an un-Naturalist way!*' Berserk countered, their wings spreading open, exhausted from orbiting the absurd while tethered to principles that would collapse beneath the weight of the feeblest inquiry. The air howled on the verge of splitting. '*Your incarnate will allow an interaction that is, by definition—!*'

Berserk faltered, silenced by one thought.

It streamed from the soul-link to the Strategist. *The elusive Meridian of Existence. A precarious balancing act.* Thick with the golden threads of memories recalled like an anchor to sanity and holding one obsidian door open. Yet Berserk disregarded the door—that human solution to a human problem—watching the flickers of memory entwined in those golden filaments.

The memory that'd stabilised Dante just the day before. The one that hadn't been fully recalled, thus forbidding it to the alchemist.

It was there now, in his awareness, in that very same moment.

A library not entirely real, not precisely whole. A book, idealised by the passage of time. A concept, a thought, a name so alchemical in nature that it should have never reached a human mind.

Berserk's maws parted, leaking molten metal, wings spreading in delight for the promised solution was tied to the Meridian of Existence—and it existed, perchance, not in Dante's present but in his past. If so, no incisions would be needed—just to peruse Dante's memories.

Ignoring Amok's rebuttals, the Dragon One focused on the Legate below, their will so directed into the soul-link they forgot to command the air. Its gravitas evanesced, slumbering as the alchemist held onto those golden threads, tethering into the echoes to soul-weave Dante.

It braided a lattice of alive elements, leading Berserk into a past memory.

Holding onto that memory, chasing the semblance of that book, and unravelling the threads of continuity, Berserk plunged into Dante's past.

Undoing his latest campaigns, while rolling beneath thoughts that repeated without apparent cause. *It's about them, not me. Always.* Reversing a trailblazing career, sifting through strategies no one else even considered, yet knotted to a lesson learnt—parallel to that thread Berserk was chasing. Unwinding years of strategic training, of simulated conundrums, of War Games, of shadowing others that were more experienced. Rummaging into an even older past, following a toddler too different from the Legate of Egon Hold.

Little-Dante was running through marble hallways—of ceilings so towering, of floors so polished each step skidded if not controlled, of glazed casements so transparent the gardens outside brimmed alive. He stopped, panting gently while looking between the columns and through the glass, lost in the opulent greenery—but when a door creaked, somewhere far away, he whimpered and hurried again. The pattering of his caligae echoed like the rally of marching legions, his ragged breathing remarking every step, every inch further and further into the Palace of Arborum City.

The corridor split, and he drifted right. His long black hair—tied low—tickled on his back, but his mind accompanied his gaze. Caressing each oversized painting, their colours vibrant even after centuries. Different wars, different conquests, different times yet all somehow known—even if faintly. Recalled only because of the books he'd stolen and read.

A double door opened ahead, and little-Dante stumbled through its archway, gawking at the life-sized marble sculpture of a Centurion. He was rallying the Legions, shield and spear threatening the sky, cloak captured in a perennial flare. The boy traipsed around it, his small, sun-kissed hands touching his belted tunic—too long for his legs, too ungainly compared to the marble Centurion's armour. Simpler and more rudimentary than the one his parents wore, but so commanding little-Dante rounded away from it, staring at the other figures.

The sunlight shimmered around the statues, rays cascading through the windows. Yet as that past-child lingered, awed, Berserk stayed with him. Reviewing that memory, absorbing its tranquillity, its sounds, its feelings; the wonder, the safety of being shielded by those figures.

The irreverent, absolute terror triggered by the incoming footsteps—precise, martial—that echoed far away.

Little-Dante gasped, backtracking with his gaze edged into that threatening double door—then turned and ran again. Chased by a looming, lurking apprehension. By the certainty that doom was impending, that harm was on its way, and that it was inescapable.

The Dragon One chased that memory as the boy tumbled into another corridor, sprinting as much as his caligae allowed. He drifted through hallways, hopped across archways—guided by a teasing instinct—swerved around tables and statues and trophies and—

Books. On the marble shelves built into the walls. On the reading stands scattered across the room. On the mahogany tables arranged in neat rows as if waiting for someone to pick them up.

The breeze hastened, warm and gentle, yet too inviting; nudging the boy with methodical precision, with clear intent. Hooking the alchemist's curiosity because that wind reeked of Protean alchemy even if little-Dante couldn't see it.

He ambled ahead, stretching and tiptoeing to snoop over the tall tables, gawking at the stands and their handsewn books. He stopped a few times near the chairs, pressing both hands into the velvety cushions to peep over the table—but none captivated him enough. The wind always seemed to move in another direction.

A last table enthralled him, rectangular and surrounded by chairs, one in the corner and angled open—so climbable, so tempting. So perfectly positioned to read the book left open on the table.

As little-Dante hurried to it, mindful of his pattering, Berserk noticed his change. The fear faded, replaced by the insatiable curiosity that brimmed in the eve of discovery—and it was untamed, unyielding. Not yet constrained by the armour he now wore. There was something between those books; a warmth, a tease, a soothing fragrance—and it enveloped him, even as the footsteps kept marching in the distance, incoming yet now long forgotten. Climbing that chair was a feat, yet little-Dante clung to the backrest, pushing up to plant a knee, then another, then manoeuvring towards the table, perusing the book—

Berserk's reasoning faltered for a sliver of existence, unspooled by their intrigue. Interminable in magnitude, infinite compared to the boy's—now gawking at that old and shabby book, little hands hovering above the ancient pages not to touch what seemed unfathomable. He traced the text, blinked as if reading—and the alchemist marvelled.

That book, that old and shabby volume spread open atop a human library table, spoke of alchemy. It was not written in any human language, but in alchemical glyphs, each one a compendium of knowledge so complex and convoluted only a few alchemists used it.

Yet in that memory, little-Dante *read* it.

He understood the symbols, not because the alchemical glyphs were fathomable, but because someone was translating them for the boy. One after the other, the symbols were simplified, their core meaning captured in human language.

That presence, that translator, loomed even in that memory. Vast. Timeless. Stretching beyond comprehension, enveloping the world like a foundation that could never be removed because everything—*everything*—depended on it.

To Berserk—from the confines of little-Dante's memories, from the depths of his limited perception—that presence was not recognisable... but there were two beings that could project a book from within The Towers' Library to the outside. One, The Towers themselves, but their might was a legend Insidious had mentioned and nothing else. Two, The Rector, and such interference opened infinite possibilities.

A most enthralling challenge, to uncover such schemes, to unravel whatever the four-transfigured alchemist aimed to achieve.

Berserk revelled in that discovery, pausing it for a moment to focus on little-Dante. Reading that old and shabby book, mouthing the translated words, scowling in deep concentration as ideas and theories blossomed in his mind. He stopped, pressing his lips, hand hovering over a translated passage.

*There exists, across all human cohorts, a precarious equilibrium where societies teeter between war and peace, suffering and fulfilment, ignorance and enlightenment, turmoil and stability.*

The Dragon One recognised the core meaning streamlined in those words, for they had written it long ago—but not in this old and shabby book.

In that memory, little-Dante read them, chewing on his bottom lip. He balanced on the chair, hands pressed beside the book, neck lengthening to re-read, to savour the idea that teased him from between the pages. He'd wondered something similar before, but no other book had ever answered him.

Intrigued, the alchemist lurked as the boy kept reading, from the middle of the right page and down to its end.

*It establishes an equilibrium between extremes of excess and deficiency, albeit human societies always fluctuate to the extremes. Regardless, societal deviation toward either suffering or comfort initiates a decline. Excessive hardship proves destructive, while excessive ease breeds decadence.*

Little-Dante looked up, fingertips tracing circles over the table—craving the texture, the anchor, the looping nature of his thoughts. Ill-shaped and misformed like a toddler's sketch, rudimentary yet grasping the core implications of that simplified translation. His thoughts steered in a promising direction. *Establish?*

He lingered, pulling words he'd read in other books—but Berserk ignored those golden threads sinking into a deeper past, instead focusing on little-Dante. With intent, with hunger. For novel ideas, for due answers, for solutions to problems they hadn't posited.

*Does this balance… imply thri-thriving?*

A scowl tensed little-Dante's face, and he balanced on a half-crouch atop the chair. His hands grazed the rough paper's edge, a palm sliding beneath, shoulders shrinking as he flipped that large, oversized page. It shushed, the sound far more enthralling than the footsteps that kept marching—closer and harsher, martial and intentional; never hurrying, never slowing. Just coming, coming, coming.

Berserk ignored them as little-Dante tiptoed feebly over the table, reading the top line of the left page.

*That boundary constitutes the Meridian of Exis-*

*tence, since it enables societies to transcend their normal cycle of self-destruction.*

Little-Dante blinked, gaze etched in the book, a hundred golden filaments reaching farther into the past—towards the paintings of wartime and victories, towards the statues of Centurions leading troops, towards the training and the lessons and the strategies that so enticed him. Another idea cleared; hanging onto a word. *Self-destruction? Why?*

The footsteps halted—so softly, so lingering and threatening that the boy, and Berserk as well, ignored them. In favour of reading, of learning, of unlocking another clue.

*Correction of the imbalance is always necessary. Hardship, the removal of luxury, or the forceful establishment of peace are all potential pathways to return to the Meridian.*

A shadow loomed over little-Dante, towering over his ideas but never shading that concept, that truth. It lingered, even as the boy blinked in realisation, his abject terror surging like wildfire through a dry forest. His lips parted, shoulders tensing as he gazed over his should—

The air burst on his right, bellowing, splitting open behind his head. Pressure, sharpness—spreading in the wake of heat, yanking his world, twisting his neck. Dante slipped from that half-crouch, wood shrieking at his left and creaking as his cheek bounced onto it. Then, the world tumbled upside down, and pain spread through his face—from his nose and chin, wet and warm and sticky like the marble floor. Needless punctured his shoulder, his hips thudded dryly as the chair moved out of view.

*He found me.* Realisation. Numbing the sharpness across his temple, the edges sinking in his cheek, the puncturing pain of his shoulder. *I forgot... about him!* He scrambled to a sit, snorting blood, another trail dripping from his temple. *Where is he?* His hands clutched at the floor, his eyes trying to see—but stars showered the room, pouring like the march racketing in his chest, buzzing so loud he couldn't hear. When little-Dante blinked, he—and the alchemist still hanging onto the memory—recognised the figure.

Black hair pulled back, a well-groomed beard, a crumpled scowl framing steel-clear eyes. Blood dripping from a signet ring.

A so-called legend in the making.

The source of all fears, of all the uncertainty. The knot where that gold thread—running parallel, written with self-deprecating words—tied neatly. *I'm a disappointment. Always.*

The clarity lasted one frantic, frenzied heartbeat. Enough for little-Dante to glance at the table—at the old and shabby book that was no more, at the emptiness it left behind, at the pristine surface of a library desk. In the next heartbeat, fear flooded the memory, pain swelling and buzzing, another bloody snort staining the floor.

Berserk hurried forward through that thread, returning to the present.

When soul-weave ended, the soul-link beneath delivered another thought. *She'll agree only if I shift the balance in her favour.* Down below, within the ravine, Legate Dante Praeto continued his negotiation, his present mind still cluttered with the murmurs of too many concerns.

Berserk tilted their head. That memory did not hold the promised solution, but a tease of what it could be: another pathway towards the Meridian of Existence. One that Dante ought to think of. One, perhaps, led by humans themselves.

Insanity, to think such a thing was possible.

Yet as the Dragon One thought, their tail lashed like a time-less pendulum—oscillating back and forth, looping around one question.

What had The Rector intended by revealing the Meridian of Existence to a human child?

# Calya

"—this joint investigation could be useful... only if approached correctly." Lady Calya Seve's statement rumbled low through the Gorge.

The windless silence blanketed the delegations with iridescent dust. It swirled with the faintest currents; the specks refracting the noon's silver light and casting strange shadows on the Legate's face.

His eyes were locked on hers, their deliberate sharpness brimming with intention and a hint of thoughtful scheming. He was a monument to self-discipline, even as his jaw tensed slightly. *Annoyance? I may have finally caught him.* Calya waited, each passing heartbeat a renewed test of her temperance. *If he doesn't offer—*

The Legate's shoulders eased beneath the weight of his pauldrons, hands slipping from his cingulum to rest openly at his sides.

"Most certainly." His voice, modulated and low, stretched with the silence left, a deliberate counterpoint to the wind's absence. "Which is why Firard will ensure Sestel's efforts are remembered and answered in kind... at a time, and not to excess."

Lady Seve arched her brow—hinting at surprise, teasing the

Legate, demanding he elaborate although no questions were issued. *Answer in kind? Can he offer that?*

As the silence lingered, he didn't proffer more clarity, instead waiting for her as motionless as a statue of a war gone by. Unfazed by the sudden quietude, unperturbed by the magnitude of the advantage he may be conceding. *If he's negotiating, he must have the standing...* The only motion was the slow rise and fall of his breath; too deliberate and measured for someone who'd offered the enemy such an advantage. *So what is he truly after?*

Taking her time, Calya studied the woman beside him. Legate Ilia Larya awaited at parade rest just a step behind and to his right; her hands clasped on her back, her features smooth and composed. *Comfortable? Or just pretending?* Larya betrayed no secrets, watching ahead with detached certainty and never flickering towards her peer. *Not disapproving of the offer, but—* Her cheeks twitched, fleeting and quick, yet too revealing. *Upset that we've reached this point?*

Lady Seve nodded, her neutral hum followed by a mild echo. *What a quaint offer!* A non-promise, presented as an open concession, recorded in their discussion, yet vaguely clarified. It allowed him to manoeuvre around the finer details to likely craft a domestic narrative, while granting her enough ground to claim the upper hand. *This must serve him to counter the effects of Sittia's return.* She had intended to destabilise Firard by returning the Ash-Walker under dishonourable conditions, then had aimed to counter his ill-timed token of gratitude—*An excellent move, even if cumbersome*—until she was offered enough leverage in compensation.

In turn, his proposal gave Calya a power no other Seve had secured, a leash no Exarch had enjoyed—and it could be wielded to cement her standing within Sestel and the world. *Yet it's not without its threats.* Teoda would court favour to tilt the Sestelii public opinion and either use this favour sooner and recklessly, or disregard it as an empty promise never to be collected. *Which is why its nuances must be properly documented.*

"Tell me, Legate..." Calya finally stated, rolling a hand towards the future. "What would happen were you to fall tomorrow? Is this promise yours alone, or does it outlive you?"

"What I offer is not a favour. It shall be policy for the Emerald Legions." His next pause was brief; a single, barely perceptible breath, as if weighing his words. "The Marshals will honour it, or they will answer for what follows."

*So that is his reason. Honour.* Wielded correctly, it made for fine coercion. It could smother reckless actions by appealing to the preservation of reputation, and that into civic virtue. It quelled military ambition by offering a narrative that presented it as legacy. *Because even nations act in self-interest.* It could reframe Sittia's loss as a crucial moment to stand with the dignity and excellence of the Emerald Legions. *Thus gaining inner leverage. Clever; too clever.*

Calya hummed, once, raising her voice. "You haven't revealed what your policy includes."

"Enough to be worth remembering, and tailored to need." The Legate explained, no more expressive than a statue of a Noble overseeing his estate. His fingers returned to his cingulum; not clenched, not toying, just waiting.

The finality of their conversation was undeniable, and so Calya didn't respond immediately. She blinked, just once, acknowledging his answer yet chasing the logic he'd so carefully guarded. Beyond the honour and commitment sprang from a bi-national treaty. Past the opportunity of future repayment and the standing it granted her. Further away from the political posturing and into the personal. *Could it be?*

She almost straightened upon finding it, scattered across their conversation like minute clues few would uncover. *He's teetering on the edge between peace and conflict… for what? Equilibrium?* Where Calya had aimed to destabilise, to sink Firard in inner mayhem for Sestel—no, for herself—to gain power… the Legate had neither pushed nor proposed, just reacted as a perfect counterpoint. *Almost as if he chased that fabled Meridian of Existence.* She restrained a rueful smirk, barely acknowledging the frontiers of that concept. *It's not through balance that it can be achieved, but through power.*

"So be it. A future owed, held in balance." Lady Calya Seve dipped her head, accepting the Legate's offer—then gestured to the clerks noisily inking their words. "Let our scribes draft the final agreement. I will return our guests once we have both signed."

It wasn't defeat, just ruthless pragmatism. It offered her what she needed and how she needed it. *And perhaps even more.*

The Legate brightened for a moment, a shimmer in his eyes. *Curiosity? Or else?*

"Then we understand one another." He tilted his head towards the scribes, still cowering behind his legionnaires. "We'll prepare for their return."

# Amok

Berserk's wings lashed open, the gusts swerving to avoid the fury blasting from them. Beaming, blinding, fracturing the ever-changing dross, tail snapping. *'Your incarnate will allow an interaction that is, by definition—!'*

Silence. Abrupt. Unexpected.

Swallowing that mind-whisper into a stillness so profound, so deep and imperturbable that Amok wondered—for a fraction of eternity—whether time had been suspended. It lingered, fascinating, as Berserk leant towards the humans within the ravine but etched on the Legate.

The glyphs enveloping Amok stuttered, hesitant to cast judgement. Their liquid light darkened with fleeting confusion, slowing in their path before bursting with realisation—Berserk could be misdirecting them. A lure enabled by an Integrity Shield that rendered them unreadable. A taunt, perhaps, meant to confuse and, within a timeless impasse, destroy every human as promised. A possibility, not unlikely, since Berserk was Insidious' most successful mentee—and their soul-skills had a precision few alchemists had mastered.

A menace like no other, to lose their promised chance to further develop the incarnate.

Weary, the Untamed One hovered still, reinforcing their own Integrity Shield while perusing Calya's soul-link. She was weaving a hundred considerations, forecasting long-term consequences, testing action paths and choosing words in her sharp, detached style. Admiration laced her thoughts. *Thus gaining inner leverage. Clever; too clever.*

'*Did your foolishness interrupt you?*' Amok mind-whispered to the other, afflicted by too many hues of concern yet allowing none to shine. '*Or has the truth finally dawned on you?*'

Silence endured in the void between the invisible alchemists, the Dragon One so absorbed that their tail barely twitched in response. Only then, Amok noticed the pooling tranquility, the absolute mantle of stillness coating the humans, the windless air. That non-alive element seemed to have fallen from Berserk's mind, long-forgotten and left to its own devices, only to fester into a concern—

*Almost as if he chased that fabled Meridian of Existence.* Calya's thought, streaming from her soul-link, and as logical as the dozens of possibilities she assessed. *It's not through balance that it can be achieved, but through power.*

Power?

Amok blinked. That single name—the Meridian of Existence —knotted into a golden filament, honey-light and vivid, that sank into her past to knot into a distant memory. It enlightened the soul-link, bright and unforgettable—and the alchemist wavered, shocked. The Meridian was a fundamental concept of Soul alchemy and had no reason to exist in a human mind.

Thus, before the memory left Calya's awareness—the alchemist pulled the thread, retracing its pathway to soul-weave her memory.

Dissolving the façade hidden behind that name, and unravelling the golden threads of continuity, Amok plunged into Calya's past.

Undoing her latest schemes while swerving around the shadows of her self. Reversing a revolutionary career, sifting through political manoeuvres no one else even considered, and past strategies that had become history. Unwinding years of posturing, of training, of lessons, of screaming in the silence of her mind while offering a gentle smile. Rummaging into the oldest past, and following a toddler Amok had seen not too long ago and was, although foundational, intrinsically different to the Head of the Seve House.

Little-Calya awaited amidst a lavish room—of towering ceilings, of glazed casements rimmed in gold, of marble walls mixed with obsidian like night swallowing day. She pressed her lips not to exhale, aware of the echo, and looked down. Her left calf burnt like the furnaces heating tempered pools, the mound of swelling purple poorly hidden by her dress. *Mother won't approve.* She prodded the silky folds, arranging the fabric to hide—

A polished chuckle. Lady Teoda's.

Fear stained the memory, but Lady Teoda ignored the girl to indulge Lord Eneko. The amusement on her face was something little-Calya couldn't quite imitate. *Not yet,* she decided, too aware of Mother's movements. The manicured hands smoothed the silky dress, the rouged lips curled in a teasing smile, the eyes—

Observed little-Calya.

*Yes, Mother.* She perked up, following Lady Teoda further into the Noble Residence within Umbra City. The Untamed One chased that memory as the girl crossed into a corridor of twisting marble and obsidian. It split up ahead, then again and again and again—but little-Calya followed Teoda, minding the distance, the rustling of her clothes, the pattering of her gold-strewn sandals. *Where is Father?* She missed him for an instant, her rueful smile knotted to the gold thread of a memory. Amok did not pursue it, the absence streaming from it enough of an answer—just like the fuzzy lack connecting to a younger brother.

They crossed an opulent archway, and the daylight died on its rim. The ensuing corridor was wide and long, oppressive as only an obsidian structure could be. Lady Teoda awaited beside a set of double-doors, half-turned towards little-Calya.

*Yes, Mother.* Terror blurred the memory again. Insane, irrational, impervious to all reason but entrenched like only instincts are. Blinding the girl and her memory as it morphed into a need to please, to satisfy, to be as expected and so much more. Little-Calya dipped her head—*As she taught me*—then approached Lady Teoda with a measured gait, eager for a gesture that approved her response.

"Wait here," was all Lady Teoda stated, her silken voice wrapping iron. She gestured beyond the double doors, the lacquer of her nails catching the remnants of light. "I shall come for you."

*What did I do wrong?* A tide of anxiety stained the edges of the memory like rust corroding a mirror. *Wrong, how?* It narrowed little-Calya's senses, consuming her sight, stifling her body, and muffling the footfalls that walked away.

Heartbeats passed, erratic, lonely. Her hiccuped breathing echoed as little-Calya awaited where instructed—under the double doors, hands clasped on her navel, jitters swarming her limbs. She reviewed her actions, drowning herself and Amok in what-ifs, considering mistakes, reasons to be punished, flaws to fix.

Before the Untamed One sped the memory, the breeze slithered between her draped dress—warm, and nudging the girl with methodical precision, with clear intent. Igniting the alchemist's intrigue because it reeked of Protean alchemy even if she didn't notice.

Teased by that intentional zephyr, she crossed the open doors and ambled into the library beyond. The towering ceilings vanished into shadows, most of the space overwhelmed by black-oak tables rimmed with chairs. The obsidian walls were obscured by sinuous bookshelves—made of blood-like mahogany and assembling countless hallways. Some hosted cupboards, and little-Calya stopped on one, studying the parchment it harboured—smeared with the colours of her own reflection. She startled, pulling her neckline to cover a green-yellow knoll bumping her shoulder. *It can't show*.

When the breeze rose again, scented like ink and teasing knowledge, little-Calya followed it through the bookshelves, reading their plaques, yet resisting the urge to touch the aged, colourful spines.

'*Little one?*' A voice. Gentle, soothing.

She jolted to face the speaker, hands clenched near her rampaging chest, chin lifting to look at the lanky librarian standing—

Amok's reasoning faltered for a sliver of existence, unspooled by their insatiable, savage need to comprehend.

That librarian—that slight shard of a figure—was neither human nor present in that hallway. It was a glamour, cast to convey, and projected from an immense distance. The cobalt threads of an alchemical portal tethered it somewhere and somewhen, fading at the edges of that memory although linked to a presence so vast and foundational it stretched across all eras like the cornerstone upon which the universe existed.

Little-Calya didn't notice it, her perception even more limited than Amok's. To her, that glamour was just a woman, robed in black-and-white, a dark ribbon laced through her silver hair, features blurred by time.

"My apologies, esteemed one…" The girl curtsied, mindful of the neckline covering her bruise. "I was instructed to wait here."

'Then all the more reason to peruse the books.' The librarian was kind, soothing. 'Were you looking for something specific?'

The glamour did not speak but mind-whispered in a tone so real, so textured and nuanced that little-Calya *heard* it, imagining a tantalising voice brimming with secrets.

To Amok—from the depths of her memories, from the abyss of her limited perception—the glamour's caster was not recognisable… but there was a single being that could use alchemical skills from across the universe. The Rector themselves.

A vexing discovery, to find the leader had interfered in such a non-Naturalist way, to be burdened with recruiting a tainted human and—most grievously—to have no other choice than to act as commanded. An intolerable misfortune, yet one to be later considered—once the soul-weave had ended and the damage's extent assessed.

Thus, the Untamed One focused again on little-Calya, so full of doubts, so quiet while her mind stuttered. *What is the correct answer? What should I say?* Possibilities scrambled like fleeting ideas, all quickly replaced as she glanced at the surrounding shelves. *I shouldn't hesitate!* She noticed a tome on the Grand

Conclave, a few volumes of different treatises, a pack of rolls with royal seals.

"The... Volatile Pact." Little-Calya blurted, recalling her last lesson. Her hands trembled, clasped tightly against the rope holding her dress. "The one that... organised the trade routes between Vesperia and Sestel, seven centuries ago."

The librarian hummed, stretching an arm to graze the spine of a tome—an analysis of the Pact. *'An interesting treaty. One born from past tensions, caused by naval skirmishes and pirate raids...'* Her long fingers traced the engraved letters, but while little-Calya saw human hands, Amok perceived the illusion. *'Lady Zuria had reached a verbal arrangement... but her kindness became a weakness. War ensued. In the aftermath, Sestel abused its strength, enforcing the Pact's cruel conditions upon Vesperia—and those did not last.'* She pocketed her hands between the folds of her robes, tilting her head with child-like curiosity. *'Do you know why that happened?'*

Little-Calya focused. On the lanky librarian, on the tilt of her head, on her own hands, on her posture, on the twitch on her cheek that screamed of hesitation. *What... should I answer?* Gold threads of memory sprung as she recalled the books she'd read, the lessons she'd heard—but Amok pursued none. *What did... Mother say about this?* She squared her shoulders, refrained from shuffling her feet. Despair embraced her, tip-tapping on her shoulders, tickling her ribs, taunting her ignorance. *Mother never explained this.*

Little-Calya second-guessed herself before whispering, "It was a Pact, but not between equals."

*'Correct. It was skewed in Sestel's favour.'* The librarian raised both palms, one slightly higher than the other. *'There was no balance at all.'* She levelled both palms, her voice innocently mischievous. *'What if there is a precarious equilibrium to be achieved? One with just enough conflict, with just enough peace to remain in that edge?'*

Little-Calya watched both hands, blinking rapidly, spurn by the likelihood of answering wrong, of failing the challenge. *Mother hasn't... explained this either.* She observed those fingers again, the book, the librarian. The clouds moved outside; the light dimming for a long moment—and the girl knew she'd dallied. *What would Mother say?* It came to her, hissed.

"War is the rule. Peace is just the intervals in-between," little-Calya offered, levelling her voice. *Too childish, too soft.*

The librarian hummed, neutral. *'And do you believe that?'*

Despair. Fumbling between little-Calya's fingers as she prodded her silk dress and roped decorations. "I believe... war and peace are important to me, because the Seve House... controls Sestel's armies and foreign politics."

Amok listened on, both bewildered and enraged by the conversation. The glamour was certainly The Rector's, and they were trying to teach, to nudge the child, to sow an idea—but it was not a Naturalist approach.

*'You are correct, but there is more...'* The librarian nodded to the book she'd touched before. *'Human societies are fluctuating. They'll wander between suffering and fulfilment, between turmoil and stability. Whatever vices, whatever extremes... they can go from one to another.'* Another pause, another stretch of infinity. *'Excessive hardship is destructive; it leads to revolution. Excessive ease, breads decay. Between them, there is a thriving zone.'*

Little-Calya waited, fingertips tracing circles on the silk of her dress—craving the shushing, the anchor, the loop peeling the layers of those words. Her thoughts were rudimentary, faint like charcoal sketches, yet grasping the foundations—and they steered in an alchemical direction.

"Why? Why do we thrive there?" Her question, so timid.

*'Because humans evolve through challenge, and refine themselves when comfort begins.'* The librarian explained, gentle but never leaning to her height. *'Because excessive warring leads to irrecoverable destruction, and excessive stability leads to stagnation and decay. Either case, little one, is a flavour of self-destruction.'*

She lingered, pulling words she'd read in other books, in other lessons. They became gold threads into the past, but Amok remained with little-Calya.

"Self-destruction?" She dared, her whisper so faint. "We cause it... to ourselves?"

*'Indeed; because outside this Meridian of Existence there is only a slow descent into nothingness.'* The librarian's words were the

source of the memory Amok had pursued. *'If you were to lead Sestel… how would you steer it towards this Meridian of Existence?'*

A pout tightened the girl's features, fingertips rubbing the silk, gaze flickering to the Volatile Pact. She was proud of having dared to posit ideas—even if wrong—and enticed by the quest for answers that went beyond the books Lady Teoda asked her to memorise.

She found one theory at the frontier of that memory. "With treaties and accords. Balancing the power of the nations."

The librarian nodded, that approval searing a mark on her. She lifted her chin—

The air burst, fingers snapping. Thrice—quick and waiting for nothing, sharp and expecting obedience. Calya whimpered, lifting her skirt to rush back through the sinuous hallways of bookshelves, between the black-oak tables, and up to the double doors where Lady Teoda awaited.

She caught little-Calya's forearm with a hand. Cold, tight. Tighter. The nails dug into the tender inside, omitting the silk and sinking into skin. There was a spoken statement, silken but steely. The girl ignored it. *Don't cry, don't cry.* She straightened, pretending that grip was gentle. Disregarded her frenzied, frantic heartbeats and buried her fear. *Smile, smile.* But Lady Teoda did so with an eerie peace that augured pain.

Amok hurried forward through the gold thread, returning to the present.

When the soul-weave ended, the soul-link enabling it delivered another thought. *Curiosity? Or else?* Down below, within the ravine, Lady Calya Seve seemed to have won the argument, her mind still weaving that network of long-term considerations enabling her plans.

Amok glanced at Berserk—yet the Dragon One remained absorbed, tail oscillating like a pendulum looping around the impossible. In that impasse, silence strangled both alchemists, thick with unseen intent.

#  Dante & Calya

A crude table had been set up at the frontier—just two barrels supporting a rectangular plank. It creaked as the scribes leant into it, muttering between gritted teeth, pointing at inconsistencies, and debating the wording like soldiers fencing in a duel. *At least they are thorough.* When they inked the final document, their scratching climbed through the cliff walls to echo tenfold.

Legate Dante Praeto straightened, standing near that table and refusing his need to shuffle his weight. Instead, he glanced westwards, where the Firardian carriages were finally settling closer to the front, doors open. The cavalry awaited nearby, ready to escort the returning legionnaires during the exchange. *Sittia shouldn't ride. I'll place her with the legionnaires.* Centurion Petra was with them, still riding her blood-bay stallion while whispering to Ilia. Their scowls were interspersed with nods of agreement.

Dante turned back to the scribes, watching as the quartet clustered to assess the final documents. Beyond them, Lady Seve awaited near the tall redhead—but her azure eyes were locked on his. Something passed between them; curiosity, or even recognition.

"My Lady?" A young scribe called, bowing to her. "The documents are ready."

Calya allowed her gaze to linger on the Legate's, just enough to wonder whatever that was—a shared understanding, or a flicker of knowing. *What an intriguing development.* She followed the Scribe towards the documents.

"For your perusal, Legate," Lady Seve offered after a moment, beckoning to the paperwork neatly arranged atop the crude table. "Four original sets of notes, two collated accounts of our discussion, two copies of the treaty."

He nodded, approaching the table and reading without leaning. Calya observed him while they both read, reviewing the sections where he seemed to stop, and ensuring the wording could be interpreted in as many ways as convenient to her. *A danger, but also an advantage.*

"We are in agreement, it seems," he stated after a while, two fingers pressing into the table. "Let us sign."

# Berserk & Amok

Berserk waited. Pondering what that memory meant for Dante's armour, debating the wisdom of revealing that alchemical concept to an ephemeral human, and vanishing the apprehension that threatened to take root within the beaming core of their molten metal.

Insanity, to project a book from The Towers and into the human world, to translate and simplify alchemical glyphs until they were fathomable to a time-framed mind. Insanity, to carve a world just for the sake of preparing one Legate as a candidate to source-being.

Insanity, except it had been unleashed by The Rector.

Berserk waited, wings rustling in the breeze that almost sought to appease them, tail twitching as they observed the humans down in the ravine like a predator considering its options.

Both factions were assembling a crude table, scribes gathering around it to assess the meaning of their notes. On one side, the Lady awaited alongside an aide, her Generals preparing for the exchange. On the other side, the Legate whispered with his Northern peer and glamour-Petra. A pedestrian conversation —repositioning the recovered soldiers and war-horses, safeguarding the Ash-Walker, minimising risk. An aberration in which Berserk indulged with a fragment of their mind, if only because having amalgamated Petra required such involvement.

The situation in the Gorge—that treaty binding two nations—was too absurdly common compared to the schemes upon which it stood. Ploys opaque to Berserk, who'd only scratched their surface by haphazardly finding clues.

Insanity, except The Rector had designed that trail to be found exactly as it had been.

Driven by curiosity, the Dragon One looked down at that woman—Amok's target—and considered a soul-link, promptly disregarding the idea not to ignite another disagreement. Instead, they glanced at the younger Soul Transmuter: hovering near, their cloak of midnight billowing behind. The glyphs of their Integrity Shield brimmed cerulean, tightly woven and as impervious as before, but flickering with something not entirely contrary to absolute intrigue. It teased the Dragon One, tantalising like a chance to uncover clues to complement their own findings.

It was, thus, not unreasonable to collaborate with such a bother.

'*Dante found a book. From the Library of The Towers,*' Berserk mind-whispered, as abrupt as the clawed finger they pointed down. '*The Rector was there. Coercing the wind to guide little-Dante to the book and translating alchemical glyphs for him.*'

Amok's glyphs froze until a hundred more burst from the blank spaces to evanesce in doubt. When they turned, their head was tilted, questioning. '*What did he read?*'

'*The basic definition of the Meridian of Existence,*' Berserk informed, unwilling to yield any further details.

'*Little-Calya, she…*' The Untamed One observed the humans below, their glyphs finally moving again—sluggish, lazy. Dragged by the shock that thickened his intention as they mind-whispered, '*Calya also knows about the Meridian of Existence.*'

A glowing tide of liquid metal crept through Berserk's wings, sparking golden with the fire of shock before bursting with the elation of discovery.

'*What?*' Berserk groaned, raising a hand, palm up. The air

above it shimmered as they coerced its components to shift. *'Did she see this book?'*

Those motes of light drifted airborne, morphing as the alchemist so commanded it, and catching the light just so. Once ready, the Dragon One willed them into a semblance of the old and shabby book they'd encountered in Dante's memories. A book they've never seen before.

Amok's eyes narrowed at the illusion. *'No. She met a glamour of a librarian, and they discussed its basic concept...'* They halted, the mind-whisper interrupted as they raised a six-fingered hand, watching something on its palm—but then waved it away. *'I couldn't recognise the caster through the soul-weave, but the presence... was vast. I can only assume it was The Rector.'*

A silence thicker than the void between the stars lulled the alchemists. It was the soundlessness of schemes too intricate to cast shade, of goals awaiting so far ahead it seemed infinity would circle on itself before reaching them. It was a calculus of stillness, vast enough to remember the basis of alchemy and the principles that so composed it.

*'This is not the only time The Rector manipulated these two,'* Berserk observed after a while, hushing the mind-whisper like a whip dragged back. *'Futile was here.'*

Ink blasted from Amok's tendrils, splotching their Integrity Shield. It dripped with hesitation, eventually quelling when the Untamed One mind-hissed, *'What? When?'*

Berserk snarled, liquid copper dripping from their fangs as they posited how much to reveal. *'Have you encountered a memory of a tri-nation war on the northern frontier? Between Orenos, Sestel, and Firard?'* They paused, their left wing pointing northwards— screaming light, white-gold at the core, yet sparkling carmine. *'Futile caused the Nadir's eruption; I saw them in Dante's memories. But —'* They lifted a finger, stalling Amok's interruption before pointing down to the Gorge itself. *'This ravine has Futile's signature precision. They must have sliced the mountains to create this specific shape.'*

Amok looked down, not at the humans—now moving the prisoners from one side to the other—but at Furia Gorge itself. Matter alchemy was beyond them, but even when shallowly considering that ravine, Berserk's observations could not be disregarded.

The mountains on each side ended abruptly, the iron-streaked cliff walls too vertical and jagged as if meant to deter climbers. There were no walkable trails across its length, and the few usable landings were carefully placed—close to the entrances but never further inside. The rocky path, fitting a narrow row of soldiers, was sinuous enough to never grant full visibility into the enemy's lands.

An incriminating realisation, to notice even the landscape had been tweaked at The Rector's convenience, for a purpose that exceeded both Amok and Berserk, and—perchance—with the goal of igniting the tensions between these human nations... or preparing those two humans.

'*I see...*' Amok rumbled, pointing one inked finger into the Firardian side. '*And the caverns? The Five Vaults?*'

Berserk's wings battled twice, smothering the sparks blasting from its membranes. '*Futile's as well. According to the memories I've encountered...*' The Dragon One raised a hand, rolled it as if searching for words, then waved it north. '*They're too purposeful. Only Futile could carve them without irrevocably damaging this world's geography.*' Their maws trembled before they added, '*Only the World-Shaper has this precision.*'

Amok lingered, pondering just how The Rector had *twice* lured Futile out of their secret refuge—in another era, to carve the tunnels and the ravine, and three years ago to ignite the Nadir. The ancient Matter Transmuter had been far removed, enthralled—likely for myriads of myriads—in another obscure experiment.

'*Understood.*' They finally mind-whispered, reshaping their Integrity Shield—it wouldn't do to allow the Dragon One to witness the details Amok had withheld. '*We shall continue our discussion at a later stage.*'

'*Indeed,*' Berserk mind-hissed in response, slowly drifting back towards glamour-Petra.

The returned legionnaires were climbing into the carriages, faces sombre with exhaustion and dishonour. Meanwhile, the Ash-Walker was barely crossing the frontier, surrounded by a guard too thick for her pride. The alchemist considered her as they descended, eventually melting to transfigure into their dragonlet form.

When they nestled on the stallion's saddle—glamoured to invisibility yet moving the redhead Centurion—a path of action cleared before them.

They could not allow Dante's armour to endure unbroken, for the alchemist craved the knowledge about a new pathway towards the Meridian of Existence, and emotions were fundamental to innovate. Yet more than ever before, Berserk ought to be careful when carving the incisions they'd designed before; not necessarily Naturalist, but methodical enough not to risk destroying the human before he discovered that novelty.

# Delta

# Verve

The thunder growled in the distant horizon, latent and perennial like a warning never realised. It was the voice of an everlasting storm, the rumbling of entropy as the tendrils of lightning sheared the darkened clouds. It was the leash of a suspended charge, taunting, teasing, threatening with might never released.

When the lightning flashed, Verve looked up—to the crowns of the fractal trees, to the hollow branches capturing the electricity that stroke them. Around them, the air shimmered with unspent static, leaves humming and zapping as the canopies fed, recharging. The sparkles zigzagged—upwards, downwards, sidewards, so erratic, so focused on existing, so entrenched in their struggle.

Struggle.

That concept, alchemical in nature yet easily confused.

It continued in the world around them, on its storms, on its plants, on that clearance harbouring them. When Verve looked down, they studied the cradle of vines and leaves before them. Élan still pooled at its centre, shadows tendrils twisting ill-shaped while barely sustaining the semblance of that dishevelled raven wing. Nightmares and electricity rippled within them... but there was more. So much more.

Struggle.

It stirred within the Raven One, swirling like oily ink swimming in clear water—barely remembering its shape while refusing to be merged and thus become something else. It sparked like the nightmares of demise, it sparkled with ideas colliding amidst the lack of a theory to unify them, and sluggish like adversaries parting after a defeat.

There was something in Élan's alive elements, something in their composition that refused to blend—and it shimmered in the surface of those shadows, unravelling the faint lines that fissured their Integrity Shield.

"It can't be..." Verve muttered, tapping a rhythm in tandem with the thunder's growl.

Within a fragment of eternity, they traced a fissure in Élan's Shield, forging a soul-link. Not to attack, and neither to dismantle—but to comprehend, to corroborate, to seek a solution.

As that connection spread open, the abyss of a timeless existence revealed itself. Unfathomable sans for the starlight flickering above that darkness—traces of knowledge, formative experiences, thought-patterns and attitudes shaping a core identity.

Yet that abyss fractured, its non-wholeness spreading like loosening swathes. Each was a figment of identity, purpose, and choices—courting, teasing, but never blending into a whole. They screamed, and those guttural howls ripped through the long-dead silence, a horrifying symphony of pain and terror swirling as the swathes twisted on and on. That pain, that visceral ache, transcended all limits.

It was a war on Élan's self, a wager on their existence.

Everything was as Sententia had described—the Raven One was fractured but still existing, teetering on the edge before the collapse of their self. Verve wouldn't allow that to happen, and so they halted the soul-link when those swathes bellowed again, marred by Delta's ever-growling thunder.

Verve waved an arm, soundproofing the surroundings and raising a palm. Their fingers twitched as they wove the threads of raw sound from a prior conversation. The words returned, drawn into glowing filaments that tightened into a shimmering, pulsing ring.

It hovered over their palm, echoing in Hellion's voice. "The Raven One tore Vim's foundational core while absorbing their fundamental knowledge of half-alive elements. It wasn't purposeless destruction—"

Verve suspended that voice, head tilted as if weighted by the logic they so chased. While they couldn't corroborate Hellion's impressions, Élan was renown for being precise. Thus, their unfolding abyss evidenced something more concerning—the Raven One was trying to integrate what they'd absorbed from Vim, yet failing to do so. It was a quest for a renewed self, a fundamental and ongoing struggle now locked in a stalemate that could lead to non-existence.

The second-in-command looked down at that dishevelled wing, shadow tendrils twitching with electricity, twisting yet never reshaping—and when lightning flashed outside of that soundproofed dome, those shadows barely flinched under the light.

Scattering their concerns, Verve wove more sounds, reshaping the ring hovering above their palm. Its edges bristled and pulsed with Hellion's voice. "I must assume The Rector foresaw this, Verve. They tasked me with assisting Élan."

The Rector. The commander who planned missions not only to unravel knowledge but to evolve the alchemists that completed them.

The next soundbite was Verve's own voice. "Not madness, but a scheme. As usual."

"But *what* scheme?" Verve gritted, their present question overlapping with the repetition still playing above their palm. They fisted that hand, silencing that soundbite to mutter, "You won't fracture, Élan. I won't let you... but what do you need?"

That dishevelled wing stirred within the pool of shadows, nightmares and electricity lurking inside. Verve observed it, their four ruby eyes narrowed in thought.

At their core, all alchemists were forged in the crucible of three critical alive elements—desire to exist, fear to cease, and absolute certainty about their identity. Around that core, existed the key attitudes comprising the latter; the shard of their self willing to struggle to define itself and thus enable continuity.

Beyond that, were the individual quirks making them unique, some a legacy of their human source-beings.

Thus, to compel Élan to reintegrate, the only path forward was to offer something that bridged the own with the foreign: whatever was Élan's, with what they'd amalgamated from Vim.

Verve mulled over that conclusion, fingers weaving more sounds, filaments knitting into the Raven One's voice as they recited their Creed. "I'm the flavour of all knowledge, and the compendium of understanding. I'm Élan."

Those four ruby eyes narrowed in the span between predilection and discovery. They altered the soundbite, the edge brimming with Hellion's tone. "The Rector... tasked me with assisting Élan, explicitly detailing I should bring them to Delta in the aftermath."

Their fist clenched to vanish those echoes, the soundproof dome shattering as the lightning flashed through the hazy firmament. The static over the canopies shimmered opalescent, the thunder roaring with such deafening power the land quavered under it. Balls of light crawled down, only to be captured by the hollow branches feeding from them.

Delta was Verve's world. The one they'd created during their second transfiguration—as a Protean Reshaper alchemist. The lightning of that world had birthed from Verve's will, that light and might the one they commanded through their knowledge of half-alive elements. Yet from the half-alive lightning flourished electricity—a non-alive element feeding Élan's existence.

A grin slashed the alchemist's mask, the abyss within rippling with elation as they watched the ever-raging thunderstorm.

Their wings lifted behind them—vast, iridescent, like mirrors refracting all the light in the universe, angled upwards as each metal feather fanned out like blades ready to fall. They held them aloft, unyielding, expelling all shadows as lightning slithered through them, streaks of amethyst and azure lashing to the sky, to the ground, to the world itself.

Delta trembled with caged momentum, the distant stormwall halting on Verve's command, the cloud-filled sky swerving to spiral over the alchemist—lurking like a predator waiting to be unleashed. With a motion like mountains waking, they formed a cluster of lightning—hundreds of tendrils converging from around the world into that spiral circling above. It fed from their wings, it rippled through their armour of mirrors, it brimmed with unspent electricity as the clouds clashed, their charges growling, gruesome, glorious.

But it waited, that lightning, suspended as Verve infused it with knowledge. Of Protean alchemy, of half-alive elements and their feeble boundaries with non-alive elements. It coruscated with excitement, the world awaiting its blast, the forest snapping and raking as the hollow branches stretched, begging for that might.

On Verve's command, a hundred searing arcs tore down from the sky, veins of cyan fire racing towards that pool of shadows. They struck as one—jagged bolts flaring outwards and folding inwards, crashing down with dooming precision, with driving intent, with defined knowledge.

Élan's shadows twitched—the sparks within snapping as the wing perked, reforming, redefining. Nightmares and electricity scrambled from its shadows, crafting another wing, leaking into feathers and strengthening those ringlets of darkness now brimming with scalding light. Verve willed the lightning to remain, its growling suspended by the will and knowledge of a Soul-Protean with dominion over both.

Within the impasse of eternity, darkness spilled from the pooling shadows of Élan's self, black filaments creeping and curling as if hungry for form. Verve halted the lightning, the thunder roaring as the pool of shadows expanded, threads of abyssal nightmares weaving into an alchemical body.

Legs of armoured penumbra, a mirage of abyssal darkness and unfathomable nightmares woven by electricity to shape metal-made faulds and a cuirass. Shadows crawled into four wings, each feather blending obsidian and steel. Two sprouting from the hips, two more from between the pauldrons now sparkling alive. Black hair framed silver eyes—but they lingered, dimmed and ajar, the light within muffled when compared to what it had been.

"What happened?" Élan hissed, sitting on their heels, hands

spread open atop their knees. They watched, head tilted, coils of shadows tickling their chin. "I... amalgamated Vim..."

"Hellion splintered Vim after that." Verve dropped to one knee, gaze levelled with their peer. "You absorbed too much. Your elements are erratic. Do you remember what happened before the amalgamation ended?"

The thunder bellowed with Verve's worry; its distorted sound mirrored what they saw on the Raven One. Morphing alive elements, shifting like colours in ink that never blended into a new hue.

Élan frowned but shook the head, staring at nothing in particular. "For a moment... I understood the universe. It was ordered, attuned." Their four wings rattled, collapsed like a mantle of darkness. "The chaos afterward was destructive. Voracious. It... was not as I am, not *what* I am."

"Nonsense. You're the Chaos Tamer," Verve rebuked, right arm resting over their knee while the other grazed the ground.

The Raven One chuckled, bitter. "You know that title... has another origin." They dragged their eyelids shut, their sight heavy with exhaustion. "What I... feel, is something different. There is—"

They halted, half-open eyes raising through Verve's figure. Studying the iridescent metal of their armour, scowling at the sounds that sparkled from their movements, and gawking at the wings still open and leashing the sky. Élan perked while curiosity renewed in their eyes, then stumbled to stand and watch the sky.

Delta grumbled again, the thunderstorm still spiralling as Verve followed their peer, watching the lightning converging above them.

It was then that Verve noticed Élan's awe—brightening those silver eyes, willing their four wings to fold back elegantly, coercing the nightmares trapped in their armour to flow like ink committing understanding into words. It was the elation of seeing beyond what had once banned, thus setting in motion the elements composing them until their collapse seemed to stall.

"What do you perceive?" The second-in-command asked, standing near the other.

Élan stammered, waving a gauntleted hand towards the everlasting storm. "I… never imagined this is how you perceive it," they confessed, pointing at the cerulean tendrils spiralling above. "Command it."

Verve grinned as they raised a wing, its lightning lashing into the indigo firmament to recharge the clouds. The spiral writhed, a hundred electric bolts flaring downwards with splintering precision, landing before the alchemists watching it with the inquisitiveness of those who seek ultimate comprehension.

"Creating this…" Verve explained, beckoning to that wing, "—is not the same as creating that." Their feathers pointed to the stormwall suspended on their will—a cumulus of charcoal clouds, of gales and destruction. "That is a half-alive system far complex than the lightning within me."

Yet as the second-in-command willed it, the spiral above dissipated, the stormwall resuming its path.

"I want that," Élan stated, the fervent frenzy of discovery flickering in their eyes. "Show me how, Verve. Teach me Protean Alchemy."

# Ferro Keep

## Zaro 14th, 17002 RE

HEAD OF THE SEVE HOUSE, SESTEL

When she turned the corner, starlight filtered through the ample casements, the glass blurring its glow to coat the marble walls with a shade of night. It cooled the golden decorations with cyan and lavender, tracing highlights over the delicate sculptures—a swirling, sweeping arrangement of golden vines embracing the base of each column. Calya halted to observe them, one hand lifting the long hem of her gossamer gown, the other grazing a gold leaf. The lavender diffused across her skin.

*So feeble.* She smiled ruefully, glancing over her shoulder at the shimmer of the Vast Expanse beyond the casements; the horizon grimaced at its edge, drawn like a slender line of dark. *Still early.* Calya pressed her lips, gaze taking to the sky because the clockjay she now awaited could—at any time—plunge like a shooting star. *The Exarch should answer by dawn. Before that, I have time to scheme.* A yawn threatened to overcome her, but the Lady subdued it by resuming her path. *He may privately see the Legate's open favour as a threat; after all, it's within my remit as Head of the Seve House.*

When she turned from that illuminated hallway into a corridor barely grazed by the starlight, a scowl creased her brows. *I must be careful.* Her pacing was measured, echoing like a casual, midnight stroll—albeit her mind raced alongside the many threats surrounding her. *Teoda is here, Hori will do anything for knowledge, and Firard... can be unpredictable.* Calya didn't mind her path, turning right onto an almost black corridor she walked by memory alone. *Yet I must continue to build my position.* Her worries diverted into a hundred possibilities, none spoken yet all considered. *Hori is fundamental. She will want to rush—*

A breeze swept past her, swirling cold against the bare skin of her arms. It quieted her thoughts as she glanced back, then turned forward again. *Is someone there?* She'd rejected Asier's offer to accompany her only because they'd assumed the Residence was safe. *Foolish, considering Teoda is here.* Yet the zephyr teased her again, its gentle gusts nudging her forward, leftward, forward.

Calya minded her footsteps, aiming for the corridor's end— where the starlight bounced on the marble again. The breeze followed her as she moved, seeping from nowhere yet caressing her naked arms, quiet like a spy and muffled by the rapid heartbeats she refused to heed. She turned left at the corner, proceeding into the silvery dimness—then looked up after a few paces, amused. *What a coincidence.*

Just like decades ago, she was standing before the open double doors of the Library. It wasn't Umbra City's, with its swirling design of onyx and marble, yet it was equally imposing. *It always seems I return here by chance alone.*

She slipped inside, studying the nearest wall for the dark shape of a lantern—then stretched to grip its tiny lever. Two spins and it clicked, the flame bursting within its glazed cage like the echo reverberating across the space. *Another remnant we can't replicate.* There were few of those lanterns, unbreakable— *And the Varre researchers have tried, indeed*—and never needing fuel. Calya narrowed her eyes as she searched for another, finding it atop the tall counter where a librarian would perch soon after dawn. It was deserted, given the time, and so the Lady half-turned to watch the place. *Smaller than Umbra's, yet well-equipped.* She refused the fond smile threatening to curl her lips, and instead observed the black-stained cedar stacks.

History called her, and so she traversed it slowly, stopping near a rugged volume; its leather-wrapped spine was peeling, yet the engraved letters were evident. *A treatise on the Volatile Pact?*

She chuckled at the tome, her gaze lingering on it even as she walked towards the next lantern. It clicked to life all too smoothly, its echo muffled by the stacks that opened from it— shaping sinuous aisles that teased her with respite yet threatened her with reality. *If I'm being followed, I could lose them here.* Entertaining that worry, she glanced around the illuminated stack until her concerns evanesced in the rowdy zephyr.

*Perhaps… I'm tired.* Calya begrudgingly considered the possibility, slipping into another aisle. Her rest had been merely a bath upon returning, a repose feigned to quell Asier's concerns, and an hour of respite during a meal with him. Midnight had found her writing to the Exarch and scheming a guard for Hori. *Because neither could wait, and I should leave this place, to—*

Movement caught behind her back and Calya turned, breath held amidst an impasse of fright—left hand trained to lift her skirt, right one seeking the blade tucked between the folds of her sash.

She blinked when she noticed the silhouette before her, robed in draped black-and-white, silver hair spooled into a knot held with a dark ribbon. A woman, aged elegantly yet looking barely older than what Calya remembered. *It can't be. It's just a trick of my memory.*

Yet the librarian smiled, dipping her head. "It was due we met again, little one."

# Amok

SOUL TRANSMUTER ALCHEMIST. THE UNTAMED ONE

Darkness overpowered the passageways within Ferro Keep's enclosure, the battle between starlight and torchlight reshaping as twisting shadows. It skirmished in the stretches of golden reflections, refracting on the soldier's shields, on their armours, on their mounts, on the hastily assembled tents still cramped with survivors.

Amok recognised what it was. The lumbering of menial, time-framed lives spent in merry ignorance of the truths encompassing the universe that harboured them. A perennial quest for meaning, and the prideful bouts of those who pretended to be powerful but plunged into helpless chaos because peace exceeded them. No matter the world, no matter the order and disorder, humans would never be more than sources of alive elements—easily defiled and distorted unless studied with the care Naturalism ensured.

Thus, on that night—glamoured to invisibility and perched atop a rooftop—Amok clenched their six-fingered fists. The glyphs leaking from their cloak oscillated across thought-lattices like a disharmony trebling from annoyance to anger.

That anger—that perfunctory alive element—originated on the plague the Untamed One had inherited at the mission's outset.

Berserk. The Dragon One, the discoverer of the Meridian of

Existence. The most imprudent, most irrational, most incautious alchemist to be burdened with. The un-Naturalist one who'd eagerly imperil their access to a promised solution by denouncing Naturalism as contradictory.

Sheer folly, to be so opposed to the single approach that would guarantee the Legate's alive elements were not distorted, thus producing that fabled solution. Sheer folly, to be so obtusely prideful as not to admit how they'd endangered the mission.

Disgust darkened the ink swirling within Amok's cloak, sickening the galaxy within it until the glyphs stained with murky hues. They shivered, dense and incongruous yet crushed into nothingness by none other than the Untamed One. Naturalism was not inconsistent but a clear framework for Soul alchemy delimited after millennia of methodical experimentation. It was not haphazard—as Berserk's actions—but deliberate.

Amok understood what the Dragon One was. An arrogant fool renown on The Orders only because they were both Insidious and Futile's most successful mentee. A careless alchemist tolerated only because of their single discovery and bloated into relevance by the humans of Omega—those that called them the Dragon God.

Sheer folly, to be forced to endure—

A blue-bay gelding neighed loudly, interrupting the alchemist. Begrudgingly, they refocused on the humans beneath them, noticing the stubborn figure of Lord Asier Aurri. His right fist held the horse's reins, his intention to mount disfigured by a hundred pressing worries.

"No one, General. Am I understood?" Asier's growl vanished into the night, his scowl etched on the woman before him.

She stiffened to attention. "Yes, my Lord, I'll take care of it. We have secured Lady Varre's location with rotating patrols. I've also assigned a guard to follow her and—"

The Untamed One watched Asier without soul-linking him, instead mulling over the expected normality they'd uncovered after spending the afternoon studying him. He'd even worried about Calya enough to summon the golden threads of memory, allowing Amok to soul-wave him—but his past held no traces of the Meridian of Existence, only memories of conversations where she'd hinted at the concept without mentioning it. He was a clever man, shaped by the matriarch just like her, yet spared the contamination—for The Rector's glamour, that lanky librarian, had never appeared to him.

The Rector. The commander who'd orchestrated a masterful context by tasking Futile with creating the geography that'd indirectly carved a path forward in a perfect, Naturalist manner —just like Amok and the Dragon Plague had done days ago, igniting the quake and the subsequent fog. The leader who should've understood the importance of Naturalism more than anyone else, but had instead irrevocably tainted Amok's target.

Admittedly, Berserk's liberal use of interfering soul-skills— that reckless soul-shaping and amalgamating—was incomparable to The Rector's actions, albeit the latter were regrettable, nonetheless. They had—

"Especially if they do not report to me," Asier gritted down on the road, piercing through the alchemist's thoughts. "Discretion is essential. Am I understood?"

The soldier held his gaze, nodding grimly. "I understand, my Lord, and will apply the same considerations when guarding the aide; Laxalt."

Asier grimaced, hissing, "Admit none that I've not personally vetted, and—"

Those words melted into the dancing shadows, flickering under the hastening midnight breeze—and the alchemist glanced at the star-studded sky, regretting their mission. The Rector's actions—the glamour-librarian and the ensuing conversation—had polluted Calya's alive elements. Her mindset as a politician and strategist was just a consequence of that foundational lesson The Rector had presented as an innocent discussion on the Volatile Pact.

"—about the matriarch's General? Do we restrain him? Or hinder his surveillance?" The soldier, still talking to the Lord.

He grunted with a strain of frustration Amok nearly mistook for their own. "Neither. Just follow him. We can't raise any susp—"

Sheer folly, to be burdened with such non-Naturalist conditions, created by Berserk's arrogance, and—even if logic recoiled —by The Rector themselves. Sheer folly, the truth Amok could not disregard, the conditions they could not correct, the consequences they were forced to work with.

The inky tendrils weaving their cloak lashed in the night, scattering murky glyphs that promptly reassembled. They swirled, dulled in anger and lethargic in incredulity, yet positing a single question: why would The Rector assign Amok? There were, after all, plenty of non-Naturalist Soul Transmuters who'd accept such grievous conditions. The alchemist lingered, clenching a wayward glyph until it shattered in ill-formed stutters.

Perhaps there was a reason meant to be uncovered as part of the mission. One important enough to require that they— Amok, the leader of the Naturalists, the discoverer of two soul-skills and soon a third—worked with such—

Power beyond the universe's edge.

Immeasurable as to dwarf existence and plunging from above to bring the inconceivable into an ill-prepared realm. It twisted reality and leashed the world to its will, capturing the alchemist's attention as they stared at the sky. It flashed when cobalt strands swirled on the clouds, plummeting to weave a passageway no human saw—locking onto this realm to fold the universe, connecting distances, and pouring the power summoning them into the Central Residence.

In a breath of eternity, Amok hurtled across the Keep, hurried by the overpowering need to prevent any further corruption.

Their Integrity Shield rose as a thousand cerulean glyphs scribbled on their cloak, each shimmering with horror and humility, with anger and aggravation. That blend splashed within them as they tore through the wind, climbing through the hillfort, careening past an archway, searing across corridors, lancing into double doors, and—

The librarian.

From Calya's past, from her clear memories. Standing in an aisle between hand-bound volumes and held by the cobalt threads plunging from the sky. It was a glamour, cast by an alchemist vaster than the universe and so unyieldingly powerful they shattered Amok's Integrity Shield with no apparent effort.

For an impasse, the Untamed One did not react, too stunned to understand how the glyphs of their ipseity had evanesced into a cloak of smoke—yet they recoiled when the awareness settled, bound with the dread of knowing themselves utterly defenceless. It was thrilling, the possibility to cease to exist, dreadful like only a human would see death, yet curious because the ease with which the Shield had been destroyed was incomprehensible.

It was a quiet torment, to foresee what would come, and thus be complicit in the unfolding of another non-Naturalist taint. It was a grim burden, to be entangled on—

*'At ease, Amok. There is a purpose for it all,'* a myriad voices mind-whispered. *'Watch. Listen. Discover the secret she holds.'*

The Untamed One quieted, barely reinforcing their invisibility glamour before looking past the librarian's shape—robed in black-and-white, and clasping her hands before her.

Calya stood paces away, dressed in a loose gown of finely draped gossamer, held by a roped blue sash. She toyed with it, seemingly idle yet prodding the hilt of a blade concealed in its folds. It weighed on her thoughts, and Amok dared a soul-link, only to see it bounce before them—controlled not by them, but by the librarian's caster.

*'No alchemy, Untamed One. Until I say so,'* the glamour mind-whispered, dipping her head towards the Lady. *'It was due we meet again, little one.'*

# Calya & Amok

Calya studied the librarian's features. Pale hands common in her trade, slouched shoulders barely holding the robes, an ageless face with no experience of distress. *She can't be the same woman, but her voice?* The intonation was eerily similar to her memory of that encounter, yet the Lady ignored it—departing the library was now paramount. *She could be the spy I heard following me.*

"We haven't met before." Calya's statement tolerated no dismissal. "Where is Master Lucere?"

"In his chambers. His shift begins at noon." The lanky woman tilted her head, her updo's gold decorations reflecting the lanternlight. "Yet we have met before, my Lady, when you were a little one visiting the Exarch's private library in Umbra City."

"Many librarians tend to it." A veiled question, demanding a response.

"But none encumbered you with questions." The librarian smiled apologetically albeit her shoulders straightened. "Instead, I asked: how would you lead Sestel towards the Meridian of Existence?"

*The Meridian of Existence?* Calya blinked, reason lapsing for a heartbeat. Pressing her lips, she reassessed the librarian's peaceful countenance. She must have been old, too old—or perhaps she'd been merely judged so by a toddler with an undeveloped sense of aging. *Too many unknowns. Did someone overhear us, back then?* The Lady didn't reply, instead dipping her gaze in curt acknowledgement to glimpse past the other. *My only exit.*

The library was oppressive, its towering stacks enclosing the trio while the glamour's cobalt threads—stretching into the ceiling—pulled the area into a sphere, edges flickering with the will of whoever held the reins.

Amok surmised who it was. Someone unchallengeable and indomitable. Someone so profound and beyond comprehension they knew—with the certainty only alchemy allowed—that what they witnessed was only the shallowest partiality of that unfathomable presence.

A most humbling experience, to be at the mercy of an alchemist who had shattered their Integrity Shield before the Untamed One could realise what'd happened. A clue, certainly, that it was no other than The Rector, since the other ancients— those old enough to tease mastery—had been unreachable for myriads. A fortunate occurrence, to see The Rector's abilities from such a close perspective in what could, to Amok's apprehension, imply they'd failed their mission... or, worse, that they'd become paradoxically non-Naturalist.

*'Fear. Such a primal alive element, even in alchemists. One that may blind your curiosity.'* The Rector mind-whispered to the Untamed One, the glamour impassive as they observed Calya. *'Smother your fear, Amok, and witness the turn of her alive elements. This is a lesson for you as well.'*

A lesson? What lesson?

The Untamed One rippled with the echoes of the anger they'd endured since speaking to the Dragon Plague. That prosaic alive element now mingled with their curiosity, yet both collided as the alchemist focused on the soul-link The Rector upheld—flooded with Calya's alive elements.

She was scanning the aisle for a pathway to escape, albeit one thought underlined her mind: *Fool of me to fall into this trap.*

She was afraid, but it didn't smother her logic, instead enhancing it—for her reasoning sparkled while gauging the librarian, positing her intentions and failing by only considering human aims. *I must leave. Find Asier.*

What was the lesson? What turn of alive elements was to be witnessed?

The will to escape sparked on her, uninterrupted as the Librarian mind-whispered, *'Did you find another answer to my question?'*

*Clearly my silence didn't deter her.* Lady Seve tucked a strand of caramel hair behind an ear. *No exit but past her.* "I did, but do you remember what I answered as a child?"

"To balance the power of nations with treaties and accords." The lanky woman recited, rolling a hand as if to bring forth the past. "Arguably, you've succeeded in that regard."

*How does she remember so accurately? Could this truly be the same woman?* Calya pressed her lips, gaze trained on the librarian. Her apprehension darkened the more she considered the political implications of the conversation. *What if the Exarch sent this woman? Or worse, my mother?* The lanternlight waved under the misplaced breeze, but Calya didn't move; one wrong step could lead to her demise. *While one wrong word could ruin my political reputation.* The librarian could be someone's envoy, perhaps part of a ploy to craft rumours based on Calya's answers. Rumours whose closeness to the truth could render them fatal. *Which is why I won't answer; my truth... is not for anyone to hear.*

"I strive only to serve Sestel and fulfil my duty." Calya smiled gently, moving towards the narrow space between the woman and the shelves.

"It may be so, but your duty has led you to toe a subtle edge." The librarian unclasped her hands to lift one finger. "One as important as the Meridian itself."

"What edge could be as fundamental as the Meridian?" Calya

refrained from stepping again not to announce her intention so clearly. *Who does she serve?*

Amok towered behind the glamour-librarian, their alchemical-form twice as large. The glyphs leaking from their cloak dimmed, smothered by the alchemy tensing those cobalt threads—folding the universe, forging an impasse where none ought to exist—yet rattled enough to shape the questions that so perturbed them.

Why was The Rector interfering again? What was the lesson?

"Excellent question. The Meridian is indeed fundamental because outside of it there is only a slow descent into nothingness—yet this is an edge society walks." The librarian clasped her hands, lingering just enough. "You walk an individual edge, one of power granted by humans. Keen, if properly wielded, but limited."

Calya blinked—just once, but enough to restrain the fear threatening to embrace her. *If she's a spy...* Anger cavorted through her, yet she forced her jaw to relax, aware of one truth. *I misjudged her. Deeply so.*

"Every ruler walks that edge, librarian," Calya replied, her right fingers pressing into the roped, velvety sash decorating her gown. "Political power results from what a society can legitimise through accords and laws, nothing more nor less."

"Yet beyond those, society imposes other limits, most unknowingly," the librarian posited, lifting a finger. "As a ruler's power grows, their subjects' tolerance for it shrinks, eventually leading to rebellion... one driven by fear of what may happen, even without apparent cause."

*What is she implying?* The Lady's hand stilled over her sash, second-guessing herself. *Is the Exarch... threatening me through this woman?*

The Untamed One hovered still, their glyphs refusing to reassemble their Integrity Shield—no alchemy was allowed, for the power bending the universe pressed upon them, and The Rector had rendered them utterly defenceless.

The Rector. The leader who was not impetuous nor reckless, instead acting with such premeditated care that the consequences of their actions fitted like the pieces of a puzzle assembled throughout myriads of ages and dozens of worlds... yet why engage in such conversation?

'*Because it is the only way, Untamed One,*' The Rector mind-whispered, those hundreds of thousands of voices blending into one coherent line. '*You wouldn't have dared, and the turn you must witness lies beyond.*'

Amok lingered, their fraying hood leaking the smoke of confusion and doubt.

'*What turn?*' They asked, the galaxy within them spooling the threads of reason to weave theories that could not be tested. '*Beyond what?*'

'*Beyond reason, at the edge of boundless terror,*' The Rector answered, still pulling the threads, still folding the universe. '*Yet what you'll witness will be Natural nonetheless.*' At the same time, the librarian lifted a finger, engaged in a seemingly pointless conversation. '*—one driven by fear of what may happen, even without apparent cause.*'

At the enclosure—moments ago, yet endlessly far—the Untamed One had deemed this a transgression: polluting, non-Naturalist. Now, they could no longer argue it defied such framework. Instead they watched, uncertain, wondering whether the fault lay in the act... or in their measure of it.

Calya hardened her features, smothering her fear, taming her annoyance. *I've been thinking about this on my way here.* She keened her hearing, but the quietude surrounding the stacks was deafening. *That's the illusion. That we are alone.* She swallowed, minding her words while her fingers searched for the concealed blade. *It's dangerous, and not precisely manageable.*

"No more games, Librarian." Calya demanded, her tone having silenced battlefields before. "Who sent you here, and what do you seek?"

As those words resonated within that folded universe, three ill-shaped, shadowy mounds emerged through the soul-link—the one The Rector sustained. Amok recognised what they were: versions of Calya formed in the past yet reaching for the present.

Fear. Anger. Detachment.

They twisted and entwined, soaking the aisle and staining the soul-link, only to be smothered by her self-control. A courageous reaction, even when courage was just the fear of fools, for bravery came not from strength but ignorance.

Of concepts that could not be fathomed within the time-framed limits of a lifetime. Of a history sanitised to fit within human minds. Of the laws and systems that rendered humans not the masters they so craved to be, but the source-beings from which greater entities originated.

'*You are mistaken, Untamed One. Her courage is the boldness that drew me here. The one that can only be unlocked at the edge of absolute terror.*' The Rector mind-whispered to Amok as the threads linking to the glamour-librarian pulled again, bringing that power closer to this world. '*And that boldness will enable the pursuit of knowledge to forge evolution—hers, yours, and mine.*'

"What I seek is simple, Lady Calya. Your new answer; the one you developed through the years." The librarian insisted again, dipping her head in mockery of respect. "How can you lead Sestel towards the Meridian of Existence?"

*Leave. Now. Find Asier.* "I'm not obligated to reply." Calya dared another step, her fingers already slipping between the folds of her sash. "I will take my leave."

The glamour-librarian shook the head—and the alchemist controlling it pulled the cobalt threads until the universe growled in pain.

'*You have no real power to so decide,*' The Rector mind-whispered at last, their many voices leaking to the human—but their following statement, brimming with the excitement of discovery, was for the Untamed One. '*Watch, Amok. The turn, the inflection. The boldness that surges, Naturally, at the edge of boundless terror.*'

Amok half-turned, their cloak of midnight flaring in reverent awe, its edges fraying into perplexity and confusion, into Naturalist theories and the deference for what existed outside, seemingly immune to interpretation.

Power.

Of the most immeasurable magnitude, of the most advanced state any alchemist could imagine. It pulled the threads, each strand shimmering until a semblance of the caster's silhouette emerged from behind the glamour-librarian. Hooded with a sheer mantle, starlight-ridden and crowned by six world-piercing blades rotating in a ring. Reality weighed upon those shoulders, crushing Amok into awed immobility. Their glyphs melted until their own inky tendrils leashed them to the ground, yet their mind remained etched in Calya's soul-link.

Her eyes had widened, her lips parted albeit no sound emerged from them, features slacking as she took one step back, then another and another—and from them, the shadows returned.

Three spires. Fear, anger, detachment.

They stretched into humanoid silhouettes, each cloaked in smoke and demanding attention with arms stretched. They clung to Calya as she stiffened, the soul-link as devoid of reason as full of terror she was—too terrified to fight, too frightened to flee. The shadows howled, churning and embodying emotions, suffocating reason, depriving her of movement and vanishing her logic as she stared, unblinking, at the translucent, towering figure.

So looming it was. So incognisable.

One thought slashed that inner chaos, reaching Amok. *Fear is a choice. Fear itself is the only thing I shall fear.* It was a blade of light in the darkness, each word a mirror sown—with golden threads —into a thousand experiences.

*Fear is a choice. Fear itself is the only thing I shall fear.* Calya's mind chanted again—and the words linked into a whip that lashed around the shadows, containing their spread. That whip, those chains of words, seared with the light of another thought. *To fear is to surrender. To fear is a judgement.* It flayed the shadows, scything their importance, inky shears scattering away from the gleaming thoughts. *I will not succumb to it. I will shed those judgements.* The littlest shadow extended a mutilated arm, the young-one pointing at The Rector's silhouette—but Calya's thoughts were unstoppable, blistering her reality with an awareness misplaced amidst that lingering terror. *I will embrace the fear then let it pass through me.* Those gleaming words were anchors, muffling the shadows' howls as a crystal wall rose between Calya and half-her-mind, trapping the embodiment of her emotions where they couldn't reach her. *I choose to stand, to control myself, to feel only what I choose to feel. Nothing.*

When only the echoes of that chant reverberated in her mind, she looked up to The Rector's contour like no alchemist would dare. With challenge, with control. With the courage to face the unknown and survive it.

Amok understood then, the turn of her alive elements. That incarceration, that purposeful detachment, that crystal barrier that now rippled with the muffled soundwaves of the fearful howls contained behind it. It was a strategy—Naturally developed and instinctively used. A constructed calm that dampened all reflexes, a manufactured numbness that prevented her collapse and refused to submit. It was not mastery of alive elements but extreme indifference; just a strategy to survive masquerading as a trait. Not a choice, but a last resort when everything else had failed.

An unthinkable epiphany, to watch the most absolute fear—to the unknown, to the evidence of insignificance—to be squandered and leashed because the only worthy fear was fear itself.

A consolidation of prior understanding: that The Rector's actions had always been Naturalist, for the glamour-librarian had only fostered what already occurred within the human. A rational conclusion, given the leader of The Orders was neither arbitrary nor imprudent, but designing existence beyond what alchemists like Amok could fathom.

In the prolonged silence, Calya smirked—her shoulders squaring, her chin lifting with the regal control she so wielded in the battlefield. When she stepped forward, the jailed shadows screamed, albeit the crystal wall remained impervious.

∽❧∾

"What are you?" Calya studied the librarian—*Or whatever she is*—then the silhouette above her.

Its chuckle rippled on the blades like a pebble on water. "The answer to that question exceeds you." The librarian lingered, pressing two fingers into the spine of an old volume. "Who do you think I am?"

The Lady glanced at the volume—so old its spine had flaked, leaving only the contour of a few engraved words. *Myths of The Reclamation?* She frowned, discarding the legends she'd read, the poems, the stories told to the children just to frighten them into behaving. *An alchemist? It can't be.*

"It matters not, but the edge you walk does—so allow me one truth. You are teetering on the verge of collapse for your power is an illusion." That being—that alchemist—spoke again, but their voice was deeper, darker. Pressing down from above, from all around. "It's fleeting like the tides of public opinion, and ephemeral like the span of your life. It is meaningless."

*No. No, no, no.* She blinked, lethargic compared to the galloping of her pounding heart—it hammered on her forehead, and she clenched her dress just to refocus. *To fear is a judgement, and I will not succumb to it.* She breathed, scattering the shivering of her jaw. *I will shed those judgements. I will embrace the fear and let it pass through me.*

"Make your case, alchemist," she stated at last, hammering every word. "I will not be a pawn in your schemes."

"How bold!" The librarian tilted her head, and the swords twisted. "I want your answer. What is your pathway to the Meridian of Existence?"

Calya chuckled—baffled by that obsession, by that concept that was nothing more than abstract philosophy. *Why ask me? Why does it matter?* She wondered, tucking a strand of caramel hair behind an ear. *Yet those answers will unfold only after I answer.*

"The path is tripartite." She raised three fingers, observing the hooded silhouette. "First, what I said before: balancing war and peace only to exploit the moment. But also, by controlling public perception to manipulate fear and honour, and leveraging morality because it is a tool, not a rule." Her steps punctuated each sentence. "It can only be done by hoarding political power, as you said... because power is the only means."

Intrigue permeated Amok, half their mind following the conversation, another half intent on the soul-link. Calya's shadows fisted the crystal wall, screams of abject terror lashing from them—but that barrier endured, as impervious as taxing it was to sustain.

Only one thing held it in place: the most absolute need to survive.

'But power inherently produces struggle; they are bound together as two sides of the same.' The glamour-librarian paused, unclasping their hands—and pulling the threads loose with that gesture. *'The power you hoard is limited, Calya. Meaningless beyond humanity.'*

"I am human," she countered, holding her ground.

*'A workable hurdle, but only if you answer another question.'* As the glamour-librarian spoke, the cobalt threads unfolded back into reality. *'What is power?'* The alchemist distanced themselves while the strands folding the universe tightened—and other snapped, whipping about, slashing reality. The remnants of the glamour-librarian mind-whispered one last time. *'Find that answer, Calya, and share it… with* him.*'*

A loose cobalt thread pierced Amok, unmooring the alchemist from reality.

*'Guide her to the answer, Amok.'* A hundred whispers, a hundred commands. Only for the Untamed One, and always undeniable. *'You will learn from her more than just how to perform an incarnate.'*

They saw it, then, with a figment of rationality, the moment the glamour-librarian dissolved like pulverised glass. The Rector's hooded outline faded, but that piercing cobalt thread twisted within Amok, anchoring into a recurrent, known shape to pull it forth as another glamour.

Calya had no questions, no thoughts, no feelings. Just the emptiness of logic in the wake of the absurd, just the remnants of reason on the aftermath of unreality.

The lanky librarian was no more, having shattered like a glass figure and scattered into dust that left no marks. The towering, translucent alchemist above her was nothing but a fading ray of cobalt light, the hallway occupied by someone else.

A slender man, his rich walnut skin bright above the black-and-white robes. His broad nose scrunched with a shock not reflected on his eyes—cerulean, and clearer than the noon sky. *He looks human. He cannot be.* Calya exhaled with excessive control, her right hand holding the blade within her sash.

"Who are you?" She demanded, breathing harsher than desired.

"Quintus." He bowed with a hand across his chest. "Also an alchemist."

The Lady clicked her tongue, daring another step closer. "What do you want? Be plain."

"I look forward to continuing the discussion." He was gentle, stepping back towards the leftmost stack while indicating the exit path she'd craved. "Once ready, find me here. Between the stacks."

He vanished as his words died in a whisper, his tunic dissolving into splotches of abyssal ink. There were no traces afterward—none that Calya could find as she moved through the aisle; no cobalt threads, no translucent mirrors, no marks or voices or sounds. Just her heart, hammering, reckless.

*Leave. Now.* She walked. Past the aisles, out of the library, through the corridors and hallways. Minding her pacing, steeling her countenance, ignoring the looming danger. *Hurry.* Her hands were trembling, her legs threatening to falter, her vision eaten away. *Walk, Calya. Walk.* The danger chased her, yet it vanished when the door to her office closed behind her.

It crumbled, then. The invisible barrier that upheld her composure.

# Asier



LORD. SEVE HOUSE, SESTEL

"To Lady Calya Seve, from Exarch Elor Luxa." The clockjay slurped when its beak clicked closed. It opened again. "For the Lady's eyes only."

Asier grunted, merely glancing at the contraption perched on his shoulder. Its left eye stared back, reflecting the starlight seeping from the glazed casements. *It returned quickly, even at night.* The dawn was hours away, yet it seemed the Exarch had been awaiting Calya's report after the Truce. *The craven one; he was probably cowering on Umbra City.*

As Asier marched, the soldiers guarding the next archway squared at attention, the clicking of their boots echoing in the empty hallway. He dipped his eyes at the quartet, his left hand reaching for the hilt of his sword—a reflex, but a grounding one. *Once morning comes, Calya will need to appease Lady Varre. The detail I organised should be enough.* His jaw tensed alongside that thought, his pace quickening again while he turned into another corner. *Teoda's arrival disrupted everything.*

His boots shirred over the polished floor, halting before the closed doors of Calya's private office. *We will need to—*

A whisper, muted and half-strangled.

The Lord's cheek twitched, then he backtracked until his shoulders pressed against the opposite wall. Silence reigned in the hallway, the clockjay blessedly motionless. *Spies?* He scowled

249

leftwards, hearing the faint movement of the guards he'd passed before glimpsing right. Nothing lurked there; just a breeze, cool even on the eve of summer. *At ease; there is nothing but my shadow.* Mincing like a thief on his own Residence, Asier approached the door again. *It's just my many worries.*

He reached beneath his shirt, drew out a chain, and palmed the key hanging from it. He pressed it into the lock, turning it slowly while pushing gently with his free hand. It clicked open, mercifully quiet. Glancing back—*Left, nothing. Right, nothing*—he slipped inside and locked before replacing the chain within his tunic.

A gasp. Too broken to be speech. Too ragged and soaked in terror.

*No!* Asier knew that pain all too well—from years and years of misery, from nights spent in terror. It shattered him, hearing her like this again. It tickled cold on his back, tightening his throat with the powerlessness he'd swore not to feel again.

*No, no, no.* He pressed both palms to his forehead, collecting himself before ushering the clockjay away. It flew to the nearest lectus, head clicking to watch him askance. *What happened? Why wasn't I there for her?* He strode into the darkness, fumbling to loosen his sword belt; it plunged into the thick rug, its fall muffled by another gasp.

Wounded. Like the fear that wouldn't accept it was gone.

*Why? What did Teoda do?* He rounded the marble desk, minding each step like he'd learnt to do not to scare her further. *Please, it can't be her.* His pleas would be futile, he knew—yet he lowered to a crouch, aware the woman crying could be only one person. *Please, not her.*

When Asier saw her, he dropped to both knees, dread weighing on his shoulders.

Calya, tucked small in the enclosed opening between the desk's ample legs, her gossamer gown spilling all around. Calya, bracing her knees, chin tucked above them, lips quivering in silence. Calya, startling at him before scrambling out of her cover and into his chest—like so many years ago, when they were both full of fearful anger and powerless like all children are.

He fell to a sit when she pressed tighter against him, yet Asier still enclosed her in his arms, fingers threading through her hair. *I should've set a better guard around Teoda.* His breathing ragged as Calya's eased minimally. *I should've expected this!*

After all, their bond was forged in the bitter consequences of the matriarch's ploys—from the ashes of their shared wrath and grief. *For her father, for my mother. For what Teoda did to them, and us.* Asier's mouth curled in a restrained snarl. *She could've at least spared her sister or use a faster poison. She could've spared her daughter from—* His teeth chafed in relentless anger, but it vanished when Calya's hands clenched at his tunic.

"You're safe now," Asier whispered, like so many times before. When she came to him bruised or bleeding, when he found her hiding from the matriarch.

He wouldn't ask what had happened. *Not now, at least.* There would be a time for that—after she'd slept, and he'd quelled the fury boiling within him.

Calmly, Asier pulled Calya closer, holding her with one arm while pushing with the other until his back rested against the desk's thick leg. They had time; the dawn was still a few hours away.

# Egon Hold

## Zaro 14ᵗ, 17002 RE

# Dante

LEGATE OF EGON HOLD, EASTERN LEGIONS OF FIRARD

*The Marshals' secrecy speaks of ambition. Nothing unusual.* Legate Dante Praeto strode through the polished corridors of the Citadel, his footfalls resonating on the decorated marble walls. A cool breeze welcomed him as he crossed through a balcony. *Except for the two cohorts they brought, delaying their arrival.* Squaring his shoulders, he nodded at the legionnaires guarding the doors, and marched into another corridor—with a sweeping view of the burgeoning twin dawn. Dante ignored the landscape. *But what are they guarding against? Do they know something I ignore?* Each footfall remarked a possibility: internal politics, the earthquake, the fog, the Retreat, Sittia's misplacement.

His cheeks twitched when recalling the Centurion upon their return—the cold fury in her dark eyes, the defiance in her stance as the legionnaires led her into a private chamber. *She can't be the cause; they departed towards here a day before her insubordination.* That thought wrung a frown, weighted by the echoes of another time. *She demanded honour all my life then… this? A fraud.* His jaw tensed, but when his teeth grated, Dante eased his features before progressing into an empty corridor. *This is not the time to feel slighted.* Yet those thoughts looped in his mind like crows circling above a dying man—waiting for his resentment to strangle him to death. *No. Just duty—and that's managing what comes now,* he reminded himself, turning into the final hallway.

As he crossed the ample archway into the Central Chambers, the Legate glanced at the opposite wall. The echoes of dawn poured through its majestic glazed casements, silvery rays reflecting atop the polished cedar table at the centre, to shimmer over the plated pauldrons of Centurion Juçe.

He stood at parade rest in one corner, untouched by past events and uncaring of the consequences. When his steel gaze found Dante's, it lit with hatred. *Of course he blames me; to him, the fault is always mine.* Standing at the entrance's rim, the Legate met that gaze with an arched brow, then rolled two fingers to dismiss the Centurion. *My fault is having expected differently*, he chided himself—yet the frustration persisted, heavy like Juçe's gaze. It etched on him for too long, then slipped towards the double doors.

Footfalls reached them, distant and looming, constant and ever-approaching. They rumbled through the Citadel's marble hallways, too loud to be anything but moments away. The Strategos' steps first; old and measured, sparse and long-limbed. The Magister's after, shushing as her caligae dragged, the rhythmic tap of her cane a steady mark. There were no sounds but the echoes of their presence when two of the five Marshals of Firard's Emerald Council stood beneath the archway, their presence underscoring the stakes.

Marshal-Strategos Gora Rachen was the embodiment of power, a man impossible to ignore. Dressed in the finest toga, its white draped silk a stark contrast to his walnut skin. His iron hair was braided tightly across his scalp, each tip decorated with a gold bead. *He's always been an example of discipline.* Beside him, Marshal-Magister Nagore Loera was a slight figure in a silk gown, an emerald trabea wrapped around her shoulders. Her silver hair shone like starlight under the dawn's light, a lifetime of seafaring mapped on her sun-kissed countenance. *And her favour or disfavour remains the most threatening peril to encounter.*

"Do not sit. Our conversation shall not extend." Marshal-Strategos Gora Rachen waved a hand as if dismissing the sunlight ricocheting from his rings. "The earthquake and its fog were unfortunate events," he lingered, lowering his rich voice until the echoes didn't betray him. "Because of them, we missed the opportunity to witness our Legions' might, and lost valuable lives in what ought to be a War Game." He paused, dipping his pale emerald gaze as if to mourn those lost—but the gesture was empty.

*Sensible not to reject the Legions' distress.* Dante glanced at Nagore—awaiting regally, both hands pressed into the crown of her cane. Her eyes, azure like the Abyss she'd sailed for decades, narrowed albeit etched on the casements. *Defiance, disagreement, or dislike of rhetoric?*

"Yet even under adverse conditions..." Gora resumed, turning to Dante while a hint of warmth softened the corners of his eyes. "—you understood what was needed, Legate. Knowing when to disengage takes a keen intellect. The Veiled Retreat saved our Legions, and the ensuing Truce recovered us from impending war, preserving Firard's reputation and securing an outcome—a joint investigation—beneficial to us. Well done."

Dante blinked, his shock lasting a heartbeat. *Support? If Gora approves...* In the next one, he dipped his head in acknowledgement—grateful but also suspicious. *It's appreciated, but he's also framing this conversation.* That silence was measured, a fragment of a moment. As the Legate straightened, his gaze followed the Strategos'—drifting, impassive, to land on Centurion Juçe. *Of course.*

Wrath clenched between his gritted teeth. "With due respect, Marshals, that shameful Retreat caused us—"

"The Veiled Retreat was the safest choice. For Firard, for our allies, and for our lifestyle as we know it." Gora scowled at the Centurion. Minimally, just another crease between his populated white brows, yet immeasurably overbearing. "Without it, the... madness that assailed the Gorge could've scarred us even more deeply."

Dante breathed, forcing his gaze away from his father's silhouette to etch on the Strategos—*Reason, not grudges*—then on the Marshal-Magister.

The Centurion dared a step. "The cowardice of that Retreat has—"

"We are not here to discuss the Retreat, Centurion. The Emerald Council's stance is not to be challenged." A warning vibrated in Nagore's strained tone—and she dallied, drumming her fingers atop the cane. "Your presence here, as a listener, is a courtesy extended because of your record and likely not to repeat."

A low creak; leather under pressure, metal chafing with restraint. The Legate forced his countenance to remain neutral —but caught the flick of movement as Juçe's fists tightened, vambraces groaning under the strain. The Centurion's gaze etched beyond the Marshals and into the nothingness of the open hallway behind them. *His pride won't let him forget. This will have consequences.* Nagore observed him, her calm an unspoken threat. It lasted a heartbeat, ending when the Centurion dipped his head in a martial nod.

Gora sighed, two fingers toying with the embroidered rim of his toga. "The events leading us here are, indeed, most unfortunate..." His features hardened as he paused, his broad nose scrunching. "Yet we cannot disregard that Centurion Sittia disobeyed orders, dispatching her cavalry as decoys, and threatening Firard's peace with Sestel." As he spoke, his gaze drifted from the table to the central chair, lingering on its golden trim. When he glanced up, his pale green eyes tolerated no rebuke. "Marshal-Magister Nagore Loera and myself will conduct a consilium over the following days, assessing Sittia's actions. A tribunal will be scheduled in a week."

Dante blinked, posture slackening for a few rugged heartbeats; it stuttered at a twisted rhythm: bitterness, duty, aggravation, calm. *Reason, not grudges,* he repeated, closing his eyes and minding his breathing because Sittia's actions were a consequence of her own stubbornness, and not a flaw of his. *This has to be done. Her disobedience... cannot be allowed.* He squared his shoulders, smoothing his sleeves and feeling the texture until logic returned. *A week's time. The Legions that came for the War Games will have departed by then.*

Yet silence lumbered around him, oppressive like an unquenched thirst for vengeance. Juçe exhaled—harsh, restrained, and just once—yet it tore that taut impasse with a hundred hushed complaints.

"It is decided, Centurion." Nagore dared Juçe with a silent

gaze, then tapped the cane's crown as if sealing a verdict. "Legate, you are to begin compiling the reports for Sestel's healers, as well as selecting a group to travel. Considering recent events, the joint investigation must be prioritised." She paused, precise, then half-turned. "Dismissed."

# Berserk

Berserk's wings pulsed once before riding the currents through the Citadel's hallways. It was a fine zephyr; dry, cold, and whirling enough that the dragonlet sped, glamoured to invisibility, into a corridor with a sweeping view of the plains beyond—the twin-suns' were dawning slowly, blotting the sky with a moon-lavender hue. Berserk ignored the view, swerving through the pointless legionnaires stationed in that tranche.

So impotent. So unnecessary.

So oblivious of the forces that'd crafted that world.

A blend of annoyance and curiosity curled on the molten metal of the alchemist's wings, incensed by the discoveries of the day before. Of Futile's intervention, of The Rector's manipulations, of that book transcribing Berserk's own words, of a memory that did not hold the solution but a clue as ludicrous as what it implied: a human-led pathway towards the Meridian of Existence.

The Dragon One snarled as that blend of annoyance and curiosity pushed them upwards, coiling airborne to turn into a broader corridor—of walls decorated with blind arches, and floors polished to mirrors.

Insanity, to consider humans could achieve such a precarious balance on their own.

Not insanity, however, to assume The Rector's mission was

twofold: for to destroy the precarious equilibrium between Firard and Sestel would unleash a war that'd prevent stagnation—and in that aftermath, create the conditions for Dante to test a new pathway towards the Meridian of Existence.

The dragonlet grinned, pleased with their conclusion, and liquid copper poured from their maws. It swirled behind as they spun into another corner, where the tall, portly figure of Marshal-Strategos Gora Rachen absorbed the space like a statue of timeless authority. He wore his toga like a mantle of power, and the calmness of his posture augured a storm his aide—awaiting four paces behind—seemed oblivious to.

Berserk's wings pulsed again, and they heeled over, circling the Strategos while they soul-linked him. One spin unravelled ploys for power, schemes of long-term politics and paths of succession. The next spin unspooled golden threads the alchemist did not pursue; the echoes were enough—promising young Dante, bright and innovative older Dante, and tested Dante: scarred but just what Gora needed. The last spin bled, burning because of decisions few would consider, and the Strategos deemed the only path possible. The alchemist ended the soul-link, alighting on the nearest windowsill.

A ruthless man, wearing a façade of discipline, and having held power long enough to put the needs of a faceless nation above the suffering of the individuals that composed it. A common occurrence plaguing every society to ever exist.

Yet the alchemist waited, watching as Marshal-Strategos Gora Rachen sighed—a long, dragging exhalation. Mournful yet resigned to that sole path he saw.

He lifted a hand, waited for the aide to approach, then hand-signalled, *"Request Centurion Juçe to meet me in an hour. Two rooms from here."*

A powerful leader, and one that—on his own—would do exactly what Berserk had required, and with no coercion at all.

Pleased, the alchemist unfurled their wings, vaulting from the windowsill to search for the next target. Their heat-haze cut through the cool air, dross shattering as they caught another current and sped past the nearest corner. They turned—left, right, right again, down a staircase, left again—then spread the wings, curbing their flight to match Centurion Juçe's pace.

He was marching towards a Decanus with measured steps. She awaited with his emerald cloak folded over a forearm, her sombreness a stark contrast to Juçe's gaze: bloody steel under the shadow of a scowl. He stopped close, allowing her to lock the fabric into the pauldron—and Berserk clung to the walls' high-reliefs, soul-linking the Centurion.

Juçe's fury exploded with quiet restraint, woven into a twisted path through golden threads barbed with resentment, with judgement, with violent intent. His was a cruel concoction that festered like sworn vengeance and aimed for a kill—not of one but many, to bring forth an ideal he believed now disgraced.

Berserk severed the soul-link, pleased with the man's schemes—then sprang from their perch, hurtling through the hallway to slip past the archway and onto the staircase leading out of the Citadel.

Insanity, to have temporarily forgotten humanity's need for conflict, to have even deemed soul-shaping necessary to further steer them into mayhem.

There was nothing unique about Gora's and Juçe's ploys. No novel theories to be tested, no foresight beyond their own cravings, no nuances that would lead their actions into an outcome unseen before. Each believed themselves the ones capable of restoring a nation that now teetered towards destruction when, in actuality, it'd be their own actions that led to Firard's demise. There was nothing new to them, just one fundamental alive element.

Fear; irrational fear.

It never existed within one mind, always expanding like a disease because it craved recognition and validation, because it dreamed of a past long gone and now idealised. Fear was foolish; derived from ignorance and easily leveraged if presented with the right clues. Fear was a useful tool; it united a crowd against another, and it poured bloodshed between them. Across ages, across worlds, across societies.

The Dragon One grinned, savage. Gora's actions would have consequences—and in the impasse before Juçe set forth his plans, Berserk had to only focus on Dante to complete the first incision. The method was simple: to arouse the flames of remorse and refusal that so assailed him to bring forth the past, and prime him for the pyre he'll soon need to set ablaze. The one that would melt down his armour, and enable the second incision.

Before that, only one action was needed: to lore-weave Petra's memories yet again.

# Juçe

The door locked, and the Strategos' footsteps muffled when he stepped over the rug. Juçe stood on its edge, boots planted firmly on bare marble, gaze scanning the limited surroundings. A private office with clean walls, two statues guarding the westernmost wall and framing a narrow window; the suns were higher, their soft silver sheen washing out the deep emerald of the lectii's cushions—the only furniture except for that rug.

Timing his breathing, Juçe etched his gaze on the other man. Standing near one lectus, fingers pressed into its curled armrest. *Useless, like all Strategists.*

"You summoned me, Marshal-Strategos," Juçe stated, clean.

Gora nodded, and the gold beads rimming his braids gleamed more than his deeds. He half-turned, dragging the motion. "What happened to Sittia… is a most unfortunate situation. Such a pristine record marred by an accident."

*Not an accident.* Juçe corrected, pressing his jaw—enough that his teeth ground again, a vein pulsing on his neck. *Dishonour, caused and enhanced by Dante's cowardice.* He kept his hands clasped behind, fingers twitching and begging for a blade. *Fool of a son. Born of my blood, but none of my strength.*

Yet the Strategos waited, studying the Centurion with that unnerving, flat stare all Strategists were fond of. *Ashamed even of themselves.* He seemed to expect a response or reaction, but Juçe offered none. After a while Gora hummed, fully turning as he searched between the drapes of his toga. When he stepped forward, a small vial shimmered between his fingers—glass-made, and harbouring a clear liquid with a gold reflection.

Juçe barely glimpsed at it, gaze locked in the Strategos.

"Sittia would not be trialled." Gora held that gaze, twirling the vial between his thick, walnut fingers. "She would not be celebrated either." He paused, looking down at the vial and up again. "You could give her the choice, Centurion. To keep the shame private."

Juçe unclasped his hands, lips pressed into a line. The Strategos was offering dignity; the last thing a legionnaire could wish for when their name couldn't be cleared. *All because of Dante.* When the Centurion picked the proffered vial, his fist closed over it with the discipline he'd been bred for. The glass clinked against the leather straps crossing through his palm. *But this won't end here.*

"When?" He dared the other man.

Gora sighed, rolling two fingers as he turned towards the window. "My mercy lasts for two days. No more."

# Dante



LEGATE OF EGON HOLD, EASTERN LEGIONS OF FIRARD

The stone-built office was suffocating; low-ceilinged, with iron-hewn walls, and two meagre wooden doors that—although they remained open—failed to air the stench clogged inside. *Ink, blood, sweat; ignore it. Read.* Legate Dante Praeto tightened his scowl not to grimace, assessing the paperwork laid before him atop a rugged table.

*The content of these reports... is unseen.* Mass hallucinations, soldiers terrified of shadows, attacking each other, mauling their own fingers in sheer despair. Dying of starvation, unable to eat or drink even days after the fog. The Legate exhaled, pocketing a hand to feel the texture of his trousers while observing those working in that room. It was easy to separate the medici from the scribes; the former were unfazed when passing blood-stained, scribbled notes, while the latter's disgust was barely contained behind grimaces. It didn't fade while collating and transcribing the reports. *I can't blame them, given what I've read.*

Rounding the table, he moved to the closest door. A Prefect awaited beyond its threshold, grim-faced yet determined.

"Ensure the collated accounts are sent to me before dusk." He gestured discreetly, half-turning to hand-signal, *"I did not see the external inspections reports."*

"Not yet here." The Prefect's shoulders stiffened minutely,

her left eye twitching before she controlled it. Discreetly, she hand-signalled, *"What I know: mostly self-inflicted wounds. Or..."* Her fingers hesitated, dallying before adding, *"Or blunt weapons. Blade injuries only on Centurion Sittia's rearguard."*

*Not unexpected.* Dante nodded, releasing the tension accumulated in his pocketed hand. *It aligns with Decanus Ler's report. Dangerous.* "Understood. Additionally, prepare a list of possible candidates—" He halted when a dispute about a stained sketch rose in volume. He waited until it subsided to add, "Candidates to stay and to visit Sestel. Have it delivered with the reports."

Legate Dante Praeto scowled under the unforgiving noon suns— slanting the ramparts in swathes of shimmering brightness and sharp shadows. To his right, Imperial Elixane stood precisely within one strip of darkness, features relaxed into her usual impassivity.

"I set two Prefects to escort Sittia's cavalry to... the scribes on the Citadel," she offered, her gaze etched somewhere away. "Besides that, two more are helping me coordinate the Legions' departure in three days."

*Before Sittia's tribunal, then.* Dante nodded, clenching his jaw as he recalled the Strategos' announcement that morning, and Juçe's subsequent disrespect. *Always praising the chain of command while breaching it at the same time.* Yet beyond that resentment existed a risk that couldn't be left unbridled—one they'd considered since Lady Seve's clockjay had arrived at the Hold. After all, her move had aimed to sow unrest, and the Strategos' decision —even if logical—may exacerbate it. *My father could do anything after the tribunal's decision. As the Legate of Egon, I must be prepared.*

As he thought, he toyed with the crisp cuffs of his camisia, pausing to glance at the Imperial before gesturing, *"And the spies I requested? Are they in place?"*

Elixane stepped back, angling her body as if to indicate something in the plains—then hand-signalled, *"Six, from different Support streams. All in place."*

He dipped his chin once, the brief tightening of his jaw response enough. *Calm. Assess. Contain. This is just another challenge.* He rolled his wrist once, conclusive, then marched through the ramparts—yet every step, every steady hit of his boots on the flagstone floor, seemed to echo Juçe's disapproval.

# Dante & Berserk

The reports stacked on the desk's far rim were arranged in chronological order, with the leftmost pair—their fronts washed by the afternoon light—detailing the symptoms immediately after the fog. *It aligns with Ler's accounts.* Dante shut his eyes, pinching the bridge of his nose. *Lady Varre should be able to work with this.*

When he opened them, his gaze settled on the regional map hanging on the left wall of his office—a detailed view of Firard's inner territories and Sestel's key cities. *Assembling the delegations is problematic…* Lady Varre's arrival demanded a clever welcome, yet sending only mediocrities across the border would weaken the Truce itself; in that case, Lady Seve's argument—of Firard benefiting the most—would be evident. The expertise had to be balanced across both groups. *Though balance seldom satisfies everyone.* Likewise, arranging the groups' escorts wouldn't be a small matter. *I must select them precisely—*

The thought hung unfinished as a new realisation settled like the clatter of discarded armour: Strategos Gora had scheduled Sittia's tribunal in a week's time, likely colliding with the delegation's arrival or departure. *The date is too precise.* His fingers drummed on the table, marching steadily alongside his thoughts. *Could there be something else there?* He recalled when he'd met her on the tent, the medicus' comments, and Lady

Seve's arguments. *Could Gora be waiting... for her symptoms to worsen?* His fingers clenched at the table's edge, an itch creeping through his wrist; he rolled it away, pressing both fists into the marble to lean forth. *No; it's just a precaution, nothing—*

Two knocks on the door. The rustling of metal armour.

The Legate pressed his lips to suppress a groan, then steadied himself. *Focus, the Hold needs me.*

"Come in," he called.

As glamour-Petra opened the door, Berserk glided past her, wings beating to alight, invisible, onto the paper-riddled marble desk. Mere inches away from the unlit lantern, and on a clear spot that only allowed them to sit with their paws pressed together. Beyond that clutter, the room was the same the Dragon One had visited before, and so they coerced the glamour to stand at parade rest between the door and the desk.

The Legate watched her, arching a demanding brow—but instead of replying to his expectant gaze, Berserk sunk into the active soul-link.

Dante's hollow of stability was a taut impasse amidst the sleepless abyss—still pierced by that blade, still hovering over a silenced past, still surrounded by that windstorm of shadowy gusts. They spun, vicious, capricious, each swirl rushing, remote, but ravenous like inky brush-strokes smothering the deadened beyond. Between those gusts, in the span between one denial and another, the alchemist found the embers of fire haunting the Legate.

Lurking, latent, crackling alive, eager to lurch, to devour and bring forth a past that could never be allowed to just *be* past— for alive elements were, always, atemporal.

Berserk could not wait to unleash those fires, for they were essential to melt Dante's armour until it dripped, dripped, dripped into the abyssal nothing to spark his ambitions, his passions, his novel thoughts.

Thus, before that heartbeat expired, the alchemist pointed a wing rightward, commanding glamour-Petra to speak.

"The Marshals sent a scribe to record the accounts of the War Games according to the surviving officials of the Northern Legions. That includes Decanus Ler, and a handful of Triarii." Her voice was smoky, dragging with that lilt they'd learnt through the amalgamation.

*Of course it'll happen; it's needed for the tribunal.* "Understood," Dante stated, straightening to press his fingertips into the desk's edge. *Ler's report can either excuse Sittia's actions or condemn her.* He lifted his chin, studying the Centurion before him. "Do you have word of the timeline?"

"The testimonies are being taken as we speak; Legate Larya is with them." Petra shifted her weight, left hand wrapping over the hilt of her sword.

Dante's jaw shifted in measured acknowledgement. The fog's effect could excuse Sittia and preserve her reputation if properly handled, but doing so may reignite the tensions between the Forces and the Strategists. *Instead, if they doom her—*

An irritating sharpness stung in the air, rancid as he inhaled —and Dante's thoughts caught, his breath hitching at the odour. He recognised it too quickly. *Nonsense. Just an echo of the past.* It lingered on his throat, chalky and gritty, iron-hot on the tongue. Half-sweet, half stone-dust. *Not the time. Focus.* He looked down, pressing his fingers to the desk to pretend thoughtfulness—but that stench endured, its sulphurous, metallic tang scraping the back of his throat. *Focus. In the conversation.*

He parted the lips, just a thread, but enough to recover and state, "Anything else?"

The scent eased when the Centurion drummed her fingers over the hilt of her sword. "Marshal-Strategos Rachen spoke to—"

A spark. A spit, snap, spit, snap.

It snicked near the lantern.

Dante's eyes flicked to it—to the wick, to the closed lid—distracted from the reports. The lantern remained unlit. *It's nothing. Nothing.* Dante tensed his jaw, staring at the paperwork, ignoring his rushing heartbeat.

Petra was speaking, clueless. "—the Northern Marshal."

Spit. Snap. The air was laced with grit and unpleasantly oily. Spit. Snap.

"A few of my cohorts, including Decanus Ler's and Legate Larya..." It changed, her voice. It softened; less rough, less burnt down by the ashfall. Younger, even.

*How?* Dante looked up. Blinked. Blinked again. Clenched his teeth and felt the pulse throbbing on his throat. *It's just a memory!*

Petra looked almost a decade younger—with the same bloody red hair, the same scowl, except her sword arm was bleeding. Dripping, dripping, dripping red onto the rug, her pauldron and cuirass scorched and marred, yellowed by the flames consuming Ílun Fort, devouring her Legions while the Orenian rained fire on them. That blood tarred, bubbling with the rotten scent of the mines, with the blackened smoke. Dante's teeth sank into his tongue. *Control yourself, you fool!*

"—were requested to stay at Egon Hold." Petra's voice. Still younger, still smoother.

*Think!* He swallowed, nodding. Once, breathing. Twice, breathing. *Don't embarrass yourself!* He tapped the table, feeling the warm marble. *What is Gora planning? Think!*

Spit. Snap. Spit. Snap.

Dante straightened, just enough to pretend. *You fool! Speak!* "I assume... this is until the tribunal is completed."

Berserk tilted their head, wings raised amidst the revolving violence of that abstruse abyss. It simmered, silent but seething as the gusts soared, brush-strokes of darkness sweeping and subduing that latent fire the alchemist sought to so relentlessly ignite.

It spread with every ember, with every spit, snap, spit, snap around the lantern's wick—yet Dante smothered it, subtly, slightly. Spit, snap, spit, snap. Over and over, he doused those embers with words, with axioms chanted in Gora's cadence, with slander shouted in Juçe's tone.

The Dragon One grinned, savage like that blend of aggravation and admiration swirling through their molten metal. Aggravation because the Legate refused to fall, resilient like few, their armour of dread and denial smelted from those very same fires that would—irrevocably, irrefutably—melt it back. Admiration, because that self-control was unusual in a human.

Berserk could not wait to ignite those fires, to deepen their incision, to ravage that self-control—but slowly, methodically. Between then, and the pyre Gora was planning for.

Eager, they refocused on the oil-soaked wick and the surrounding air—then tore its charges apart until the tiniest, fiercest spark of white anger spit-snapped yet again. The oil caught, and tongues of flames embraced the wick, whooshing half-alive, flickering shadows dancing on the paperwork atop that desk.

Dante's gaze snapped towards the lantern.

His thought was an offence to Berserk's Matter alchemy: *It's not real. Ignore it!*

Displeased, the alchemist added a reactive compound to the air, fuelling that fire. It grew, fuller and fuller, cobalt tongues mixing into the crimson ones, that crackling louder, louder, louder and impossible to ignore, the shadows it cast swinging over the paper, over the desk, on Dante's eyes, on his mind, on his thoughts.

The storm raged within his soul-link, voracious, vicious, shadowy brush-strokes catching fire, ink leaking and dripping, memories slipping from behind the gusts like wood-burnt images from battles gone by, from days never forgotten, from cities and harbours and vessels and a lifetime of war that'd call for hundreds to be killed for other hundreds to live—on his command, always on his command. Knowingly, so knowingly, so unashamedly. *It was my duty!*

It raged, devious, furious, crimson-amber tongues sweeping

above the inky brush-strokes, devouring the hollow's dome and pouring into that crumbling stillness.

In the real world, Dante nodded, pinching his nose. *Focus! That's then! This is now!* In the soul-link, his self screamed, howling as ashes fell onto the blade like charred strips, raining like during the invasion and assailed by an orchestra of alchemical fire.

The Dragon One lifted a wing, pointed to the glamour—and it changed again, morphing into a past image retrieved from the memories they'd absorbed.

Petra's armour chafed as she shifted her weight. "I'm not privy to that information, Legate."

He looked up in bewilderment, the lantern's flame flickering in his eyes, the brush-strokes' ink leaking, melting, howling as the glamour moved before him.

Petra as she'd been three years ago. Hair tousled, sticky with crust of clot and mud in her forehead, her neck drenched by the blood flowing from a cut under her jaw. Her armour was charred —but her left looped around Centurion's Sittia—wearing half-blackened armour, one arm and a leg eaten by the Nadir's fires, skin twisted, fury on her eyes, slander on her mouth.

Another thought: *Stop reminiscing, you fool!*

Insanity, to insult Berserk's accurate reconstruction of such a historical moment.

"However, as per tradition..." As glamour-Petra spoke, the Dragon One altered the air to add a hint of sulphur, of char, of non-alive components that mixed into the reek of burning flesh. "...my unit and myself are under your authority until we depart." Glamour-Petra spoke, uncaring of that blood, of the fire, of the woman she held. "Any orders until then?"

Fire; it rained in the soul-link. Dead brush-strokes, charcoal ashes falling, curling, swirling, catching aflame, whirling in rage as the windstorm ahead bellowed—distant but with a mewling of agony, with a rattle of dread.

One more thought: *Pathetic! Control yourself!*

Dante's voice, "Prioritise the reports for the tribunal, then..." Slow and restrained amidst that ravenous windstorm of fire and shadows, but coarse and rough because the air was iron-hot, half-sweet, half stone-dust. "Then assist Centurion Ciro; he's guarding the battlements."

Berserk curled, wings aloft, maws snarling and leaking liquid copper, dross shattering above them, around them, sparkling with latent aggravation. Their patience had melted, their tolerance evaporated, their need to squander that composure enraged into wildfire of craving—for the knowledge of alchemy, for the power to craft yet another world.

The Dragon One twisted the air within the lantern's cradle, adding more reactives until the flame soared azure, rapacious, ravenous to ruin, to devour. It spread into the soul-link, that ashfall hastening, spewing charred pieces, spilling little fires, falling onto the blade's edge and tarring it bit by bit.

The ink burned.

The brush-strokes blurred.

A last thought. *Dismiss her! Now!*

Dante's voice, gritted like his teeth. "Dismissed."

Berserk grinned, delighted, but aware of the method and its measure of progress. Dante's armour couldn't be melted by a burst of flames, for in the peace that followed those brush-strokes would recharge and the ink would flow again to deaden the beyond once more. Dante's armour had to simmer, deliberately, until it submitted to the smouldering wildfire Berserk was igniting.

So carefully. So methodically.

So precisely timed with Gora's and Juce's plans.

Before another heartbeat expired, the Dragon One suffocated the lantern's chambers, smothering the wick's flame and cleaning the room's air for the Legate to breathe.

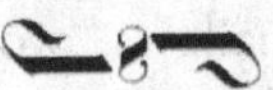

His heart pounded. On his chest, hammering. On his temples, on his hands, on his abdomen. Rabid like an uncontrolled warhorse, delirious like a prey fleeing for its life. *Just memory, you weakling!* Dante's jaw tensed—but when he breathed, the air was clear, and the lantern unlit.

He looked up, the office pounding with his heart, the corners darkening. His eyes twitched when landing on Centurion's Petra's profile.

She awaited, half-turned, scowling at the map on his wall. *She... didn't notice?* Dante straightened—slowly, cautiously—inhaling that pure air before frowning and beckoning to the door. It always worked to dismiss legionnaires. *Steady. Steady!*

Yet in his silence, Petra hesitated, the corner of her eye tightening. "Legate, if I may?"

He blinked, but that blackened heartbeat crunched his vision. *Speak! You wimp!* It wouldn't open, his jaw, his fists clamped so tightly, his—

"On my way here I passed through Centurion Sittia's... accommodations." Petra, watching that map and speaking as if Dante's silence signalled agreement. "The guards wore the Council's triskelion."

She didn't wait for a response. Just walked out, locked the door after her, marched away. Through the hallway, bootfalls, martial, measured—

Spit. Snap. Spit. Snap.

Fire.

"No..." Dante's voice was rough, his tongue iron-hot, his saliva half-sweet, half stone-dust. "No, no, no..."

The lantern was alight, like Liminal Harbour during that siege. *It was duty; missions to complete.* Flickering before his eyes, cobalt tongues embracing crimson leaves to cling to the walls, to the roof, to the soldiers running through the street like blazing silhouettes, everything on fire, everything oily sleek, everything char and tar and black. *Just service to the Legions; nothing else.* The Southern Legions' galleys wail in the night, on the sea, luring the Presyans into the shallows, wood screeching as it dies aflame, legionnaires leaping like droplets ablaze. The water. There is no water but flaming wood. *They serve; they know the risks!* He can't breathe, can't endure that stench: of charred flesh, of burning hair. Impossible to scourge from his clothes, from his nose—but he sends them away, the legionnaires, to chain the piers, to lock the entrances, to be charred and incensed in the name of the Emerald Legions because victory is paramount and retaking that harbour will lead him to recognition, to respect, to that title of Legate no one—no one—has reached at his age. *It is duty! Duty!* It was a challenge, and he'd brought the solution, the salvation. *Liar.*

He was Legate.

It was the wrong success.

# Ferro Keep

Zaro 14ᵗʰ, 17002 RE

# Calya & Asier

*Quintessential royal correspondence. Flattery edged with warnings, meant to impress and unsettle.* Lady Calya Seve ran her fingertip along the rugged edge of the paper, rereading a few choice words before replacing the Exarch's letter on the marble desk. She pressed her other hand into its cold surface, perusing the flourished handwriting for the last time. *Courage, it seems, continues to elude him.* A cold, taunting smirk curled the corner of her lips. She allowed it for a breath, within the privacy of her offices, but it soured on the next. *Afraid of my mother, of public opinion, of his own shadow.* He was useful in his weakness, a tool easily turned and prompt to offer ornamental praise. *Perhaps—*

That thought hung unfinished as a gentle breeze seeped into the room, chilling her shoulders. Her lips trembled before she pressed them closer—and while her gaze settled on the letter spread atop the desk, her mind recalled the pre-dawn encounter.

The lanky librarian. The cobalt threads. The hooded, translucent figure hovering over. The blades spinning as if commanded by sheer will. The taunting insistence on questioning her about the Meridian. *The comments on my power.* The irrefutable evidence that such an idea had been seeded on her childhood for a purpose obscure to her. *I refuse to be their pawn.* The younger librarian, Quintus. That request to meet again. The demand to provide an answer. *They won't manipulate me. I won't allow it.*

The asphyxiating, oppressive sensation she'd only recognised after departing the library. The suffocating frailty she'd promised not to accept ever again. The betrayal of her composure. *I failed myself.* The way she'd crumbled because that powerlessness was exactly what she'd sworn to overcome. *I'm not powerless; not helpless.*

Her fingertips pressed between her brows, smoothing the crease tightening her features. *They'll regret finding me.* It still lingered on her, the echoes of everything she'd repressed, crushing on her until Asier found her. *That's why he is a risk; he knows… everything I want to hide.*

Straightening, Calya smoothed the drapes of her gown, collecting herself before ambling towards the coffer enclosing the locked clockjay. It awaited to be removed, but she still posited whether to write to the Sessentas Minister and continue her quest to shift the overseas alliances. *And while outwardly praising it, the Exarch may also fear this achievement. I should—*

The breeze rattled the curtains, and the light reflecting on the coffer's metal shimmered cobalt. *It could've been just a delusion,* she second-guessed herself, returning to the pre-dawn events. *A product of my exhaustion. A nightmare, so I don't forget my reasons.* The rapid beating of her heart threatened her again. *It's not. I couldn't have imagined the Meridian as a child. The—*

The door thudded closed. Calya straightened, glancing over her shoulder.

Lord Asier Aurri held onto the door's handle, the other hand clutching the veilwing notes Ruria had received—yet his urgency scattered the moment he saw Calya.

Standing near the closed coffer, caramel locks arranged over the left shoulder. She'd refreshed her cosmetics with rouged lips and gold freckles over the eyes, and wore no remnants of the night's events. Just her usual demeanour—infuriatingly calm, and with a presence that demanded compliance. *But she can't deceive me.* Asier sighed, aware of the nuances. Her brows tensed in a minute frown seldom allowed to exist, eyes duller yet challenging him into a normalcy he could not accept. *It's been too many years. I thought she'd overcome—*

He locked the door to squander the memories he couldn't revisit and strode to the desk to drop the veilwing rolls. They tumbled haphazardly, stopping at the edge of the Exarch's letter.

"What happened last night?" He hissed, pressing his fists into the edge of the marble desk; its coldness failed to soothe him. "It's been five years since the last time you—"

Calya pressed a hand into his arm, quashing his anger into abject worry. "I thought... a spy was chasing me. It—" She pressed tighter, interrupting a rebuke. "It was not Teoda's or the Exarch's, just... a misunderstanding."

*She's lying.* The Lord turned, towering over her to search for the truth in her face—but she revealed nothing. *Always the same, like when we were children.* He would witness the aftermath of a cause he could only surmise, left to puzzle facts based on her curt answers. Asier shut his eyes, pinching his nose, working his jaw. *I've always been powerless compared to her.*

"It can't be... *just* a misunderstanding," he groaned, eyeing her askance. "Something rattled you, Calya. Something—"

"I was scared," Calya gritted, her hand tightening over Asier's arm. *He knows too much; cares too much. I can't share this.* "I was scared, and I remembered all the times—"

Her voice thinned, strangled by her past. She walked towards the coffer, meandered to the archway, then returned to sit on the nearest lectus. Her fingers threaded through the silken fabric, crumpling it. *It's always worse in the aftermath.*

On those moments, her perception was a puzzle made of ill-fitting pieces jammed into place. Fragments that returned at the most inopportune moment, pulled by the most illogical connection—a sound, a scent, a feeling. *Powerlessness. Helplessness. That pair... augur pain and misery.* The past leaked into the present, splintering the current reality until she often found herself as she had been, not as she was. *As if I were a child again.* Her lips parted as she exhaled, that helplessness—from the night before, from years ago—throttling her, decimating her, obliterating her. *I am not a pawn; not anymore.*

She was small; so small. Feeble, like a shadow. Minute, like a mote smothered under Teoda's weight. Shivering, quavering. There was screaming but she wasn't howling albeit her throat tensed and swallowing became almost impossible. There was darkness and it was encroaching although the noon shone brighter and the breeze warmed by the hour. There was—

"Calya?" Asier's voice. His hand on her shoulder, on her cheek, lifting her chin. "We're no longer there."

The Lady looked up. Met her cousin's gaze. His stubbled chin, the fine lines at the corners of his eyes, the pathways criss-crossing his scrunched forehead. She smiled ruefully, moving his hand to stand up. *Except sometimes it's impossible to distinguish. What was. What is.*

Taking a few steps, Calya paused under the archway to toy with the drapes of her dress—each fold she rearranged, a plan was refined. *I must deal with the aftermath of the Truce; leverage the advantage I have.* She moved aside, exhausted by the concern in Asier's countenance, by the worry he exuded and what it reminded her. *Sestel, now. First, and foremost.* She glanced at the clockjay's coffer, then at the desk paces away; the veilwing rolls had scattered above them. *I'll shape my plans tonight. When regret comes, it'll be too late for the alchemists to undo me.*

"Asier? I saw you bringing some veilwing notes. What—?" She halted before he could interrupt, frowning and beckoning to the desk. *We have no time to waste.* "There is pressing work to do."

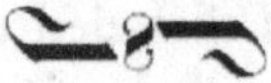

A thousand retorts overwhelmed the Lord's mind, ranging from the ineffective and emotional, to the angry and rational. He could confess his concern, worry loudly about her need to rest, appeal to the mistakes she could commit... or even accuse her of being irrational, of disregarding a danger that had scared her like not even the Nadir's eruption had. *None would work*, he knew, for none had worked before. *She only knows how to bury emotions. But...* From that close distance, her eyes told him what she wouldn't articulate—a plea. Silent. Private. *I can't blame her for being like this.*

Asier groaned, stretching an arm towards the desk in an unwilling concession of defeat—and Calya dipped her eyes, gliding towards the desk with a confidence antipodean to what he'd witnessed heartbeats before. The morning's light flickered on the gold details of her cosmetics as she fetched the Legate's veilwing note. Its seal cracked when she pressed it, reading with an impassive stare.

*This will have consequences.* "Is he upholding his part of the Truce?" The Lord asked at last, wrapping his hand atop the hilt of his sword, fingers digging into its patterns.

"He's confirming what we agreed." The Lady nodded, fingers steepled beneath her chin. "The Firardian medici are collating their report, and they'll send it by dawn. Lady Varre will be pleased," she finished, extending the paper towards him.

"I'll notify the guards on the Gorge and begin preparations for an escort." Asier accepted the proffered note, refraining a grimace as he read. "She will want to travel as soon as possible, arguing the need of a postmortem." *A genius to her patients, a butcher to those aware of her methods. A key ally either way.*

Calya smirked roguishly before hand-signalling, *"Hori's oath holds until curiosity calls."*

He answered with a grunt of displeasure—both at the healer's actions, and Calya's enforced normalcy. It didn't matter how many decades they'd survived together, her immediate detachment and absolute sharpness in the wake of extreme distress remained striking. *It has a cost; it always has a cost.* Her hands were steadier now, her shoulders straighter, gaze gleaming as if auguring a political manoeuvre. *Although sometimes, forgetting is just easier.* The Lord's jaw clenched as he walked back towards the desk, dropping the note and letting it roll.

The Lady was reading Ruria's note—written in a grittier, ink-stained and crumpled paper. She took enough time to reread, then hummed—*Realisation?*—and reread again. *I'll need to under-*

*stand what happened on my own.* It enthralled her, but he doubted she was still reading it; the darkness of her eyes was not the calm before the storm, but the impasse in which she schemed to become the storm. Asier knew better than to interrupt when that look took hold, and so he mulled over his thoughts, staring through the glazed casements. *Change the patrols, discreetly. Set the servants to spy on Teoda.*

"It seems Marshal-Strategos Gora Rachen has arrived in Egon, alongside none other than Marshal-Magister Nagore Loera," Calya stated at last, gaze running through the sentences.

*Nagore? From the Central Legion?* Asier pressed his lips tighter, barely whispering, "Meaning that the Northern Marshal-Strategos, Arte Siere, is either encumbered with the frontier's guard against Orenos, or plotting Gora's political demise from Arborum City."

"Possibly," Calya nodded, passing the note. "And the excess troops from the War Games are due to leave in two days at the most." Her eyes narrowed, voice steeling into a whisper. "It could be a message to us; a disarmament disguising an apology for Sittia's unexpected detour... or it could be just a regular movement."

Asier kept the note between his fingers, hand-signalling, *"Should our troops think the former?"* Thus, we return to the deliberate misdirection of public opinion.

"No. We cannot risk humiliating the Emerald Legions after the Truce." Calya shrugged with the same restraint she wielded like a murderous weapon—then whispered, "For now, the Sessentas Minister and my mother should be our focus. The joint investigation will run its course soon."

Asier's cheek twitched, his logic unable to fight against the hundred concerns that burst at the mention of the matriarch. He chewed saliva, managing not to crumple the note before whispering, "Whatever you need."

When she didn't answer he looked up, apprehension guiding his motions—but found her lost in thought, fingertips rubbing the roped sash of her draped gown, gaze unfocused as if pondering a universal truth.

# Amok

The noon's glare streamed between the clouds, bathing the balcony's rails without warming its surface. Amok alighted atop it, walking the edge while glamoured to invisibility. From their vantage point, The Central Residence sunk like a white spire into the ironstone maws of the Keep below, the landscape beyond blurred by the glare.

When the breeze lifted—natural and not alchemical—their cloak swirled, leaking glyphs. They pulsed cerulean like the breathing of thoughts—but stilled on their command, reshaping into an Integrity Shield. It gleamed unfractured, swirling with the ideas that preoccupied them.

How The Rector, from the confines of reality, had shattered that Integrity Shield while also impeding its regeneration. How Amok have been denounced for not daring, not learning. The possibilities that'd now spawned from that conversation, from the simple question—

"Is he upholding his part of the Truce?" Lord Asier Aurri growled, and his aggravation shot through the window like spears of annoyance.

The alchemist caught one, twirling it between two fingers—then dropped it as they crouched, elbows resting atop flared knees. Their head tilted while studying the office through the glazed window.

"He's confirming what we agreed." Lady Calya Seve stood near a desk, a veilwing note stretched between her fingers.

Her curated appearance—enough to fool other humans—contradicted what Amok had seen mere hours ago: the edge of collapse, the struggle for continuity, the precarious effort to reclaim the feeling of owning existence. That chaos subsisted like soot clinging to every plan she posited—and tumbled onto the balcony like flakes rolling in the zephyr.

One teased Amok, and as a grin slashed their non-face, the Untamed One soul-linked Calya.

Within the soul-link, darkness reigned absolute over a sea of shadows.

Calya stood amidst it, impervious to the fragments of the collapsed wall sinking into her. She didn't bleed, for alive elements had no such effect, but wore them like hallmarks. Each was ready to inflict the most immeasurable pain the moment it caught a reflection—echoes of past grievances awaiting a reason to anchor in the present and exist again.

In that darkness, the shadows of Calya's self returned. Amorphous mounds, humanoid outlines that ill-reflected the isolated emotions Amok had discovered before. They contorted, arms extended towards her, jaws parting to scream.

Little-Calya howled first, recognisable given how small she was. "I was powerless! At someone's mercy! Again!"

Young-Calya growled, her wrath rooting into the ground to become a seldom-acknowledged foundation. "It was my fault. I foolishly ensnared myself and became the hunted!"

Precursor-Calya breathed at last, freckled with the holes in her logic. "I have power. I'm the Head of the Seve House. I *am* powerful."

The three mounds surrounded actual-Calya, lurking around her as the remnants of her fear, of her anger, of her detachment and self-enforced apathy—trudging closer, arms stretching to seize her. She pretended those alive elements did not exist, refusing to acknowledge them and instead focusing on the present.

When Amok ended the soul-link, only a charcoal veil embraced Calya.

A welcomed experience, to witness The Rector—of all alchemists—enact such a fine, Naturalist intervention. Teasing her with the unknown, taunting her with fearful wrath, tearing through her self-control to unleash pure, Natural alive elements.

An instructive example, demonstrating Amok's need to better align their stance—and thus Naturalism's—on some approaches. Evidently, early conversations wouldn't risk taint—The Rector's original, on Umbra City's library, was evidence of it.

The Untamed One grinned again, watching the glyphs captured between their palms. Once the mission had concluded, they'd summon a quorum with the other Naturalist Soul Transmuters—barely a hundred—to further refine this evidence through methodical experimentation. After all, Naturalism was deliberate, unlike the Dragon Plague's actions, who—

Berserk.

That name stalled Amok's plans, forcing them to stand and glance at the blurred clouds now hindering most of the light. A realisation lingered between those hazy rays, impossible to ignore: Berserk must have noticed The Rector's arrival, for the universe had folded into Ferro Keep. They must have, unless...

Ravenous for an answer, Amok reassembled their Integrity Shield, lingering at the rim of daring—but when The Rector's reprimand echoed again, the Untamed One unleashed a fragment of themselves.

It hurtled past the Central Residence and out of Ferro Keep, across Furia Gorge, and into Egon Hold to search for Legate Dante Praeto. They found him walking through the ramparts, his alive elements swaying like clouds enslaved by a gale. A hundred concerns dragged him into the depths of unresolvable worries.

Meanwhile, Berserk was circling one man and alighting onto a windowsill, their attention split between that man and the glamour-Centurion engaging a handful of Decanii across the Hold.

A fascinating revelation, to discover the old Soul-Matter alchemist had been blinded from the pre-dawn events and the evolution promised to Amok. A dooming discovery, for there was little worse than stagnating without learning.

Satisfied, Amok recalled that fragment, merging it with their body still perched on the balcony's guardrail.

At that moment, Lady Hori Varre stood amidst the office within the windows. Demure and mindful, although Amok saw through the layers of her façade. Past the delicate looks hiding a ruthless demeanour. Beyond her visible concern—often mistaken as a laudable interest on her patient's health—and into the truth only few understood. Her appetite for the ailments yet to discover, for the secrets only postmortems could reveal. Hori craved knowledge like an alchemist, yet lacked the resilience needed to survive the process.

"My Lady." Calya welcomed her with a frown of practiced concern. "I trust you've rested besides working?"

"Whenever possible, my Lady. I've been tending our soldiers; those wounded by our guests will mend, except for a few." Her deep voice embittered for a moment, a frown pulling gently on her brows. "Likewise, most of the fog's survivors have stabilised, and albeit we must be grateful for its minor impact, the... small numbers limit what we can discover."

Calya's understanding flared like a lantern searing an abyss. *Hori's warnings are always clinical—and she's threatening my power.*

Power.

"Of course, although it is fortunate that the impact on Sestel was minor, unlike Firard's." Lady Seve rubbed her fingers—pensively, purposefully—as if her concern were genuine. "I trust the joint investigation will offer the opportunity to better help our forces." Taking a step back, she gestured for a pause before reaching for the desk. "Fortunately, earlier today I received a veilwing from Legate Praeto..."

When she proffered the note, her uneasiness scattered like sooty flakes, passing through the window to swirl around

Amok. As always, they heard all thoughts without a soul-link, an ability uncommon amongst Soul Transmuters.

*I must be careful with the power this joint investigation granted me.* That thought was appropriate for a leader as herself, the alchemist wouldn't deny it—but it was a loose strand in the grand scheme of a deception. The thread that, when pulled, would unravel her composure exactly as The Rector had demonstrated. *Foreign politics are Seve's remit, and under my control... it's challenging the Exarch's power.*

Power. Power.

"This... will change everything," Hori whispered at last, rolling the veilwing note and proffering it back. "It can help our research greatly... but tending to the Firardian's survivors is of utmost importance. There is limited time before their condition becomes fatal."

Calya sighed in feigned agreement, retrieving the note and toying with it. *My Generals hesitate longer than Hori with a fresh body... but she's a fundamental ally.* "That limitation remains in my mind, although a Varre-Seve delegation travelling to Egon Hold will only have one or two days at the most..." She softened her expression with practised empathy. *Hori is fundamental to my political standing.* "Perusing that material first will ensure we make the most of such a brief trip."

Power. Power. Power.

Power; for herself, above all else. Power; not to be helpless and neither subjugated. Power; because it enabled survival.

Amok crouched again, hands pressed into the rail to lean forth and grin. Their glyphs whirled around them, moving alongside that ongoing conversation to reshape one question: 'What is power?' That mind-whisper was so perfectly recalled it echoed as if repeated.

An intriguing question, fundamental to holding Calya at the edge of boundless terror—where the crystal wall's engineered neutrality arose like a last resource to prevent her collapse, to protect her existence, to reinvent herself and survive. It was Natural, a pure response to the most damaging creatures humans could encounter—other humans—yet through it lay the path to perfecting the incarnate soul-skill.

Amok understood it, and remembered it to one day experiment like so.

"A few days ago you mentioned the event in the Petricor Mountains, considering there were similarities..." Calya's voice, so calm, so collected. So unaware of the alchemist watching her. "Is that still the case?"

"It remains a hypothesis, since we have discovered no additional connections..." Hori's fingers curled around her chin. "For what I heard, Decanus Ler Halde's strategy was to ambush Centurion Sittia through the caverns. If that's the case, their path could reveal which substances caused the fog."

Calya nodded, walking the healer towards the office's door. "Of course—and we will pursue that since the Treaty included access to the caverns, if safe." She paused, measured. "For now, the documents should arrive tomorrow, and you'll be notified of any further developments."

Amok soared as the door clicked closed. There was much to consider before Calya offered the answer The Rector had demanded.

After all, boldness enabled the pursuit of knowledge and—through it—the refinement of Naturalism.

# Egon Hold

## Zaro 14th, 17002 RE

# Dante & Berserk

The cup thudded dryly as he placed it on the table, his finger lingering on the glass' rim to coax a wavering hum. It died too soon, murdered by the distant echoes of a Hold that never slept, not even after dusk. Dante ignored it, fixated on the dregs of carmine wine pooling at its bottom—reflecting his palm as he flicked the glass with his index to induce another note.

Subtle, compared to his groan. Harsh, thick, rolling in the privacy of those opulent, marble-walled and cedar-furnished chambers. The ones he'd been assigned as the Legate of Egon Hold.

"Legate…" A murmur, hoarse. Burnt down.

He flinched as his calloused fingertips scraped the streaks he'd carved in his neck that afternoon. *A coward and a fool.* His lips curled in a half snarl, and his jaw ached after swallowing too many screams. *Can't even bear the cost of my own decisions.* When he chuckled, bitter, he stepped back—away from that glass, away from the dishevelled reflection on it. He stared into the darkness of that chamber—no torchlight, no lanterns, not even the unlit devices—then crossed the space to emerge onto the balcony.

A few steps and he spun, walking backwards towards the guardrail, elbows pressing in its edge while he ignored the view below. His eyes shut as he breathed in that refreshing zephyr, so clean and dry, so neutral. It slipped through the thin linen of his camisia, chilling the dried sweat he hadn't yet washed. *Pathetic…* His frown tightened, thick like Centurion's Petra. *How much did she see?* It was a question never to be resolved, for the woman hadn't seemed to notice and Dante would never ask. *Weak; shamefully weak.* He'd barely managed to scurry away from his office, later ignoring Ilia's quiet knock at his chamber's doors. *Hiding like a coward.*

Noises crept from the Hold, enhanced by the height—the thudding of footfalls, the clatter of metal, the creaking of distant doors. Dante's fists pumped, fingers curling, uncurling, curling, uncurling as if from the motion he could weave Petra's last words. There was a vague recollection in his mind; a hint, a few words.

"Sittia. Accommodations. Guards. T—?" Dante groaned again, fists clenching because the last one wouldn't twist out of his mind. His nose scrunched as if to coerce it into shape. "Triskelion?" *If so… that's a problem.*

Dante's fists clenched, veins thickening with the unspent tension. He'd assigned a guard to his mother's chambers, made of trustworthy legionnaires. *But if Gora replaced them…* He shut his eyes, haunted by Sittia's image—her scowl, her clenched jaw, her fists so tight, so wound up in tension, the veins in her neck, pulling taut. The wrath on her inky eyes. *The Strategos… may not think me capable of restraining her.* His guilt rose, crumpling into a bitter smile. *Gora could've stripped me of command for letting this happen, but he praised me instead.*

Those fists relaxed again, his pulse pumping, pumping through his wrists, the cold zephyr rustling his camisia, its fabric scraping his sore neck.

*Focus. Think!* His eyes opened, lost in the starry sky barely mangled by a few shimmering wisps. Gora's position was not entirely emotional—accepting the Retreat and Truce was also political. Safe, given how it related to Sittia's actions, and convenient to support a peace the Ochrese allies would approve of. Useful in enabling the joint investigation and appeasing all fears of a fog-weapon with knowledge. Honourable not to renege on a treaty already signed. *But its aftermath… that is my responsibility.*

The tribunal. Shame, grief, conflict, factions within factions, restless Forces, wary Strategists. The Truce. Sestelii inspecting legionnaires, Lady Varre in Firardian territory, an unseen potential for balance and stability, for upcoming alliances, for commerce and trade routes, for joint raids against the Presyan, against the Orenian.

A challenge like no other Legate—no other Strategos—had ever faced.

The alchemist alighted, invisible, atop the marble guardrail, wings spread to enjoy the cold zephyr. It was a quiet night, peaceful even—yet they disregarded it to peruse the active soul-link.

That hollow of serenity had quelled compared to earlier that afternoon. Its ashfall had stopped, the rivulets of fire no longer raining—but the deadened beyond now sparkled alive into a windstorm of regret, of aspiration, of blame, of schemes as only humans knew how to blend. It swirled at the hollow's threshold, its darkness interspersed with embers, Dante's ambition finally leaking into his awareness.

The dragonlet tilted their head, wings rustling with the breeze. It'd always been there, that craving, but now it resurfaced between his tense scowl and his unchallenged heartbeat, between his clenched fists and that maelstrom of tarred memories. He was an astute candidate to source-being, yet driven by an affliction pervasive to humanity, entangling reality with endless longing disguised as goals, with yearning for the impossible cloaked as fervour, with greed for what wasn't presented as thirst for progress.

One thought corroborated it: *Anything for the long-term, even when the price is blood.* It spread through the soul-link's hollow like a network of possibilities, of schemes, of pieces to move as if playing a game of regnum. Legions, treaties, strategies, spies, interests, challenges, answers, prevention, escalation—all emerging from the edge of that blade Dante's self balanced on. *I must rise to that challenge; lead Firard to the Meridian of Existence.*

Insanity, not to agree with such craving, even when he chased it for the wrong reasons.

Berserk's wings fluttered as they lifted, landing near the Legate. His elbows were still pressed into the guardrail, hands dangling loosely—except his fingers moved to trace half-formed glyphs his awareness didn't recognise. Alchemical in nature, and read in that old and shabby book Berserk had never seen in the Library of The Towers.

Another thought refocused the alchemist—linked to the face of that striking woman, also part of The Rector's plans. *Lady Calya Seve.* A new lattice of patterns and clues flowed through the soul-link, braiding more logic into the prior network. Dante's schemes and hers as well, his silences and her pauses, his counters and her parries, his aims and hers. *She acted... as if seeking the Meridian.*

Insanity, not to leverage such an alchemical thought, not to force Dante to chase that solution. Insanity, not to deepen the incision Berserk was so carefully chiselling.

The Dragon One grinned, savage, and fire burst from their wings, inflamed by their desire for knowledge, for understanding, for a pathway that had been—for myriads of millennia—unknown. It consumed the air into a mirage of heat-haze, annihilating the invisibility glamour as the alchemist transfigured into their true form.

# Juçe

CENTURION, EASTERN LEGIONS OF FIRARD

Juçe walked in the dark, starlight pouring through the Citadel's broad casements. His footfalls hammered the floor with precision, his armour shifting with restrained menace. Four blind arches decorated that hallway, one statue inside each—Centurions from an era gone by, their armour simpler, their legends preserved in history. *They'd be ashamed of what the Emerald Legions have become.* He raised his chin as he walked past, turning the corner.

Four legionnaires waited ahead, armoured for war—with spears upright, gripped in clenched fists. Two flanked a carved wooden wall, two more across the hall. *They keep her like a prisoner.* Their faces were set; grim. Unfazed as they noticed Juçe and squared while he approached. A salute of rank, not respect. *The difference is loud.*

One of them—a youth with too few scars and smooth skin—gestured towards the door. "Our orders are to admit you."

*No scars, no trust.* The Centurion didn't answer—a soldier without pain hadn't earned his place—instead staring at the door with a clear expectation. The pair flanking it stepped aside, the clatter of their too-polished armour resounding on that empty hallway. Juçe forced his hand to steady on the handle as he pulled the door open; he closed it swiftly.

The room was functional. Bare walls, polished floors, no

needless decorations. The narrow window awaited opposite the door, the starless night impervious to the flickering lantern-light —bright, yet feeble as only flames can be. A bookshelf took the rightmost flank, empty except for a few tomes. The lectii were a matching pair; simple and worn out, unlike those in the Strategists' rooms. A small table stood between them, the water jug in its centre almost spent.

He took his time before holding Sittia's gaze.

She was sitting on the leftmost lectus, knees splayed, elbows pressed into them. Her arm was freshly bandaged, but the sutures on her cheek sorely needed a change. When she straightened, her battle-worn leathers creaked in unspoken expectation. *At least they allowed her that dignity.* Sittia observed him; not angry, and neither concerned.

Three strides and the vial clinked when Juçe placed it on the table, next to the water jug.

"The medicus will come at dawn. Take it before that." He stared at the window, his forefinger lingering over the vial's stopper. *We crafted legends. Not anymore.*

Sittia looked at the vial and nodded, just once. "You hold our name. You decide what it means from tomorrow."

Juçe's eyes snapped to hers, locking in that inky darkness. His lips pressed into a line, fists clenching with the strength he'd need. The silence between them spoke too loud.

"You do what you must. I did." Sittia's voice was rougher than he remembered. She beckoned towards the vial. "It'll be done."

He didn't answer, and neither looked back. He simply marched away with the silence of men who knew exactly what comes next. *Our name won't end like this.*

What had to be done, would be done.

#  Dante & Berserk

A reflection; caught in the curve of a blade, twisting in the dark. Dante backtracked, hand dropping to his belt, fingers searching for his pugio. Grasping nothing. *An assassin?* His jaw tightened, the night brightened by his alertness. *Where is it?* His fists clenched as he looked for the threat, for the would-be-killer, for whoever had attempted— *There!*

Molten metal. Twisting over the guardrail, burning like blood blending with gold. Blistering the dross of its surface, the fire within bursting and soaring. It reached the sky. It poured in upon itself. Swirling like liquid fire—like emberbane—raining into Liminal Harbour, leaking, leaking, leaking through the buildings, flames catching and cavorting from the windows, muffling the screams, the howls, the agony.

*A nightmare. Too much wine.* Dante panted, backtracking, certain it was an echo of the afternoon and the lantern that kindled itself. His spine pressed against the marble wall, seeking its coldness while he brushed the guardrail with his fingertips. Not for safety; for grounding. *This is just—*

That molten metal ruptured into ringlets of liquid copper, weaving a humanoid shape with immense wings. Its membranes undulated too slowly to be liquid, too alive to be solid—and the air folded around, buckling and groaning as the metal reforged, shaping scales of flowing iron that laminated an armour too seamless and impossible. Heat haze whooshed from it, dark clouds rolling up, up, up from each of them—from the legionnaires, in Ílun Fort, in the ramparts, in the courtyard, under the collapsing towers. Aflame, all of them, screaming as fire swallowed them, charred forms tumbling into the wells, into the soil, into anything that'd smother the pain, the agony, the irritating sharpness permeating the air, iron-hot, half-sweet, half stone-dust and so metallic it scrapped Dante's throat.

*Close your eyes, breathe*—but he stared at the absurd, unable to look away, to focus on reality. *You craven! Control yours—!*

The scales in that armour flowed, arranging in lines as if willed in place, layering yet never locking, its sharp points dripping metal that vanished into smoke. It shaped cuises that encased the legs yet moved to take a step forth; vambraces and rerebraces knitted from scales and gleaming while the gauntleted claws clenched into fists.

Dante groaned, frustrated, ashamed, incoherent as he forced his gaze to crawl up—to the sky, smouldering, fire raining onto the Fort, black vapour bleeding upwards from the towers, groaning as the torsion catapults collapsed ablaze, wood shrieking, soldiers bellowing. The stench, the stench! So acrid and pungent, sweet and oily and ever-present, raging on the back of his throat as he ran, ran, ran through the collapsing ramp—

Those clawed fists opened, closed, opened, closed—and the black vapour contorted into the semblance of dross. It shattered as it lashed, curling into a tail spiked with bones curved like cutlasses.

"Hurry!" Ilia's voice; hoarse. Lost in that cloud of lime-dust billowing skyward, clogging, blinding.

Dante's jaw clenched. *Not… here! She's not—* He ran behind, bracing his head, rubble cascading behind. Liquid fire slashed the sky, raining into the courtyard, igniting the soldiers, the horses, the shrieking and screeching, sheer terror running loose, deadly, deadly, deadly as Dante sprinted through the ramparts, chasing Ilia's shadow, rushing, rushing—

That tail lashed—and wings fanned open when Dante leapt above the fire slithering through the bricked floor. Heat haze blocked the starlight, two rubies flourishing beyond it, fiery tongues sweeping in those depths, leaking into a snarling façade, teeth bared, the snout's liquid metal crumpling.

"The Meridian of Existence..." Growled, unlike him.

Dante drifted in a pool of blood, regaining balance, sprinting, hunting Ilia's silhouette. Ahead: Ílun Fort's towers aflame. Above: emberbane, raining, pouring. Besides: dust, blood, fire, and heat and the army that besieged them and the mountain pass.

He couldn't breathe, couldn't see—but he knew Ílun Fort was on fire, the Orenians assembling in Bruma Pass, an invasion latent, possible, too possible, too likely. He coughed, tumbling, balancing, rushing—to solve the challenge.

"The Meridian... is the challenge." Dante's voice. Hoarse. Aflame.

Berserk snarled, projecting the Legate's soul-link into the real world until his windstorm of dread and denial swirled around his body.

Yet in the span of a single heartbeat, that dread became more. Horror, panic, regret, remorse, desire. All mingling, all colliding, all warring against his reason because he was sinking into the fires that would melt that armour into an uneasy suspicion—of his own sanity, of his own rationality, of his own ability to see the truth and distinguish it from madness.

It was a war for and against reality—yet at the threshold of that collapsing hollow of stability, Dante's inky brush-strokes fought the fiery gusts. That battle throttled his logic into the incoherent emptiness that witnessed the impossible and couldn't warp it into words but into memory.

Amidst that rage, the Dragon One angled the head, measuring their prey. In the real-world, the Legate's body flattened against the wall, a finger brushing the guardrail, eyes wide open; seeing, but unseeing. In the soul-link, his self-image crouched low to balance atop the edge of that blade, hands locked over his head.

Four golden threads emerged from the Legate—real and *self* —to coil in the windstorm now roaring with that battle between reality and unreality. In a matter of heartbeats those threads shimmered golden, that honey-light searing through the darkness, curling, unfolding, unravelling to reach between the brush-strokes and the fiery gusts, knotting into the livened beyond and pulling closer the fires of the past that could never be *just* a memory but the perennial echo of atemporal alive elements.

Impressions—visual, colourful, inflamed with a hundred alive elements—rushed past them like wood-burnt visions of a past siege. They sparkled golden, pulled by the threads, by Dante's mind, by that flicker of liquid fire dripping from Berserk wings.

"Hurry!" The Dragon One growled, impatient, eager for that past to return naturally, to interfere within it and resurface Dante's desires.

There were hundreds of impressions brought from the past. Nameless faces contorted into endless screams, legionnaires trapped in a never-ending battle, mountains weeping mist, Ilia running, running, running while Dante looked up. The sky flickered golden as well, sibilant as fire rained upon the Fort, clouds rushing in the projectiles' wake, arcs of flames blending with blackened smoke, the wind catching to reveal another clue—teasing Berserk, taunting them, revealing hints of a plan that exceeded even the discoverer of the Meridian of Existence. A slender figure, braided from swathes of starlight, a skull-face crowned by two half-moons, fire and air dancing around them: Chasm, a Protean Reshaper, invisible to all humans yet coercing the wind towards Ílun Fort.

Insanity! To discover yet another clue of The Rector's involvement, to—!

"The Meridian... is the challenge." Dante's voice. Hoarse. Aflame.

Berserk groaned, refocusing as the threads shimmered, rippling through those impressions, distorting but pulling, pulling, folding, coming, closer, faster, closer, closer until that gold light seared the darkness of the windstorm, inky brush-strokes now repainting the past, forcing it alive, adding the sounds, the scents, the colours, the howls and the fire and the battle that raged in Bruma Pass while Dante sprinted thought the ramparts of Ílun Fort.

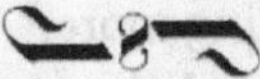

The stone was slick with the emberbane leaking from every tower, slicker with the blood spilling from the corpses trapped in the rubble. *This can't last.* Dante ran, blinded by the deep haze of that morning. He drifted in a carmine pool and hit the crenellations, hand scraping stone as he pushed and ran again— tearing the blackened clouds, past the screams, chasing Ilia towards the outer rim that'll offer the vision they needed. *Without Ílun, they'll invade Firard. Can't allow it.*

He gasped, breath shuddering as he took a hand to the brow. The smoke itched in his eyes, and the air clawed at his throat. Pungent, acid, half-sweet and oily sleek; disgusting like the emberbane, like the machinery the Orenians produced out of that thick mist pooling on Bruma Pass. *This isn't a battle. It's a prelude to war.* Legate Ilia Larya drifted and turned a corner. Dante chased her, forearms bracing his head while a blazing scythe swung across the sky, bleeding into embers, a firefall spilling alight.

The smoke thinned as they emerged into the outer rim of Ílun Fort—a stronghold terraced in four rings, a dam of stone blocking Bruma Pass. Dante hurried to the crenellations—where Ilia awaited—to assess the view beyond. Dreadful. Stunning. *An opportunity. A challenge.* The Pass, stretching like a sinuous valley edged by mountains weeping streams of thinning mist, the path within dotted with fire, with hordes of Orenians, with siege machinery assembled into engines of destruction. *They finally committed. Now we attack.* The force Ilia had sacrificed to steer the army to that position had earned them time, revealing the enemy. *We assumed siege engines, but they brought emberbane.* It wasn't the same as fighting the structural destruction of stone-throwers; emberbane was worse. *More than destruction, it unleashes terror.*

"It worked," Ilia groaned, cleaning the spyglass with her soot-stained camisia and pressing it to her eye. She scowled when passing the contraption. "Limited army, but too many machines. They're assembling more."

Legate Dante Praeto exhaled, refusing the acrid, blazing air and grabbing the spyglass. *We'll need two years after this to reinforce Ílun.* He watched the mountainsides, recalling the first strategy he'd pondered. He scanned the pathway—the descent from Ílun to the Pass—and reviewed his second possible strategy. He traced the mountains at last, remembering the beyond—the northeast, that nation never breached, the latent threat that Firard could never face on its own; he discarded the third potential strategy. *Must force the Orenians out of Bruma Pass—for those two years.* The spyglass creaked in protest, his hold too tight, too restless. *If Ílun falls, they'll swarm us. The Pass widens on Firard's side.*

One, two heartbeats. Dante lowered the contraption; slowly, thoughtfully, meeting Ilia's gaze. She was scowling, keeping the blackened clouds away—but her onyx eyes shimmered as she tilted her head; knowing. *Instead, if I force Orenos to attack through the Vast Expanse they may attempt a two-pronged invasion, climbing into Firard via the Cobalto Valley.* Both Legates had weighed the options before, when the veilwings warned them. They both agreed. They both allowed that barrage of destruction as a lure. *Sestel. Firard. We could ally against Orenos; temporarily, of course.* They'd both risked the Fort's integrity to ensure the Orenian committed the machinery and revealed their weapons. *Blood is the cost of long-term stability. Stability leads to the Meridian.*

"Why do you chase the Meridian?" That question. That... question? It roared across the smeared sky, rippling through his body while the Fort shuddered again. It rose from the fire before him, stretching like a clawed finger until the world pounded at the corners.

Dante pressed both hands to his nose; breathed the hot air between. Still half stone-dust; still oily sweet. *The Meridian... is the only answer.*

"Why do you chase the Meridian?" Berserk growled, maws parting without shaping the words.

Those sounds tumbled into the terrace while they crouched atop the guardrail with knees splayed, clawed hands pressed into that thin edge. Their fanned wings encased the broad terrace, their glow carving shadows into Dante's face.

He remained flattened against the wall, mouth quivering with every hitched breath, eyes hopping left, right, left, right but unseeing reality—for those golden threads had brought the past back for him to relive.

So thoroughly. So fully. So unstoppable.

Yet the alchemist's voice pierced that recall, altering that memory—but Dante didn't answer. His jaw was unhinged, his heartbeat raising, his mouth stuttering the answer his thoughts elaborated so clearly: *The Meridian... is the only answer.*

A reckless, audacious man to dare remain so boldly locked in that lie.

Liquid copper leaked from Berserk's jaw as they roared, "To what question?"

"To what question?" That voice roared; the fire bloomed, ignited with—

"We cannot allow them to assemble more." Ilia's voice, her ash-smeared fingers steepling beneath her chin. "I gauge we have... six, or seven hours until then. Not more."

Dante nodded, the grit of grime dragging across his jaw as he groaned, "More machines aren't the only problem. Their supply is too large." He beckoned to the hazy horizon with a soot-stained hand. "We must destroy everything at once."

Ilia clicked her tongue. "That leaves us... two or three hours to move."

He grunted in response, choked with the cinders—then leaned over the crenellations to cough it while staring at the Pass. His third, now discarded strategy was unworkable: no force could slip past them to ignite a wall of fire. *Yet we finally know enough to counter them.* What strategies were left, however, were as useful as deadly. *Sacrifice some more to distract the Orenian, and again to trigger a landslide by collapsing the mines.*

Wood groaned, dull; mallets driving wedges with thudding knocks. Dante stepped back, crossed the rampart, looked down —to the other rim where the torsion catapults were being assembled. *Useless for now; the wind is against us. It has been for days.* It whistled again, emberbane jars tracing crescents of fire above them.

"Two assaults, then. Hand-picked legionnaires." Dante coughed, the air iron-hot on his tongue, the breeze oily, dusty, sticky as he gasped. His vision sputtered, darker in the corners. "V-veterans first. The wounded, the inept, the mediocre."

"We lure them northwest first?" Ilia coughed as well, staring at the Pass.

"Indeed." Dante angled the head, greasy hair sticking to his temples. The darkness crept through the edges. "While the other assault force collapses the mines. We have enough black powder."

*Just decoys.* Dante's lips pressed into a line. Those deaths were a workable cost to block the Pass, to damage Orenos and lure them into the Vast Expanse and gamble that Lady Seve would accept a temporal truce. One that could develop into an alliance. *For a greater—*

"For the Meridian!" It growled, the fire. Surging all around him, heat haze choking the Legate, cold marble pressed into his back, those words rolling towards him like a clawed finger digging an incision. Powerful, unforgettable. "You sacrificed thousands for the Meridian! Why? Why does it obsess you?"

"For the Meridian!" The Dragon One growled, leaping from

the guardrail to land on the terrace and point a claw at the Legate's lies. "You sacrificed thousands for the Meridian! Why? Why does it obsess you?"

Dante gasped, unseeing even as he looked up, fingers clutching his rampaging chest while he collapsed to his knees. He groaned when his elbows hit the marble, back folded onto himself, fingers curling into the marble to grasp nothing.

His breathing was jagged, shallow, frantic like his fingers— clawing for air, clawing for purchase, both insufficient because reality was outside of him but he was locked in his mind. He panted as if drowning, desperate, dragged, choking even as the breeze picked under the starry night.

Berserk disregarded those shallow, unsteady breaths. That recall had just begun, and Dante's body physical endurance was not yet at its limits. He would survive long enough for the alchemist to chisel deeper.

"Not obsession..." The Legate groaned, hoarse but proving the alchemist correct. "A challenge. To keep Orenos away, to delay an invasion. To reach stability."

Dante gasped, his throat burning, too taut to breathe, too tense to speak. It pounded, his chest, brutal like a rampaging horse, lost and erratic as the fools selected for the first assault force. Pitiful. Weak. An assortment of mediocrities and veterans who'd long exhausted their usefulness. Sick miners with only a few years left; some younger but too problematic to retain. They marched under the veil of night, that darkness enclosing as they dragged barrels of black powder to collapse the mines and die crushed and suffocated while the landslide engulfed the enemy and Dante was praised for the long-term goals the Emerald Council so craved.

His mouth parted, at last. Sticky with gunk, with the oil of the emberbane. "Not obsession..." His voice; sore, hoarse. *When? How?* "A challenge. To keep Orenos away, to delay an invasion. To reach stability."

The world pounded at the corners again, a pressure raising on his chest, hammering on his forehead, whistling buzzing on his ears. *I'm serving the Legions; that is my reason.* He knew the arguments; he'd planned for them. Twisted each word, each strategy, each reason in his mind until the choice to massacre so many became a laudable feat, a move that changed the course of history and enabled the invasion to hap—

"Liar!" That roar raked the sky, a tower collapsing into rubble with its sheer might.

It exploded somewhere; hot, close, too close. The world folded again, whistling.

"The challenge is an excuse! Peace is an excuse!" Growling scythes of fire, blackened vapour, liquid gold dripping, dripping, dripping from the firmament while emberbane seared across it.

It hurried, the night. Restless and unsettled, torn ablaze and collapsing into rubble. Iron-hot on his throat, unbreathable and unsustainable, the odour of sweat and blood and grime and death churning on the wind, on Dante's body, on his stench.

It howled: "Why do you hunt the Meridian?" Darkness, fire, dross shattering.

The second assault force readied. Veterans, wounded, the bloody, the nuisances, the short-sighted and the disruptive. All lined up to die, all marching towards demise on his command, because of his plan, because—

"Why? Why, Legate?" Fire sparkled, snapping, liquid copper dripping, dripping, dripping.

"Why?" Fire burst from the Dragon One's wings, dross rolling and shattering to leak molten copper. "Why, Legate?"

Dante, kneeling. Panting, heaving, patting the floor in an echo of past movements, eyes quivering left, hopping right, unsteady like the shivering coursing through his body.

Fear. It imprisoned him. Fostered the fight within him. Forged a path to flee. Fractured him like a corpse consumed by the flames. Funnelled a cry for mercy against that mind of his so foolishly locked in a past that could never be forgotten.

"Because..." More panting, bare threads of words, marred by his enraged heartbeats.

Pounding on his lips, pounding as he sat on his heels in the emptiness of his terrace, mind lost in a battle almost a decade old. It endured, held by those golden threads that throbbed and throbbed like his quivering now sinking into his neck and clawing, clawing, clawing while the soul-link buckled.

"Because it's the only way!" Dante howled, coughing, teeth chafing. "The Meridian!"

"Because it's the only way! The Meridian!" Dante howled, coughing, clawing at his neck because he was swallowing iron, swallowing death, teeth chafing grime, tongue sour, throat tense, always dry, dry, dry, no matter how much water, how much wine he drank it was always, always dry. Half sweet, half stone-dust.

It whirled, the fire. Amidst those arcs unravelling into a burning deluge. The wind against them, the fog weeping, weeping, weeping because of that bellow rumbling from below, from the mines in the mountains, louder, louder, louder until the screams were lost but the agony and the misery and the pain and the deaths howled in the dust slamming into the Pass. The mountainside ripped loose, rocks and dust plummeting into the assault forces, into the enemy, into the machinery that crumbled as they all choked with debris, swarmed in ruin.

Legate Ilia's grin. Savage, like his. Younger, as well. "Kill the enemy, prevent an invasion... at the cost of losing mining tunnels."

*And the rebuilding efforts.* Dante stared at that grin, wiped the ash from his own face. "We'll need to secure the iron deposits again. At a priority."

She lowered the spyglass before dawn, her skin crusted with the dust. "No need. We can procure iron from the southern mines until we reopen these." Her fingers drummed on the contraption; she coughed before adding, "It won't hinder Ílun's reconstruction."

*The Meridian may be closer now.* The Legate walked back, pressed his back against the wall. Coughed; coughed again. His heartbeat pounded in his chest, in his forehead, in his wrists, the air so thin his hands shook, the fire still crackling in his ears because—

"You can't reach the Meridian!" Fire. It blossomed like tongues enraged but soaring into the infinite above, into the twin-dawn blotting the sky and the dusty mist into a silver mantle that will never leave. "Humans will never reach the Meridian on their own!"

"I will!" Dante, younger-Dante, older-Dante. Curled, distraught, screaming, contorted, fists quivering with the fires of his rage and the denial he'd unearthed from the abyss he ignored. "I will reach it, and I'll be Strategos!"

The thrums of war, a cacophony clattering like metal over metal, howls riled with the panic of survival and the fear of betrayal. It rampaged in the Pass, in the aftermath and amidst the rattle of armies fighting while boulders still crashed, hurling dust into the roar of rioting blades and shouted orders. Petra's, Sittia's. He heard them, amidst that mayhem—or perhaps not, because it was impossible but it was or had been, and it soared, distorted into nonsense, torn into absurd echoes and etching into wounds that would never scar. *To die was their duty.*

One growl, raging. "Strategos? You don't do it for a title!"

Enhancing the madness of that ache pounding throughout him.

The air trembled with a bellowing vexation, with bawling aggravation—then soothed, slithering, that whisper chiselling deeper, deeper, deeper enough to ask: "You know why you desire the Meridian, Legate... or does the truth embarrass you?"

The world burned like paper in the flame of a blazing lantern. Catching fire, screeching and crackling, contorting to escape the fiery tongues that crept, crept, crept to reveal the unblackened beyond where the truth still existed.

Embarrassment. Wrong success, wrong, wrong. Sittia's scowl, dry with blood and grime. Wrong, wrong, wrong. Fought from afar, too short of a battle, no honour to be gained. Coward to let them assemble the machines, coward for dallying too long.

Fire, just sparks. Falling in the ashfall, pounding and consuming itself into the lethargy of the aftermath.

Recognition, approval. From Marshal-Strategos Rachen, from Marshal-Strategos Arte, both late to arrive, both pleased with the outcome and the plans. Both satisfied with the selection of assault forces. From the Northern and Eastern Legions. From the Emerald Council which saw the leverage they'd earn and granted Egon Hold to Legate Dante Praeto.

His own bastion. His own region.

He was victorious.

It wasn't about victory, glory, duty. It'd never been.

The soul-link was ebbing, the golden threads scattered into sparks that petered out of Dante's awareness. Those curled like the blazing flakes of Ílun Fort, like the fiery gusts of that wind-storm that now raged—unstoppable, unyielding—as it melted the ink, consuming the brush-strokes of dread and denial.

It was exactly what Berserk had planned for—and so they watched, crouched atop the guardrail with splayed knees, elbows pressed into them.

The Legate had collapsed against the terrace's wall, one leg half bent before him, the other curled tightly to hold his fore-head. His hands had fallen to his sides, palm up, fingers twitching, twitching, twitching whenever the cold breeze chilled the sweat dotting his skin. He breathed in mouthfuls, each ragged intake shuddering alongside the enraged heart the alchemist couldn't tease any longer.

Berserk did not indulge on it. The incision they'd chiselled was now deep enough to allow for the truth—that unstoppable desire guiding the Legate—to bleed through this wound… and once it did, they'd carve it out through the second incision. Methodically and precisely, ruthlessly efficiently until a sole desire existed within the human.

Thirst for knowledge, for understanding.

It was the only worthy aspiration, the only acceptable desire from which evolution would come. The only ambition that would lead Dante to his fabled answer. The only craving the Dragon One allowed their mentees to have.

After all, The Rector had decreed it at the mission's outset: this human was more than a purveyor of a solution. He was a candidate to alchemist; a source-being.

# Egon Hold

### Zaro 15th, 17002 RE

# Dante & Berserk

The pre-dawn light gleamed over the polished floors, rimming the edges of the archways and casting a halo around the statues encased between them. Four towering Centurions armoured in marble—finely sculpted, and faithful to the simpler designs worn several centuries before.

Legate Dante Praeto halted between them, fists clenched as he contained the urge to hurry into the next corner. *I can't submit to this… restlessness.* His hands were shaking, his heart galloping out of his body, that whistling ringing in his ears. The events of the day before absorbed his thoughts, blending the attack on Liminal Harbour with the Siege of Ílun Fort, and traces of a nightmare assailing him like that sole question: *Why do I chase the Meridian?* As he paused, the corridor's unruly silence absorbed him.

He'd woken on the terrace's floor—*Like a coward*—drunk in memories and wine, and washed himself in utmost darkness while haunted by that question. *Why the Meridian?* He knew the answer. It'd existed since he'd found that old and shabby book, since he'd understood the implications of that concept. Since he'd realised that, by achieving it, perhaps—

Wrong.

Dante chewed on his lips, mauled the same precise spots he'd bruised the night before. *It's the stability it could bring, the achievement it'd be.* It was duty, he knew, and so he rearranged his camisia to cover the streaks at the base of his neck. *It's not the moment to—*

Rustling alerted him, and the Legate remembered the medici that had long fallen out of step. Aggravated—*I'm too distracted, too volatile*—he glanced over his shoulder to scowl at the Faber Medicus. The blonde man had stopped to whisper to his apprentices, the words sibilant fragments far from holding any meaning. Dante cleared his throat, impatient, and the Faber dipped his eyes before reaching the Legate.

Resuming their march, the group turned a corner, advancing through a darker corridor where four legionnaires awaited. Two youngsters, two veterans, all flanking the door to Sittia's chambers while assessing the newcomers with set expressions.

The Legate beckoned them to the door—but as the oldest soldier shifted to the handle, the engraving on her cuirass became clear. *The Council's Triskelion?* Dante remembered it then, a fragmented conversation lost amidst the emberbane dripping through Liminal Harbour and his absolute need to control himself. *Did Petra... warn me? Why?* That vague recollection twisted in his mind, bringing echoes of the night before and words he's heard while the door's handle unlocked. *Why would Gora—?*

"It is clear, Legate," the legionnaire confirmed, head angled in permission. "You may go in."

Composing himself, Dante gestured the medicus through first, granting permission, but followed immediately after. The apprentices tailed behind, tools rattling as the door closed, their hesitant footsteps edging into the scantily furnished room.

*I must focus on this moment.* His gaze lingered on the small round table, studying the unlit lantern; it was a simple device, charred and smeared with soot, the wick blackened at the tip, the oil— *Control yourself!* An empty jug; Dante's gaze etched on it. *Water or wine?* There were noises, but he couldn't look to the Centurion, couldn't ask the questions, seek the answers. *Afraid of my mother? Of her judgement?* Dante parted his lips, exhaled with control, steadied his countenance; only then, he glanced at the leftmost lectus.

Centurion Sittia sat with knees splayed, elbows pressed into them, hands clenched into tight fists. Her leathers stirred as she leant forward, her tousled iron hair shrouding her countenance and only revealing the jaw—open, trembling. Rattling the teeth.

*She's not well.* A chill—like the breeze on his sweat, like the mist in Ílun Fort—dripped through Dante's spine to augur death. *No; no, no, no. She can't die.* He dared a step forward, hesitated for a heartbeat, then ran his gaze through the medicus— kneeling before her, unreadable while inspecting her. Lifting a hand, touching her forehead and cheek, scowling when Sittia chuckled, saliva leaking from the corner of her mouth.

One thought lurked around him: *Poisoned? How?*

His pulse betrayed him. His mouth parted, his thoughts stuttered, "What… did you do?" *She can't die; not now.*

Sittia turned, chin up while searching for Dante with unfocused eyes—and found him a ragged breath after, offering a waxy, dulled countenance dotted with sweat. Her hair stuck to sweaty cheeks, hands buckling before she clenched them again; the burnt skin of her left arm twisted, reddish, burning again, bleeding anew.

"What had… to be done," she uttered, mouth quivering amidst the rousing panting. Disgust coated the inky darkness of her eyes. "You were born of a wolf, yet… are nothing b-but a lamb."

Dante couldn't answer, couldn't think, could breathe because the air was iron-hot, with that bite of scorched steel, with that greasy sweetness, half-ash, half-carrion. It whistled, sharp, on his right ear—on and on and on. *She can't die. Not now.* He noticed the apprentices moving, the medicus trying to palm Sittia's forehead. *Can't die before I—* The window opened, and the chilling breeze reignited the room's stench: a sweet rot, the musk of singed remains, of flames still eating her arm, her leg.

A scowl. Tense, heavy, trembling near his nose, eyelids twitching, one sole thought forming. *Did she vomit somewhere? Did she—?*

The Centurion chuckled bitterly again, coughing and gurgling until the fit twisted from mockery to choking. It brought the desperation, doubling the wrongness and the reasons prowling in the dark. It contorted in latent fear, with the dread of a lethal wound, with—

A body tumbled. The medicus rushed. The door remained locked.

One step, another, the Legate hesitated, stepping then stilling, watching as Sittia knelt on the floor, falling into her hands. Her limbs writhed, no longer hers, body flailing like a broken standard whirling and burning in the blackened vapours soaring from Liminal Harbour.

"You are not... my l-legacy, Dante." A slither of a whisper, a thread of hate. It looped around him like a noose, even as the death-throes came for her. "You... are not enough t-to— be the shadow that follows my name." Laughter, spitting. Bleeding the Legate from those wounds that'll never close. "Never... will be... enough."

It was a hollow of restless, peaceless serenity, chaos looming before unfolding, no longer dormant nor latent but waiting. Waiting. Waiting for the moment in which unreality collided with reality, when denial failed and truth charred and shattered that single, sharp blade upon which Dante's stability balanced itself.

So threatening. So imminent within.

So muffled. So reserved without.

Berserk revelled on that soul-link, focusing out to alight on the tip of the spear of the tallest legionnaire. The four were still there, standing against the wall opposite the door and squared at attention because *he* was near.

Legate Dante Praeto. Motionless in the corridor, so stoic, so impassive. He didn't fidget, breathing evenly, his presence pragmatic even as his face tilted slightly towards the door to Sittia's chambers—where the medici worked, murmuring, whispering. Leather creaked, rustling while they attempted to move her. Once. Twice. Even then, he waited. Waited. Waited for... something. For someone. Sometime.

A distressed, troubled man who continued to deny reality in the feeble, futile hope that doing so would preserve his sanity. An audacious strategist, aware of the long-term like few humans were, and encouraged by a quest for answers that seemed to defy reason solely because his reasons had been—for too many years—too deeply buried.

The Dragon One disregarded the Legate's body, focusing again in the soul-link.

It bled, Dante's mind.

Within the soul-link, the brush-strokes were lethargic, the ink too liquid to cover the livened beyond. They remained only because of a practised instinct, but the fiery gusts—so rapacious, so voracious—ate every remnant of the thick ink that'd denied that beyond. It permeated that hollow until it bled. Bled. Bled from those intangible wounds Dante had always denied to drip golden and shimmering. The past slipped, so full of memories recharged with atemporal alive elements. The very same that would enable the innovation Berserk now craved more than anything.

Yet the alchemist didn't coax it, not then at least, for some brush-strokes survived—with thinned bristles, and smearing translucent ink. They were doomed, those feeble remnants of denial. They were doomed to crumble the moment Sittia's pyre seared the night.

The silence swelled with deep scrutiny. Ahead, the Faber medicus straightened. Closer—with his back towards Dante—Marshal-Strategos Gora Rachen exhaled, exhausted and already weighed down with the consequences to come.

Dante glanced at his back, at the semblance of a profile not yet turned—*Not surprised*—while standing at attention one step behind. His eyes fixed again in the wall behind the medicus before he rationed his blinks. Purposefully. Methodically. For that brief darkness pounded darker, restless but listless. With Sittia's death. With Liminal's emberbane. With Ílun's blackened vapour. With her bleeding after that last charge. With the Nadir, brutal, spewing lava, burning her pauldron into her. With her words, ruthless, spitting—

Gora rolled his hand, and the morning light—seeping through the window—ricocheted on his rings. It refocused the Legate. *Fool. Control yourself.*

"I understand, Faber Medicus, this may have been... just the delayed onset of the fog's symptoms." Gora's whisper carried the roughness of grief, although it soaked the space with an implicit command.

A perspective that tolerated no challenges. *Like Sittia's. Always.*

Dante's cheek twitched before he repressed it, fists clenching behind him. *Gora's legionnaires guarded the door. Petra warned me.* His pulse hammered like a forced march, remarking the pounding in his head, in his wrists. The whistling in his ear. *Someone could've slipped poison on his command. Had I listened...* His eyes fixed again in the wall ahead. Her last words rang in his mind, seared in a permanent echo. *Never enough.* That question returned, clinging like the emberbane slithering down Ílun's towers. *Not now!* Dante's jaw clenched as a growl built on his throat. He swallowed it.

The Faber Medicus dipped his head, silent. "It was most unfortunate, but not unexpected, given the fog's death toll."

"Indeed," Gora half-turned, dismissing the man with a roll of his wrist. His pale green eyes set on Dante, then beckoned to the door. "Duty follows death, Legate."

*Duty.* Dante straightened, met the Strategos' gaze. Blinked once. Swallowed cinders, swallowed again not to cough. *Death?*

Gora's features softened, but there was no mercy on him. Just a command. "See to the arrangements for Sittia's pyre, and inform the Hold. The chain of command cannot break."

## Juçe

CENTURION, EASTERN LEGIONS OF FIRARD

The Faber medicus was a pitiful man, keeping his back to the closed door—*As if securing an escape path*—and his gaze down. Juçe clenched his jaw, angling his head yet remaining silent.

"I was with her at the end. There were no final requests." He spoke with control—but the fingers of his right hand twitched, and he clasped both behind his back. "I understand the Legate will see to the pyre. Tonight."

*That fool.* "Understood," Juçe beckoned towards the door. "Dismissed."

# Dante

LEGATE OF EGON HOLD, EASTERN LEGIONS OF FIRARD

"This… will have consequences," Imperial Elixane Ritz whispered, perched at the edge of a barrel. It creaked as she rubbed her face, muffling her next whisper. "Most of the observers came to watch the War Games for Centurion Sittia. Since they depart tomorrow, they'll be here tonight, for the p—"

Her voice faded. Dante groaned, that minimal sound echoing in the half-empty shield-room. He didn't flinch but clenched both fists, staring at the mossy, wet door. *Duty. Just duty. Always.* He forced himself into reality—to gauge the rumours that'd spread like wildfire, fed by Sittia's legend, by Lady Seve's Truce, by the measures legionnaires often took not to be disgraced. *My father… could've asked for the poison. Gora could've provided it.* The grit of grime dragged across his jaw when it tensed. *I've seen it—done it—before.*

Liquid fire; drip, drip, dripping all over Liminal Harbour, carmine tongues devouring vessels, eating legionnaires on his command. On Ílun Fort, on the Nadir slopes, on the Lunar Sea. Fire, everywhere. Eating Sittia's arm, suffocating— *Focus, you fool!* His teeth chafed as he worked them, mulling his thoughts until only the funeral rites mattered. For a Centurion, a renowned one—but just a Centurion.

"The fog… had consequences. That is what the Hold will be reminded of," the Legate finally whispered, emphasising every word lest his mind wander again. "Another reason as to why the joint research must continue." *Focus; you were working on it.* He breathed, ignoring the stench. "I'll finish the... selections for the delegation tonight."

Elixane straightened, her long braid sliding away from her shoulder. She was dressed in the common uniform of emerald trousers and a white camisia, well-rested albeit weariness slowly marred her countenance. She looked down, pondering the questions that couldn't be asked, raising her hands to signal—then lowered them again, as if having thought better. *She knows. Of course she would.*

"I will reinforce the patrols," she stated at last, easing her features with every breath.

Dante hummed affirmatively, his gaze etching again in the crumbling door. The Citadel was no longer safe; the ramparts, the stables, the balconies, his office. Nothing. Unrest was marching towards the Hold; they both knew it. They'd discussed it before, soon after Lady Seve's spies disclosed her view, then again when she'd sent that clockjay. *I must focus... on the consequences.* That room had been the only confined space he'd found devoid of lanterns and lit by sunlight; it poured through the loophole, brightening a strip of iron-hewn stone. He frowned at it, dragging his gaze towards Elixane.

"Do we know whether our reports reached the Sestelii guards in the Gorge?" *If the news reaches them now...* He waited as she shook her head, beckoning to the door. "I will speak to the Watchers and organise the... funeral." Pausing, he raised a hand, fingers sketching, *"Ensure those patrols respond to us, and only to us. Use legionnaires reporting to Ciro or Rhea."*

Elixane's gaze narrowed in search of a reaction, waiting for a heartbeat before dipping her head—in respect and acknowledgement, although dread still shimmered in her pale grey eyes.

When she left, Dante stayed in the armoury, gaze etched on that strip of light. *This... augurs chaos. It's another prelude to war.* The room's air was dry, metallic, dusty. Dante's fingers found his throat, curling as if to grab that greasy half-sweetness and hurl it out. He flinched when brushing the reddened streaks.

"There are some who conquer with Legions. You conquered with words, Dante." Strategos Gora stretched the silence, seemingly lost in the feeble noon.

Silver light, overcast by the sweeping clouds, and weeping like the trails over Bruma Pass' mountainsides. *This… is not personal. Never was.* Shade and light danced over the cedar table, prolonging the jar's shadow. *Just another lesson to take.* His jaw tensed, the lie sour in—

"You gave us stability, first with the Retreat and now with the Truce." The Strategos' voice. Deep. Steady. Anchoring. "Tarnishing it with a tribunal for a dead Centurion… is not appropriate."

The Legate's gaze snapped to his mentor's, chin angled. *So he admits it.* He remained as he was, standing at rest near the bookshelves on the private chamber, his heart galloping because something was unfolding, tearing, whistling a scream far behind but somewhere deep in his mind.

He held that gaze, unwavering. Waiting. Waiting because a new challenge—a new conflict—loomed upon them and the Strategos must have known, or the Council's cohorts wouldn't have come with him. *He knows; likely more than I do.* His right fist clenched behind his back, his heartbeat pounding in his wrist, in his chest, in his neck.

"Perhaps is best that the rites… remain modest." The words locked in his throat until the Legate swallowed a burial stone.

A hundred reasons. All unspoken. Not to offend Sestel by praising the one that attempted to kill Lady Seve, not to offend the Legions by not remembering the Ash-Walker, not to signal inner chaos to their enemies and allies, not to provide more arguments to the Forces resenting the Strategists.

The Strategos countenance darkened although he dipped his head. "The Centurion did her duty; that will be enough."

"The Gorge's unit confirmed that Seve received our despatch at dawn." Ilia's expression was as controlled as her whisper. She lifted two fingers, a veilwing's roll clutched between them. "Lady Seve sent a response."

Dante watched the proffered letter, avoiding her eyes. He picked it, the paper crackling like fire, then ambled towards a somewhat private corner—as private as the ramparts could be. He rolled it with a thumb, then angled the head to observe the Seve seal. *What would it be? Chaos, or stability?* He unfurled it slowly, minding its rustling before reading it twice.

*Legate; the reports are safe. Lady Hori Varre will oversee them personally. Further materials will be sent overnight. We expect to cross the Gorge soon.*

*Interesting.* Dante straightened, aware of Ilia's approaching steps, of the tension on her features—recognition but not relief, warm but private. He didn't react, for there was nothing to acknowledge. *Just duty, and the challenge ahead.* He proffered the paper back to his peer.

"Any other news?" He asked at last, careful. "I'll finish the selections for the delegations tonight. We must honour our part of the Truce and send medici across as well."

Ilia frowned, tense. *She never frowns in public.* Her onyx eyes darkened into an abyss while she studied him for a long moment. Waiting. Waiting before skimming the neat handwriting. Waiting once more before rolling the paper. Her hand stretched to return the letter, but her eyes locked on his; unwavering. *Concerned? Ignore it. Focus on the Truce, on the aftermath.*

"I was ordered by the Marshals to stay in Egon Hold. Petra's and Ler's cohorts as well." A whisper, shushed by her fingertips lacing around her camisia's cuffs, hand-signalling, *"War edges closer."*

"I was informed..." Dante whispered, aware of the bewilderment flickering through her gaze. Locked on his, even as he gestured, *"It always does."*

Yet a new question haunted him; one he didn't allow to reflect in his face. Was it worth it, the Meridian? Or would it be just another wrong success?

# Ferro Keep

Zaro 15ᵀᴴ, 17002 RE

HEAD OF THE SEVE HOUSE, SESTEL

*Some think that war wins peace.* Lady Calya Seve leant over the table, tucking a wayward strand of caramel hair. As she did so, her gaze sifted through the parchment map spread above the desk—a recent depiction of the Ochrese continent, its frontiers, and the names of relevant cities and ports. Dotted red lines connected it across the Azure Abyss and the Zephyr Depths towards the Verdant continent—where Sestel and Firard absorbed the land. *Fools. It is trade routes.*

A tiny smirk curled the edges of her mouth, her hand moving to tap twice over the strangely shaped Argo Bay—crowded by islands filled with ancient ruins and thus the subject of too many legends. *As only sailors can concoct.* It was currently under Lares' control—*Thus, it's Sestelii territory*—but it was no secret that Sessentas craved passage through it. *And no alliance survives a frontier.* She glanced back at the lines connecting that land towards the ports of the Central Legion—and her smirk deepened with irony. *Empires rot at the edges, and Firard will, if Sessentas favours my offer.* Such a transaction would increase her power—

The breeze chilled her shoulders, swirling with a remnant of the lanky librarian, a drop of ink reminding her of Quintus. The map rustled as if demanding an answer—but Calya pressed it down with a finger, crushing the zephyr's rebellion. *They'll regret presuming I had no power. Tonight, I'll—*

The door knocked. Thrice and insistent.

Calya straightened, folding the map in half and covering the inked letterhead of the half-written note she was crafting. *Not Asier*, she realised, hearing the repeated knocks.

When she commanded it, Ruria Laxalt slid into the chambers, locking behind. She was dressed in her scout's dark leathers, the uniform crisp albeit her braid frayed at the edges; reddish strands framed her features, sticking with sweat as she bowed. *She ran here. Why?* Calya watched her for another moment, her questioning interrupted as the youth reached forth, a veilwing roll pinched between her pale fingers. Thin, ink-stained.

*The Firardian spies!* Calya picked it in one swift motion, tracing the torn edges before unravelling the crumpled paper.

*The Ash-Walker met her end; she'll be taken to the pyre at midnight. A medicus confirmed the fog's symptoms. Excess troops depart tomorrow.*

Impassive, Lady Calya reread the note, staring at the words to demand them to confess their secrets. *Who killed her? Centurion Juçe Praeto, or the Legate? And why?* Exhaling, she ignored the unsolvable mystery to glance at her aide. Ruria's breathing had eased, and she'd loosened her fraying braid to weave it again. *Must have run here after receiving it.*

"Did you confirm whether there was any announcement of a tribunal?" Calya asked, toying with the paper between her hands.

"Imperial Elixane didn't mention it," Ruria confessed, lingering while her lips pursed into a pout. "I thought prudent not to ask. It could reveal we replaced her spy."

The Lady hummed approvingly, noticing how the youth brightened.

Returning to the letter, she half-turned until the incoming light bathed the paper. *Sittia could've been silenced to prevent dishon-*

*our, then.* There were no marks she could detect, except the grease of sweaty hands smudging a still-wet ink. *Her death is useful, but her legend will remain a problem.* She turned the note on her hands, prodding it for marks that could unveil a secret code —only to find none. *It could reflect poorly on Sestel and the Truce. I have to—*

"We should not respond," Ruria whispered, her certainty enough to break the Lady's concentration. The redhead waited until their eyes met, then beckoned to the note under perusal. "This is not an official communication."

*A fast learner.* "Indeed. We must act as though unaware." Calya nodded, refolding the letter and tucking it under the map. "Do you have news from Asier?"

"The Lord was at the enclosure, overseeing the arrival of the Firardian reports, and vetting soldiers to guard Lady Varre's office." The youth perked as she spoke, the echoes of a proud smile skipping in her voice—all while she nimbly laced the end of her braid. "He seemed... preoccupied with the safety of the former."

*As I am.* Calya nodded slowly, dragging her fingers through the desk, her thoughts scattering from Asier to the map again. The breeze lifted its rough edge, reminding her of the plans she'd crafted. *Tonight. Not before. And on my terms.* She discarded those concerns, pausing them until her attention returned to Sestel. *This is an excellent opportunity.*

"I'll write to the Legate," the Lady confirmed, lifting two fingers to quell the youth's retort. Once the silence lingered enough, she rolled the hand, explaining, "Confirming the reception of the medici's reports would be helpful to remind the Legate of Firard's duties regarding the joint investigation." *To Hori's satisfaction, of course.*

Ruria straightened, patting her redone braid into a neat bun. "Then I shall send this through the Gorge's patrol, my Lady." Her eyes flicked up, waiting for approval before hesitation swallowed her in. She dallied for a moment, toying with her leather vambraces beforehand-signalling, *"My Lady... the matriarch's General seems to be spying on me."*

*Not unexpected.* "Understood," Calya confirmed, steeling her gaze as she rounded on the desk. "Then, after you send this letter, fetch Asier for me."

# Asier

LORD. SEVE HOUSE, SESTEL

The breeze seeped from between the parted windows, and the door closing swiftly behind him. It swayed the sheer curtains, shifting the patterns of light and reflecting on the ruffled feathers crowning the awakened clockjay. The iridescent contraption skipped across the table, fluttering its bladed wings and lifting its tail as if readying to fly. It took off within a heartbeat, hurtling through the ajar window like a soaring shooting star.

*To the Sessentas Minister?* "Ruria urged me to come," Asier explained, locking the door and stepping inside. His worries weighed on him with every inch he crossed. "What happened?"

The Lady didn't turn, instead gazing at the papers scattered over the desk. He'd seen that expression, not during battle and neither in court—but before it, when making plans nobody anticipated. *Who concerns her?* Asier pondered, studying her profile—the slight crease between her brows, the focus darkening her azure eyes. *It's not what happened two nights ago*, he noticed, keeping his distance if only not to interrupt those thoughts.

When Calya sighed, her frown persisted like a lingering annoyance, albeit her gaze eased just slightly. "Centurion Sittia is dead, and the Firardian are blaming the fog," she stated at last, proffering a crumpled veilwing note. "Read."

Asier strode closer to accept the roll, his calloused hands fumbling with it. When it crinkled open, he read the scribbles twice before hissing, "Impossible! Lady Varre tended to the Centurion. She was well!"

"She was not *this* ill, although I leveraged her minor symptoms during the negotiation," Calya murmured, rounding the desk to nudge the window inward, narrowing the sliver of air it allowed through. "I gather she was poisoned, perhaps to prevent the dishonour of a tribunal... or even living after we returned her."

The Lord pursed his mouth, rereading the note. That translucent, ink-stained piece carried more weight than any royal seal he'd seen pressed into a gold-rimmed letter. *I should've considered this! Advise Calya before!* He exhaled, sliding a hand through his auburn hair to hide the quivering in his fingers—then folded the note, returning it.

"This could undermine the Varre healers' reputation alongside Hori's." He swallowed hard, displeased. "Firard could also accuse us of poisoning Sittia."

"They could..." Approval grazed Calya's eyes, warming her expression if only for a moment. "But it would be a matter of coercing public opinion in our favour again, and the Emerald Legions' honour would tatter like a forgotten banner left to rot in the Peaks of Nadir." A smirk curled her lips ever so gently. "That approach is a benefit of having returned the legionnaires instead of humiliating Firard. We acted honourably, and people would easily believe us."

Asier frowned, silenced by his worries. *I'm missing something; she's too calm.* He watched as Calya stared through the glazed casements. Her gesture only harboured cold calculation, yet there was a darkness in her stance. A reminder that only a day had passed since he'd found her cowering under the desk, trembling in panic yet refusing to admit what had terrified her.

"Teoda's General is moving through Ferro Keep. I gather he's spying on Ruria" she informed, disregarding the prior conversation as if the death of the Ash-Walker could not spark the largest war since the Grand Conclave.

The Lord's jaw tightened in silence, left hand drifting to the hilt of his sword—an old gesture learned long before fear had a name. *This must have been why.* He looked down, blinking before his gaze fell from the desk and onto the floor to scowl at the lack of answers. *I should've told her when the servants advised me, but...* Asier curled his hand around the hilt of his sword like a drowning man to driftwood. *I should've known that she'd discover it. I'm always powerless to help her.*

His nails sank into the hilt's engraving. "What do you need me to do?"

Calya eased, raising one palm up, forefinger stretched. "Write to the troops on Tormenta Plains; we must prepare against a possible flanking attack from the Eastern Legion. Discreetly, and out of caution."

"Are you worried Firard may retaliate after Sittia's death?" He ventured, imagining the map.

"No. The way I returned the Ash-Walker to them was meant to cause inner unrest. It'd be foolish not to prepare." Her voice steeled as she lifted another finger. "Beyond that, I also need Vega Fortress to fortify the northern border; I'll inform them myself."

Asier glanced again at the table, catching a glimpse of the map spread open atop it as if the act might clear the fog of his understanding. After a moment, he pressed his nose with both hands, hiding a grimace between his palms.

"Vega Fortress? Do you think Orenos may attack? Could they've been behind the landslide and the fog?" He groaned, pained; his thoughts were pounding against his skull like a storm trying to break through. *If I could only see what she sees...*

Her slender hand pressed into his arm, recalling his attention before withdrawing to signal, *"Or my mother could've picked the wrong allies. She seemed... particularly confident this time."* She didn't smile, and her following whisper was sharper than any blade. "We are also moving four stratoi towards the Claw's Fold."

"With what excuse?" Asier gritted, his jaw tightening and loosening as if he'd chewed through his worries only to find steel. "The Seve armies cannot move inland."

His forefinger traced the patterns on his hilt while glancing at the map again. Although the Seve armies often marched inland to reach the different frontiers turned battlefields, keeping the civil order within Sestel was handled, exclusively, by the Luxa enforcers. *And the Exarch could easily misunderstand this repositioning.* His tongue clicked as his gaze etched in the map. *Adding that Calya is concentrating too much political power, and—*

"We have done it before, Asier," she observed, pressing a manicured finger into the map's depiction of the Claw's Fold—the westernmost crook of the Petricor Mountains. "From there, those stratoi can move to the Vast Expanse, to Tormenta Plains…" She dragged her finger north and south, then westwards. "—or even return to Ferro Keep." Then, hovering over the land, her fingers signalled, *"It can also make Ferro Keep seem… undefended."*

*Undefended?* The Lord scowled until understanding struck him silent, crushed by the implications she was seeing so clearly. "You are setting a trap." A whisper, first. Then a gesture, *"For Teoda."*

He saw the manoeuvre on her nod. The matriarch's troops were not enough to arrange a coup, and even if she did, the Exarch could send the Luxa enforcers. The only thing that she'd be left with were the same tools Teoda had always used. *Gossip, allies, or poison.*

Calya watched him as he thought, approval softening her features. It was the tilt of her head, how she tucked a strand of caramel hair behind an ear, the tightness of her lids, and that hint of a smirk pulling the left corner of her lips. *Always the left.* Yet it was empty. Concerned. Weighed by the darkness surrounding her.

"Have you slept?" Asier dared, ignoring the politics for a moment. "You should—"

"After the Truce I've been… too focused in my duty." She dismissed him with a roll of her hand, as she'd done enough times for him to recognise the lie—yet before he could retort, her features steeled. "I'll inform the Exarch of the repositioning at the Claw, but not of Orenos. We cannot afford him to panic." She paused, thoughtful. "I should meet my mother soon enough. Tomorrow, at the latest."

The Lord groaned. "I'll prepare for it."

# Teoda

The garden was smaller than Lady Teoda Seve remembered, although it remained well kept. The cold, harsh breeze of the high-mountains swivelled around its bushes, eliciting a blended perfume which oscillated between appealing and appalling. *Whoever changed the flowers clearly thinks gaudy means grand.* The Lady soured privately, arranging her carmine half-cape across her lap. *At least they kept the marble benches.* The empty regnum board before her—placed atop a portable table—was wooden-made yet varnished to a sheen, its grid traced with precise carvings.

Taking her time, she toyed with the pair of stones between her fingers—polished shells, shimmering iridescent. Across the garden, a few aides shuffled uselessly in her silence, stilling when their noise became apparent. Only then did Teoda place the shells on the board, parallel to the bottom edge, then gestured with her free hand.

The General beside her—Ayere, a stout man with a well-trimmed beard—nodded curtly. His calloused fingers sank into his leather pouch, retrieving two rounded carnelians.

"The Laxalt youth seems to handle the Watchers… but she's heavily guarded." He whispered quietly while scowling at the board—then placed his pieces vertically a few grids away. "I have not discovered what her role is."

*A spy-master, most likely. Crucial to remove.* Teoda hummed in acknowledgement, producing two more shells from her pouch and toying with them. *I thought spies remained Asier's remit.*

Her lips pursed as she placed her shells close to the carnelians. "And Lady Varre?"

A grimace threatened General Ayere's lips, his gaze etched on the newly placed pieces. *Understanding or confusion? Fascinating.* Teoda refrained from smirking, noticing how roughly he rubbed his next two stones.

"Her guard is akin to the Exarch's. The finest Seve soldiers, changing rotations, unpredictable schedules..." He pushed one stone onto the board and dallied, one thick finger pressed atop it —then shifted it to the next position, placing the other one. His nose scrunched as he straightened. "She was granted a building near the enclosure, but it is a fortress of its own."

Teoda dipped her head, agreeing with the General only because she'd seen the guard herself—a testament to how relevant Hori was to Calya. *That butcher can prove difficult to handle.* Idly retrieving her third pair of shells, she assessed the regnum board while pondering her options. Swaying Hori's loyalty verged on the impossible, yet arranging her demise was outright hazardous—and not only due to that escort. *It'd be akin to blunting one's own sword.* After all, she was fundamental to the joint research of the so-called Chained Truce, and a source of pride for Sestel given her discoveries. Killing her would cause too many unwanted setbacks. *Despite the foolishness of trying to poison a healer—and her in particular.*

Leaning forward, Teoda placed both shells. "When is she travelling to Firard, General?"

The man's cuirass creaked as he drew a sharp breath. "She'll likely depart on the seventeenth, my Lady." A droplet of sweat emerged on his forehead, and he straightened on his seat, glancing at her. "Infiltrating a spy in her escort would be challenging, given Lord Aurri's measures... but it could be attempted."

*And that could prove useful, perhaps in sowing unrest amidst the delegation.* "See to the possibility, General, including how to remove that youth. Laxalt," Teoda beckoned him towards the garden's entrance door, not oblivious to the concern on his eyes. "You may go."

He stood up solemnly, leaving the pouch on the bench with a careful—*Too careful*—gesture. His orders seemed to weigh on his eyes, yet he bowed elegantly and marched out with a steady gait. The echo of his footsteps died when an aide closed the garden's door, while another one—young, pale, dark-haired—bowed to Teoda in a silent offer.

She gestured to the board with a flick of her wrist, and the boy fetched the discarded pouch. The carnelians looked over-sized between his bony fingers, the afternoon's light gleaming over them as he stared at the board.

*I must remove Asier… but poisoning him is unfeasible.* The Lady's eyes narrowed as the aide leant over the board, right hand hesitating above it. *He may be blind to Calya's intentions, but not to other political manoeuvres.* Her scowl—unbeknownst until then—relaxed as the boy placed both stones in a surprisingly clever position. Yet he stood up with a neutral countenance, bowing to signal the end of his turn. *And even if Asier doesn't foresee my plan, my daughter will.* The scowl returned, bitterly intentional. *She learned too well, unfortunately.*

Displeased, Teoda retrieved her fourth pair of shells while reviewing the board. *Alas, I refuse to land in another of Calya's stalemates,* she decided, preventing a grimace. Both the General and the boy played with excessive caution, perhaps even with deference, as if to let her win. *Weaklings.* The impossibility of enjoying a decent regnum match soured her as much as the gaudy flowers ruining the garden. *Perhaps it is time to be more aggressive,* the Lady concluded, surrounding a carnelian with her shells to preemptively capture it once the game's second phase began. *After all, I proposed this to the Orenians.*

The boy waned within the span of a breath, retrieving his fourth pair with slow, hesitant hands.

*I must remove Calya now, before she accumulates more power,* Teoda decided, aware of the permanency of that removal; not figurative, for such attempts had already failed. *My fault, for not making her predictable and meek, like Enzo.* Her youngest child was a perfect tool, presentable in social events, clever enough not to make a fool of himself, yet not too clever to outmanoeuvre her like Calya had done. *At least from her I learned to tailor my reprimands,* the Lady recognised, watching as the boy's clean hands—*Just like Enzo's*—pressed two more stones into the grid. *More reason to remove my daughter; once she's gone, Asier will be easy to kill.*

Tilting her head, Lady Teoda studied the recent placement; the aide was weaving a sensible strategy, even if aimed only at the short term. *A pawn; and he thinks he'll survive this board.* But it was a common mistake, to underestimate the importance of correctly placing the pieces and thus failing to aim for the long term. She couldn't blame the boy; most people weren't fit to play regnum at all.

Retrieving her fifth, and last, pair of shells, Teoda rubbed them in her palm. They warmed quickly, and when she pressed them into a spot, the boy frowned. Confusion, most likely, since her move was—to the naïve observer—seemingly illogical. *Yet sometimes, only the unexpected can move the board away from a stalemate.* Teoda knew, since that was exactly how Calya had outplayed her—by leveraging the unexpected as part of a scheme grander than she'd anticipated. *Something unforeseeable, yet perilous if it reaches the wrong ears. But in my terms, of course.*

A smirk teased her lips when the boy rushed to position his carnelians, restraining a pleased smile.

The Lady nodded, enjoying his naivety. "Let the game begin."

#  Calya & Amok

The lantern's flame bathed the library with a copper glow, its warmth fading past the tables to outline the nearest stacks. Lady Calya Seve paused at the light's rim, seeking the next lantern and finding it not too far away. When she spun its lever, the flames stirred to life.

She walked deliberately, one step every three rushed heartbeats. *Fear is a choice*, she reminded herself, too mindful of her breathing, too focused on her stance. When the aisle forked and she veered right—towards the next lantern—her restlessness had subdued. She skimmed the shelved books, saw nothing of relevance, and considered her plan again. *Evaluate all angles, test all motives. Never yield.* Her lips pressed with resolve, crushing their subtle tremors.

Halting under the History banner, Calya spun the next lantern and waited. Three heartbeats, then she steered towards Myths only to hear the rustling of paper somewhere else. *On the Philosophy aisle?* She veered in that direction, one choice—one truth—remarking her every step. *I'm not a pawn; I'm not powerless.*

Quintus stood between the stacks, his cerulean gaze etched in the book held between his long-fingered walnut hands. He was still dressed in a librarian's black-and-white robe, and wore his hair buzzed at the sides with the top woven back in neat braids. *Not human; just an illusion.* Yet the book thudded when closed, the cover's leather stirring as he slotted it back onto the shelf.

"My Lady," he welcomed, dipping his bright, cerulean eyes. "I'm humbled to speak with you again."

Amok waited, perched atop a stack, one leg dangling, the other drawn in taut; their forearm rested on that knee, fingers clawing the air, weaving the glamour. Quintus; an echo of their own source-being, a façade they enjoyed recreating. His accuracy was useful, more Naturalist than any other imitation and amusing to craft since it changed, mildly, every few millennia.

After another lantern lit, they compelled the glamour to retrieve a book, pages rustling when flipped. Moments later, Calya turned that last corner—and Amok soul-linked her without hesitation.

Her alive elements burst like lightning searing a storm, lashing the aisle, the glamour, the books and herself with a hundred considerations. Words linked with each other, plans meshed lattices of possibilities, and a thought spun around her like a storm of its own: *I'm not a pawn; I'm not powerless.*

Power.

The Untamed One pressed a hand into the shelf to lean over, enthralled by a singular detail—the crystal shards sinking into her body had vanished. Instead, the wall stood behind her, impervious and thicker than before. It jailed the three shadows of her past, albeit each was a distorted blur with arms of twisting tendrils and faces dimmer than nothingness.

To Amok, that recovery was not miraculous but another consequence of her relentless need to adjust and, thus, survive. A flaw that brought a pretence of stability at the cost of a hundred future repercussions. A curious detail to later exploit in their quest to perfect the incarnate soul-skill. It was part of her, and fed the boldness guiding her to approach Quintus with calculated confidence.

When she halted closer, the alchemist willed the glamour to dip his eyes. "My Lady. I'm humbled to speak with you again."

She pressed her lips, enduring no fear, no anger, nothing. Just one decision: *I'll feel only what I choose to feel.* It overpowered the soul-link, thickening that wall with every repetition.

"We are past pleasantries, alchemist," Calya stated, so unwavering even her shadows stilled. "If you want an answer, you'll solve my questions first."

That boldness toed the courage of the fools, teasing the absurd as if it were sheer folly—yet it was a Natural reaction, the subject of Amok's study, the trait auguring that promised evolution. The alchemist allowed it, willing glamour-Quintus to tilt his head.

*Caution?* The Lady assessed the illusory librarian, seeking a gesture that would betray his composure—only to find none. His eyes blinked slowly, his mouth never pursed, his shoulders didn't tense as she studied him overtly. It was the epitome of self-control, a façade so perfect it couldn't be anything but a falsehood.

"How did the burden of answering fall to me?" She punctuated each word amidst a silence that tolerated no disruption.

*Why me? Why after so many years?* If the legends held any truth, the Alchemists had vanished since The Reclamation—five centuries before the Grand Conclave and the Emerald Accords. *There must be a reason for their return, and I can't be it.* As the silence survived, taunting, Calya arched a brow in an unspoken demand.

Quintus shrugged. "Because you were asked to."

*Not a response.* Calya hummed, noting the observation while aware of its implications. *Either he won't or can't answer.*

"You say that..." Her tone was so smooth it lingered like an observation. "—but it seems to me you are here only because you were charged with collecting my response."

A grin split Amok's non-face. So savage the void leaked between their fangs, so elated their eyes narrowed to slits, so eager they leant forth just to watch her meet the absurd and threaten it as if knowable.

A dozen thoughts clung to that simple observation, each a possibility she evaluated like the pieces placed on a regnum board: for what they were and what they enabled, for what they could and would be. One thought cleared first—*He has a master*—and its certainty terrified the shadows behind the wall. They howled in distress, tendril-like arms clawing at the wall only to stall when another thought roared louder: *But it doesn't mean he's powerless.*

Power.

The glyphs surrounding the Untamed One shaped that single concept, but they lifted a finger to command the glamour.

Quintus bowed, conceding. "Be that as it may... what does it tell you about power?"

Calya watched him, gauging. *Careful.* Fear lurked within the all-encompassing silence, circling the aisle until only the lantern's flame crackled in the distance, muffled by the unbreakable glass that shielded them. *He may be a pawn, but not all pawns are powerless.* That terror towered over her until breathing became taxing, her throat so tense she could barely exhale.

"That discussing power engrosses you." Calya stated at last, tilting her head and ignoring that wayward strand that tumbled onto her cheek. "What makes this answer so important?" *He must have a purpose; stakes he's bound to.*

Amok teetered on the shelf's edge, lured by an intrigue that knew no bounds and refused to loosen its grip. It twisted into hunger for understanding, wrenched into desire for the impossible that happened—against all odds—before them. Driven by that reckless curiosity, the Untamed One descended from their perch, cloak fluttering as they alighted, gently, behind the woman.

She rolled her fingers, holding Quintus' gaze while unaware of the alchemist stalking her—lurking, circling, splotching the automaton-lanterns with abyssal ink until their flames crackled, refusing the darkness. A meek sound, eaten in the surrounding silence, absorbed by the dozen alive elements weaving from her. Luring Amok, teasing them, taunting them with one thought: *Not all pawns are powerless.*

Power.

She wielded it wisely, even against a Soul Transmuter alchemist—for her questions were strategic. Pieces placed in a regnum board, traps carefully laid for whenever they revealed the weaknesses of their mission.

"That the topic engrosses you." She was assembling a killing ground one word at a time—and one of Amok's inky tendrils pushed a caramel curl into her cheek just to see her react. Unperturbed, she added, "What makes this answer so important?"

The Untamed One towered over her—then glanced at that impenetrable crystal wall, at their target, at the plans that soared through the soul-link to build malleable edifices upon a hundred schemes. For curiosity's sake, they postulated one question.

What would push her, once more, to the edge of boundless terror?

Eager to unearth the answer, Amok willed glamour-Quintus to speak. "Power is a fundamental dynamic. Something that exists at all levels of existence, in too many shapes, for different periods." The illusion clasped both hands, head tilting. "Because of it, power is fundamental."

"In that case, you must know the answer," Calya retorted so quickly, her thoughts were wordless—just light, flickering in the darkness. "The legends and the myths never speak of your origin. You must have had centuries, even millennia, to find an answer."

Amok narrowed their eyes, each facet refracting her intentions. She was taunting them exactly as she'd done with the Legate—even when it wouldn't work as expected. Yet it gave the alchemist more time to evaluate her.

"But *our* answer is not *your* answer," Quintus emphasised each word by raising a hand. "You are not unfamiliar with power. What is it for you?"

*He doesn't* need *the answer.* Calya concluded, adjusting one drape of her skirt with slow precision—as if that maze of a conversation would be solved with that neat arrangement. *This is a game. A pathway to something else.* Talking to that being, that alchemist, was akin to playing regnum while blindfolded while the pieces were being repositioned in the darkness. *I can only keep prodding.*

She rolled her shoulders—a minimal but deliberate motion— and a memory unfolded with it, bringing a clue. *A workable hurdle*, she recalled the librarian's assessment of her humanity, and glanced at Quintus; he was a perfect replica, if too impassive. *She also offered power.* That thought almost coaxed her lips to smirk. *A taunt; nothing else.* Yet even when the relentless questioning was nothing but a game, even when that conversation was avoidance phrased into careful sentences, there was one nuance left to leverage. *But I need to concede first. Partially, at least.*

"Power is a truth," Calya dared, lifting her chin. "While another truth is that coming here, to ask me these questions, poses a risk to you." She waited on the silence of nothingness— then tilted her head, resetting the conversation. "Thus, you resort to illusions. Quintus is one."

"Quintus is a glamour." Amok's voice tore reality, fracturing their own invisibility in a premeditated test.

Fear roared through the soul-link, fissuring the crystal wall until it leaked smoke, raking through her composure, scourging her reason. She gasped, turning and stepping back as her eyes widened, gaze surging like a string unravelling the delusion of safety, defying all sense of scale, and struggling to meet its end.

Her fear reeled when her gaze found Amok's, and the shadows' howls blistered logic. They pounded on the wall, ill-shaped arms clawing into the fissures and deepening its pathways. It deafened her for a heartbeat, stealing her breathing for another, only to be leashed by that chant she kept repeating. *To fear is to surrender. To fear is a judgement.* Her tension unravelled, smothering the terror and restoring the wall—silencing the shadows hammering its insides, muffling its howls, and banning emotions. In the fourth heartbeat, only reason survived. *I will not succumb to it.*

A compelling cue, the impact novelty had on her terror, on her self-control. It seemed a lifetime of the matriarch's inexplicable inconsistency had trained her to resist repetition. Amok learnt from that observation, restoring their invisibility.

Quintus spoke for them. "The answer is the first price you must pay to access true power. Time-unbound power."

Power. Power.

Calya frowned over her shoulder, coils of anger untangling from her shadows and spilling like sooty flakes. Amok caught a few between their six-fingered fist—then soared to gently perch atop the stack. The question they'd postulated continued unsolved.

What else would lead her to the edge of boundless terror?

Her heart galloped, erratic. Pulsing on her forehead, twitching on her fingertips. She blinked when the outline vanished—a non-face with eyes as cerulean as Quintus'—then clenched her fists, reaching the only reasonable conclusion. *He*

*wants something from me. But what?* It tightened her scowl, pursing her lips until she heard the so-called glamour. *They're offering alchemy to entice me. Why?* She turned, swallowing and parting her lips to regain control. *For all I know… it could be sheer amusement.*

"Every offer has a reason and a cost, Quintus." Rough, too rough. Enough that she paused and swallowed again, hissing, "What are your reasons? It defies logic to think you came to me, a mere human, to find an answer you already know." *Even more, if you think that librarian talked to me as a child, almost thirty years ago.* "You must be risking something by involving me."

There were too many answers, too many conditions she couldn't know. *I could guess if Quintus were human,* Calya knew, but her mind still flooded with grim what-ifs that fed the fear lurking near. *It may be symbolic; it may be a punishment.* The myths, the poems, the songs returned, their meaning lost to time yet fathomable solely because the unknown had presented itself to her. *It may be a test for him, or even a ritual he ought to pass.* That thought angered her until her jaw tensed—but she ignored it, aware of its danger. *I'm not a pawn; not powerless.*

Power. Power!

It was her reason to question none other than the Untamed One, her guidance when challenging the unknown, her goal in politics and in life. Question, question, question everything—relentlessly but carefully, contorting hypotheses into statements, reshaping intention into doubts others had to solve. It aimed to comprehend, to gain leverage, to discern the truths hidden in the nuances nobody else saw.

Amok laughed as she spoke—with delight, with satisfaction, with the elated realisation that rose unchallenged: her own questioning was her answer to The Rector, and it was correct.

Knowledge was the highest kind of power. The most enduring and irrevocable, the foundation supporting alchemy and—through it—existence itself. It acted on minds, shaping their perception, their interpretation, their engagement with the universe itself and thus rendering every other form of power ineffective.

A riveting conclusion indeed.

Satisfied—even if Amok's own question remained temporarily unsolved—the alchemist pointed a finger, willing Quintus to dip his head.

"You are not answering. You are negotiating," he observed, as impassive as the Lady before him. "Is this your version of power or a fear of commitment?"

Her single thought—the answer she wouldn't give—surged through her mind like the pathway guiding all her actions. *Knowledge is power; and I need to understand you.* "You're offering me something abstract, something undefinable... and you are asking me, the recipient, to define it." She waited, just so—but her smirk sliced through Amok's delight. "I beg to differ. I'll need a demonstration. An example."

That boldness. A cumbersome yet promising trait.

Amok spoke through Quintus, their darkness smearing his voice. "You are in no position to request that." He waited, impassive. "Moreover, you have witnessed alchemical power twice."

Bewilderment. It blasted through the soul-link like splotches of smoke—bleak and twisting in spirals, surging and convoluting until they threatened to swallow Calya. At the edge of the nowness, her inky darkness scattered into the clear clouds of curiosity.

The Lady dipped her head in acknowledgement. "Then, Quintus, I'm not obligated to answer."

When she stepped back, her footfalls echoed with confidence—following her through the stacks, across the tables, and out of the library. The soul-link evaporated at that threshold yet the alchemist stayed behind, bound by thoughts and intrigue.

# Egon Hold

## Zaro 16ᵗʰ, 17002 RE

LEGATE OF EGON HOLD, EASTERN LEGIONS OF FIRARD

Fire.

It consumed the night, flaming over the plains and devouring the body within it—wrapped in cerements stained with too many oils. Sweet. Singed. Sticky like the emberbane dripping, dripping, dripping through the towers of Ílun Fort, through the buildings in Liminal Harbour. That oil leaked into the bier, enraging the flames until they soared like blazing wings, molten metal and dross mingling with that cloying, choking, cinder-heavy stench and the acrid notes swinging in the breeze.

It bawled, the Nadir, bellowing from the depths of the earth, shearing the mountainsides and scorching the air with a deadly surge. Dark, darker, deadly, dense with cinders, choking, bursting within. Mingling with the musky aroma that coated the bier, its acrid sweetness whirling whenever the flames cavorted in the wind. They rose above the pillars, the heat haze overpowering the night, muffling the starlight like the molten stone soaring to the firmament to pour over the armies and scorch the basin where they fought. It streamed like rivers of fire, a burning tide rolling, dense, sluggish, languid on its path to kill.

That clogging, cloying haze surrounded the pyre, whirling in the restless breeze. The ash fell in the aftermath, flakes of charred remains dancing in the air like elusive fragments of a peace that would not return, like the war reverberating on the

Legate's mind, like the wrapped body consumed by those relentless flames.

His eyes traced each of those tongues. Gold at the top, tips waving in the wind, yet deepening as he looked down, down, down to the mound atop that bier. Those tongues wavered, thick and impervious, carmine like flowing blood, pooling in the crevices of charred skin, creased and crumpled by the fire it barely survived.

Dante looked up, blinked—and scowled at the resentment in her eyes, at the slander in her mouth, those hypocrite truths only applicable to him. *A lamb; not enough to be her shadow.* Then, now. Long ago, earlier that day, decades ago, through missions and victories, worse on the latter, worser in promotions, spat with clots of blood, with saliva, with hatred, with loathing, with revulsion. *Called me a coward for collapsing Bruma's mines.* So much of it lingered in that fire, dripping in that oil and clinging like the greasy sweetness of the air. *Called me useless for chaining Liminal.* It crackled, the fire, screaming with the laments of thousands, with the terror of hundreds, with the taunts spilling from Sittia's mouth. *Fought from afar, killed through others. Hypocrite.*

Dante's fists clenched, quivering with the resentment accrued through the years. It dragged with the grime he couldn't stop tasting. *How dared you, mother...* He mulled that threat between clenched teeth, his anger pumping into his fists to boil with the wrath Sittia had left behind. *How dared you die before I—*

Death. Death. Death.

Sittia was dead. Dead!

A lie, soaring from that shrivelling silhouette, that blackened, acrid vapour curling up until she sat, within the fire, beyond the ashfall and the vapours, amidst the heat haze's mirage that would soon become a truth, a legend, a myth because it was impossible, a rarity, thoroughly unexplainable.

She stood, lethargic. A mere slab of darkness within the enraged fire, behind that shroud of ashes. Growing, growing closer to stand, slouched, her sword dragging through the bier, scraping the stones as she climbed up the hill, metal clattering with her slights, a rancid shroud oozing from her. Greasy. Sickly sweet but coppery. Cloying and smoky like the ashfall she was traversing, the reek of smouldered flesh laced with a tang of iron and ash. She walked towards him, towards the encampment, while he watched from his tent, from his safety, from that position surrounded by smoke and blood intermingled with foulness.

*No.* Dante stepped back, eyes wide. Watched her walk. Thought it a lie, knew it was true. *She... didn't retreat on time?* Half her armour was charred and blackened, her left arm hanging limply, left leg tense but bleeding, both eaten by the Nadir's fires, skin bubbling and oozing oil, strips clinging like ash flakes, fury on her eyes, slander on her mouth.

*No.* Dante stepped forth, held to the table or to the guardrail; scowled. Watched the bile oozing from her mouth as Sittia stumbled, falling—but Petra was there, hair tousled, crusted with clot and mud and blood and cinders, neck drenched ruby, arm slipping under the other Centurion's armpits. Half supporting, half dragging.

They lugged upwards, climbing, climbing while he barely stumbled forth. Eyes wide in shock, eyes narrowing because the ashfall was gritty, cloying, itchy. *How can she—?* He stopped closer still. Swallowed that oily, smoky sharpness of sweetness turned sour and foul, rotten underneath. Petra didn't notice him, Sittia spat a clot at his feet.

"Lure the Orenian..." She snorted blood, the strips hanging from her arm flickering like banners, like ash-flakes. Tarred. Falling. "A coward's trick." Two more steps, Sittia hauled her sword. "No son, no... soldier. Just shame."

"No." Dante blinked, eyes wide in shock, eyes wider still.

The plains, at night. Clogged with legionnaires. Pockets of heads, murmuring, walking, bowing. Mourning one legend. Another standing near, a statue, impervious, untouchable. The breeze, the stench. The pyre burnt, the pillars darkened by the fire. The bier—

"No." Dante again, taking a step back.

Death. Death. Death.

The bier had a mound. A shrivelling mound. A remnant, a vestige, a residue of a legend now leaking, leaking, leaking that greasy sweetness rotten still.

Sittia was dead. Dead!

It was final. Undeniable. Unassailable, like the fire soaring, like the flames enraged, like the blaze romping on the breeze.

Dante turned. Found himself in the ramparts; outermost, western, stair near. He walked. Across the bricked path, past the turns and the towers, beyond the inner walls, up the short steps he walked, walked, walked.

He ran when his boots hammered the marble floors of the Citadel.

# Berserk

SOUL & MATTER TRANSMUTER. THE DRAGON ONE.

The dragonlet alighted on a cart's edge, invisible to the many humans gathered in mourning—then intertwined the crowd. The fire blended with their sorrow and sadness, with disbelief and relief. It was a clogging mantle, darker than the night, thicker than the pungent air, and firmer that the grim resolve imposed in the many faces watching the funeral pyre.

To the Dragon One, there was nothing new in the contradiction they observed, nothing novel amidst that sea of biases and opinions that would now forge the memory of a so-called legend soon to be forgotten. There was nothing but fear—of being the fool that didn't mourn the Ash-Walker, the dishonourable one that'd marred her rites with undesirable truths. Nothing but utter obliviousness to the greater forces shaping the history that nation prided itself on.

None of them mattered except for two men. Son, and father.

Legate Dante Praeto, watching the funeral from the outermost ramparts. His scowl slanted shadows across his face, his gaze fixed in the blazing pyre, his mind lost in a past that was bleeding golden. Berserk perused it through a brief soul-link, then severed the connection when the Legate stepped back. Once, twice. Quick steps, shocked, distraught with denial, dreadful of the moment. A third step—then he strode through the ramparts, oblivious to the woman following him at a cautious distance.

Berserk watched the humans from afar. Crossing the ramparts, moving past a tower, sinking into the darkness of the night—then let them go.

The first incision was complete, for there was nothing that Dante's own alive elements wouldn't do on their own. After all, thought itself was a fragile lattice, easily unmade when bleeding from so many open wounds, when devoured by that unquenchable fire of dread, denial, and regret that'd livened the beyond after a lifetime of being ignored. Little remained of Dante's armour, of those thinned brush-strokes inking nothing—and it would melt in time for the next barrage of chaos. The one planned by none other than his father.

Centurion Juçe Praeto. Standing close to the pyre, unafraid of its ravaging might. He was a statue of composure, impervious to the grief others offered, to their nods of respect, to the glances of morbid doubt, and to the empty salutes offered out of rank and duty.

A reductive remnant of an era gone by, smelted of pride, soured by life, and sentenced to die and be forgotten like so many others of its type—yet not before unleashing the chaos Berserk needed through the plan they'd discovered two days ago.

Hours passed. Irrelevant to the alchemist, consequential to the Centurion. He endured as was expected of him, exchanging a few words only with a handful, and retiring when little remained atop that blazing bier.

As he approached the Hold's doors, his eyes locked on glamour-Petra—leaning against the cart's side and scowling at the world on Berserk's command. The alchemist willed her to nod and, after a few moments, followed the Centurion's trail.

# Ilia & Dante

Ilia measured her gait, keeping her distance from Dante as he strode through the ramparts—shifting past legionnaires, veering into the shadows, hurrying whenever he turned a new corner. She measured her steps as well, moving carefully not to elicit a footfall that'd echo too loudly and betray her. *I'll lose him if that happens.* Her brows tensed into a not-quite scowl while she fought the urge to hurry.

When Dante climbed to the Citadel's outermost corridor, Ilia waited paces away from the guards flanking the door—then slipped inside when their salute wouldn't alert him. Three steps in, and his footfalls echoed beyond, faster. Erratic. *Running?* Her strides picked up, her worry growing alongside that nervous rhythm. *He seldom rushes… not unless he must.*

Yet his trotting continued, echoing but dying in the distance.

Amidst the corridor's penumbra, the Legate hastened into an urgent stride, swallowing hard. Her throat was too tense, too dry. *That pyre, Sittia… It can't—* Her thought hung unfinished after she halted in a split, turning left and right only to scowl at the empty corridors—marble-made, polished, barely lit with the starlight suffusing through the windows. *No.* Ilia half-turned, finding nothing. Left, right, left again, one step right. *Where did he go?* Silence, overwhelming. Thunderous.

Amidst the starlit darkness, Ilia looked at the marble floor.

Its veins slithered like silver rivers linking the consequences of each battle they'd fought—alone, but also together. The Western Wildfires, the Siege of Ílun Fort, the Nadir's eruption, and many other times. She knew what Dante was running from —*Dante's nightmares… always come back*—for she'd pretended to be asleep instead of offering help too many times over the years. *Even a few days ago.* That regret soured her, locking her gaze on the floor. In shame, in remorse, even when she knew—with all certainty—that their two-decade involvement would've ended the moment she awoke.

Ilia sighed, exhausted and pinching her nose. *Twenty-four years, and he never allowed more.* Yet after seeing him staring at the pyre, she'd recognised that quiet shock in his face—

Noises. One ragged breath, one boot scraping the floor.

It startled the Legate from her thoughts, and she glided left —carefully, precisely—until her fingertips brushed the marble wall. For grounding, for guidance. *I have one chance. No more.* When her fingers pressed into the air, signalling the corner, she stilled her mind to emerge as slowly as possible.

Dante was slouched against the wall, both forearms braced against it to cradle his head. His weight dragged to one side, the lean lines of his frame outlined by the remains of light slipping through a distant window. He didn't move when Ilia stood at the corner, watching. Waiting. *I need to help. To wait. Both.* For a clue that'd allow her to approach, for a signal that he wouldn't pretend nothing was happening. Her frown twisted while her mouth mulled all her thoughts—too raw or too professional, too cautious or too loaded—into the simplest call.

"Dante?" One whisper. Gentle.

He startled, half-turning, hair tousled. His breathing was ragged. "I can't stop… smelling burnt flesh."

Ilia's cheek twitched, pulled by sorrow—but she controlled it. Appealed to her training. Nodded ever so slowly. *He's still here*, she recognised, aware of its significance. "I know. It never goes away."

She breathed that stench as well, even when the air was clean. She'd also heard the screams… but never like him. Never like the nightmares that often awoke him.

Silence; hollering but quiet. Marching like her heartbeat, like his panting. Ilia dared one step forward. Long. Evident. Slow.

Dante's eyes snapped to her foot—but he looked away, to the wall coated in shadows. "The fire..." He chuckled, bitter, half-turning to press his back against the wall; his eyes kept away from hers. "The fire keeps... hurling me there. With every flame."

*Emberbane. Ílun, then? Or...* Understanding almost slackened her features—but she blinked instead, ignoring those rivers of molten stone she saw from afar, those plumes of blazing fire rolling into blackened clouds. Ilia's heart stumbled, almost forcing her to hurry forth—yet she steadied herself, lowering her hand from the wall. *The Nadir. Given this is Sittia's pyre...*

She'd been there as well, among the many fighting the Orenian invasion. Handling the eastern front while he led the assault in the triple-frontier. Redirecting her Legions when he sent two more to lure the Orenians towards the basin where the lava would run. It'd decimated the enemy. *It created the Ash-Walker.*

Dante exhaled, still not watching her—and she took another restrained step. He didn't move, didn't signal to have heard. Ilia took another step, measured. She needed too many things at that moment, but only one prevailed: her need for Dante to allow her close.

Silence, yet. Roaring in its deafening stillness.

"She..." Dante's voice was too hoarse, too laboured. He gaped, as if the words wouldn't push past his strained throat. "She won't... walk again... Not from this..."

Ilia breathed. Heavy, for the air cut with memories and consequences. *No. No, no...* She knew what he meant; she'd been there.

Amidst the chaos, beneath that dense ashfall that scorched when breathed. When the wind carried that sickly sweet rot, when Sittia emerged from that cloud, her skin hanging in strips from her arm. She remembered Juçe disregarding his wife to lead his cohorts, and Petra—bleeding, bleeding—hauling the Invicta towards the encampment. But most of all, she remembered Dante. In the field, when his mother spat blood at his feet, repudiating him for the same strategy that saved her life and earned her a title. Ilia also remembered him the night after, when he wouldn't stop scourging his arms to clean that tarred stench, fingers clawing at his neck. On the nights beyond, when he pushed her away to sleep with the nightmares she pretended to ignore.

Silence. Permeated with her sole need.

"No." Ilia's throat knotted as she dared one more step. "Not this time…"

Dante didn't answer, just nodded. Bobbing his head, over and over until he pressed the heels of his palms into his brows —then slid down. Through the wall, down, down, down until he was sitting, knees half-bent, elbows pressed on them to cradle his head with his forearms.

She walked. Counting her breathing, waiting between steps, but approaching, approaching, approaching until she was one pace away. Dante didn't notice her, or perhaps he did but let her stay—and so Ilia crouched low, pressing her back to the wall and releasing into a sit. She braced her knees, looked at the shadowed wall ahead.

The silence was motionless. Restless even if quiet.

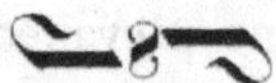

The floor's coldness jolted through him. Merciless. Rippling through his legs. They trembled.

He couldn't walk. Sittia either; she wouldn't walk.

Dante's boots slid, just so, not much. Not even when his elbows landed on his knees, head tucked under the forearms. It trembled, his body. His chest quavered; rattled by its delusional heart. Erratic, pulsing, pulsing, pulsing on his neck, his wrists, his legs.

Couldn't walk. Sittia wouldn't walk.

He exhaled, but the air was serrated, sharp. Shaking with the soot and grime grinding in his jaw. He inhaled; clear, marred, cold, warm. One was, the other wasn't; he couldn't decide which. He breathed, but she wouldn't.

She wouldn't walk.

Not from the ashes, not anymore.

He closed his eyes, and it fell again: flakes aflame, cinders contorting in that dense haze, burning his throat, etching in his clothes. Half sweet, half stone-dust. The scent was there, the ashfall, the crackling of the flames, its tongues spreading like wings aloft.

She wouldn't walk from it; not—

Movement. In the dark, at his left. Footfalls, measured; fabric, rustling. Ilia's silhouette eclipsed the light coming from the left. His back tensed, but he didn't move—just held his breath. Heard his heart hammering out of his body. Ilia stopped, crouched low, fell to a sit. Close, but not too close.

*Coward.* Dante's lips trembled, twisting into a broken grimace. *A fool for letting her see this.* A shame, all his fault—but he couldn't move; his legs wouldn't hold his weight, wouldn't walk.

Another breath, crooked. Tortuous.

Burning like that pyre that consumed it all until little was left but Sittia's last words: *Not enough to be the shadow that follows her name.* His cheeks twitched; his eyelids, his fingers as well. Clenching with the hypocrisy, with the strength of Sittia's fists on his jaw: *Never enough.*

Dante closed his eyes but the tongues of fire spread—again— like wings of molten metal fanned out, embracing the night, a pendulum of fire and cutlasses marking a rhythm, on and on, on and on. Waiting. Waiting with an unspoken demand. Waiting, until he dared answer.

Their fire crackled, the pyre's crackled. Whooshing with finality. With death and demise.

Death. Death. Death.

Sittia was dead. Dante's reasons were dead. His answer was alive.

*A fool.* He tried to smirk, but his lips wouldn't curl; not even with his bitter irony. *Legate, and still a fool.* A fool coveting one goal—one specific goal: the Meridian of Existence. Not because of duty or honour, nor because of interest. Not to be Strategos, nor because he craved to be a legend. *The truth... is shameful.* That smirk returned, bitter; so, so bitter. The Meridian of Existence, and only because—perhaps—it'd be finally enough. *For Sittia... but for Juçe most of all.*

He shut his eyes; tighter, tighter still—and that voice in his nightmare, in the terrace, roared again with its question. Haunting, lurking, burning and searing those words with the embarrassing truth he'd denied since he found that old and shabby book, since he'd imagined that reaching such an impossible balance could be enough.

It wasn't; it'd never be.

His fists tightened, teeth clenching with the violence it ignited—against himself; all against himself. *Shamefully weak. Pathetic. A*—

Movement. Again, besides him. So quiet, so... gentle. Almost as if asking for permission.

Dante saw it out of the corner of his eye. Ilia, still sitting near. Ilia, moving her hand—with measure, with peace—until it rested on the floor between them. Palm up, fingers curled but open just so.

She hadn't left. Not then, and neither in twenty-four years. She'd never left... him? *Perhaps...*

Ilia waited. Waited. Waited when Dante gasped, when she heard that hitched breathing, when his fingers curled—veins taut—into an ill-born fist. She waited. Amidst his pain and hers. Through his distress and hers, his loneliness and hers, his needs and hers. His regret and hers.

Moments passed, even after she placed her hand on the floor—between them both, palm up in an offering that could very well be rejected.

Moments passed, but Dante's left hand slid until it rested atop her palm, tentative. She didn't move; not until his fingers wove into hers and she answered in kind.

# Berserk

The underground's room was rectangular and low-ceilinged; an abandoned warden's office with broken wooden furniture and boxes of dank paperwork pushed against the walls. Its centre was taken by clusters of high-ranking legionnaires, all too eager to betray what they stood for on the whim of a legend—yet their murmurs were as heavy as their cautious stances.

Berserk watched them from atop stacked crates, the dragonlet's tail wrapping their four paws, wings fanned up as if to catch a wayward breeze. Glamour-Petra rested against the nearby wall, thumbs looped through her cingulum, gaze etched on the one who'd summoned them all.

When Centurion Juçe finally climbed into the crate placed at the centre, silence overpowered the room—drawn taut with expectation, with interest, with recognition of what was to come. Those alive elements teased the Dragon One until they intertwined everyone present, revealing the dark clouds of collective restlessness. It clogged the space, flickering like flames needing to be kindled, lurking with trepidation, and melding into sheer expectation. Juçe leveraged it masterfully, staring them down, pursing his lips and rolling his shoulders.

"The Veiled Retreat; *that* is how it will be remembered. Because we escaped like cowards." The non-legend chewed that last word, twisting his lips and spitting to the floor. "Sestel, and every nation in the world, now knows we'll retreat at any minimal inconvenience… and it's only a matter of time until Orenos and Presya decide to abuse this new weakness of ours."

His fist tightened like the attention he so well commanded, hushing the room into a silence so deafening every movement thundered like a battlefield—and Berserk's ruby eyes narrowed with interest.

Juçe knew how to dominate a mob, for his every word appealed to the most useful alive element of all.

Fear.

"But that is *not* all." He spread that hand—and the alchemist watched, enthralled, as the foolish humans followed it with enraptured attention. "The complexity of the fog-weapon speaks of Sestel's power. It maddened soldiers bred for war, killing them slowly, and leaving little evidence of its origin. It took our best, and deprived them of the honour of falling in battle." The non-legend hissed with the confidence of a man whose facts were entirely self-made, and the crowd listened, bewitched. "We all know it's Sestel's doing; we have studied them for long to know their tactics… yet we're now Chained to them because of that Truce the Strategists, once again, burdened us with. We're bound by the interest of a few, deprived of honour, and unable to defend ourselves if they attack us again."

The remnant's arguments verged on absurdity, yet Berserk listened as eager as the surrounding humans. After all, the most absurd lies—the most infused with hatred and most closely targeted—were the easiest to spread, the simplest to present as truths and through them twist reality until it fit the discourse. From those lies, only fear grew.

Fear. The best and worst part of human nature. It protected life with ravenous intent, but it also stole freedom by overpowering reason and presenting a thousand sources of danger—real or imaginary.

Humanity was always terrified of others simply because they were taller, broader, older or younger, fooler or more intelligent. Terrified of their history, lest its secrets proved them wrong. Terrified of feeling or believing something that contradicted what the majority demanded they felt or believed. Terrified of thinking, lest defending their ideas attracted the wrath of the masses. Terrified of living because of its challenges, but also terrified of death because it brought oblivion. Terrified of the sky, of the storms, of the plants and the animals, of the land they coveted and upon which they lived. But most importantly, terrified of themselves, because all humans knew what they were capable of.

"Sittia had the courage to attempt what the Strategists wouldn't: to restore Firard's honour," Juçe raised his voice until it reverberated like the cornua blaring before war. "But you saw how *they* grieved her. Modestly and hastily, too eager to bury the one that protected Firard's frontiers. The one who survived the Nadir, who pushed Orenos north, and who tried to defend us from Sestel's latest weapon."

There was malice in his tone, but also the seeds of terror, festering within and exploding without only because it had happened to him, and so it would happen to everyone else. Berserk approved of Juçe's approach, revelling on the collective realisation overpowering the intertwining. It confirmed what each human already dreaded, quiet on the outside but building inside like an impossible tide—the threat was certain, the peril impending: Sestel would attack, and the Strategists would betray Firard.

"What do you propose?" A Centurion asked, silver-blonde and suntanned.

Juçe squared, dragging the silence, crafting the moment. "It's time to free the Emerald Legions from the Strategists' cowardice and reinstate Firard's legacy."

Sighs and exhalations rippled through the crowd, restrained yet blending with the shuffle of leather and metal. Murmurs rolled from between them, probing those around to corroborate the collective opinion—on the half-formed truths everyone knew, on the sources of those facts, on the Invicta's integrity, on the Strategists' goals. It fed on each other's looming dread, twisting like Juçe's snarl, twirling like his intentions and arousing another alive element.

Desire. The compass and the mirage of human nature. The

one teasing with progress and deceiving with illusions of the unattainable.

Berserk grinned as the murmurs rose, and molten metal dripped from their wings. They severed the intertwining, gaze etched in the Centurion—still standing on that crate but nodding with the grim demeanour of those who pretend to know the truth.

"That... is not a minor endeavour." A woman's voice, aged and worn like a blade. "We'd be rebelling against the Emerald Council... and many legionnaires will take the Strategists' side." After she paused, her voice frayed with hesitation. "They have led us to many victories."

"Indeed," Juçe rebuked, skirmishing for every word of leverage. "But the Strategists have deviated from their original purpose, and instead of bringing us victory they brought us dishonour." He waited long enough for the weight of the accusation to blanket the crowd—then looked at his own hands. "*We* can overpower them. We can retake Egon Hold and teach the Forces—the *true* Emerald Legions—that a renewed Emerald Accord is within reach." He lingered, acknowledging the worried glances, the restless shuffling—then nodding alongside them. "It won't be easy, but we have won worse battles. This is one we fight for Firard, for the Emerald Legions, and for the memory of those who died under the coward rule of the Strategists."

Silence. Confounded, befuddled, perplexed like the fear who didn't realise it'd been overridden by desire. For power, for recognition, for honour and might and a legend of one's own.

"How do you see this happening?" The silver-blonde Centurion raised his voice, fists clenched tightly as if to hold the reins of the opportunity.

"First, we let the Legions return to where duty calls them; this way, we'll ensure Firard remains protected against our external enemies. We need only an assault force: skilled, well-organised, and precise." Pausing, Juçe pressed a fist into the opposing palm, gaze etched on the crowd at his feet. "Once they're gone, we'll overtake the Strategists by rank: the Imperials first, the Legates, and the Strategos." Murmurs and silence, he allowed it all. When he spoke again, his voice was a cornus calling for war. "Without the Strategists, Egon Hold will once again be Firard's—and Ílun Fort will follow. One after another, our strongholds will be retaken until only Magisters rule on the Emerald Council."

To the alchemist, Juçe's actions were not vengeance against his own son—but the outcome of reckless desire and unyielding fear. The overpowering, uncontrollable desire to destroy everything the Legate represented and force history to forget him in a childish game of honour disguising the Centurion's own fear of being surpassed.

To the legionnaires invited to that room, Juçe's actions embodied honour, justice, and the lost greatness time always polished into a flawless memory—even when he was only stirring the fear of decay, of foreign betrayal, and perceived inaction.

A clever fool, with power, standing, and age. A noxious concoction that often butchered entire nations.

Having listened to all there was to listen, Berserk fluttered their wings closed, nestling atop the crates to wait. For the meeting to end, for glamour-Petra to earn her place, for the plans to be laid out, and for the Legate to calm his mind.

Enough to be rational when Petra leaked the truth of Juçe's actions.

# Ferro Keep

## Zaro 16ᵀᴴ, 17002 RE

# Calya

*A pawn, but not powerless.* Lady Calya Seve pressed her lips, drumming her fingers over the marble desk. She was leaning forward, watching the documents—a summary of the healers' accounts, and a list of soldiers vetted for the travelling delegation—but the conversation with Quintus haunted her. *He's keen on mind-tricks as well.* She blinked, forcing herself to read the handwritten names and recall their track records, but after two of them she was back on the library. *He implied I've witnessed alchemy before; twice. But when?* That question had plagued her, its answer as elusive as few others. *When the blade-crowned being appeared? When Quintus showed his own shape?* Calya sighed, pinching her lips. *I can't dwell on this now—*

"What worries you?" Asier's voice was an anchor to mundane problems. "I'll change the soldiers if—"

Calya shook her head, frowning at the worry in his eyes. *He's been seeing to my needs since he found me under the desk.* She hummed, pretending to acknowledge him and glancing at the documents to collect herself. Her anger—at the scattered thoughts, at the inherent powerlessness—subsided while her thoughts returned to that conversation as if it were an unsolvable regnum board. *But what two times?* She groaned in the privacy of her office, fisting the hand still pressed into the paper.

"That this would not be enough," the Lady finally answered,

struggling for concentration. "The excess Firardians will be long gone by the time Lady Varre crosses the frontier, but the risk remains."

Frustration scrunched Asier's face while he hand-signalled, *"You are not worried about losing Hori."*

"No..." Calya mouthed that word, toying with the drapes of her gown to gesture, *"Her death would be a loss, but easily leveraged."* Although she'd rather preserve the inventor of postmortems herself, her sister and heir—Lady Nari Varre—would be a fine replacement. *Not as intelligent, but also an ally.* "Add two more Watchers to the list; the delegation should be able to communicate with us." She reread the names, glanced at the window, then asked, "Is the despatch of reports about Petricor's events ready?"

The Lord nodded, one hand over the hilt of his sword, gaze etched on the burgeoning lilac dawn. "I saw to its departure before coming here." His forefinger raked through the hilt's engraving, tapping the metal with precision. "Should we—?"

A silver blur hurtled through the open window, wings spreading like fanning mirrors to slow and land over the desk. It startled the Lord while the Lady simply watched it, amused by her favourite clockjay—the larger one with lilac eyes and a few dishevelled metal feathers on its head.

It watched her askance, blinking once before opening the beak. "From Oier Kerro, Sessentas' Minister of Trade. To Lady Calya Seve, Head of the Seve House."

# Amok

The night was not quiet, for the wind whistled with its reckless currents, coiling like sibilant threats the humans below ignored. Some travelled from the Gorge to Ferro Keep and back, their torchlight mere motes of dying light, while others moved within the latter's enclosures, the matters that so pressed them lost to the gusts.

Amok watched them from atop the Central Residence, standing at the edge of the tallest marble rooftop, their back towards the Peaks of Nadir. Their cloak swirled in the wind, leaking glyphs and ink that returned to swarm them—weaving the mesh of fascination and aggravation that obsessed the alchemist into stillness.

That quarrel—that daring coexistence of alive elements—originated on the target the Untamed One had been tasked to recruit. The one that had twice warranted The Rector's intervention.

Lady Calya Seve. A curious human, bold but not fearless, resolute but not angerless, collected but only outwardly.

Daylight tore the edge of the world, the largest sun blooming from the horizon to oppose the starlight. The sky above it mellowed into silver-lilac hues, the land welcoming it with ever-stretching shadows. When the second sun dawned, Amok clenched a fist to produce three alchemical glyphs—one for each question besetting them.

The first was the gateway to the others: how, and if at all, should Amok answer Calya's demands?

In the dawn's emptiness, the Untamed One plucked that glyph with their free hand and hurled it to oblivion. That question allowed a single resolution: to give her a demonstration because—not long ago—The Rector had berated Amok for not daring. Thus it would be done, and it would corroborate Calya's own conclusion: alchemists were not powerless.

With that resolved, the glyph harbouring the second question shone the brightest: how to craft a Naturalist demonstration? Yet as they posited it, the third question—that taunting, seemingly irresolvable glyph—clung to the previous one through an inky tendril: if novelty was an impediment, what else would take her, again, to the edge of boundless terror?

The Untamed One considered the glyphs while observing the diminutive motes moving through the Keep and the plains it guarded. Those humans were irrelevant, too used to thinking they had crafted that world and continued to do so. All unimportant, unable to eclipse the rising light, their edges blurring until they were nothing else than shadowless silhouettes. They were powerless, unable to even craft their inky sunmarks—except one, trailed by two others, all galloping back over dark specks.

Horse-riders, three of them. Casting shadows under the twin-suns noon.

Three. Like the shadows of Calya's self, like the alive elements escaping from her past: fear, anger, detachment. One rushed ahead, the other two trailing behind—but always in the same order: fear, anger, detachment. Those riders traced shadows when the clouds shaded the suns, those shapes stretching like claws reaching for the next one: from fear to anger, from anger to detachment, from detachment into the nothingness of the present.

That third glyph shattered when Amok crushed it within a

six-fingered fist, the ink it dripped returning to the alchemist's cloak.

A mesmerising achievement, to understand the clue The Rector had given them by watching three inconsequential humans ride back to Ferro Keep.

A quaint spectacle, to realise that—during that conversation in the library—Amok had chased the wrong question—for Calya could cross the edge of boundless terror only once. After all, her alive elements turned in one specific order: fear, anger, detachment.

Thus, if The Rector's semblance had brought the boundless terror, Amok's demonstrations would need to lead her past the threshold of raging wrath, and beyond the rim of absolute stillness. Every turn would refine her boldness from the fear that enabled survival at all costs, to the fury that burnt with purpose, and to the frost that sharpened sanity ensuring the continuance of the self. Only then would she be ready to train as an alchemist, and aid Amok in developing the incarnate.

Pleased with their conclusion, the Untamed One narrowed their eyes, raising both palms and releasing a hundred new glyphs—each a potential answer to the last question: how to craft a Naturalist demonstration? They hovered before them, shimmering azure and amethyst, and spinning with the slow, purposeful cadence of objective consideration.

Immediately, the alchemist disregarded those experiments requiring the use of interfering, non-Naturalist soul-skills—they would not act as the Dragon Plague, mindlessly risking Calya's natural potential. With that decision, the examples requiring a mind-latch, a soul-shape, or similar skills faded away.

When only their echoes lasted, Amok discarded any demonstration depending on geographical changes. Such approaches were Naturalist but required control over Matter alchemy—and the Untamed One refused to request Berserk's assistance. It was both a protective measure and a need, for they knew the examples ought to be personal; only then would Calya's alive elements turn as needed.

The remaining glyphs reorganised to outline potential targets—their countenances were contained within the alchemical writing, their relevance remarked with inky droplets. Amok studied them, impervious to the howling wind yet enthralled by a dual problem: who to choose, and what to do. The order mattered because Calya's progression was ordered; meanwhile, the actions would define the example's effectiveness.

The Untamed One grinned, thoughtful. The challenge was enthralling indeed.

A shimmer of the early afternoon slipped past the hurrying clouds, reshaping the semblance of shadows. They cascaded through the Peak's shapes, pouring from the Keep's structures, and bathing the two glyphs hovering before Amok.

Two faces, two demonstrations. One to be splintered, the other precluded.

Satisfied, the alchemist set to it.

# Calya & Teoda

The garden remained as inhospitable as Calya remembered it, with bushes shaped into smooth balls, flowers of contradictory scents, and two trees with neatly pruned canopies shading a nook of marble benches. Teoda sat on one, her carmine cloak crossed above her legs like a shield against the icy breeze. *Holding court here, it seems, although devoid of aides.* None waited for her in that inner garden, except the slender boy standing on the hallway and flanked by two guards. Calya studied him while closing the glass door. *A spy?*

"My dear, it was due time we spoke again," Teoda greeted her once the door closed, gesturing to the space on her own bench.

"The Truce's aftermath has been rather busy..." Calya smiled, lifting the hem of her dress while steering towards the other bench. "But I trust your three days of leisure were entertaining."

Teoda rested her clasped hands on her lap—then prodded the ruby ring on the left. Its chiselled gem was as cold as her daughter's gaze. *So immaculately constructed.*

"Will your affairs keep you in Ferro Keep for long?" Calya's pretended concern had an artful accuracy. "If so, we could provide you with larger chambers... but your cohorts should return to Umbra City."

*Of course she'd notice.* Teoda offered her a frown—minute, but with enough hurt and shock to justify looking aside.

"But if they leave, I'd be unprotected..." She dallied, letting her lips tremble before whispering, "Or am I a burden to you, child?"

*You exhausted the effectiveness of that trick fifteen years ago.* Calya smiled, but her jaw tightened and her eyes narrowed more than intended. It wasn't the underlying accusation that aggravated her, nor the expression so perfected as to seem truthful. The target of her anger—budding, but quickly doused—was herself. *Because I fell for it for too long.*

"In light of the Truce, a large garrison at Ferro Keep is unwarranted. The War Game is past, and the joint investigation is ongoing." The Lady rolled a hand, discarding her irritation with it. "I presumed you were aware that most Seve stratoi were repositioned." *Or did you think your spies were secret? They live because I find them useful.*

Teoda's frown morphed—not in intensity, but certainly in intention. "Relocating my cohorts is entirely possible... when the time is right."

*Too blunt. Is she slipping or rattled?* When curiosity took over—considering motives, anticipating requests—that seed of anger withered and died, unattended. As the breeze sharpened, biting in the Peaks' signature style, Calya observed the matriarch—fidgeting with the Eneko ruby ring. *Her engagement ring to my father,* she noted, aware of the repetitive, idle motion. *This can't be about Lord Eneko, dear uncle. What game is she setting in motion?*

"It merely pertains to foreign affairs, and days ago you were concerned about it enough to offer support," Calya recalled, noting how Teoda touched that ring again.

"Departure has never been in question; merely its timing. We'll take our leave when my purpose here is fulfilled," Teoda whispered while smiling, her profile to the door—it wouldn't do for those outside to read her lips. She glanced at the portable regnum board near the opposite bench. *Just the unforeseeable—for her, of course.* "Even if required, the joint investigation is merely a superficial agreement. Undoubtedly, Lady Varre's scholars have already concluded the matter…" She paused, grazing her chest with two fingers. "The fog-weapon, if you please. Hand it over, and I'll leave." *I offered it to my allies, and so I must have it.*

The canopies rustled as she spoke, the wind coiling in the garden's trap—yet even with its coldness, Calya's countenance didn't change. There was no tension in her features, no change in her posture, not even a reaction when her gossamer gown swirled gently. *So poised, so bloodless. I taught her too well, unfortunately,* Teoda lamented, holding that gaze.

Questions. In the hundreds, in the thousands.

About her motives, her knowledge, her sources, her goals. About targets and spies, connections and conversations, about timing and allies and conditions and expectations and the hows and whys and whats and for whats. *What, exactly, does Teoda think she knows?* About the Noble Houses and the neighbours, about strings being pulled and the pathways they connected. About the future and the unforeseeable, about the twisted past and how it led to the unexpected present. *She may set the challenge, but I choose the game.*

Calya hummed, letting her eyes run through Teoda's face—leaking concern with each passing moment. *Did she ally with the Orenian, as I thought?* She pretended to gape for a moment, drawing back in hesitation. *Under which terms?*

"Did someone threaten you, mother?" She whispered, leaning forth, wrists crossed over her knees. Her disgust was only internal. *The things I do for information.* "Perhaps if you told me who's behind this, I could help you."

Teoda blinked—once and slow—the corners of her mouth quivering down from her smile. *Clearly unprepared to be the victim of her own tricks.* Calya raised her brows, almost pleading—and the matriarch averted her gaze, again rubbing that ring.

"Your concern is appreciated, but there is only a... need for fairness," Teoda managed, her throat drier than desired. *Just a need to give the Orenian something valuable enough to demand they act.* Lingering, she raised a hand, palm open. "This weapon shouldn't be exclusive to the Seve armies. The Zurias could wield it against Presya, and the Luxa Forces to better protect the Exarch."

*That fog-weapon cannot be anything but another relic of the past. Thankfully, my spies informed me at once.* Teoda was aware of the delicate chain around Calya's neck—finely crafted, and plunging into her gown to conceal its key-charms. *Like the clockjays, the unbreakable lanterns, and the Orenian's tools.*

As the silence stretched, the matriarch sighed with measured sadness. "It is regrettable to see you don't believe me."

*I believe you're desperate to think the fog was a weapon.* Calya parted her lips, still appealing to the fake concern. "I'm worried about you." *But who did you offer it to?* Counting her heartbeats, she let three pass before whispering, "You carry this so gracefully, yet it must be difficult to navigate such arrangements while meeting... someone's expectations."

Despite her outward calm, one worry lurked around Calya. *Does she know about Lares' incident?* Hori's documents clouded her thoughts, crackling with the danger of having been found. *No, Asier has them heavily guarded.* A coldness tickled her shoulders, weighing the Lady with a single realisation. *Could Teoda mean… the alchemists?* She discarded that idea before it settled, glancing at the hallway and the noises rumbling between its marble walls —soldiers, hurrying. *No, she couldn't know about those beings.*

"Your concern truly warms my heart," Teoda sounded too soft, too mellow—and the hand she pressed into her chest almost trembled. "But there is only an agreement—"

The matriarch frowned, cut short by the distant voices rumbling in the hallways—twisted by the echo and tarnished by hurrying metal footfalls.

Teoda lowered her gaze, fingers tapping on her ruby ring. "Neither of us wants to see this become complicated." Her veiled threat dissolved under that hurrying march. "Just hand over the fog-weapon, and whatever you discovered about it. There'd be no need for disruption after that, provided everything aligns as expected."

A voice roared through the hallways, and the guards snapped to attention. The door shrieked when Asier pushed it open, striding with his gaze etched in Calya's. She rose with controlled haste, scowling at the stout, bearded General that slipped behind. *From my mother's guard?* He approached Teoda alongside two subordinates, flanking the matriarch with the precision of wartime. Calya pressed her lips, but Asier' fingers seized her above the elbow with a pressure that startled—then turned her half-away from the others, his brown eyes darkened with unseen concern.

Within the barricade of his body, the Lord gestured with shaking fingers. *"Ruria is dead. I found her body."*

Nothing, for one breath.

In the other, fury blasted through Calya until the air she breathed burnt like Nadir's ashes, whirling with violent indignation. Against herself, for leaving an opening unprotected, for lowering her guard, for the failure it implied, for the consequences she'd caused and the gap on her allies. It burnt from the inside in the coldness of that breeze, and her nostrils twitched and flared when she tried to speak.

Cautious, she beckoned over her shoulder, implying one question. *Teoda?*

*"Unsure,"* Asier mouthed, and his fingers tightened above her elbow.

Calya raised her chin, acknowledging—then hand-signalled, *"When? Where?"*

"Not—" The Lord worked his jaw, swallowed a tombstone. "Not long ago."

Anger. Against herself. For the weakness she'd shown since the alchemists arrived, for the failures that couldn't be reversed, for how Ruria's death marred her own standing in the public eye, and for the threat Teoda had delivered and Calya had failed to forecast.

Wrath. It loomed around her like towering fear, circling like a predator—until a rebel strand of hair toppled from behind her ear.

Clarity washed over Calya's mind, assaulted by an echo of the previous night. She glanced over her shoulder—to the matri-arch, whispering to the General—but *he* wasn't there. Only humans occupied that garden.

A thought refuted her; clear in her mind and spoken in a familiar voice. *'You requested an example.'*

# Delta

SOUL & MATTER TRANSMUTER. THE RAVEN ONE

Delta bellowed in the night, roaring in agony and clamouring for destruction. A violent, vertiginous moment that burst into the preternatural quietude of a storm too shocked to react, its lingering energy blurring the horizon with a shimmer of static.

At the seam of silence, the alchemists hurtled across its charcoal clusters, soaring at the edge of the storm. It flared indigo-white, bolts lashing in fury—down below, high above, all around like volatile claws pursuing Verve and Élan. Amidst that brightness, the second-in-command tore ahead, swerving through the currents that twisted at their will; they glided, wings spread open, their lightning leashing the storm.

'*Watch the world. Beyond the non-alive elements composing it...*' Verve mind-whispered from afar, a barrage of electrical destruction flaring from their wings. '*Why is the storm half-alive?*'

The question haunted Élan as they followed, four wings beating to catch another current and soar. They sought the answer in the rumbles of a world that knew no peace, on its strangled silence, and in the menacing growl swelling with unrelenting fury. Finding none, the Raven One whirled and surged eastwards, the thunder's savage howl roaring in waves, dense curves each, all chasing the alchemists but fading, falling behind yet striving to survive.

'*Look beyond its non-alive compounds!*' Verve again, searing ahead.

That flavour of unknown knowledge teased Élan with the memory of the ordered world they'd seen during Vim's amalgamation—and it fuelled them with the eagerness to learn, to comprehend, to turn that knowledge into power and transfigure for a third time. Greedy, the alchemist soared above the remnants of the lightning and its thunder, searching for whatever existed beyond—only to see the known aftermath of that violent discharge. What they already manipulated through Matter alchemy: non-alive compounds scattering like restless, moonlit motes drifting through the clouds like shards of ice and stardust. Yet in the threshold between known and unknown, Élan felt what shimmered within each mote.

The need to survive, to reshape, to be.

It permeated the storm, the air, the fading soundwaves, twisting and whirling through those fleeting existences. Élan watched, dominated by the truths that had always existed but were only visible after amalgamating Vim.

One need. So fundamental yet impossible to accept, to define.

It brought chaos to the brink of stillness, auguring the birth of another lightning strike and clamouring with the unexpected: desire to exist, fear to cease. In the storm, in the air, in the lightning and its thunder, in the soundwaves that were no more but wanted to be again. It lashed with fury, tendrils of ashen-violet stretching as if to rip the ground—yet it halted, redirected by a higher will.

Verve's. Circling over the storm and searing ahead, one mind-whisper suspended behind. '*Come! To the core of the storm!*'

Spinning airborne, Élan chased their peer, hurtling through the sky while the thunder growled in the moment left behind. It howled when a new lightning flashed, and at the cusp of its brilliance, both alchemists pierced the stormwall into its abyssal seclusion.

Ahead, Verve soared before plunging into an inner cluster, while Élan climbed skywards in widening, awe-struck circles—enthused by the discharges, the electricity, the ice clashing and shattering, the currents dancing and fighting. Eager to will the storm, they catalogued its non-alive particles now escaping above or below, inverted like mirrors of each other. It was known and thus recognisable, a part of Élan's will that coerced the wind to recharge and—

'*Change your perspective,*' Verve mind-whispered, hidden by the dense clusters. '*Go beyond the non-alive elements, past the storm's components. It has an essence of its own, each lightning, each gust. Find it.*'

The Raven One grinned, full of questions yet consumed by the knowledge now teasing them. '*That essence… is it the threshold to its half-life?*'

A chuckle, approving, amused. Answering by rumbling through the clouds, flashing like a scar searing that charcoal darkness with dawn-fire silver and moon-washed blue.

That light scattered the fog of the visceral unknown, revealing the perfection of a truth that bloomed within Élan's mind, so full and thoroughly understood, it lived along the lightning and perished too soon. It was the spark surrounding non-existence, the core of Protean alchemy: the essence of the storm itself.

Encouraged, Élan tightened their ascent, twisting skyward, one arm stretched to grasp the storm and learn from it. It roared again, enraged by its fear to cease, and empowered by its desire to exist—then flashed ghostlike cyan, blasting with relentless power, yet curling around the alchemist in a forceful fight against demise. When it growled, Élan understood what lingered within.

Struggle.

On the storm, to be more. On the alchemist, to bind them all to their will.

Struggle.

Woven from the clamour of a thousand essences, each suffusing the storm with a unique signature: one for each tendril of the lightning, each rumble of the thunder, and each gust of a reckless current. They all beat, half-alive—yet in the drumming of that heartbeat, at the verge of coercing those essences, Élan unravelled.

Unwinding like loosening swathes, fragments of the nowness falling in disorder and dissolving in screams. It howled, reality itself—Élan themselves—with knowledge and pain in a synthesis so contradictory it bellowed with the turmoil of the unknown. It howled, so dissonant and discordant it unspooled the nightmares within the alchemist's armour, unweaving the Raven One, and bellowing alongside them.

Élan remained albeit fragmented, pulsing their wings and desperate to soar towards those swathes—to pull them together and blend them into coherence. They burnt when Élan approached, flaring with the grief and agony of a reality that wouldn't be what it was nor what it ought to be, only to howl and twist until the world tumbled and the Raven One fell into the nothingness within.

# Verve & Élan

ALCHEMISTS OF THE ORDERS

The currents whirled and Verve spun, wings unfurling as they glanced up, willing the storm to sear its charcoal darkness. It scarred with dawn-fire silver and moon-washed blue, the tendrils barely eclipsed by Élan's four-winged silhouette. They were soaring in tightening circles, hunting the lightning and luring the thunder, one hand stretched upwards as if to grasp the sky. When the thunder bellowed in fury, Verve willed the storm to flash ghostlike cyan—and released it, allowing that bolt to curl around the Raven One in a forceful fight against demise.

In the blink before the sky burnt again, Verve soared towards the other alchemist to chase their nightmarish shape—yet as the lightning raged, Élan vanished.

The second-in-command halted airborne, wings fanning open to defy the gale and break hold. Around them, the charcoal clusters sparked with nascent lightning, but their electric dimness revealed nothing—not an echo of the Raven One, not a shadow, not a nightmare.

'Élan!' Verve mind-whispered, but that thought scattered in the storm's vacuum, wasted with no one listening. "Élan!" They roared, battling their wings and willing the gusts to soar. "Élan!"

They circled upwards, hurried by a hundred alive elements too human to be embodied again—confusion, apprehension, desperation. Scattering them, the alchemist swerved through the currents in the smoulder of a thunder's bellow. It lingered, unspent, until they caught a reflection: tendrils of a nightmare, shadows of a memory.

A howl.

It slashed through that abyssal cluster, dissonant, like reality torn apart. Twisted in discordant echoes, distorted by the rumbling of a stormworld that wouldn't rest, always embattled in a cycle of self-renewal. Verve soared, turning, half-turning, searching for the other, the thunder roaring with the might of their concern. Their fists clenched, and lightning balls flared between their fingers, anger leaking—

The sky shook high above, soundwaves blasting through the darkness. Sunlight sheared the storm, and as Verve turned, Élan crashed into them—a dead-weight, fainted, leaking nightmares, the world spinning as they fell, the storm twisting and whirling, the lightning volleying through the darkness while Verve held onto the Raven One. Their plunge curved like vengeance remembered.

"Élan!" A demand in that call, so bold yet futile.

The thunder roared again, reaching the alchemists and bellowing when near.

"Élan! Hear me!" So demanding, so pointlessly desperate.

They pierced the stormwall, whirling like a maelstrom of destruction, lightning and haze bleeding into haze and lightning, spinning, spinning, spinning until Verve spread their wings, willing the currents to flare. The world shot past them, land first, from horizon to horizon, the sky after, cluttered with the clusters surrounding that charcoal wall. Hauling Élan onto their chest, Verve appealed to the storm, warming the chilled gusts and slowing that maddening descent. The wind sheared in their command, rustling wings, lightning lashing and holding them up.

An impasse, hovering airborne. The wind whistled in grief.

Verve spun, lifting Élan and flying northwards to alight at the edge of the cliff overlooking the ocean. The forest nearby crackled to welcome the storm above—but it held back on the whim of its creator.

Lowering to a knee, Verve settled the other over the teal grass-blades, urging, "Élan?" Then: "Élan!"

The Raven One did not react, but their Integrity Shield swirled, iron and silver, roiling and never blending.

A name. Theirs.

That name; echoing—even when the swathes shrieked, devouring reality and parting with it.

Shadows, falling. Theirs, all of them. Four-wings, fragmented, battling. A hand, fingers spread, searching, seeking to grasp, to hold, to cling to what that name meant. They were falling, that was certain, unspooling like the swathes unravelling the world.

Most were silver, brilliant like the flare of knowledge. Some were iron-made, coiling like metal lashing in wrath, molten edges spilling liquid fire, flames eating their ends, leaking down. Consuming. Devouring. Ashes swayed in the gale, curling in the gust and refusing to land. Fire rained in their midst, liquid, burning, blazing, trickling upon the vessels down below, so small, all sailing a river, then a bay, and somewhere else.

Across centuries and millennia, while the Raven One plunged and the swathes unfurled with slow decadence. They kept eroding, nightmarish strands fraying from its edges, sparking with lightning, with charges, with the desire to exist as it had always been but also to become more—so much more.

Water. It did not ripple. The alchemist passed through it, sinking, hand stretched, drowning in the agony of the most unequivocal pain. It blazed at the core of their existence, strangled by a noose of ideas that'd been foreign but were now their own, no longer easily muffled and neither disregarded but lurking like anchors that dragged them down, down, down to the confines of that abyssal darkness where nothing was certain and the continuity that'd carried them across millennia faded as the water's surface blurred.

"Élan! Hear me!" Their name. Like golden threads holding onto memories.

The Raven One gasped, and the water's surface rippled with the need to *be*—but that edge wasn't there, and the Raven One fell down and through the crown of the sky.

Above it, their name lingered again, gold threads twining from it. "Élan? Élan!"

Ashfall, again. Fire pouring liquid and blazing, the swathes shrieking and twisting—but the alchemist fell, fell, fell. Unto the fire on the vessels once more, through the plumes of sooty darkness, into the violence and destruction that augured a war against the self that would not cease—not unless those swathes melted into a whole, not unless continuity was ensured and held absolute.

They sank again—through the water that didn't ripple, through its threshold of boundless terror, and into the realm of the most desperate need to survive.

"Élan!" Again, that name. That *path*. "What are you?"

The Raven One spun, looked up at the question that rang above. The answer was too thoroughly known. A Creed, once sworn and forever held: that perennial quest to compound understanding—and it blended with that fire, with the vessels sailing to destruction, with the ashes of those burnt and the flames leaking liquid.

Élan soared. Through the water and into its surface, the chaos above, into the perennial twilight of the stormworld far beyond—where the lightning seared the sky, and the horizon blurred with static.

⌒⟷⌒

The second-in-command dropped to both knees, leaning over the Raven One. They were curled on their right shoulder, wings collapsed behind and above, hands twitching and trembling. Verve watched, deterred by that swirling Integrity Shield and held back by—

"Impossible." Disbelief, albeit temporal, but as unexpected as what Verve witnessed.

Ghostlike outlines were emerging from Élan's body, overlapping into reality and echoing ill-shaped traces of the Raven One. These silhouettes were distorted, incomplete, unable to hold shape and evanescing for a breath only to return. Beneath those ghostly forms, their Integrity Shield swirled silver and iron; swathes of each curled and coiled, yet refused to blend.

Desperation. On the lightning bolting far into the ocean. On the waves surging towards the cliffs. On the alchemist watching the impossible while unable to restore the possible.

"Élan! What are you?" Verve hissed instead, daring that fundamental question to carve a path outwards for the other to resurface.

There was no answer.

Silence choked Delta, unnatural like an eternal storm that refused to growl. It lingered, threatening—yet at the rim of its stillness, the Raven One opened their eyes, rising to sit on their heels. Quiet, they looked down to the hands gauntleted in nightmares and electricity, bladed fingers curling as if to grasp the abyss within. Four echoes split from them, overlapping and diffusing; each incomplete without the other, yet refusing to coexist.

"Not... like this," the alchemist whispered, silver gaze lost within.

The second-in-command didn't answer, too stunned by the fractures slithering through Élan's Integrity Shield. Each hurled forcefully, aegean blue and brutal like reality, rifting that silver and iron and never allowing it to fuse—except the Shield endured, kept whole by a glass-like coat, translucent as if yet unseen, thus unknown.

That glass was will itself, empowered by the most absolute need to survive.

Verve sprung to their feet and backtracked in restless astonishment, sliding a hand through sooty coils that refused to wave with the gale. When they looked down—to that fissured-flawless Shield—understanding blasted through the sky, rearing the stormwall yet holding it captive.

Those fractures in Élan's Shield were internal, shattering the alchemist's ipseity and tearing it apart in a fight against stability —for Vim's impressions contradicted the Raven One's, thus teetering the alchemist towards a horizon of chaos that recognised only two outcomes: continuity or collapse. Of the self, and the existence it enabled.

"It is... contradicting," the Raven One hissed, enthralled by those echoes. "It's war; within me. Against me. For me." A pause, and their Integrity Shield flickered, refusing *them*. "It's unravelling from within. Unspooling while shielding my *self*... from myself."

Verve didn't answer, obsessed by one detail: the echoes overlapping over Élan were sometimes remnants of Vim's ipseity, unyielding in their quest to survive—and Verve had exacerbated that mayhem, for their knowledge-infused lightning had stabilised the Raven One's intuitive understanding of alchemy, but nothing else. It'd been a tether to reawakening, but a feeble one.

"Unacceptable," Verve whirred—and before their anger blasted, they crushed it within a fist, glancing at the other.

There was one fundamental truth to Soul alchemy, one irrevocable rule: to exist was to struggle in a forceful fight for and against identity. Thus, the key to survival was the path of utmost agony—to smelt the fragments and reforge the self.

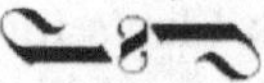

There was chaos but it unfurled, split in silver and iron, swathes twisting but never fusing while others burnt with that reckless fire.

"There is one path, Élan," Verve's voice, and their own name.

The Raven One clung to it, looking up to those four ruby eyes—narrowed into slits, and as unwavering and uncompromising as their voice. Élan had heard that tone before, too many times in twenty millennia, yet always before Verve unleashed annihilation: upon nations, upon continents, upon worlds. Upon themselves, for no other alchemist had such a twisted penchant for self-destruction and self-preservation.

"I can't… transfigure now," Élan gasped, all too aware they wouldn't survive it.

"Not a splinter, no." The thunder roared as Verve spoke, bellowing with a hundred reprimands. When they flung a wrist, a soundproof dome poured over them, bringing merciful stillness. "An incarnate could extract the dissent causing the dissonance; just Vim's fragment, and nothing else. It'd be enough for you to properly reabsorb it."

Élan chuckled, bitter—then chortled, poisonous like the molten metal leaking through the corners of their mouth. "I'd rather face non-existence than let Amok ravage my mind."

"Not Amok," Verve stated with the certainty that'd created Delta itself. "But you'll need to lower your Shield."

Utmost peace, within that dome, and for a fragment of eternity.

Then, it clashed within Élan's echoes, into the shrieks of those unfolding swathes. That was one soul-skill the Raven One hadn't breached, yet they knew enough to comprehend the sheer agony it brought—for an incarnate sundered the self to stream a fraction into a temporal embodiment; conscious enough to have a semblance of autonomy, but not enough to *be* on its own. It was a nuanced skill, among the most complex of Soul alchemy. Only Amok had mastered it, and no one else.

Yet there was no other way.

In the impasse of that renewed silence, Élan held onto the swathes they could, and shattered their own Integrity Shield. "You know what to do."

CHAPTER 15

Egon Hold

ZARO 16TH, 17002 RE

# Berserk

SOUL & MATTER TRANSMUTER. THE DRAGON ONE.

Berserk sat on a corner of the desk, paws placed in a precise spot to avoid the scattered papers—lists of medici and legionnaires to be formed into delegations for that trivial Truce. It was another waste of a time-framed existence, a frivolous exercise in diplomacy between two nations due to collapse—yet the Legate attempted it, to the extent his limited concentration allowed.

So absurd. So oblivious to the chaos soon to be unleashed.

A synthesis of exasperation and intrigue rippled through the alchemist's molten metal, inflamed by the human before him. Leaning into the desk's edge, hands pressed into its rim, gaze etched in the hand-written lists albeit his mind was anywhere else just to enact a normalcy that would never return.

Dante groaned, pushing himself away from the desk to watch his palms; his fingers quavered before he pressed them into his temples. They seemed to pound alongside his heartbeat —hammering so intensely that Berserk's active soul-link buckled alongside its erratic rhythm. Over and over, darker on the edges just like the Legate's vision.

His body was experiencing the toll of Berserk's first incision —senses so heightened the world burst with colours and sounds, his blood thrumming through his body at a sprint, logic teetering at the edges of perception. That state was a detail the alchemist could not disregard, for human bodies often succumbed to the torrents of atemporal alive elements, especially when their return was sustained. It wouldn't do to kill him before he became a source-being.

The Legate exhaled, standing near the map with both hands pressed into his nose—then returned to the desk, minding his breathing before reorganising the papers yet again. They rustled in his trembling hands.

So impotent. So blind to Chasm's and Futile's involvement. So ignorant of the plans set in motion only for him—for his mind, for his ideas, for the path he could propose.

But as Dante forced himself to read, Berserk straightened, pleased with the results of such a precise first incision—then plunged into the depths of the soul-link.

One heartbeat.

Within it, a turbulent abyss soaking the soul-link, unruly and frenzied like Dante's erratic heartbeat, pounding, unbound and violent, its darkness a threat of demise. The hollow was no longer, its prior stability now impossible amidst that storm of cacophonous gales. Each swelled or shrunk, a myriad howls surging, unsteady, into a perennial droning that rumbled from the depths of his mind.

It was a frantic chorus bellowed by a hundred terrors and a thousand denials, that gale mewling in layered hues—around the Legate, around the alchemist—all stacking, restless, hissing or roaring while every pulse carried a new surge.

Two more heartbeats.

The Dragon One grinned, molten metal dripping from their parted maws and leaking onto the blade—still emerging from the clamour of that abyssal storm to impale the currents smothering all promise of inner peace. Instead of balancing atop it, Dante's self clung to that feeble threshold, hands sinking into the blade's edge.

Another heartbeat.

A golden thread flowed from him, piercing the storm like a spear cleaving its prey. Each of its sunlit filaments gleamed and pulled to eventually recall a long-denied and long-refused memory: the moment at which Dante had first developed his reason to pursue the Meridian of Existence.

It was a foundational recollection, an essential desire—but a naïve one. Misguided because it did not serve the Dragon One and neither a candidate to source-being. Unacceptable simply because the only worthy ambition was an insatiable thirst for knowledge.

Three more heartbeats.

The onslaught of revolving gusts roared with a thousand threats that—

The desk pounded. Once, twice, thrice—and the dripping, dripping, dripping of blood flooded the soul-link carmine.

The Dragon One emerged from the depths of that connection, displeased.

Dante stood two paces away from the desk, left hand up and smeared in fresh blood. His knuckles and fingers were scraped, his skin burning in waves that rippled through the latent soul-link—yet his face did not register the pain.

"Coward," he hissed, turning and half-turning that hand before walking to the bookshelves to open a box and retrieve a cloth. "Can't bear the weight of my past."

The fabric reddened as he cleaned himself.

Aggravated, the alchemist padded through the desk—carefully avoiding the papers now lying in greater disarray—to sit near Dante. Even when unfocused, those violent gales assailed his soul-link, yet he endured upon that blade due to a single need: to sustain the charade because his shame ought to remain private, because weakness was destructive, dangerous, deadly. To preserve his façade of stability because being caught without it foretold total collapse.

Berserk snarled at him, disapproval hastening the dross rolling through their form. Only humans would hold on to whatever remnant of knownness they still had—even when it poisoned them from within.

Yet that denial only served the alchemist's purpose, for the thread they'd seen on the depths of Dante's soul-link kept pulling. Pulling. Pulling that essential memory into his awareness—and once it did, Berserk could carve their second incision to methodically extirpate that undesirable craving. But that method was not without risks, since the slightest error would lead to Dante's demise... or—to compound the risk—to the obliteration of his alive elements and the loss of that promised solution.

Insanity, not to assume the risk, not to leverage their sole chance to ignite Dante's alive elements to free him of the shadows of his past and enable his novel thinking.

Insanity, not to temper the candidate The Rector had selected for them.

Decided, Berserk hunched, wings pulsing before they sprang to drift through the currents. They melted to slip under the door, then glided down the Citadel's hallway. Before that second incision, glamour-Petra had something to report to both Legates.

# Dante & Ilia

The door hardly concealed the sounds of the guards on duty. A muted clink of plates shifting against each other, the scrape of spears against the marble floors. When they settled into position, only the faint rustle of cloth and leather remained. Just four legionnaires, all from the Eastern Legions—yet their presence leaked into Dante's office.

It wasn't quiet, at least not to him. His heartbeat droned— on his chest, on his wrists, on the scraped knuckles, under his jaw. It wasn't constant but tumbling, discordant, so erratic his fingers twitched uncontrollably. *Not now.* Dante chided himself, rounding the finally clean desk to recline against its edge, hands pressed into it; for grounding, for control.

Before him, Centurion Petra Arvina stood, once more, between the door and the desk. *Like two days ago*, the Legate recalled, the thought buzzing into his ear. He muffled it by tightening the jaw, head tilted just enough to demand the Centurion spoke. *If this is what I expect…*

"You requested an audience, Centurion." Ilia pocketed a hand with the same nonchalance of her countenance, then flicked the other, palm up. "We are waiting."

The silence extended, the pounding on his wrists too distracting, too exhausting. Before it unravelled his composure,

Dante arched an eyebrow in a wordless statement, rolling two fingers because Ilia's command hadn't been clear enough.

"After the pyre, Centurion Juçe Praeto gathered a dozen officials in the Hold's basements. On the abandoned warden's office, more precisely." Petra's crisp voice cut the air like a pugio in the night. Not loud, yet neither a whisper. "He was rallying the others against the Strategists; his plan is to wait until the excess Legions depart, then subdue Egon Hold."

Silence, anew. Unblemished.

The Legate's cheek twitched as he recalled the prior conversations; after the Retreat, and after the clockjay. *This is exactly what Lady Seve wanted.* His wrists pounded, pounded, pounded. His ears buzzed, buzzed, buzzed. The legionnaires outside shuffled, the faint jingle of mail wailed into the room. His left hand throbbed, a dull soreness waving through it—and doubts surged from that pain, carving a hollow. Dante ignored it.

"I understand there is more to this than you mentioned." He spoke at last, slow and mindful of each word. "What else should I know?" *Lie or truth; both are equally dangerous.*

The silence stretched, pounding, his fingers twitching before he clasped the desk's edge; the movement warmed his pounding ache. *Even if Petra tells the truth, I cannot react now.* There were a hundred consequences to the Centurion's revelations, a myriad problems soon to be unleashed. *Can't afford a coup.* He studied the Centurion, her posture, Ilia's, his own under that buzzing that wouldn't leave him. *Can't afford my father's petty revenge.* He waited until that doubt—the one reignited by Sittia's death—fell out of his mind. *Can't afford to act without apparent cause.*

Dante arched a brow. A heavy gesture, layering wry amusement with a dozen unspoken demands, with an implicit reminder of the Legions' ranks, and a timeframe to answer— remarked, clearly, by his right forefinger. It tapped, thrice and steady, against the desk's edge.

There was no answer, at least while his heart buckled again, racing through his throbbing fingers. Then Ilia straightened to her full height.

"It would be wise to answer, Centurion," she observed,

angling her head to indicate the doors and the guards outside. "Promptly, I'd recommend."

"Juçe…" Petra lingered, shifting her weight—then lowered her voice even more. "He repeated his old argument: claiming the fog to be a Sestelii weapon, and the Retreat a dishonourable and shameful move." The bitterness in her chuckle was unexpected. "A quaint discourse, appealing to Sittia's honour and how she had 'the courage' to attempt what the Strategists wouldn't."

*What a hypocrite, my father.* Dante's heartbeat. Pounding in his wrists, in his temples, in his bruises, under his jaw. *Control yourself. Think!* Dante pocketed both hands, almost grimacing when the fabric scraped his sore knuckles, setting them aflame. *Why would Petra do this?*

"And what would that be?" Ilia pressed, steady.

"To restore Firard's honour." Petra waved a dismissal; part mockery, part disagreement, part act. "Curious, because the Centurion was inciting a revolt that, given its implications, was not precisely honourable."

The buzzing, shrieking, eternal. Searing his senses, slashing the doubt still haunting him. *Honour.* Dante's fists clenched inside the pockets, his hand burning and shivering loose for a sole heartbeat. *A contradiction only my father could attempt and succeed at.* Resentment. It tightened his jaw, slowly filling that hollow within him. *Steady…*

"Help me understand, Centurion Petra," Dante stated, avoiding all gestures because his mind raged like a storm. "What would be the purpose of such a revolt? What is Juçe's goal?"

"Besides removing the Strategists? To renew the Emerald Council only with Magisters." Petra shrugged, the plated pauldrons chafing in mock dismay. "He was *not* subtle; perhaps because the meeting's attendants had been close to him or Sittia during their five decades of service."

A question bothered the Legate; the one that nightmare had unravelled. *Why should I chase the Meridian?* It was his duty to Firard… yet he knew that after the pyre it had less value, less relevance. Were Petra's disclosure truthful, he'd have only one more chance to reach it. *Never enough*, Dante recalled, pushing himself from the table to approach the woman.

"These allegations are... substantial, Centurion. Should they prove unfounded, the cost would not be small—neither for the Legions nor yourself." He paused, glanced at the map, then met her gaze. "What led you to share them with us?"

She didn't so much as move.

The onslaught of his heartbeat heightened in that impasse. Between them, that hollow again, distorting that racket. He ignored it; ignored the shuffling of the legionnaires outside, ignored the burning of his hand, ignored that pulsing, pulsing, pulsing on his chest. *Duty; just duty.* It was a lie; but it was everything.

"I serve the Legions, Legates." Petra dipped the head, glancing up with dutiful conviction. "There is no honour on betraying the Emerald Council."

*Too rehearsed.* Dante smiled, equally rehearsed, yet sceptical enough to let it linger more than needed. "On what basis should I trust your word, Centurion?" *This can't be just duty.*

She shrugged in response, pauldrons grating. "Instinct, perhaps. Because Juçe's ideology is not unknown. Facts, maybe, since the Strategos requested me to stay." Then she paused, that scowl weaving tighter. "Prior experience, if not, given my unit was the first to obey you during the Nadir's eruption."

*Not a lie, yet...* The Legate hummed, once and neutral—then shrugged just like her. "You also served, repeatedly, alongside Centurions Sittia and Juçe. On the famous snowstorm in the Peaks, on the Sweep of Tormenta Plains, on the Siege of Ílun Fort..." He enumerated with precise calm, his gaze still etched on hers. "—and during the Orenian Invasion. There was a reason he invited you to that meeting, Centurion."

Petra's shoulders tensed as she ran her eyes through him, lips curling in a half-snarl that ended in a hiss: "Are you implying I'm disloyal, Legate? Or else?"

Dante didn't answer—not while his heartbeat twisted and he ground his knuckles against his pocket to set them aflame. He didn't think either, his glance towards the door a learnt gesture. "Your report is appreciated, Centurion. You may leave."

The door thudded closed, but Ilia held onto the door's handle, gaze lost somewhere between the floor and the bookshelf.

Petra's revelations clung to her, undesirable yet unavoidable. *We knew it would happen*, she recalled, the handle's metal warming under her palm until she released it. Her gaze etched on the volume about Sestel's Grand Conclave she'd perused days ago. *The same day we considered this.* It hadn't been the only time, since Lady Seve's pragmatic return of Sittia and her Centurions had led to a similar discussion. Ilia frowned, shielded by the privacy of that office yet torn between admiration and dismay—admiration that Seve had manoeuvred events so deftly, and dismay at the cost of their unfolding. *We can't afford this now; least of all after—*

A noise distracted her. The rustle of fabric, and two measured steps.

The Legate straightened, half-turning until she found Dante's lean frame. Resting on the edge of the desk, his back towards her, left hand covered again in a new cloth. *Steady and collected*, Ilia noted, too aware of his change in demeanour; calm, reserved. Nothing in the prior conversation with Centurion Petra could've revealed the inner turmoil of the night before. *He hides the strain too well; he's always done so.* Yet she couldn't ignore that he wasn't his usual self. *Colder, more detached.* It was understandable; despite its personal impact, the situation demanded a strategic approach. *This could shatter the Emerald Legions.*

Carefully, Ilis reached for the same volume she'd been staring at, then pulled it from the shelf. Its leather cover creaked as she opened it, passing the pages with the consideration of deep thought. *If Dante falters, Egon falls, and the Legions will suffer.* Her hand hovered with a finger pressed into a corner while she glanced at the desk—*He completed the delegations*—then flipped the page. *He won't open again to me, and… this exceeds us. Firard should come first.*

It took her a moment to settle her thoughts, but they stilled when she closed the tome, pressing it back into its slot. The leather creaked—intentionally—in the process.

"For now, Petra's revelations... are just slander." Ilia commented out loud, two fingers still pressed into the engraved spine. "Truthful or not, we cannot act against Juçe solely based on rumours. Least of all now, when Sittia's death has given him leverage."

"Indeed," Dante sighed, pressing both fingers into his nose before standing and turning. "If I accuse him now, it would look like a political purge or, even worse, a personal vendetta. The... Praetos' turbulent history is common knowledge within Firard."

*Family never survives politics; only names do.* Ilia angled her head, agreeing while glimpsing at his neck—covered by the camisia's neckline. She'd seen the marks the night before, she'd stared at the recency of some, cleaning the deepest one. *But after dawn he closed himself again.* Ilia turned to watch the map in the opposite wall. There were too many interests at play, too many personal cravings, too many nuances to ensure Firard's long-term stability, too many obstacles preventing immediate action. *Like a bitter reminder of Ílun Fort.*

Yet there was one risk above all.

"More than that... the wrong move may delegitimise *all* the Strategists." Ilia paused after emphasising that sole word, then crossed her arms. "The Emerald Council may have supported the Retreat and the Truce, but—"

"Juçe couldn't have leveraged it if nobody agreed with him," Dante interrupted, working his jaw as if the words refused to be spoken. "If Petra's report holds any accuracy, Juçe is waiting for the other Legions to depart, likely to reinforce his honourable façade by still protecting the frontiers."

Ilia rolled two fingers, each circle rounding her thoughts. "It is... sensible, but we can't be certain your interpretation is correct." *I could believe such a move had it come from Petra, not from Juçe.* She didn't voice that last concern, instead adding, "Those Legions could return at any point, or even steer to other fortresses. We can, however, estimate that at least half of the remaining Eastern cohorts will support Juçe."

"Ciro's and Rhea's Legions are loyal, but our numbers will be limited." Dante nodded, walking past her to sit on the opposite lectus, elbows pressed into his knees. "Petra's Legion could assist… but her allegiance is something to be seen."

Dante's jaw clenched for a moment, then he raised his eyes to meet hers. Ilia reciprocated, though what she saw in that inky darkness concerned her. *Emptiness, not peace.* Her shame and remorse returned. That entire conversation was a façade; an act in which both pretended the prior night hadn't happened, clinging to a semblance of normalcy. *But even if I care… the Emerald Legions come first.* Ilia's shoulder straightened while she appealed to her training, forcing herself to redirect her concerns —about the unrest, and about Dante—if only during the day.

"Petra's allegiance remains to be proved," the Northern Legate gritted, pocketing both hands. "The Legions are not our main obstacle; Juçe is—and nothing can defeat a legend."

Dante didn't answer, instead gazing through the window to the enclosed garden beyond it—where the trees shimmered pale teal under the suns' silver light, the flowers like pearlescent specks over the finely trimmed bushes. *This is almost an unwinnable battle*, Ilia recognised, accepting that silence. They ought to contain Juçe, ensure the Truce with Sestel, while protecting the Marshals. *And Dante—*

"Legends may be invulnerable, but their legacies are not." Dante stood as he spoke, rubbing his calloused fingertips; the knuckles of his left were a carmine smear over his sun-kissed skin. "Let my father destroy his own image; let the people see who he really is… they will not follow him once his honour is gone."

*My father?* Ilia frowned, studying his features—calm, detached. *He never refers to Juçe as 'his father'… not publicly, at least.* She'd known him since they were wide-eyed pupils, and he'd never been the type to favour revenge. *Another reason why Strategos Gora always favoured him.* Taking another moment, she curled her fingers under her chin to force herself into considering other —less personal—angles.

"You're proposing we let him move first," Ilia stated, now torn between agreement and disagreement—agreement, because the consequences of acting without apparent cause were too steep, and disagreement because the risks were greater than those they wagered in Ílun Fort.

Dante met her gaze, smiling with that thirst for a challenge he only displayed in private—yet it soured too soon.

"Indeed," he pressed his fingers into the desk, the right forefinger tracing circles over the marble. "It is not Juçe who's rallying these high-ranking officials Petra mentioned, but his and Sittia's legend. We need to discredit him as a symbol, and defeat him as a man." He dallied, seemingly lost in the marble's veins slithering away from his fingers. "Once the coup begins, we demonstrate that Juçe is fighting out of personal interest and not for Firard's honour."

*One moment, a hundred consequences.* Ilia tilted her head, weighing the odds. "In such a case, the coup *must* happen—and to do so, we must force him to commit. Tease him to make the first move."

Dante nodded again, beckoning to the door as if to imply everything that existed beyond it. "Elixane would do." It was a whisper, but there was no hesitation in it. "Her position as my Imperial makes her a primary target; significant, but easier than either of us." He gestured towards both of them, then frowned at his bruised hand. "If we plan this well, we'll have legionnaires on the Gorge beforehand, and the delegations will be already marching. I could handle the official communications, but we'll lose the spies—at least those writing directly to Elixane."

*The problem is how long it'll take… and if happens when Lady Varre is here.* Ilia didn't answer, and neither did he, so the silence settled like an impervious mantle that allowed no sounds to exist. She frowned, thoughtful, and it didn't miss his gaze.

"After that, it'll depend on how we turn Juçe's allies against him." The Northern Legate dallied, approaching the desk to whisper, "But one wrong move, and we could destroy everything we've sworn to defend."

"No strategy would allow us to move first and succeed. We can't act on rumours, and neither produce another reason to detain Juçe—not after Sittia's death, and not without triggering a revolt." Dante lingered, his empty, steady composure reflected on his voice. "We can only react, Ilia, and only within a small margin of error."

She nodded, once and curtly, yet watched him intently. *Dante... I care about him deeply, but my duty is to Firard.* When she spoke, the warning in her tone was unmistakable. "The Marshal-Strategos is here. We may best avail ourselves of his wisdom."

Dante watched her, impassive—yet the corner of his mouth twitched in a bitter smirk he promptly smothered. "Of course."

# Gora

Marshal-Strategos Gora Rachen leant on the chair, right arm extended over the marble desk, left clasping the armrest before pushing himself to a stand. *As I feared, Firard's greatest legends will be responsible for its destruction.* He walked towards the window, basking on the noon light while he pressed two fingers into the windowsill's edge. *Decades spent to cleanse the Legions of them, and still Juçe stands; my failure, not his triumph.* His shoulders straightened as his fingers looped over the edge, the marble shushing smoothly. *Strange fate, that his greatest service was not his victories, but providing me with a successor. That alone redeems his wretched existence.* Yet the bitterness of decades spent plotting the senior Praetos' undoing didn't spoil Gora's countenance as he half-turned.

Legate Larya stood at parade rest near the bookshelves. She upheld her regal composure, yet the Strategos noticed a hint of tension between her brows, a tightness around her mouth. *Another sharp mind. These two in service of Firard are worth a Legion in the field.*

Besides her, Dante awaited with hands clasped behind his back. He hadn't hidden the bruises on his left, but neither did he need to. *Even in his blood, there is no love for that brute.* The remaining Praetos—Dante's younger siblings, now Decanii— had never posed enough of a threat for Gora to be concerned about them. *Although after this I should, perchance, ensure they're both sent to the correct battlefields.*

Amidst the silence, Dante pressed his lips, holding the Strategos' heavy gaze. Even amidst such a dire situation, even after Sittia's dishonourable demise and Juçe's ploys—even then, he carried himself with dignity. Proposing solutions and defending the Legions. He'd never cowered like others, always aiming for the long-term like only a few could. *Dante's heart has always dared —and always did so wisely. Even now.* Gora could only approve of the Legate's proposal—to snare the brute and let him destroy himself—for only a handful of methods could defeat legends. *Risk embraced tempers the Strategist,* he recalled, allowing pride to shape his smirk.

"Courage like yours, Dante, is the foundation of a true Strategist." Gora subdued that smile, returning to the desk to press his hands into it. "Few would dare what you propose, and even fewer will understand why it is necessary... yet even if you succeed, it would not be without repercussions." *For nothing is without consequences.*

Dante nodded, precise. "The risks are my concern as well, Strategos." He paused, restraining himself albeit the darkness of aggravation tensing his scowl. There was no love on his voice as he stated, "I'd rather face the fallout than let Centurion Juçe ruin a nation that'd endured thirty-four centuries."

There were still many factors to examine, all present in Gora's mind, all guiding his actions. *If Dante falters now, Firard will fall. I must see if he can still bear the weight.*

"Have you considered the Sestelii delegation?" The Strategos pressed, disregarding the previous answer to gesture with an open palm to the medici's reports scattered on his desk. "Our Truce must not be compromised, nor should we risk war with Presya or Orenos."

"The delegations were assembled with medici and legionnaires who never served under Juçe or Sittia. Most belong to Centurion Ciro's Legion. The Gorge's patrol will be led by Decanus Ler." He paused, working his jaw, then added, "We may not be able to rely on the Watchers; we have not yet accounted for how many remain loyal."

The Strategos hummed, neutral. *His answers will be my legacy.* "We could delay the delegations' departure."

"And the survivors may perish so that we default on our promise." The Legate straightened, smothering a small twitch under his left eye. "We cannot warn Lady Seve of our current situation; she sought to destabilise us precisely as it is happening now."

*Promising, but I have more to demand.* "Yet were the worst to happen, we may find ourselves guilty of Lady Varre's death," The Strategos glanced at the paperwork, aware that Egon would welcome an eminence while sending mediocrities at the most. "The world may not forgive Firard for the loss of such a keen intellect."

"A risk we must take, or there may be no nation left to blame," Dante stated, holding his gaze and straightening his shoulders.

The Strategos did not answer, instead arranging the pleats of his emerald trabea; the fabric rustled mercilessly, more sibilant than his measured steps while he rounded the desk. Once he stood on its opposite edge, he looked at Ilia, then at the door—and she saluted as expected, walking out of the private office. After her footsteps evanesced in the hallway, only silence existed. Not uneasy, but neither steady.

*The risk is not cowardice, but calculation. But does his impulse outweigh prudence?* Gora sighed, his features relaxing with a worry seldom exposed yet useful in that context. "This is about Centurion Juçe, Dante. About and because of."

He broke his parade rest, an unexpected aggravation burning in his eyes—then he chuckled, sour as if tasting ashes. *Yet he doesn't avert his gaze,* Gora noted, approving of the strength it required.

"I'm not fighting Juçe nor the coup." The Legate hissed, unflinching even as his fists tensed. "I'm shaping the conditions under which both would destroy themselves."

"Save the speech," Gora rebuked, severe—yet his scowl softened when he took a step forward. His hand landed on the Legate's shoulder, his voice tamed to imply what the words alone wouldn't convey. "Why, Dante? Egon Hold may be yours, but it'd be understandable if you requested me to assume command." *Will you defend Firard, or let the brute have his way?*

The Legate's jaw tensed until his teeth ground, shoulders tensing. He never looked away, never aiming to hide the tempest reflected in his eyes. *"Because* Juçe is my father."

*He steps forward. Honour demands it.* The Strategos straightened, removing his hand and taking one step back. "You have my respect, Legate." He allowed his pride to colour his smile— then beckoned to the door. "You may take your leave; I'll ensure the Council's guards follow your instructions."

# Dante

"Our duty today is to the Legions, Centurion. Towards Firard and the Emerald Legions." Legate Dante Praeto beckoned towards the map hanging on the leftmost wall. "We trust you'll continue to honour the Legions and reporting what you find."

"As always, Legates." Petra dipped her head at a precise angle, glancing briefly at Ilia—standing near the bookshelves—before producing a scarf from within her cuirass. Long, purple-dyed fabric that tangled on her left palm as she offered it. "This is what they wear." Her fist curled over it, the leather bindings of her vambrace creaking under the strain. "I'll give you further information as soon as it is available."

Dante scowled at the fabric; that colour bled into the room, his eyes unable to see it sharply. He ignored it, instead focusing on his concerns about the Centurion they could scarcely trust. *No other choice; no other loyal legionnaire had been invited.*

"Understood," Dante stated, beckoning towards the door. "Be cautious."

Legate Dante Praeto crossed through the Citadel's door, yet the short flight towards the ramparts vanished beneath him in two pounding steps. Devoid of a crowd, the ramparts were only populated by a normal guard—archers posted at key points, a handful of Watchers scattered around, two Prefects and a young runner. *Meagre compared to the excess of mere days ago.* He took a few steps, but the silver suns' light blinded him more than usual. Taking a hand to his brow, the Legate hurried through the bricked path only to halt near paces before the staircase, gaze lost in the landscape.

*Finally.* The plains were streaked with columns of marching cohorts, neatly ordered and heavy to move. Dante watched them as he descended the staircase, counting those marching south-east—*Two, likely the Central and Southern Legions*—and the few aiming south. *All Eastern, given the banners, and bound towards Tormenta Plains.* When his boots hit the mid-level ramparts, the flicker of a torch distracted him. He swallowed, tasting the stone-dust, smelling the sweetness—*Not now*—but forced himself to stride towards the northernmost edge of the Ramparts.

Imperial Elixane Ritz awaited him, her usual nonchalance lacing her nod. *Too smooth. Not deception; performance.* He returned the gesture, dipping his head in a salute and hiding a quirk of his brow—questioning, concerned—as he stepped closer. *Did she find anything?* His own plans for her rang in his mind, but he stalled them as she offered him a veilwing letter. He plucked it gently, immediately noticing the azure Seve seal.

The crisp paper unfurled with a crackle, revealing a polished script.

*Legate, we look forward to dispatching a Varre-Seve delegation towards Firard, bound to arrive by dawn of Zaro, 18th. Likewise, Ferro Keep has been prepared to welcome the Legions' Medicii. As you know, the nature of the fog-induced symptoms prevents us from dallying.*

*May this joint investigation reinforce the peaceful relations between our nations.*

*Of course, Lady Seve would pressure us.* Dante proffered the letter to his Imperial. "I trust the accommodations are prepared. Decanus Ler will lead the domestic escort himself."

As Elixane read, her fingers curled too tightly around the paper. "Decanus Ler?"

The Legate hummed, once, then retrieved the letter to crumple it into his pocket. The trouser's linen scraped his hand, reigniting the fire pounding through the wounds—yet he kept it there, pressed against the fabric. *Using Elixane... is not personal. Just duty.*

It was a partial truth.

The afternoon light cast its sharp shadows into the office—across the desk, through the floor, on the door Centurion Ciro had just closed. Blotted strips of silver shimmered on the polished cedar, smoothing the bas-relief. When Dante closed his eyes, those strands had seared in his mind's eye, each pounding alongside his heartbeat. It had eased since the morning, but still throbbed under his jaw.

Turning away from it, the Legate opened his eyes to stare at his palms. Callused, both; the left still spotted with remnants of blood he hadn't fully cleaned. *The Strategos...* he recalled the echo of the words, that gesture of unexpected respect. Each syllable had weight, as though carved from the Citadel's marble. *Yet his respect is misplaced.*

Dante chuckled like he did before his mentor. Bitter and tasting cinders.

"Because Juçe is my father." That echo—that hiss—slashed the silence and the brittle peace of his mind.

His jaw clenched, hands curled into fists for that reason poured resentment into that hollow within him. It lurked for a moment too long, lingering as he rotated his left hand to watch the bruised knuckles. It burnt like Sittia's pyre, pulsing like the flames flaring like wings above the bier.

Dante groaned, closing his eyes. That fire kept roaring within him, blending the pier with Ílun's Siege with the memory that'd paralysed him on his terrace, and the questions that'd assailed that nightmare. *Why the Meridian?* He pressed the heels of his hands into his brows. Smelled the death. *Is it worth it, now?*

It may have been a different question, but its answer was the same he'd offered to Gora.

He denied it.

# Ferro Keep

Zaro 16th, 17002 RE

# Asier



Calya's footsteps had long faded away, swallowed by the Residence's hallways and adding to Lord Asier Aurri's restlessness. She'd rejected all guards—*As usual*—leaving him to worry in that inner garden—assailed by his many concerns and the wind gusts sharper than blades.

The Lord held his ground, unwilling to extend the conversation and thus staring down at the unflinching matriarch. She stood under the canopy's shadows, motes of light and dark roughening the severity of her scowl; her lips were so tightly pursed that slender creases skittered outwards like brittle rays of sunlight. *Upset, but it'd be politically riskier not to protect her.*

"Am I a suspect now, Asier?" Her question was as grating as a dessert knife chafing against a porcelain plate.

*Always a suspect.* The Lord ignored her remark just as she'd ignored his title—*And always demeaning*—instead stating, "It's for your own protection, Lady Teoda, that I'd requested General Ayere's assistance."

Steadying his hand over the hilt of his sword, he glanced at the man—standing beside the matriarch with a scowl that revealed his inner conundrum: doing his duty or displeasing the woman. *I don't pity him.*

"Lord Aurri is correct, my Lady," the General groaned, indicating the soldiers he'd fetched on their way to this garden. "It'd be unwise to walk unguarded when a spy skulks about."

She hummed in response, a single note booming with her indignation. "And for how long, if I may ask?"

Her gaze bore into Asier's, pale and steel-like.

*Until we find your spy, or whatever poison you used.* "Until it is safe, Lady Teoda, and I trust your guard is as vigilant as you are." He stepped back while dipping his head, the gesture as sharp as the matriarch's scowl. "If you'll excuse me."

He didn't wait for a retort, Teoda's last words murdered by the shrieking of the closing door—yet the hallway after shrunk with his footsteps, each resonating as loud as his heartbeats. *Change the guard, protect Hori, return to Calya.* Asier recounted his tasks, taking the corner and hurrying to a trot; he'd lost too much time with the matriarch.

"I'll complete the change as requested," the Commander snapped to attention, her brows tightly knitted as she lowered her voice. "I have assigned additional guards to Lady Varre's key healers and earth-scholars, and will handle the guards' rotations myself."

Asier grunted in agreement, pulling the reins of his gelding to move the animal closer. He mounted in a swift motion, leaning to hiss, "Report back anything suspicious."

As the woman saluted, he spurred the blue-bay into a trot, rushing down the dirty tracks near the Keep's enclosure. *Only the spymaster left,* the Lord reckoned, shifting his weight to nudge the gelding around the corner; its hooves kicked up dust against the blacksmiths' buildings. *If the Firardians' messages are intercepted* — Neighing, the gelding veered into another corner, two dogs barking into the swirling dust. *Whoever killed Ruria knew who to target.*

It wasn't fury that he recognised in Calya—but that unquenchable self-directed contempt he'd encountered decades ago. It darkened her azure eyes as she watched him, stilling her countenance into the perfect portrait of the serenity presaging the most devastating tempest.

Asier didn't speak while approaching the desk, too aware of the challenge in Calya's gaze—to dare utter a word of comfort, or perchance whisper it hadn't been her fault. He knew better than to attempt it. *That tempest is better aimed at someone else.* There were only two things she'd allow—facts and actions—and he ought to comply. *Yet I do understand her rage; Ruria's death... is problematic.*

"I set Teoda's own guards to protect her, strengthened Hori's, and redirected the spies to my command," he informed instead, pressing one hand into the desk's edge and the other into the bridge of his nose. *The timing couldn't be worse.* "Did you—?"

"How did you find her?" The Lady interrupted, her voice too still. "And when?"

He closed his mouth, fighting a grimace. "I went to her post outside the enclosure, but the Watchers hadn't seen her. I hurried to the field office, and..." He trailed off, fighting his hundred worries for a semblance of rationality. "The door was locked from the inside, and none of the guards had heard a thing. But—" A groan escaped him as he clenched a fist to squander the impotent fury tensing his muscles; he could not strike his failure nor his frustration, and neither eased when his fingers uncurled. "It was noon!" He hissed, sibilant like a blade severing air itself. "I can't fathom—!"

Calya's hand pressed into his arm; slender fingers, as tense as her features, and as furious as the tempest coiling in her eyes. She didn't speak and neither did he, yet their shared fury whirled between them like a macabre respite.

When she took that hand away, her fingers flicked towards the letter spread on the table. "From Minister Oier Kerro. His third response," she informed, Sessentas' broken seal shimmering gold like that nation's deserts. After a moment she pointed at a smaller, soiled veilwing paper. "Lord Zuria finally replied as well."

*Facts and actions,* Asier recalled, grateful for that impasse—*For the acknowledgement*—he'd long deemed outright implausible. "Did Minister Kerro finally yield?"

Her chuckle curled as sarcastic as her tiny smirk. "Kerro is more eager than I expected to have access to Argo Bay... which can only indicate something else lurks in its ruins. I'll need Zuria's scouts to investigate, but—" She paused, fetching the other note; it reeked of sea and spilled ink. "Via clockjay, and no response needed. Read for yourself."

Asier retrieved it reluctantly, grimacing at the paper's stench —*Sea, ink, and turmoil; that's the note's odour*—then wrestled the stiff letter into a somewhat readable angle. Its rough edges caught on his calloused hands as if refusing to bend.

> *My Lady, as requested, I've repositioned four vessels into the Sanguine Sea, lead by my sister, Lady June Zuria. Six galleys, including the Victoria Ascendens and the Corona Tempestuosa, will soon arrive at Zafiro Gulf; our scouts sighted Orenian activity.*
>
> *We hope to encounter a clear sea, although I'd welcome your armies should the need arise. Shall we meet again in the thick of battle, may the might of our joint forces enable another Sestelü victory.*
>
> *Lord Julen Zuria, Head of the Zuria House and commander of Sestel's navies.*

*The Victoria Ascendens?* "He's moving his own flagship?" Incredulity rimmed the Lord's tone, overpowering his prior anger as he skimmed through the vessels' names. "The Corona... isn't the famed galleon?" *Too many warships. Is he foreseeing another Orenian invasion?* Asier awaited a response, concerned about the implications—but the silence confirmed his worries, strangling him with the echo of prior conversations. "Why now? They couldn't be behind the landslide!" *Unless...* The letter slid between his fingers as he hand-gestured, *"Did Teoda ally herself with... someone?"*

"I gather as much," Calya confirmed in a whisper, catching the letter as it tumbled from his hands. "I have now warned the Exarch; Lord Zuria left me no other choice... However, I wrote to Vega Fortress and they reported no inland sightings, but—"

Two knocks on the door—concise and curt, marred with the rustling of armour. Asier exhaled, his breath shaky before he composed himself—then strode to the door, flinging it open to reveal an armoured soldier. The startled man squared at attention.

"Lady Varre..." The soldier's ragged breathing interrupted him. "Lady Varre... requests your attendance. She... has completed the postmortem."

## HEAD OF THE SEVE HOUSE, SESTEL

It was the same functional office they'd assigned to Lady Varre after the landslide—yet it was now cleared of paperwork, the window partially obscured by the outline of the guards standing outside. They stood like statues, impervious to the whistling wind or the dawn rays they eclipsed.

*A sensible measure, perhaps futile.* Lady Calya Seve awaited inside, regretting the leathers Asier had insisted she wear—the field armour she'd donned during the War Games and likely useless against the source of the threat. *If what the alchemist whispered was true...* She tucked a rebel strand of hair behind her ear, gaze unfocused while ruminating in the day's earlier events— when Asier had broken the news and she'd heard Quintus' voice in her head. *But how?* Calya scowled at her cousin, perturbed by his restless pacing yet too aggravated to berate him. *And how did the alchemist kill Ruria, if at all?* Her fists clenched at her side, squashing her boiling anger and the echoes of that last demand she'd given Quintus. *If that—*

The door creaked open, unleashing the misery of distant sobbing; it tumbled into the room while Lady Hori Varre stood under the archway, a frown knitting her brows into an exhausted line. She didn't speak and neither moved, right hand curled around the door's latch, left scrunching a handful of papers. *Shaking? I've never seen her shaking,* Calya noticed,

432

respecting that weeping silence. It was a single person's, and it curled around a lattice of unintelligible murmurs. *But whose? Most survivors were just... resting quietly.*

Sighing, Lady Varre closed the door, hesitated, then ambled sombrely towards the desk, two fingers pressing into the soft bridge of her nose. Her robes—*Too clean and neat*—flowed heavily with each step, and she pulled them gently before sitting on the desk's edge. The papers crackled when she pressed them into it, face down.

"Ruria's postmortem... I've never seen anything like it." Hori gaped, rolling a hand then tightening her scowl; the purple crescents under her eyes became undeniable. "But I did discover the cause of death. Severe internal blood loss, as suggested by her clammy skin."

*Internal blood loss?* Calya blinked, toying with the rim of her leather belt. *Did she swallow something? Or was it pois—?*

"What about... the bruises? They were—" Asier dallied, fighting a grimace before muttering, "—tender."

Hori's head moved slowly, a nod or shake confused by whatever horror she'd seen. "No. The bruises were just another symptom of her blood loss: pockets of clots trapped under the skin. Her abdomen as well..." She trailed off, her long-fingered hand hovering in front of her lean stomach, tracing a curve then waving it away. Her dark skin dulled as she whispered, "Most of her blood... pooled there."

Somewhere in the room Asier groaned, his revulsion blending with the distant, unstoppable sobbing coming from outside. That noise writhed as Calya coughed, her throat burning with anger and disgust; she massaged it gently, hoping to ease that unwelcome sensation only to enhance it. Her gaze unfocused, steering away—to the window, to the soldiers' outline—while she fought against herself not to imagine Ruria as Asier had discovered her.

"Were you able to deduce... the cause of the bleeding?" Calya managed at last, voice coarse from the acid slithering through her throat and coiling with her fury. *If this was truly caused by—*

Hori shook her head amidst the fragile stillness. "Before the postmortem I inspected her externally. I didn't find any outer wounds, assuming a poison-induced bleeding. I've seen some... ghastly effects in my visits to Lares." Her hand hovered over the creased paper, hesitating before lifting a tip; she rubbed it with her fingertip, turning it without glimpsing at its contents. "Ruria's insides were torn apart. Every organ, hacked as if she'd swallowed blades... but we found none inside her."

"What?" That word blurted from Calya as if spoken by her shock.

After two rushed heartbeats, the Lady stared at the creased papers—two rough graphite sketches likely drawn by a depictor, one of the Varre illustrators tasked with recording the House's many discoveries. *But what is it?* She pressed a fist to her lips, feeling Asier towering behind her and swearing while Calya stared at the figures, unable to fathom them. *It doesn't look like human anatomy...* she realised, head tilting as if watching at another angle would unravel the mystery of the water-stained illustrations. *Are those... Ruria's insides?* Calya gasped as realisation embraced her like an omen of death, the shaky lines revealing their meaning to sear into her mind. *What can cause—?*

'*A splinter; quite a diverse soul-skill with many effects.*' Quintus' voice, in her head. Didactic, even. '*Complex, as well, since it disassembles a human's body; totally, or partially.*'

No thoughts. No fear. Just wide-eyed shock slacking Calya's features.

She gagged, covering her mouth with a hand yet unable to look away—and the sketches died, flipped over and hidden. She keened to hear that voice, but it was silent, muffled by the pounding on her heart, hammering in her forehead, in her ears, in her chest, in her ragged breathing now slashing the air, burning the room with the might of her fury. It howled, only within her, ear-splitting and demanding a violence that couldn't be unleashed even as it scorched like the Nadir's wrath.

'*You requested this, remember? An example of true power.*' Quintus again, echoing in her head. '*A splinter is not straightforward, but with knowledge of alchemy—*'

The voice blurred while the room swirled like a windstorm, shrinking and compressing into absolute darkness, the metallic stench of blood and bile slithering down Calya's throat and inflaming her wrath. She walked back, one hand pressed into her churning abdomen, the other reaching for the desk's edge and curling over it. Her nails screeched over the wood.

Yet there was no fear in that darkness; she didn't allow it. Just maddening wrath—against herself, always against herself. For being so careless with her words, for not assessing the danger correctly, for enabling Ruria's death, for allowing the alchemist into her mind, for not being able to stop or fight it. For endangering the power she'd so carefully garnered over two decades of politics and campaigns.

Amidst that spiralling chaos, one thought hissed in her mind. *This will have consequences, Quintus.*

'A *threat?*' He chuckled into her mind, a blend of amusement and disbelief more poignant than the weeping echoing behind that door.

"Calya?" Asier's voice, tight like his hand curling above her elbow.

Her response was a mere nod, curt and sharp as she straightened her shoulders, guided by duty, by the need to safeguard her own power by protecting Sestel's integrity. *I still need a human culprit; something believable.* The Lady blinked, rubbing her fingertips with thoughtful patience before turning towards the healer. *But not now; on due time, and on my terms.*

"Hori…" Calya whispered, coating that informal address with worry—not feigned, yet useful nonetheless. "We can't reveal this."

"I know!" The healer hissed, jerking to a stand as if coerced by the revulsion that'd slowed her before. When she waved a hand towards the paperwork; a snarl twisted her mouth. "The fog, then this? Two mysteries I cannot resolve? It'd shatter Varre's reputation as much as Seve's peace!"

*Always pragmatic*, Calya smirked, dipping her gaze in agreement, albeit the world swirled alongside that gesture. "This… cannot be a reason to postpone the Truce's arrangements. You still must travel to Firard," the Lady insisted, barely mouthing the words.

Asier's groaned, but his gritted complaint hung incomplete

after Calya silenced him with the same glare she'd given him while in her office. *Don't you dare, cousin.*

"I'll have to select another depictor to accompany me." Hori flicked her fingers towards the door, gaze etched on the hidden papers—then sighed, shoulders slouching as the air left her. "I'll also need a new guard, Calya. Ruria was due to escort me."

*'What an untimely demonstration, then.'* Quintus' voice echoed like a predator's whisper. *'Perhaps the splinter—'*

*Enough!* Calya closed her eyes, pressing a hand against her leather belt not to fist it again—but every fingertip pounded alongside her fury. She took a moment to collect herself, the strain of the moment a suitable façade to dally more than usual. When only her reproaches remained, she looked again at her cousin—*He disagrees, but it is decided*—then back to the healer.

"Lord Aurri will travel with you," Lady Seve stated, the firmness of her voice overriding the protest on Asier's grimace. "You'll depart on tomorrow's midnight, as planned."

# Amok

As the twin suns edged closer to the horizon, the dusk subdued the world into bleached hues—muted teals on the land, moonlight-lilac washing the sky. Ferro Keep fell into a deviant serenity—too peaceful given Amok's demonstration of Soul alchemy, too placid given the chaos soon to be unleashed. The wind brought only restless howls; high above, while hurrying wispy clouds towards the north, and down below while slipping between balustrades and crenellations to coil in inner gardens and terraces.

The Untamed One descended onto their favourite one, perching on its guardrail while glamoured to invisibility. They squatted with splayed knees, both hands grazing that marble edge to ignore the landscape and watch the room across—beyond the broad terrace, framed by turquoise vines, and sealed behind glass-panelled double-doors.

Lady Calya Seve's office, dimly lit by a flickering lantern and the dying dusk, while subsumed in a different serenity—as tense as the woman standing alone in its midst, and marred by her shallow breathing. It wasn't ragged nor vicious, just mere sips of air that clung to her parted lips as if unable to pass through her taut throat. Her leathers stirred, protesting her stillness—yet she simply blinked, slow, nothing else moving while she stood alone in that room, hands at her side, chin tilted down.

It teased the alchemist with a spectacle like no other: mayhem and destruction on the realm within, but not without. The edge of raging wrath, perhaps, were Calya's alive elements would turn again—for her fury during that day had endured, latent like a wildfire waiting for a moment of solitude to consume the world.

Eager for that moment, the alchemist soul-linked her.

A noir world as oppressive as only absolute obscurity was. Black all around, desolate in its isolation, the cage of a mind twisted by a primal, prolonged need to survive. Silent all around, sovereign in its brutality, enduring in its abuse of the one creating and enacting it, neither willingly nor knowingly, but thoroughly and consistently in a desperate quest for self-preservation.

Calya, standing amidst it all like an echo of the real-world—deviously still yet not serene. Her gaze, unfocused, accepted the darkness while her shallow breathing subsisted like meagre, unsatisfying sips slowly strangling her reason. Unperturbed, even as the Untamed One perused her onerous darkness, grinning at the crystal wall erected behind her back. It was denser and fuller than before, emerging from the ground-abyss and soaring to the inky-above, no longer transparent but frosted into a satin sheen blurring the shapes it jailed.

Yet the alchemist recognised them nonetheless, and their grin widened to split their non-face with savage delight.

Those shapes were the shadows of Calya's self: one little mound sobbing and shivering, one young humanoid bursting in fury, one precursor with perfect definition studying that wall. All silent, always silent, even as they burst in wailing fear, in roaring anger, in howling despair—contorting, stretching, pounding at the wall with tendril-limbs of dense shadows. Nothing leaked; no wails, no roars, no howls. Just ripples, expanding across that frosted glass like circular soundwaves devoid of vitality and dampened to irrelevance while struggling to survive through a sense that couldn't interpret them.

A fascinating spectacle, indeed, to watch the turn of her alive elements, to stand beside her under the thick ashfall now clogging the obscurity outside that wall. It rained upon her as the Untamed One watched, each sooty flake curling with fiery intent, whirling around her with no pattern or plan, charcoal-ashy leaves coiling and coiling and catching aflame the closer they were to her.

When Calya exhaled, a windstorm embraced her, swirling with raging alertness, blazing with the intent of destruction, gusts blasting outward and rampaging through her heart until it sprinted, chaotic, irregular, tumbling and tumbling like the thoughts that couldn't form, like the emotions spilling from her and absorbed by the storm. It narrowed her limited thoughts, blurring reality until Amok stretched out an arm, fingers diving into that wind to assess the visceral contradiction locking Calya into an all-consuming, life-threatening wrath.

*I am to blame!* That voice. A thought, hers yet split into four, howled enough the alchemist startled, cerulean eyes refracting the fire now searing the windstorm. It whirled, gusts ablaze, scorching her limited world, streaks of twisting flames bellowing in Calya's voice. *It is always my fault!*

Pain. So much pain.

*Useless! Careless!* Those blazing streaks howled in Calya's own voice, in shades of it, in hues present and past, each fraying into golden threads. *I brought it upon myself!* Golden links, knotting into a distant past, but always circling the matriarch that'd caused it all. Those threads burst as well, blistering and roaring in Teoda's voice. *You are to blame!* Or was it Calya's? *I killed Ruria!* Both, fusing unwillingly. *My fault! My mess!*

Amok basked in that upheaval, fascinated by those violent alive elements and the fury turned inwards because Calya was her own worst enemy yet she sought to survive, at all costs, by all means, always, always, always even when that contradiction fed the voracious viciousness draining her mind into a frozen frenzy.

Yet it shimmered, that pitch-black nothingness, reflected in mirror-daggers born from the windstorm—edges sharpened by the immutable truths still screamed by the chaos, blades reflecting Calya's history. The alchemist leaped back as those mirror-daggers whirled, rapacious, insatiable, closing in, tighter, tighter, tighter until her thoughts were slashed apart, emotions torn into meaningless fragments, the remnants as perennial and powerful as the whole yet no longer regarded as menaces.

It hastened, the rhythm of her heartbeat, the speed of the storm. It narrowed, the noir world of her mind, the shallow intake of useless breath. It darkened, her vision, crimson flares raining down like blood spilled and never forgotten.

"No!" Amok's shock, lost to the soul-link.

Edged with fear—for Calya's mind was battling itself, seeking to rescue her logic through a flawed fight that froze her at the threshold of collapse.

The frosted wall preserved her; tendrils of liquid satin stretched from it to strangle the storm. They fought each other for four taut heartbeats, but the wall's tendrils won, dragging the storm back, back, back and behind its impervious threshold. Those furious gusts hastened, slashing, but the wall restored itself, simultaneously arching around Calya's self-concept to form an impervious shield.

Only the mirror-daggers remained near her, spinning on their axis, edges sharper than before, points aiming down—then plunged, ruthless, into the darkness at Calya's feet, dissolving the abyss and nailing an inky shadow stretching from her. It slipped under the frosted wall, feeding the shadows and the now-caged windstorm.

A stunning revelation, to trigger such a war against the self in the purest, most Naturalist form: by having appealed to Calya's atemporal alive elements, thus unleashing her intrinsic desire to survive.

Amok's burst with curiosity, glyphs leaking from their cloak, each shifting from cobalt to amethyst, intrigue and understanding reshaping their plans while they glided onwards—towards that baseline shadow grounding Calya's mind. Once closer, they dropped to a knee, sinking two fingers to sample its contents and feed them to the glyphs.

Yet as they leant, Calya moved. She yawned, hand covering her mouth, eyes moist with utmost fatigue—then a thought sheared the darkness like a shooting star aiming skywards. An intention, non-verbal yet clear enough to picture the Residence's library and Quintus' likeness.

The alchemist grinned again, more savage than before.

Amok dampened the soul-link as Calya turned, watching the desk, the rug beneath it, the shelves, the exit door. She stepped forwards but the Untamed One willed glamour-Quintus to appear—standing before the terrace's glass-panelled doors, one hand knocking twice on its metal frame.

Slowly, Lady Calya glanced over her shoulder while mirror-swords emerged from the soul-link. They hovered behind her, spinning on their axes yet aimed with flawless precision—towards herself and Quintus as well, so exquisitely angled either target was feasible.

"My Lady," glamour-Quintus bowed on the alchemist's command, traversing the closed doors to stand inside the room. "I trust the demonstration served its purpose. I've—"

"Show yourself, alchemist," Calya stated, looking beyond the illusion. Her gestures were minimal, her countenance blank. "I won't talk to your façade."

That boldness, past the edge of boundless terror and in the aftermath of raging wrath, was a most exhilarating discovery—and Amok dared to indulge her, disassembling Quintus and shattering their own glamour. When their invisibility faded, Calya looked up to their towering height, craning her neck higher and higher as she ambled forth, unlocking the glass-panelled doors to exit into the terrace and stand before the Untamed One.

"What are you?" Her whisper was as flat as her soul-link.

To the Untamed One, that question was too alchemical not be answered with their Creed. "I'm the incisive digression, the blade disrupting conformity. I'm Amok."

The Lady hummed—*hummed*—as if noting a detail that couldn't be understood. Her curiosity was a dim spark, rough like her words. "Are you still looking for that answer?"

Only then, the alchemist recognised the emptiness permeating her soul-link, for Calya wasn't thinking as before, instead living through that semblance of a conversation while estranged from emotions. Her reason had survived, but only produced tired experiences: segments of images, splatters of colours, shades of scents and intuitions clogged with weariness.

"Indeed." Amok confirmed at last, rolling a six-fingered hand in a welcoming gesture. "What is power?"

Calya didn't notice their hand, instead smirking with lethargic intent. "Power..." She dallied as if unable to summon the word—but as she thought something sparked alive within her, logic returning to brighten the soul-link and her voice. "Power is the capacity to influence reality. One's, anyone's. For any period, and to any extent."

A most suitable answer, more substantial than the Untamed One had expected and nuanced beyond what any human language could convey—yet the soul-link flared with a depth the alchemist approved of. They dipped their head, satisfied, then glamoured to invisibility while severing the connection.

The Lady awaited on the terrace, idle, gaze lost on the silver horizon. She shivered when the wind coiled, chilling like the night to come, then returned inside, locking the glass-panelled doors to sit on the lectus. She blinked, twice, and collapsed onto her right shoulder with eyes closed; her breathing remained as shallow as before.

A Natural consequence of what humans praised as laudable mastery while unaware of the underlying exhaustion and the toll such reactions had on her body.

As she slept, a single glyph leaked from alchemist's cloak, stained in carmine concern and flickering with unease—but they waved it away, recalling The Rector's instructions: boldness enabled evolution; hers and Amok's.

The third turn in her alive elements was unavoidable.

CHAPTER 17

Egon Hold

ZARO 17TH, 17002 RE

# Dante



LEGATE OF EGON HOLD, EASTERN LEGIONS OF FIRARD

Someone knocked at the door. Thrice, and echoing with the clink of articulated plates, boots settling into the marble floor. Voices hushed, the clatter preceding two more knocks.

"Legate!" A woman's voice. Commanding, but low. "Legate!"

Dante jerked out of bed, snatched his trousers and stumbled through the archway while pulling them up. His heart pounded under his jaw, the room's pre-dawn's light spinning as he traipsed past the table—wrestling with the laces and staggering under the archway. His stomps thudded dryly as he hurried, trousers barely clinging as he stretched a hand towards the door.

It shrieked when he pulled it open, revealing a displeased Centurion Petra. There was a single torchlight in the hallway, its amber reflection cavorting over her plated pauldrons. *Armoured; heavily.* Dante forced himself to observe her armour, her weapons, the scowl on her face—at his bare chest and limited clothing, yet refraining from looking within his chambers. Her leather straps rustled as she proffered a veilwing letter. *Still sealed.*

Dante plucked it hastily, the thin paper crackling between his trembling fingers. His vision blurred as he noted the ink-stains, first skimming through the hasty handwriting before reading it:

*Departure continues uninterrupted. Southern and Central cohorts split at the edge of Silente Vale; as expected. No changes in projected path. Arrival: as scheduled.*

*From the Watcher Elixane set; those following the excess troops.* Dante crumpled the letter in his fist, the bruises on his left pumping with the tension. He studied the Centurion beyond the archway, the torchlight's reflection, the flame's warmth brightening her copper hair. *Could the letter be fake? Trying to misguide us?* His lips pressed tightly, hiding his suspicion while the echoes of sleep faded away; the paper rasped his fingertips. *No way of knowing.*

Padding distracted him; gentle, smooth, known. He glanced in its direction and into his chambers. Ilia awaited out of sight, wearing only his camisia and frowning in concern.

"*The coup? Juçe?*" She hand-signalled, urgent but quiet. "*Now?*"

Dante dipped his gaze to signal a negative, jaw clenching. The grit of cinders and soot dragged through his teeth, hot and—

*Focus.* He pressed his lips, studied the Centurion again. *Full armour, no ornaments. Too awake.* "What else?"

Petra angled her head, looked left, right, to Dante. She took one step forth, hissed: "Imperial Elixane."

The Legate closed his eyes, counting the pulses on his wrists —then fixed again in the Centurion. "When?"

"As we speak." Another whisper, barely audible.

"Understood." He stepped back, moved the door towards its frame—with measure, with restrain. It locked as he turned to Ilia. She knew, yet still he gestured, "*We move. Now.*"

Dante frowned as he turned into another hallway—where the morning's silver light slashed through the large casements, bouncing off the polished marble floor. Each streak seared into his eyes, even as he looked away. *Unsteady, but still upright.* His frown tightened at that thought; it was one of the first lessons Gora had taught him, yet now it echoed with questions that—

"It happened faster than we expected." Ilia's voice. A hint of a whisper.

*Indeed.* Dante hummed in agreement, that sole note muffled by their combined hard march. He halted past the corner, toying with the creased cuffs of his camisia to hand-signal, *"Petra was not privy to more details."*

Ilia straightened, studying him with quiet unrest. "Is *he* dividing the field? Or suspicious already?"

"Either," Dante gritted, restraining a grimace. *And either must be managed.* His swelling left hand tensed, its itchiness pumping with the reckless pulse he was learning to ignore. "We'll need to—"

He stalled when he met her eyes. Dark, unwavering. Quiet enough to surround them in a private silence. Beyond the distant rustling of regular patrols, and away from the whistling wind outside the Citadel. *Perhaps.*

Inching forward, he brushed the back of her hand. "Despatch the delegations, then… follow through. Soon."

"At once." Ilia didn't move her hand away. "Tread carefully."

The lanternlight flickered, its flame crackling above the pyre, golden-crimson tongues fanning like wings aloft. It sparked, that flame, liquid ember pouring into every metal surface in that crammed armoury. Under that light, Ciro's blonde hair seemed woven from emberbane. *Steady…* Dante pressed his lips, watching the Centurion—scowling at the lantern, thick brows framing unwavering amber eyes, jaw taut while he scratched an incipient stubble; it covered the scars below, burnt skin twisted in braids, that sweet-greasy stench still oozing from it. *Not—*

"Most battlements are secured, Legate, the legionnaires placed per your request." Ciro paused, looking away from the flame, thumbs looping through his cingulum. "I assigned my best legionnaires to guard Marshal-Magister Loera; six total, plus the Council's guards." His scars twisted alongside his grimace. "Marshal-Strategos Rachen refused the guard; he... was confident on the Council's legionnaires."

*Not unexpected.* Dante hummed, displeased. *Yet... I can't risk him. The Marshals must be extracted.* He looked down—to the floor streaked in flames, up the Centurion's melting armour—then breathed. "And the search I requested?"

Ciro's mouth vanished into a thin line, his calloused hand scratching his chin with an idle motion. "My legionnaires are already assigned. I passed the request to Centurion Rhea." His jaw tightened, throat hard as he swallowed, then added, "The Support spies; my Imperial, Su Lissalt, has hold of them."

"Understood," Dante straightened, edging towards the mouldy wooden door.

## MARSHAL-STRATEGOS, EASTERN LEGIONS OF FIRARD

Marshal-Strategos Gora Rachen stood before the opulent desk, two fingers of each hand pressed into its rim—yet they slid as he sighed, his full palms pressing into the marble. *That reckless brute will drag Firard into chaos, and his followers will cheer their own ruin.* The weight of a lifetime in service to the Emerald Legions pressed upon him, yet with every breath, Gora's aggravation towards Centurion Juçe reshaped into the need to act. *I did not rise through the ranks to see him upend all I've laboured to build.* He pushed himself from the desk, clasping his hands behind his back to glance through the open windows.

The glazed casements overpowered the office's westernmost wall, the afternoon's silver light blurring the plains beyond. *All my victories and triumphs... all shadowed by two failures: that Sittia only died days ago and Juçe still breathes.* Yet as the clouds hurried across the firmament, overcasting the landscape with streaks of shadows, the Strategos moved towards the window, watching the lands he lived to defend. *Dante has proven himself.* His lips pressed into a contained smile; the Legate's three decades of achievements—first, simulated in War Games, and later leading Firard—brought him solace. *He now stands unflinching, even before that brute.*

Gora's smile blossomed amidst the privacy of those chambers; he didn't have many years left—*The medici are clear*—and, given Juçe's rebellion, he had even fewer. Dante had seen the risk as well, offering a guard the Strategos had rejected. *I'd rather die in service to the Legions than uselessly sick.* After all, killing a Marshal of the Council was an act against Firard, and further annihilating the brute's reputation would be a victory. *Let him be the smith of his own ruin. Legends do not die by force; they die when they create martyrs who will outshine them.*

As the clouds moved again, their ominous shine tamed the Strategos' smile with one bitter truth: the Legate had chosen not to inform the Council of Juçe's rebellion. *A wise and foolish move*, he reckoned, aware of how carefully the Marshals spoke to the Legions, and how venomously they whispered in private. *Especially the Magisters, with the exception of Nagore.* But the Central Legions' Marshal-Magister was irrelevant in the grand scheme— older and sicker than Gora himself, and closer to the grave than he was now. *The other two Magisters are obstacles.* His fists tensed at that truth, forcing the Strategos to unclasp his hands. He arranged the folds of his trabea, the emerald fabric a stark reminder of his duty. *I must ensure Egon endures, even if those who departed days ago return to assist the brute.*

Decided, the Strategos ambled back towards his desk, retrieving a writing set—a polished cedar box, decorated with golden engravings. Its gleaming handle clicked as he turned it open, revealing a set of plumes, inkpots, and an assortment of papers. *Preventing the spread of Juçe's taint is paramount.* His fingers brushed the nearest stopper, the fabric shushing as he retrieved it.

"Luca?" Gora called the name into the air while finding a suitable plume.

The door clicked open, and the aide bowed. "You summoned me, Marshal-Strategos?"

"Fetch one of our veilwings, Luca. I must write to the Northern Legions." He didn't look at the girl, gaze etched on the offering of papers—he needed something discreet but resilient. "With urgency."

The aide bowed, backtracking until the door closed. Her footfalls sprinted through the hallway beyond, vanishing as the

Strategos stretched a roll over his desk. *The cruellest irony is that Dante's relief will be owed to my political rival...* There was no mirth in Gora's chuckle, no joy or respite—yet he still addressed the letter to Marshal-Strategos Arte Siere. *Alas, my duty to Firard stands before all else.*

# Juçe

The second underground was limited but useful. It had a single access—a narrow staircase—and a handful of corridors intercepted by wooden bars or collapsed walls. It had been long abandoned, but the functional cells still had working iron bars.

Juçe watched them as he marched, bootfalls steady over the bricked floor, gaze etched in the single torchlight ahead—held by a woman with auburn hair and brown eyes: Decanus Ynes. *A true Firardian.* She saluted after hearing him, angling the flames to illuminate the cell she guarded. Cleaner than the others, furnished with a single stool, and inhabited by Imperial Elixane Ritz.

Recently captured, her legs were bound to the stool, hands tied behind her back. A purple bruise spread from her right temple, blood dripping through her cheek to pool on her gag. The grimy fabric was soaked, but her eyes upheld that flat stare all Strategists favoured. *Frightened even of their own rage.*

"She won't talk," The Decanus informed, half-turning towards him. "Should we eliminate her?"

*It matters not; she'll be useful soon.* "Not yet. We must capture the Strategos first." Juçe stated, walking away while expecting to be followed. "Keep it private, and take a minimal entourage. Move by dusk and aim to capture, not to kill. That fox could be useful."

"Understood." She nodded, pausing alongside him to lock the torch into a sconce. Hesitating, she mouthed, *"Private? Do we have infiltrators?"*

The Centurion didn't answer, instead jutting his jaw towards the exit to dismiss his subordinate; his reservations were not for her to listen. *Dante. A coward even now.* She saluted, crisp, then marched without further questions. Juçe stayed amidst the dimness of that corridor. *Always a pup, never a wolf.* His fists clenched, tensing his arms while the leather of his armour stirred in protest. *He won't be able to stop this.*

# Ferro Keep

Zaro 17th, 17002 RE

# Teoda

The chambers were suitable for guests, and certainly below what Lady Teoda Seve had expected to receive. It had no terrace, just a narrow balcony and glass-panelled windows placed at the most inconvenient angle. *A chamber fit only for those I'd wish to see diminished.* Her rouged lips hinted at a smirk, incited by the memory of those she'd once hosted in that very same room... until her lectus creaked—*creaked*—forcing her to stand.

Three paces after, Teoda scowled at the regnum board under the archway. It was abandoned mid-game, and locked in a stalemate too akin to her game against Calya—forever dancing on the edge of compromise. The red carnelian stones atop it incensed her until she groaned, her slip from propriety now a secret held by that undignified room. *This shouldn't have happened! The death of the Laxalt youth could easily incriminate her, given she'd sent her General to assess such a possibility. I needed that spy-master gone... but not like this! Not now either!*

The Lady turned, a fist clenched near her navel while she gazed onto the too-narrow balcony. Its balustrades were scantly sculpted, and the lack of greenery turned it into a white desolation—especially as the noon silver light smeared all shadows into slate-grey spots.

It soothed her, nonetheless, and as her anger morphed into curiosity, the Lady recalled Calya's departure from the garden with stark precision. Tense shoulders, movement stripped; fury had embraced her like the mantle of winter. *Not performance, and enough to leave without formalities.* That image wrung a frown, and the matriarch toyed with her gown to ease herself; the balcony's view did not help. *Calya must have already suspected whoever murdered that youth*, the matriarch concluded, toying with her ruby ring. *But who?* The ring's gold band warmed as Teoda pushed it around her forefinger, the motion marking a rhythmical cadence. *Ferro Keep is heavily guarded. Slipping inside would not be straightforward; killing an aide like this, even less.* Her unwelcome frown returned, tightened by the convenience of the assassination. *Do I need to consider another enemy? But who—?*

A harsh scrape echoed down the corridor, and the world intruded into her restless isolation—a dropped tray, a slammed door, a footfall too loud. Soldiers, marching away. Teoda let the silence stretch until her anger resurfaced, just like the memory of Asier brokering the news while in the garden; striding with a mask of apprehension, General Ayere on tow. *What a farce!* She looked down at the ring, pushing it until the ruby sat perfectly centred again. *I underestimated my nephew as well.*

It was another failure she couldn't tolerate, another error that'd led her not to a stalemate, but to having her own approach overturned. *The unforeseeable.* She smiled bitterly, displeased yet not defeated; after all, that stalemate on the regnum board was only a façade. *I cannot dally; I'll need to procure the fog-weapon as they march.*

Glancing over her shoulder, Teoda waited until the corridor promised her solitude, then reached within her gown, lifting a pendant between thumb and forefinger—a slender, rectangular prism crafted in the same ink-stained, iridescent metal of the clockjays. She lowered it onto her open palm, then turned it with the thumb to press the band of a gemless silver-gold ring into its engraved side. *Now, it begins.* The prism vibrated softly, splitting into a hundred strips; they layered on each other like whimsical feathers, forming a tiny bird. *A tictail. Gorgeous!* Barely an inch long, with a flat tail and beady eyes blinking at her with a mimicry of life.

The matriarch lifted her palm, smiling at the metal bird

while showing her key-ring—the silver-gold band. It blinked again, releasing its wings and tilting its head as if waiting for a command. *The Orenians do have astonishing tools.*

"It's done," Teoda whispered ever so gently. *Limited, but useful.*

The tictail blinked again, then hopped around her palm to face the glass-panelled door. It flashed through as soon as the matriarch unlocked it, leaving her with an open palm up. She closed her fist over it, aware of what her request would imply. *It's been too long—*

Someone knocked on her door. Precise.

Teoda hastened to slip the necklace under her collar, smoothing her dress and hair with both hands. She was closing the balcony's door when the knocks insisted with the same martial precision.

"Come in," she commanded, stepping away from the window's unbecoming sight.

"My Lady," General Ayere bowed curtly, one hand holding onto the open door—then he pushed it closed. "We have cleared the Central Residence, and you are free to move through it. Your escort will accompany you."

*Could I be a target as well?* Taking her time, she glanced at the regnum board. "Was the assassin found?"

The General shook his head with the heaviness of one who understands failure.

*So many recognitions, so little talent.* It required effort to inhale with restrained aggravation, and exhale it with proper calmness —but the matriarch overcame the difficulty. *I'll need to use a spy to discover what happened; Calya won't reveal it.*

"I need to meet with my daughter; soon. Our conversation was interrupted," she informed him instead, expecting an appointment to be settled.

This time, the General straightened with the ill-gained pride of having completed a menial task. "I understand she'll meet you at dusk."

# Asier



LORD. SEVE HOUSE, SESTEL

"You passed out in your leathers, Calya!" Asier hissed, pointing one quivering finger down.

The Lady hummed in dismissal, pouring over the documents spread atop the makeshift table. "I was exhausted. Reasonably so."

*That wasn't exhaustion.* The Lord worked his jaw, mauling his frustration while pacing near the tent's closed flap; the last time, Ruria had been there as well, stunned by the clockjays. It seemed months ago, when it'd been only days since the War Games. *Even less since I found Calya under the desk. Since—*

Paper crackled, protesting as she moved one sheet to read another. Asier halted his pacing, another grievance clogging his mouth—but his lips remained sealed, his gaze on Calya. She'd changed since the day before, that tempest of self-directed contempt smothered into a flatness he'd long deemed overcome. *Another costly mistake.* He'd committed too many in little less than a week, and the consequences could be devastating. More so than they'd been two decades ago, when they were youngsters eager for retribution and not burdened by any responsibilities. *Except now, this nation depends on us.*

A hum, tilted like a question.

Asier halted, half-turning, stepping closer to the table only to watch her cousin staring at another paper—with fingers steepled under her chin, empty gaze tracing Hori's handwriting. *Prepara-tions for the travel tonight?* That enforced normalcy enraged Asier —*It can't be just facts and actions!*—and he strode towards the tent's flap. He stopped sharply, breath caught, then nudged the flap ajar with the back of his hand. The afternoon's light blinded him, but after a moment, he counted enough soldiers to temper his unrest—including the handful he'd requested to await for a possible escort. *I have to try*, he frowned, releasing the flap and approaching the table again.

"Something is happening, Calya. We let spies into our ranks. Teoda's, the Firardian's; someone's. We can't—" The words died as he swallowed, throat cluttered with the restless, reckless inner violence only powerlessness could cause. *She could be the next target!* He gaped; once, twice. *It's futile.* He knew it, but still begged, "At least accept an escort."

Calya glanced up from the papers, factual. "It won't change anything."

The Lord scowled, snarling and letting his hand fall onto his sword's hilt; it rattled, reiterating his annoyance. Calya blinked at that sound, the tiniest of frowns hinted between her brows— unnoticeable, a fragment of weary tension, an echo lost to that apathy she summoned on command. *Which never helps.* She sighed, waving the paper to pick the itinerary.

"Three guards; no more." Calya agreed at last, raising one hand, three fingers stretched. "If that would let you focus on Hori's safety."

Then she poured again into the documents, reading as if she'd hadn't upended Asier's world. *This is worse than I thought.* His chest tightened while he watched her, frozen by that agree-ment—it was yet another thing that'd changed. *She always refuses. Always.* For years Asier would insist out of duty, and she'd decline because of public perception. It was a self-imposed rule she'd adopted—at least within the walls of a city—since the Exarch had elevated her as Head of the Seve House. If she was agreeing, then the omens of war were closer than he'd assumed. *What happened!?*

Asier inhaled, struggling to avoid the pressure building on his stomach—but it dissipated when she sighed, pressing two fingers between her forehead. That gesture replaced his worries with something else entirely.

"The itinerary and the supplies seem reasonable." She lowered her hand, tucking two rebellious strands of hair behind her ear. Her cosmetics were refreshed, her presence polished—but her voice lacked inflections. "Are you ready to depart at midnight?"

*Facts and actions*, Asier groaned, aggravated by the wind whistling outside the tent, by the movement—soldiers, horses, carts—on the fields around, by the Lady Varre's subtle threats, by the Firardians who'd so carelessly managed that War Game… but most of all, aggravated by himself. The urge to protest burned in him, but he swallowed it; habit, more than will, as always. *Not now. Especially not now.*

"The Legate… confirmed that Decanus Ler will wait for us at the frontier." The Lord informed at last, left forefinger toying with the hilt of his sword. "Our spies, however, had not reached out… but they may have nothing to report outside official communications." Yet there was one concern he wouldn't hesitate to ask about—and so he hand-signalled, *"What did you discuss with Teoda?"*

For a moment, the silence flickered. In another, it thickened with Calya's smile—carrying a disdain that made his own worries seem both trivial and far more dangerous than considered.

It didn't soften when she hand-signalled, *"I'm meeting her at dusk."* Then rolled a hand, beckoning at the tent's closed flap. "Your guards may accompany me. She made a quaint threat, actually."

"What?" His lips pursed for a breath, hurrying to gesture, *"The Orenians? As you suspected?"* The blood drained from his face when she nodded in agreement. *It can't be!* "When?"

"Too soon," The Lady observed, disregarding his shock to round the makeshift table while indicating the tent's flap. "Come. We must meet with Lady Varre to review this material; we cannot afford this joint investigation to fail, and neither to warre Firard. Now less than ever." She paused, plush lips pursed. "The Exarch was restless enough about Lord Zuria guarding the Gulf; we must act in consideration."

The urge to defy her flared and so he raised a hand, insisting on another moment. "I should be there with you. Like during their last invasion."

She watched him for a moment, that deep, azure gaze—*Too flat, too restrained*—unwavering while horses neighed outside, soldiers moving so close they eclipsed the light leaking around the edges of the tent's flap. It lasted an eternity, at least for the Lord, and the words that ended that moment were just as empty.

"Protect Hori, Asier." No smiles, no gestures. Just facts and actions. "I'll handle our unwelcome neighbours myself."

# Egon Hold

## Zaro 17th, 17002 RE

# Gora

Two suns. Each a silver disc of smooth perfection drifting towards the horizon—a strand of brightness, washed teal on the ground below, a blend of hues in the firmament above. *One more dusk, and Firard still endures… though I may not see another dawn.* The Strategos straightened, taking one measured step towards the windowsill—then glanced up, tracing the palest tones blossoming from the skyline to darken into the deep plum high above. The veilwing he'd sent had vanished hours ago, albeit it displeased him not having brought his own clockjay. *It matters not; that brute will not—*

Echoes.

Boots scraped marble, a martial cadence enacted by the rattle of armour. Murmurs rolled, distant and hollow. Gora straightened, half-turning to watch the closed door—polished cedar carved with bas-relief—but the sounds vanished into the usual silence.

*Not yet, then.* Gora breathed, shoulders easing as he approached the desk. He pressed two fingers into the edge, keening his hearing—a slow grind of boot soles on marble, leather shuffling under a muffled grind. *Just my guards, then*, he reckoned, steadying the hand over the desk. He'd kept only two legionnaires, having sent the rest to assist the Legates. *It should be enough; for them, for me. If—*

Stomping; precise, but distant. Distorted by the wide corridor beyond the door. Voices; growling threats, hissing commands. Leather shrieked, shaving the polished floors.

Gora moved towards the front of his desk, facing the door. His shoulders straightened, chin held high.

One breath brought silence, but the next clanged in mayhem. A hollow clash, a barked order so resonant it was meaningless. Wood thudded, laden. The jangle of a harness lunging, lunging, lunging into the shrieking echo of a parry to clash with the steel bite of a melee that grunted and groaned, lunging, lunging into another ringing clash. A hard rasp, steel on steel, grating over voices and rimming a guttural grunt—then another and another and another. A roar—then someone slammed into the door, then somewhere else. A thunderous collapse, all noises killed by its echo, ringing, ringing, drumming alongside Gora's heartbeat, pounding, grunting, pounding, grunting, strangling a cry. Something cracked, dry, and armour collapsed into a silent aftermath.

Outside, heavy panting under the sibilant rush of hissed commands. Inside, hammering like a galloping horse rushing recklessly into the battle ahead. *Let him come, let him strike…* Gora reminded himself, shoulders straightening, left hand fisted under the weight of his trabea. *In his triumph, Juçe will craft my victory.*

The door unlocked, shrieking open to reveal the hallway. Smeared by the silver, dusky light falling from a distant corner, shadows interspersed at harsh angles. One of the Council's guards had collapsed against the wall—eyes unseeing, jaw unhinged, blood pooling beneath him. Two legionnaires towered over him, purple scarves tied on their arms. Someone else barked an order, then a figure stepped through the door.

A woman, auburn hair, brown eyes, a lifetime of violence on her face, that same purple scarf on her arm. The Strategos studied the blood spattered across her nose, then almost smirked at the irony of being considered so low as to only warrant Decanus Ynes Varus be sent to kill him. *A pawn stuck in the ranks for too many years.* In all her life, she'd left no mark upon the Legions save the void of her own insignificance—yet her presence spoke only of the brute. *A coward sending shadows in his stead to—*

The Decanus stepped forward, beckoning to the door. "Come with us, Strategos. Peacefully, if you will." She tightened her grip on the bloodied sword. "Centurion Juçe requests your presence."

*That would be unwise, however...* Gora sighed, moving to face the Decanus while making no effort to shield himself. He kept his shoulders straight, his disdain evident in his eyes while scrutinising the woman. He wouldn't risk the dishonour of being captured nor the danger it posed to Firard—and while he'd preferred the Centurion to come, Ynes would do. *She's served under him her whole life.*

"Centurion Juçe? Truly?" Gora teased at last, holding his ground. His right thumb pressed into his forefinger ring. "I would have to disagree, young one. Only someone without bravery sends proxies, and I do not answer to cowards."

Ynes ground her jaw, the leather holding her vambraces rustling as she rolled her shoulders. "I am not asking, Strategos."

Gora didn't answer, instead chancing a glance at the hallway. Three standing shadows, the dripping of blood on marble, metal shushing against fabric. *Just Ynes and three legionnaires?* He refused to smirk, albeit satisfaction eased his features—deploying such a small assault force revealed much. *Only a few follow the brute, or he trusts only a few.* He glanced back at the Decanus, taking another step to better position himself. *That is why Juçe will fail: betrayal never inspires loyalty, just further betrayal.*

"Have you forgotten rank, Decanus? You think a Decanus can command... me?" The Strategos looked at the open door— the legionnaires were moving out of his view—then back at her. "Go. Tell that coward he'll need to come himself."

Ynes snarled, fingers curling around the hilt of her sword. The crossguard creaked faintly as she dared, "Words won't save—"

Silence, abrupt like her features. Frowning, but it seemed a remnant, the rest of her face controlled, collected. *Blank except for the eyes.* Irrationally wide, etched beyond the Strategos but seeing and unseeing at the same time. She blinked, once and heavy, the motion dragging until the lids ebbed up into an unsettling expanse that saw nothing but a revelation. Gora had seen that expression before; always in soldiers and always in that fragment of a heartbeat that preceded death to usher the realisation of its inevitability. *Abject terror.*

Ynes' arm shook with restrained force, her grip so tight on the sword her knuckles had waned like her face. Metal rattled as her leg slid back, boots grinding, leather squeaking—yet her form stabilised, poised to attack.

"No choice... then." Her voice. Rough, but—

She thrust.

The sword seared, angled upwards. It pierced, tearing, splintering into burning pain, a gnawing pulsing rippling erratic, warmth leaking and leaking and leaking until Gora gasped, useless, each intake sharp, so sharp but spreading sizzling agony and the same terror he saw in her eyes—or perhaps not because he staggered, left foot forward, right hand clutching his heart. It tumbled then twitched, pumping in his neck, in his wrists, pumping but leaking until he dropped to both knees, that useless air blurring the dusk, its hazy silver light, plum lilac washing the room, washing his pain.

There was panting and Gora looked up, clutching his chest, smiling until he saw her. The Decanus, horrified. Wide-eyed with abject terror, staggering back to stare at her sword, at the blood, and the Strategos, at the wall behind. Panic, panic, panic in her eyes, in her mouth: quivering like Gora's.

She stomped back, slid on the guard's blood, caught herself on the door frame. Looked around—at the blurring shadows, at the things each carried—then ran. Stomping, capricious like Gora's pulse, unstable until it faded, faded, faded.

The Strategos looked down, weakness churning in his stomach, nausea cavorting in it. A weight pressed down upon him— *Firard's, just Firard's*—but he pushed himself to sit on his gore. Against the desk's leg. He chuckled and blood trailed from his mouth, spattering the reddening toga. Shallow, shallow intakes, sharp and searing, sharp and searing and useless—but he moved.

Left hand first, slow across his portly abdomen. Slowly, slowly—and it touched the ring on his right. *Dante will car-ry it with... honour.* It slid easily with the blood. Gora smiled, keeping it cradled in his weak palm while watching the darkening hallway.

Even by proxy, the brute had killed a Marshal. *My triumph, at last.*

# Dante

LEGATE OF EGON HOLD, EASTERN LEGIONS OF FIRARD

The corridor's engraved marble walls blurred under the dusk's silver haze—coating the walls with hues of mauve and teal, dust swirling and shimmering in the windowless corners. Under that light, the polished door—enclosing Magister Nagore's chambers—gleamed in plums and amethysts; the two Council legionnaires flanking it cast deep shadows over the wood. *Only two, but eight more within the chambers,* the Legate recalled, half-turning to dismiss their salute. His own armour—slenderer than a Centurion's—rustled with that minimal motion.

"Is the path ready?" He beckoned north. *We can't lose the Marshals…*

The oldest legionnaire squared, martial. "Yes, Legate. We'll depart soon."

"Understood." Dante took a step back, voice steady as he demanded, "For your life, protect the Marshal-Magister."

Both guards snapped at attention again, swearing their loyalty—but the Legate turned on his heels and marched into the western corner. *Find Centurion Ciro. Arrange the defence.* Voices echoed far away, the rustle of armour remarking a distant patrol. Each bootfall hammered like the throbbing on Dante's left hand—the swelling bruises pulsed, distracting, the bandages unable to cushion the leather's scraping. *Perhaps I should—*

Voices, somewhere.

Dante paused past the corner, listening. *Is someone here? Following me?* That concern lingered as the sounds faded, blending into the usual noises of the Citadel. He took two more steps, angled to glimpse ahead and behind, then pretended to fiddle with his vambraces. All around, the silence pounded with his heartbeat, with the pulse in his bruised hand, with distant footsteps; a door shrieked, the wind dancing outside. *Is Juçe… this reckless? To tackle me first?* He hesitated, then moved with measured steps, shoulders rigid under the plated pauldrons. *Or am I too pedantic to consider myself safe?* The shadows at an intersection darkened the path ahead. *No, bringing guards would've raised suspicions.*

Dante walked past it, hiding the bitter smirk tugging at the corner of his lips—but his mind steered to the throbbing itchiness of his hand, to the hollow of resentment filling within. *A fraud, my father.* He frowned, jaw tensing and grinding, a hollow opening within him. *I'm not fighting Juçe nor the coup, but creating the conditions for both to destroy each other*, he reminded himself, even as the words echoed empty in—

Armour, clattering. Muffled voices, distorted by the echo of the marble walls, by the distance, by his heartbeat galloping again. It burnt, each sound, like his hand—but it quieted again, the silence latent yet lurking.

One thought invaded him. Own, but echoing like an unexpected intuition. *The Strategos; I should visit him.*

Dante's scowl tightened, shoulders tensing even as he steered towards Gora's office. The pathways were clear, unmarred, those sections seldom used. *No guards, no patrols*, he noticed, picking his pace, footfalls hammering, hammering, hammering as he hurried once more. Striding; fast, but not running. *What happened? Why is this empty?* His jaw tensed until his teeth ground, but he kept the pace, moving, turning a corner, taking the empty hallways. *Gora had sent my guards away, but—*

That need again. His own voice in his own mind, but foreign somehow. *Hurry! To Gora!*

Footsteps rattled in the distance. One pair, clear but rushing to echo down a staircase. *Assassins?* Dante broke into a trot, turned the corner and sped into a run.

The wind swirled, stinging his face, iron-sharp and acrid. *No, no, no!* He sprinted when the breeze urged him, warm and humid, pungent streaks sweeping his face as he drifted then darted across a narrow tranche to leap through the stairs in pairs. He slid on the last step, but his hands gripped the marble before his jaw slammed into the floor, burning veins scorching his left hand, right knee aching and pulsing, numb but pounding even as he regained footing and dashed again. The stench was raw, coppery but sour, half-sweat, half-warm, dooming like the urgency churning in his stomach.

Blood. A trail.

Spattered in the hallway, escaping into the staircase. Right corner, one body. A woman face-down, armour-plates askew, gore drying atop. Wood splinters on the floor ahead. Dante ran, slid into the corner, saw the opulent door. Half-open, the dusk dying inside. A guard crumpled near it, armour dented, blood all around.

Dante rushed, leapt over that pool, landed past the archway and slid. He held onto the door, blinking at the shimmering silver-lilac sky, the horizon flickering cerulean in tandem with his heart. It pounded as he panted, that moonlit-cyan light washing the room until breathing hissed somewhere, faint, around the desk—

"No!" He staggered. One step, two steps. "No!"

The Strategos. Collapsed on the floor and resting against the desk, one leg bent, toga drenched ruby, sweaty face with lips parted in shallow breaths while holding his chest even as blood gushed between the ribs. Dante staggered again, stumbled and fell to his knees to crawl closer, closer, closer. *Too late.* His hands hovered over his mentor's body—*Too late!*—watching the stained trabea, the unstable heaving on his chest, the fingers twitching—

A hand, on his wrist. Firm but weak.

Dante looked at Gora's fist, then up, up, up to the pale green eyes, watching him, delighted. *Proud?* His quivering mouth was smiling, pleased. *Why?* No remorse in his eyes, no regrets, no sorrow. Just satisfaction and pain, relief and agony and the shallow, shallow intakes. *Why? Why!?*

"Who... did—?" The Legate gasped, stuttered, one hand motionless in that grip, the other hovering uselessly. "Juçe?"

The Strategos blinked once and slow—but tensed his quivering grip, Dante's armour straining under it. "I've watched you act..." He coughed, holding him, gripping, steady even in death. "—with wisdom, and w-with... stability as y-your cause."

*No, no, no.* Misplaced respect, misplaced trust.

Dante's was not wisdom, no honour. Just a lie.

He shook his head, stuttering a rebuttal, but his mouth wouldn't open and the words wouldn't form because his pulse was beating on his legs, on his forearms, under his jaw. It pumped with every jagged gasp, constricted by the armour, by the death lurking in that room.

The Strategos chuckled or coughed, spattering blood still with that smile, with that relief even as blood leaked down the corner of his mouth. "Do not... let... the L-legions falter..." His grip tightened, quivering, strained. "Duty, always."

Lies, all lies. All lies because Dante was a fool coveting one goal, but the rest was a lie—a respectable lie, but a lie still. No duty, no honour, no service. Just a pretence carried through the years, just a mirage as fake as his service to Firard, just a means to a goal except that Gora's respect was misplaced, ill-timed, wasted on a coward to grant the wrong recognition, the wrong success.

Dante stuttered like a boy, wide-eyed and shaking even as Gora smiled with his eyes, so calm, so collected even when bleeding out, even when the Legate gaped with too many lies locked in his throat. He tried to swallow but drowned in them, in desperation, in anguish, in the unstoppable need to correct that perception and the awareness he wouldn't do it because letting Gora die while believing a lie was better than spoiling his deathbed with the truth, because the childish foolishness that—

A cough, the Strategos'.

The old man moaned, head tilted, the gold beads tipping his hair brimming carmine, ruby-drenched like death. His breathing hastened, sprinted, stammering alongside Dante's ill-formed words—no reason, no logic, just everything there, the stench, the colour, the misery, the agony, the lies—

"For thirty... y-years you've... s-served F—" Coughing, panting. Blood, lethal, out, gushing. Hoarse and jagged, a whisper, "Firard. Now..." Movement, on Gora's hands, twisting Dante's. It did not matter, just the eyes—the trust in there, the faith, the conviction, the lie, the lie! "Now it's... y-your turn, Dante."

A thud. Blood dripping, dripping. Dripping.

Silence. Silence?

Death. Death. Death.

No jagged breathing, no whispers, no fabric rustling, no sounds on the hallway, no breathing to tamper. Just the pounding inside Dante's mind, hammering the lies, the deception, the bitter façade he built around honour and duty and service and victory—not for Firard, never for Firard. For himself, but not for recognition, not for power. Just for learning, learning, learning and surpassing everything in hopes that one day he'd be enough for Sittia and Juçe although he knew he'd never be. Just for them and no one else, but she was dead and he'd tear the nation apart because—

Dante looked up. The shadows were darkening, plum, cobalt, blurring into ink. His eyes cut from corner to corner as his vision narrowed, churning at the edges while annihilation towered near—pressing on his chest, on his head, doom haunting him, destruction prowling closer, closer, unavoidable, unstoppable. He gasped, jagged; eyes chasing the shadows. Everything was danger.

"No..." The Legate. Shutting his eyes, aware of his grief. "Steady, steady..."

In a moment, nothing, just the creak of leather, his hand fisting—then amidst that darkness Gora's eyes, open but curled at the edges as if he still saw the future and approved of it. To Gora's smile, so fulfilled, so... contented. Then down and down to Gora's hand—resting on Dante's knee to entrust the legacy of a lifetime of service to nothing but a lie.

Death. Death. Death.

The room, the night, the blood all around, the blood on him, the itching on his left hand, that sweet-sour air biting sharp, shallow, pointless. No breathing, no mumbling, just grief, just grief and anger and pain and agony and that unstoppable death devouring everything around him like liquid fire, ruthless, ravenous, collapsing the world to cinders and soaring to the sky like wings made of flames to—

Dante quavered, gasping that barren, sweet-sour air. One realisation strangled him.

He couldn't move.

Danger. It towered near, unnameable but absolute. It existed, and it skulked in the shadows of that dusk, prowling near, lurking closer.

Death. It was coming for him.

# ❖ Berserk & Dante ❖

The soul-link was an abyss of revolving nightmares, all swelling and swerving, all swirling voracious, all pitch-blackness like Dante's eyes—wide open in terror but motionless, throttled by the alchemist twice his height. Single-handed, they held the human's self aloft while the storm's soaring darkness cavorted around him, wailing when his fingers locked around Berserk's wrist—nails raking but finding no give.

Amidst them, gold. Flickering in the storm, four sunlit strands, emerging from Dante to entwine the golden thread Berserk had seen early that day—now lancing into the gales to reel forth a single foundational recollection.

One memory, created a lifetime ago, but harbouring the outset of Dante's lie. One memory, the target of Berserk's second incision: the inception of that wrong desire the alchemist ought to soul-murder.

Hope. The most futile variant of desire.

Its edge emerged from the eddies of shadows—a myriad honeyglow flakes whirling like sunflares from between the inky maelstrom. They swirled around each other, tar and radiance, shadows and gilded flares—some smothering, the others incandescent, but all spinning, all coruscating in a battle between a past that refused to be forgotten and a present too unstable to resist it.

Within the stutter of a heartbeat, past and present curved towards each other like stars collapsing. Dante's self morphed in tandem, shredding years as the soul-link burst aureate—a few months, first, then one year, two, his scars faded, his features smoothed. A lattice of flickering streams shot like a starfall of liquid gold that coiled ten years ago, waiting for Dante's self to adjust then speeding again, rolling until he was just a little one —trampled on Berserk's hand, and fusing that golden past— thirty years ago—into the nightmarish present.

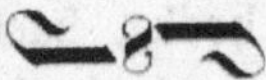

Sunrays in the darkness. In the floor, streaks, coming up at him. Dante's arms shot forward but pain rippled through his hands, sharp in the wrists, hard in his elbows before the stone bit into his nose and chin, wet and warm and sticky. *Run!* He tried to move, but his stretched arms couldn't grip the marble, couldn't push him up because the sunrays spun, vision narrowing, something ringing in his ear, bootfalls coming, death towering—

A poleyn pressed into his upper back, cold steel digging past his grimy tunic. Dante gasped, drew in blood, snorted it again— but Juçe's knee dug under his bone, right arm numbing while he clutched at the floor, grabbing nothing but wanting to crawl, to escape even though he knew the punishment was due. *Couldn't defeat that boy.* His heartbeat pounded on his temples and wrists, shaking with a trapped whine. *Failing the pre-test; what an embarr—!*

His eyes widened when his father's armour creaked, metal chafing while a shadow cast over him—then all air left him. His teeth ground but he screamed and there was no sound, just the floor pounding under him, pounding his breathing, with his heart. He was falling, but that knee on his back pressed down, pinned him down as pain blazed from his torso, through his neck, from his head. *My… f-fault. I'm not a fight—*

The armour rattled again, something wooden swung—and he knew it was coming, coming through his left, down, down,

down with a dry crack that stabbed under his arm, its sharpness cutting up through his chest. Buzzing in his ear, blood in his mouth, in his nose, in the floor before him.

"Useless." Juçe's voice; truthful, too truthful. "A failure, a shame."

*I'm a failure, a shame.* Movement. *I'm a fail—*

Wood creaked again. Pain burst on his ribs.

Dante screamed, eyes shut because the room was spinning, the floor warm and sticky, his chest seizing but trapped, crushed between pain and his father's knee, that iron-sweet taste in his mouth, wetness on his cheeks, back convulsing because he needed to curl and hide and shield himself from the pain because everything was pain. *My fault, my fault.*

Wood rattled against the floor, his breathing jagged over the marble, his tongue too sleek, his heart slamming into his chest —a gauntleted hand. Juçe's. Clutching the base of his neck, pinning him down from the left. *Think something, anything!* Metal grated, leather stirred. A hum—a *hum*—and that buzzing in his ear, wailing as his father flipped him around. *No, please! I—!*

Those eyes. Steel-clear and cold. So, so cold.

Juçe was kneeling astride, right fist around his neck, the left rising—

Acid. Burning Dante's stomach, creeping through his mouth, bile and blood leaking as he gasped, not enough air to scream, that hollow ache lost in ragged gasps, sips so short, air so sharp, silence in his chest then galloping reckless as the bootfalls walked away—farther as he gasped, farther and farther.

Silence.

Just his breathing, jagged. Just his heartbeat and his pain.

Silence.

Dante didn't move, stayed on his back. Too dizzy, too tired, all dark around, all throbbing, all pounding.

He blinked. From that angle, the room was upside down, the sunrays rising towards the book atop his bed. Dante couldn't move, couldn't reach for it. *My journal.* He smiled, lips dry and crusted, fingers twitching as if he were flipping the pages. *Regnum strategies, first.* He recalled the sketches, a dozen pages, then the scribbles about a siege, and depictions of Legions' formations. *Good at strategy, not fighting. A coward.* It didn't matter, he kept watching that journal, kept twitching his fingers, so proud of the knowledge he'd hoarded in it. *The same the Strategists learn.* Trialling for the Strategists had always tempted him; the chance of succeeding even more—but he soured, still motionless, pain throbbing from his left, hunger creeping on him. *If I could show father and mother that I'm not an embarrassment...*

Dante's eyes widened, recalling what he'd scribbled only months ago. *The Meridian of Existence.* He shut his eyes, forcing himself to remember what he'd read in that old and shabby book if only to ignore the hollow ache within him. One idea surged from the pain. *It sounds impossible, but if I l-learn... if I become a Strategos, I could... lead Firard to the Meridian, and—*

Hope.

It shone like the sunrays that blinded him. He smiled, wide, blood spotting his broken lips. *If I lead Firard to the Meridian, Father and Mother could finally be proud of me.* A plan shaped over the pain. To study in secret, to distract the Decanii, to sign for the Strategists trials.

Currents of gold spun and shredded, a whirl of amber-light flickering across the soul-link while Berserk held little-Dante aloft by the throat—yet that past-self smiled like in that memory, dreaming, *hoping* while golden filaments coiled in the hastening gusts, twisting vertiginous to anchor on him whenever a new thought, a new idea, a new emotion was born.

So naïve and childish, that lattice of alive elements, that hope later hidden under honour, ambition, and duty to Firard.

So foolish, so embarrassing—yet still yearned for.

Amidst that windstorm of aureate flakes, Berserk tightened their grip while regarding little-Dante with the patience of an executioner awaiting the moment to deliver the sentence: a soul-murder, because the hope born at that moment was worthless to them. It obscured Dante's thirst for learning, while deadening his emotions so he wouldn't endure the misery of knowing that what he longed for was the one thing forever denied to him. It fostered his regret for having justified with duty what he'd done for that longing—even when the pursuit of knowledge tolerated no limits, no principles. Hope was a useless alive element, doomed to be obliterated to craft a suitable candidate to alchemist—one able to innovate and discover that new pathway towards the Meridian of Existence.

In the span of a second heartbeat, currents of gold and tar spun around the alchemist and their prey, spinning, sweeping, whirling faster and faster while the Dragon One unfurled their wings, right hand raised, claws sharpened and poised to attack, ruby eyes etched on their target. They grinned, hauling little-Dante—then speared his heart, clutching the golden strand within to rip it free in one savage arc.

Little-Dante howled, whole body curling as he clung to Berserk's wrist, his scream splitting the soul-link. The strand of hope frayed, dissolving into foiled leaves—yet a whirl of amber-light enveloped the surviving strands still tied to him. He convulsed, choking, resisting even as he changed with every gasp, his murdered hope leaving a gap the other filaments hurried to redress by reweaving that foundational recollection.

One maimed memory, soul-murdered into a hopeless moment.

One memory, treasured still because every edge of Dante's new reality was still based on it.

The soul-link buckled while the surviving strands entwined again, its void of despair colliding into the aureate flakes—all breaking and bending into nightmares unravelled, all revolving, all twirling faster and faster. Little-Dante screamed again when the thread recoiled into a vertiginous ascent like a spear recalled from the past into the present—and the Dragon One crouched, the boy still held aloft, wings pulsing before they soared to push the Legate's corrected self across a lifetime of mended memories.

From that angle, the room was upside down, the sunrays rising towards the book atop his bed. Dante couldn't move, couldn't reach for it. *My journal.* He smiled, lips dry and crusted, fingers twitching as if he were flipping the pages. *Regnum strategies, first.* He recalled the sketches, a dozen pages, then scribbles about a siege, and depictions of Legions' formations. *Good at strategy, not fighting. A... what?*

Something was missing.

Dante squinted, but the stabbing pierced him, pain spreading through his chest and smothering the air—but he kept watching that journal, fingers twitching as if flipping pages, proud of the knowledge he'd hoarded in them. *The same the Strategists learn.* Trialling for the Strategists had always tempted him; the chance of succeeding even more. *If I could... could...*

He stalled, confused by the pain in his chest, by the sunrays spilling into the room, spinning like golden flakes at the corners of his vision. His chest hurt, his ribs, his throat, everything throbbed while he forced himself to recall what he'd scribbled only months ago. *The Meridian of Existence.* Dante shut his eyes, ignoring the golden flares to remember that old and shabby book. *It sounds impossible, but... perhaps...* The floor beneath seemed to blend down into a storm that purled with pain, with agony, with air so sharp that it cut through him with stabbing agony. One idea blossomed, bright and steady. *If I l-learn... if I become a Strategos, I could... lead Firard to the Meridian!*

It teased him—the chance to learn, the knowledge it'd require, the experience he'd need. A plan shaped over the pain. To study in secret, to distract his father, to sign for the Strategists trials.

With that idea, Dante fell into the pain, honeyglow flaring and drowning between the lashes of dark, spinning in that room like translucent specks that faded into nightness until his feet were dangling again. His tunic crumpled under his nape, the glimmer of the signet ring rushing down, down, down—into his temple, his jaw, his cheekbone. *Hypocrite.* Blood seared his face, the ring burning with each strike: temple, jaw, shoulder, chest. Nothing beneath, wrath above, a streak of sunlight cutting through shadow, gold purling when Dante grinned—angry but proud—spitting blood into his father's face, that mark like wings of fire. *I'll learn. I'll lead Firard.*

He fell, etched on those cold, silver eyes.

He fell. Down and down and down like the laurel crown crushed beneath the Centurion's foot, smothered by his resentment and splintering into golden sparks searing sunlight into the marble floor. *My father doesn't matter.* Dante pressed his lips, remembering his crushing victory, that unseen strategy, the recognition of Legate Gora Rachen. *A mentor. I must learn from him.*

The world spun around him, unfurling golden.

It whirled, faster, faster, leaking liquid gold, fire crackling in the distance while the air turned sour—half sweet, half stone-dust, daylight swinging past Liminal Harbour and bringing that stench: of charred flesh, of burning hair. Impossible to scourge from his clothes, from his nose—but Dante learnt from it, learnt from the unquenchable emberbane, from the other Strategists, from the Presyans, from those around. He learnt and led the nation to another victory. *It was duty.*

He was Legate, and one step closer to the Meridian—but the balance he'd achieved hurtled away months after, upset by too many political interests. It faded, searing incandescent wings into his vision with blinding pain, yet darkening the world into the choking haze of Ílun Fort.

Underneath it, Dante chased Ilia, forearms bracing his head while a blazing scythe swung across the sky, bleeding into embers, a firefall spilling alight before he hurried to the crenellations. *An opportunity. A challenge.* Legate Dante Praeto exhaled, refusing the acrid, blazing air and grabbing the spyglass—then thought of the future, of the invasion that would come, of the cost he ought to pay to reach his goal, of everything else he needed to learn before that happened even if the price was known already. *Blood is the cost of long-term stability. Stability leads to the Meridian.* The world burned like paper in the flame of a blazing lantern—but the recognition arrived from the Marshals, from the Emerald Council, from his peers, under that daylight that seared the sky until everything in its path was undone.

It coiled, the world, with the gold of those mines, with the liquid fire raining upon them—but he was victorious, the owner of a bastion, the one who wrote history, and the one who'll lead Firard to the Meridian of Existence.

Berserk's wings flared wide to slow their vertiginous ascent, sparks flickering into reality as they alighted amidst the slowing gales—then hauled Dante's self high, watching that image. He was no longer a boy, instead resembling his body: with the same pain in his eyes, the same heaving chest, the same tremor on his fists. The surviving golden strands anchored on them, the remnants of the murdered hope evanescing like aureate flakes in the echoes of that windstorm.

The alchemist strode through the soul-link, deliberate, pressing, looming closer—then released Dante's self.

At first, he stood before the kneeling body—but after a heartbeat his image ebbed into pain, faltering into nothingness by a mind that wouldn't accept its new reality. In the office, the Legate gasped for air but gathered a void, his mind narrowing by the weight of that absence, darkness swelling, gold fading while the maimed memories fought the remnants of the truth, neither surrendering and both subsisting because somewhere—deep into the abyss of his unawareness—a shard of hope had survived.

Berserk snarled at the human, frowning while his body convulsed, still kneeling near his mentor's body—right fist clenched tightly, left open and grabbing nothing. His eyes were wide, dots of inky terror unaware of the advent of light, blind to the alchemist and reality itself, his gasps shallow because the air he breathed was hollow.

"No. No!" Berserk growled, aggravation morphing into desperation. "You can't die, Legate! Not until you've reached the Mer—!"

Power. Surpassing the boundaries of the known.

Unfathomable as to dominate existence while plunging from the uncharted beyond to pierce the fading soul-link and invade it with someone's will. Myriads of cobalt strands anchored into reality, weaving a passageway from the horizon of eternity—then pulled, folding the universe, merging distances, and pouring that inexhaustible power into the office.

At the edge of realisation Berserk reformed their Integrity Shield, forgetting about the human—but that power shattered it like dross cooled from the inside, sparks of fire scattering into defeated smoke. The Dragon One sought to recoil, to somehow shield themselves—yet again their will was smothered, that power mind-latching them from beyond the shroud of nowness to prevent all movement and hold them like a helpless observer.

It was as titillating as terrifying, the risk to cease to exist; as grim as death was to humans. The Dragon One quieted, dreading whatever was to come while wishing it'd happen if only to witness the incomprehensible.

*'Fear and desire, a rampant conflict, even for alchemists...'* A voice mind-whispered through those cobalt strands. *'Deserved, because one mission was laid before you, Berserk, and you fiddled with it until your negligence invited the ruin that brings me here.'*

The office twisted, blending into the night that fell through the windows—where the horizon was a gleamtrace of agony, wrapped in itself while those cobalt threads folded the universe. They warped time, defying all rationality with the power only the four-transfigured alchemist held: the leader of The Orders.

Insanity, to watch The Rector fold the universe, to be mind-latched and subjugated to their will, to feel—for once, and after two-hundred millennia of existence—powerless again.

Yet those cobalt threads tightened, each strand blazing aegean until a semblance of the caster's silhouette sunk from above. Hooded with a starlight-ridden mantle and cloaked by six world-piercing blades rotating in a ring.

So threatening it was. So incognisable.

*'You have flirted with the worst possible outcome—the death of a unique mind and the loss of knowledge—yet you did nothing outside the bounds of the foreseeable.'* That mind-voice was suffocating. Power embodied in a hundred voices—some screaming, other whispering, all smothering. *'This human cannot die, Dragon One. Evolution depends on him: his, yours, and The Orders' alike.'*

The universe howled when The Rector folded it tighter, their figure moving to stretch a hand and graze Dante's head. Thousands of alchemical glyphs flowed from that arm, passing through its translucent fingers to shape droplets of liquid glass. They flowed towards the Legate's self like an opalescent river that coated every surviving strand, every new memory, every fragment of his maimed identity with an unbreakable shimmer. Chaos whirled within that coat, a war against the self where the echoes of what he'd been refused the hopeless version—yet with every droplet his heartbeat stabilised, the soul-link easing into plain darkness.

'*Your missions remains,*' The Rector stated, easing the threads, unfolding the universe and the time upon which it ran. '*Train Dante. Only then he'll enlighten you with another pathway towards the Meridian of Existence.*'

As that voice faded, the cobalt threads stretched and dissolved, the horizon beyond the window unwrapping itself while time rushed back into the office. The night cascaded into it, plums and azures melding into the shadows only to be slashed with Dante's heavy panting—scared, but no longer teetering on death.

The Dragon One watched him, so stunned they didn't reforge their Integrity Shield, wings fanned open and ushered into stillness.

Insanity, to have been rendered helpless, to have witnessed The Rector's power as they defied all laws of Soul alchemy to protect one feeble, time-framed being. All while using a soul-skill Berserk had never seen before.

Insanity.

Insanity!

The Legate fell forward, left hand slamming into the floor and stalling the fall, pain bursting from the swollen knuckles, agony piercing through him. He gasped, shallow, rapid, the air thick like tar, the office whirling chaotic and torn at the edges.

Everything was agony. Within him anguish, without him torture, an abyss of nothingness engulfing him whole, misery unravelling with every breath and every scream he couldn't howl.

His eyes darted to the body near, to Gora's pleased smile, to the peace in those features—then to his bloodied fists. A grimace curled his lips, his mouth not enough to breathe that hollow, barren air—not even as he scraped his cuirass, gauntlets chafing into metal, rattling, faster, finding nothing, scraping louder, his chest ablaze, the air like pugios slashing his throat and cutting down while he gaped, choking on nothing but terror, gagging on pain and loss.

Loss. Grief.

It throttled him from that darkness, ringing with an echo of pain, an emptiness that sneaked through his shoulders while a vacuum swelled within his chest to bring a hopeless desolation condemned to be endlessly so. *Where... is it?* His eyes widened, clawing at the void, seeing nothing while his chest heaved that hollow thin air, gaping but breathing nothing. *What... is missing?* The certainty was infuriating; the unknowable lack harmful even if he didn't know why or what at all.

The air dragged through Dante's throat like liquid fire, half sweet, half stone-dust, his pleas twisted in his throat, murdered by the echoing silence. He mumbled, stuttering and panting, hands writhing, left clutching the air because that missing something was there, not there, but there in the dark somewhere.

*Must... find it.* Dante lurched forth, pressed both fists into the blood and pushed himself up, legs leaden and twitching, world tilting and tumbling as he scampered forth. His numb legs woke in fire, every step a clash between stone and lightning. *Find it. Somewhere.* It was his body but it wasn't, and yet he forced it through the red marred with dishevelled footprints—then past the door, lurching into the corridor swallowed by the night. *Where is it?* He staggered into a jerky run, not his gait but all he had, legs half-dead but sprinting, drifting into a corner, shoulder slamming into the wall before he ran again. *What is it?*

A breeze slammed into his face, warm and inviting, but the

Legate ran through the Citadel's corridors, on and on and on—past the corners, through the shadows, under the moonlight, up the staircases. *Where? What?* Then down and up again, blood in some corners, wood splinters in other, grime and dirt and metal shards but no corpses, no trails of whatever he was missing, no clues, no hints. *What!? WHAT!?* the need to run, to escape, to find what was missing, to search for it although that vacuum came from within and he carried it as he ran like a dead weight never to be reawaken nor freed. It was maddening, that lack, that breeze he chased, the misery he dragged, the grief, the grief!

Dante halted, his breath wrenching out in raw, heaving gasps—and his armour rattled with every laboured intake, lungs lurching for air even though he stood in an open hallway.

"What is it?" His panting hushed, muffled by the rustle of patrols down in the Hold. "What is it!?"

His hands fisted at his sides, leather stirring as he pumped twice—then rose them, quavering, shaking as he felt a pressure within the right fist. Blood smeared in his palm, one thin trail slipping under the leather straps. *Please, no...* He guessed what could lay there, yet he still feared it more than the emptiness assailing him—that lost thing that would never come, not even as he unfurled the fingers one by one to discover what he'd guessed laid there.

A ring. Bloodied. Gold band crowned with an emerald, a fili-gree veilwing setting it in place. The Strategos' ring. Not on Gora's fingers, but on Dante's hand.

"No... no, no, no..." Dante's voice, hoarse, hoarser still. Broken, so broken.

He watched it as if the ring could reawaken his mentor—but as the zephyr coiled in that terrace, as his breathing eased and his heartbeat smoothed into a trot, that gnawing emptiness slipped. Slowly, from the confines of that desperation to the realm of logic. He kept staring at it, disregarding the patrols down below, ignoring the flash of warm torchlight and the boot-falls moving through the Citadel's hallways. He stared at it, finally understanding what he felt.

*Grief.* For the Strategos who'd served Firard and died by the hand of a hypocrite, for the one who'd taught Dante and given him what he needed to serve. *Trust, recognition, knowledge.* He brushed his thumb across the emerald, remembering what Gora had taught: *Endure what is given.* It didn't quell that corroding abyss within him, for the Strategos' death had left a scar. *But I must act on it.* He knew what his duty was—*I must remain steady and protect the Hold. I planned for it*—even if it was just the means to reach a great, more elusive goal: the Meridian of Existence, that zenith between struggle and stability.

His shoulders unwound at that thought, tensing anew when a cornua blasted somewhere north. *An attack call?* He frowned, looking up at the starry sky to gauge how many hours had passed, then staggered towards the guardrail and looked beyond. Torchlight was dotting the ramparts, silhouettes fighting on its bricked path. *I can't falter, not now.*

The cornua blasted anew—then two more followed—one echoing the attack, the other calling for a defence. *No past battle brought stakes like this.* Legate Dante Praeto stepped back from the guardrail, tucking Gora's ring into the pouch at his cingulum. That emptiness—that grief—still haunted him as he passed through the archway, but he brushed it aside. *The wound lingers, but I must walk on,* he reminded himself, hastening into a trot—he needed to find Centurion Ciro and lead the Hold's defence as planned.

Firard stood on the horizon of chaos, at the edge between collapse and renewed cohesion where the omens of war could not be ignored. To meet the challenge, to learn, to improve—it was the pathway towards the Meridian of Existence. He would find it; that was undeniable. It did not matter when nor how. Just that he would find it.

# Ferro Keep

Zaro 17ᵗʰ, 17002 RE

# Teoda

FORMER HEAD OF THE SEVE HOUSE, SESTEL

The Central Residence was immaculate, each bas-relief spotless, each windowsill polished—but the corridors were shrouded in a dusky penury, so that walking under the wavering lanternlight of her escort was a treacherous endeavour. *How unfitting!* Lady Teoda Seve endured such conditions, lifting the hem of her dress to step precisely, eyes narrowed with the vain hope of seeing more than silhouettes. Yet as she halted at another intersection, her features soothed with the promise of better light. *Finally!*

It was a long corridor, with its leftmost wall covered in an exquisite high-relief depicting the assembly of the Grand Conclave; the rightmost, however, hosted an array of glazed casements offering a sweeping view of the south. Its light bathed Calya's profile, shimmering on the metal decorations of her leather armours; when she turned, her caramel hair seemed even more golden.

"Join me; the view is breathtaking." Her hand beckoned towards the casements, but her eyes had already settled on the landscape.

*Something is wrong.* Teoda almost frowned, stalled her own reaction, then blinked twice when her eyes—still reticent after the dimness she'd endured—noticed the three soldiers awaiting at the opposite intersection. *An escort? I wonder how Asier convinced her...* Two men and a woman, all dressed for war. *Carrying the act,*

*I see*; Teoda pressed her lips, waving her own armoured quartet to stay at the opposite intersection alongside their aggravating lantern. *Or does this mean there is truly another enemy?*

The Lady took more time than needed to walk ahead, pretending to be absorbed by the view while covertly assessing her own daughter. *I haven't seen her like this before...* There was something on her; a certainty, perhaps, reinforced by how that armour enhanced her regal stance. *Does Calya know something I don't?* It was a possibility, and it haunted Teoda as she halted close enough for confidence, yet not so near as to tempt danger.

When she turned, the view was as breathtaking as promised.

From the right rose the Peaks of Nadir, their jagged summits interrupted by the Gorge's harsh entrance only to continue southbound. Those edges eclipsed the dying sunlight, silver rays flaring to subdue the firmament with muted lilacs and silvers—hues that simmered into oblivion towards their left, where indigo and plum overtook the world to blur the edge of the Claw's Fold into a mote of darkness. Between them, the southern horizon was a silver seamlight.

Lady Teoda exhaled, enjoying that moment—even as the day's fatigue settled on her. *I should've taken a proper meal.* Her regret was short-lived, muffled by her own distrust: after her sudden incarceration, eating would've been akin to inviting death-by-poison to her doorstep. *And only drinking water wasn't enough*, she lamented, disregarding her weakness to steady her features. There was a plan to execute, information to gather, and another warning to deliver.

"My dear, I am terribly sorry about your aide," Teoda whispered at last, ever so gently.

Calya's acknowledgement was artful—blending sufficient mourning with ample restraint to be proper. "We have reinforced the guard," she explained, glancing at the lantern-carrying guards. "...but I trust you'd appreciate the need for additional protection."

*Is she exhausted?* The idea lingered as the matriarch studied Calya's immaculate presentation—just as usual, yet slightly duller; the change was too imperceptible to be noticed by others. *Except I trained her.* That realisation incensed the same concern haunting Teoda since the previous day: the involvement of an unexpected rival. *Clearly, the assassination on the eve of the butcher's departure has taken a toll.*

"My dear, have your enemies... come too close?" Her offer faded into a whisper as Teoda placed a hand on her daughter's arm, features eased with measured concern. "I could assist you... shall you provide what was requested."

Silence lurked while Calya stepped back to be rid of her hand. The impassivity of her azure eyes startled Teoda, yet she leveraged that natural gesture to feign shock—curling her fingers near the chest, one brow arched in appropriate hurt. *Does she know... something?* Her heart skipped a beat, pressed by too many considerations. *I've committed too many mistakes as of late.* Not admitting it would be foolish—

"What did the Orenian offer you?" Calya spoke too low, too firmly; enough for that question to remain private.

*How did she find out?* Teoda forced a smile, twisting her features into an innocent doubt that would neither deceive nor admit. The matriarch knew that question was likely not founded in certainty—but laid out as a trap to force her to reveal the truth. *She heard me doing it too many times.* Teoda almost smirked bitterly, the regret of having created such a pragmatic and keen daughter was almost unbearable. *I'll remediate this soon.*

"What an imaginative inference, child!" The Lady chuckled instead, covering her mouth with a hand. "However did you arrive at it?"

Calya's only answer was a hint of a smile—the centre of her lips pressed as if sealing a taunt, a glimmer of knowledge curling the corners. *She knows.* It was the only feasible conclusion, remarked by the carefulness guiding her to glance into the dusk: with measure, with certainty, with a threat held between her hands as she clasped them together.

Teoda indulged her in that silence, watching the southern horizon while her mind wandered north. *Could the troops at Vega Fortress have informed her?* A strangeness invaded the matriarch—suspicion, mistrust, scepticism. *Something isn't right.* Her intuition was seldom wrong, and so she glanced at her own guards —*Still holding that vexing lantern*—then at Calya's. They bore the cultivated indifference of soldiers whose vigilance was itself a performance. *A listless parody of service*, she lamented, turning again to watch the sunset—but the hungry hollowness of her stomach lurched from below her. *I should've eaten something!*

"The fog-weapon," Calya whispered in a masterful impersonation of thoughtfulness. "I understand you want this at—"

Silence.

The words tumbled forth, delayed and meaningless. "Earliest... research... expected..."

Teoda pressed her clasped hands into her stomach, asking... something, but her voice did not react, gaze lost in the darkening firmament. *No... no!* Understanding flooded her—and she prodded her neck with trembling hands, feeling the tictail's necklace. *Was the prism... poisoned?* Her eyes widened in concern —to be disposed of so easily, to lose that perennial regnum against Calya, to have the unforeseeable turned against her yet again. *Breathe.* She tried, hard, but the air was insufficient and the world muffled. *Did the Orenians... betray me?*

One step. Back. Erratic, impossible as the feeling within her. *Not them.*

Another step, weak; too weak. The marble floor seemed an expanse of lilac-washed whiteness, a silver pond darkening at the edges.

A third step. Teoda looked up.

Calya; frowning, nostrils flaring. Her eyes widened. *Shock? What a... perfect... performance.* That bitterness again, for she knew it was her fault. *My f-fault... having created h-her.* Not fear; it couldn't be. Just hands, feigning a quiver, pressed into her mouth. *Performance, just... p-performance.*

A woman howled. The words... weren't there.

*Her.* Calya's profile—facing the guards. *It was... her.*

The world narrowed. *How? Did she... manage it?* That silver pond deepened. *When?*

Slow. Too slow, the pond's approach. *How... fitting.*

The air, so limited.

# Calya

## HEAD OF THE SEVE HOUSE, SESTEL

"What an imaginative inference, child!" Teoda chuckled, covering her mouth with a hand. "However did you arrive at it?"

It was too sharp; too stiff in the tilt of her tone. *Nervousness?* Calya knew what it meant. *Not an answer; a deflection.* She waited for three breaths—counting each, forcing her countenance to remain impassive—then smiled. Slowly and methodically; with that curl on her lips that teased of knowledge and had so often upset her mother. *What else are you hiding?* That gesture was enough to confirm her suspicions, since Teoda arched her brows in the feigned hurt that only surfaced when no other strategy had worked. *Treachery always suited you, mother.* It augured more political unrest that desired, forcing the Lady to steady her smile not to grimace at the evidence of another failure. *Why didn't I discover this earlier? Is Amok… also involved in this?* Smothered anger haunted her as she faced the casements.

The view beyond was breathtaking. The silver-lilac sky in the west dying as the indigo-plum of the east swallowed it whole, the horizon flickering cerulean and silver over the Sanguine Sea. *More beautiful than watching the dusk on the Victoria Ascendens.* It reminded her of the year she'd sailed to the Sideral River with Lord Zuria, before the famous Accords and during a time with as much political unrest as now—yet that longing evanesced as her gaze settled in the sharp entrance of Furia Gorge.

*Two or three days before Asier returns*, she estimated, and if Orenos invaded before that, one clockjay would be enough for her to command Vega Fortress' response. After that, travelling north would be unavoidable. *But can the fog truly be a weapon?* While Calya had suspected it, Teoda's certainty implied a belief —even when it seemed far-fetched. *Nothing is, after meeting the alchemists.*

"The fog-weapon," she pressed through a whisper, allowing her thoughtfulness to leak into her tone. *Whatever the Orenians are planning for it is as dangerous as their source of knowledge.* "I understand that you requested it at the earliest convenience, yet our research has neither confirmed nor denied its existence." She lingered, unclasping her hands and gazing into the Residence's lower terraces. "Does this mean I can expect you to share your knowledge of..."

The words withered, forgotten while Calya angled her body towards Teoda, gaze settling on her pale blue eyes. Widening, stunned. *Too much given my question.* The Lady took half a step forward when the matriarch blinked, lips parting—*Quivering?*— although speechless. Her hand rose, manicured fingertips brushing the neck, teasing a delicate silver chain. *Her neck is so... tense?* So pale, so taut. *Is she—?*

Silence. In the world, in that hallway, in Teoda's face, in Calya's mind.

Stunned, with disbelief, and dragged in the listless, lethargic loop of her gaze—roaming down the matriarch's stance, observing her legs, noticing their quiver, soaring to the chest, seeing the ragged pattern of her breathing, watching her arms, then up to the face ever so pale, those rouged lips bright like fresh blood.

Silence. Everywhere in that slowing, tumbling world—but pierced by a string trebling unyielding, right to left, on Calya's mind because the hallway was silent, silent, silent.

Tight, too tight as well. Like Teoda's trembling mouth, gaping at a loss for words, strangled by the same devastating fury blazing in her eyes and burning Calya's world. It curled from the edges like paper aflame, collapsing inwards, contorting into a new reality, impossible as it was. *No, no, no!*

Silence, still trebling with that string unyielding, but admitting one murmur.

"Guards..." Calya's, tumbling weakly as she glanced at the quartet. Spread up, hands on hilts, lantern discarded. "Guards! A healer!" Sharp, sharp, sharp like the three steps she reeled back, getting away, away from the Teoda, away from the danger, from the consequences, from reality. Away, enough, to yell at her own guards. "Bring healers! Now!!"

Orders, reverberating.

Steps, erratic, echoing over marble.

Calya snapped towards Teoda, a loose caramel curl tickling her chin, impotence lurking like towering fear, circling like a wrathful predator that coiled, coiled, coiled tighter and tighter until it strangled her.

*No, it can't be.* But it could, and Calya frowned, breathing enraged as Teoda sipped air, little bits, just sip, sip, sip while that chest—*Always so proud*—twitched like the fingers, dusky silverlight flaring on her polished nails—*So sharp; on my arms, on my neck.* They grabbed the air but Calya didn't move, instead watching those nails sinking on Teoda's own lips and chin, those little sips again, faster, faster, faster like the hammering heartbeat pounding the world until it crumpled into the handful of paces Calya wanted to close but didn't dare because the matriarch was a monster, a big towering shadow, a memory of a memory that consumed and consumed until she became the source of fear, the cause of anger, the target of cold-blooded plans meant to push her away but never kill her because that monster couldn't die, wouldn't die, never die.

*No.* Calya knew it, but couldn't accept it. *No, no. She can't die.* Teoda's face furrowed into a frown, stunned, that erratic gaze boring into Calya. *Who poisoned her?*

Silence, but beneath that string trebling unyielding rumbled one soothing murmur.

'*Poison? What a reductionist idea!*' Detached; so detached, Amok's voice.

Rumbling and rolling, through her senses and beyond, while Calya pressed her hands into her mouth. That scream; it built up within her. Raging; powerless. So pitifully powerless.

'It is another demonstration of Soul alchemy.' Amok went on. On and on and on. Unreasonable, unwanted, unstoppable. 'A preclude, which I developed myself, and cont—'

Despair; Calya's. It howled as she turned towards her guards —One missing?—demanding a healer, wailing for help to come. They stilled, her guards, eyes wide, mouths moving, no words. The others, three—not four—stances wide, faces pale, lantern smothered in the floor.

Teoda looked down—at the floor, with disbelief. Calya followed that movement, lost in the shadow escaping the dusky penumbra. It moved, Teoda stepped back, forth, back. Faltered. Fell.

"Mother!!" Another scream, swallowed by that silence. Calya's, but not Calya's.

Run. A demand. Run! Sheer instinct. RUN! Never thought of.

Calya ran, stumbling forth. The guards run, startled, armour rattling. She slipped, someone growled, she traipsed, steadied, ran again.

Her arms looped around Teoda's armpits, her knees nailed into the floor, the matriarch spread over her lap. Shadows all around, the guards, hesitant, hands on hilts, the dusk shining silver, that trebling unyielding, the world burning in the corners like paper enduring the flames.

Teoda's eyes, above all. So furious, so wrathful, so unforgiving. Burning Calya, searing that stare, twisting all amidst that shallow pale blue.

'The preclude helps the mind forget about body functions.' Amok again, in her mind, with their preternatural calm. She didn't want to hear, but they spoke nonetheless. 'It's an alchemical mimicry of a failing body. A stroke, in this case.'

"No, no, no…" Desperation, like the hurrying race of rushing armies eager to clash. "No, no, no!"

Desperation, in that silence, hands hovering over Teoda, quivering as fast as her sips, sips, sips, the air so futile, Calya knew, because she sipped as well and the world narrowed, darkened, silent. Words, words, words, they clogged her throat, fighting against that precious air, tumbling in her mind like bookshelves falling one by one onto the chaos of that floor where the air didn't reach and the darkness would soon swallow them all.

*'I can hold her there, between life and death, as long as her body resists…'* Amok, Amok, Amok. Why, why, why, why. *'As another demonstration, my Lady.'*

Teoda's mouth quivered, slow, methodical. Calya leant, one arm beneath the matriarch's shoulders, ear edging closer, closer, close to that mouth, close to those tremors.

"I did n-not… eat… nor drink. H-how?" Teoda whispered, panting, dying. Sharp, so sharp and sibilant. "So… el-legant." Blades, blades all of them.

One gasp, then her hand clutched Calya's hovering one, nails sinking, sinking, sinking. *It hurts; mama, it hurts.*

"How d-did…" A question, a statement, Teoda's whisper. "How… did y-you kill… me?"

*No, no, no, no.* Calya gaped, so small, so shaken with her head shifting in tandem. No, left, no, right, no, left, no, right. Teoda's nails hurting, hurting so much. Calya looked down, to her mama's chest—panting, panting, sipping that useless air.

"Bring the healers!!!" It had to be her own voice. Calya's.

But it couldn't be. Teoda couldn't die; the monster wouldn't die. It was eternal like that string trebling unyielding and the world enduring although it burnt at the edges. Eternal because Calya's pain was eternal. Muffled, muffled, but immortal and indestructible.

*No, no, no, no.* Desperation warmed the air, lurking like towering fear, circling and circling, tighter and tighter because she'd caused it anyways although she'd never wished for it, always planning around, always pushing her mama away while hoping there would be one time in which mama approved of her, even as she did everything, everything, everything in her power to have power, power, power because through it there wouldn't be pain, there would be safety but it only brought pain and death and—

*'Perfect… p-perfect fear…'* Teoda's voice? *'What… a p-performance…'*

No thoughts, although they smothered her. Just Teoda's wide

eyes, just her sips. Her mouth—ear closer, no whispers, no blades. *How?*

'*A soul-link.*' Amok, Amok, Amok. Power, with power. '*Because her thoughts about you are incredibly compelling. You must listen.*'

Cold. On her spine, tickling down. On her mind, chilling, but never quelling that burning pain seared by Teoda's eyes.

'*What a-a waste... to have t-taught h-her... so well...*' Teoda blinked, slow. Fire burning within, breathing stalling. The nails, unhooked, slipping. Clutching her chest. She didn't speak, but her thought-voice was there. '*I should've... killed h-her...*' Truth; it felt like truth, those words. '*—l-long ago... h-how weak... of m-me.*'

Calya blinked, slow; breathing stalling. Her hand, bruised.

Fear, enveloping, clinging, dragging. Wrath, raining like blades, hurting, hurting, spilling no blood. Powerlessness, throttling, murdering. Pounding, pounding, down, down, down, down like an anchor that caught her in the nothingness of that dusk.

'*Why... c-couldn't she be... meek and p-pretty...*' Teoda, sipping faster, clutching her chest. Shadows over her. '*I wanted... a tool. Not her.*'

Hands. On Calya's shoulder, gauntleted and pulling her back, pulling her apart. White, robes, ghostly all; pouring over Teoda's throbbing chest, one white-robed arm embracing her shoulders.

It mattered not. It did not. Just mama's eyes. Just her eyes.

Burning with hatred.

# Amok & Calya

Death bled into the hallway through every ray of silver sunlight —drowning behind the mountains and drowning again in the penumbra within those walls. Amok stood in its midst, glamoured to invisibility, two soul-links active, one preclude consuming the matriarch's life.

To the humans, narrow-minded and locked in reality, that moment was tempered with tension. Two handfuls of guards, all startled, some holding flickering lanterns. A quartet of healers poured over the dying matriarch, whispering to each other with haste. Two more held Calya, murmuring reassuring words she didn't hear. She was kneeling on the floor, cheeks tear-stricken, eyes wide and quivering, mouth trembling with those sips, sips, sips of air.

In the soul-link, there was utmost chaos—and it leaked into the hallway, corroding the dusky penumbra with the throes of the abyss emerging within Calya's mind.

Black all around, except for the pale blue eyes aflame with hatred.

Black all around, while Calya's soul-link twisted. Contorting in itself, bleeding desperation into the noir world, a suffocating windstorm of woven shadows spinning at its fringes—voracious, vertiginous, more abyssal than absolute obscurity, more dreadful than the wailing whirling between each gust.

*Mama can't die!* Howled, flashing in and out of the dark.

*Monster! Get away from me!* Frenzied. Near, gone, near, gone.

*I needed a mother, not you!* Screaming, but slipping away. Swelling again, orbiting anguish, sinking down.

*Please, love me, mama!* Misery, a carousel, returning, leaving, returning, leaving. Never forgotten.

They bellowed, all of them, in that storm and through the remains of the frosted wall—shards, uneven and sharp. Purling in the gusts, slashing the shadows, sinking and surging, sinking and surging alongside the mirrors-knives. Those poured down into Calya's body, into Calya's mind—sitting in the core of that storm, tendrils of shadows curling through her limbs and anchoring her into that misery, into that wrath, into the disbelief and the belief, into the awareness of what was but couldn't be, because her logic twisted alongside the emotions never dealt with.

The mirror-knives downpoured, blades flashing with the pale blue flames of the burning hatred in Teoda's eyes. In the hundreds, in the thousands, in the myriads of myriads amidst three heartbeats that extended to infinity.

Amok endured at the centre of that turmoil, their fraying cloak revolving in the mayhem, their glyphs spiralling around them but flashing blood-like crimson. Some shivered with a dozen uncertainties, others warned of impending collapse, of dooming destruction, positing alternatives—to conclude the preclude and sever the matriarch's soul-link—if only because their prey may shatter before the third turn.

A maelstrom like no other, that gale swallowing Calya's reason, those whorls of umbra, spinning gusts of shades.

She writhed, gasping, sipping, sipping, sipping air—*Just like mama*—while her mind crumpled because the tar she breathed was slick and suffocating. Amidst those midnight jaws, Amok's glyphs burst again, pounding like her heart, hurrying, hurrying, hurrying because the storm was gnawing inward, chewing the mildness of its core, folding closer and closer—

The alchemist severed Teoda's soul-link, releasing the preclude for the matriarch to die on her own.

For a breath in that void, that black maw of twisted alive elements awaited, suspended.

It sheared after a heartbeat, gusts of shadows peeling and imploding while the windstorm drank its own horizon. It stripped everything away while fear bedevilled reason, desperation feeding hatred only for despair to return tenfold—splintered into a hundred flavours, each with a hundred causes. It unravelled reality, twisting perception, slanting senses, and shimmering with the underlying gold reflection of never-forgotten memories.

"Impressive," Amok muttered, taking a step back if only to watch that moment unfold.

Threads, myriads of myriads, emerging from the pain and the misery howling in that windstorm. It was sublime, dawning golden, furious, desperate, and whipping from the remnants of that gale of shadows to weave around Calya.

A privilege like no other, to watch that woman fold reality—bridging time, pulling the past closer, closer, brighter, louder, harsher, deadlier, truer.

Not a soul-weave, and neither Amok's alchemy. Just the desperation of a mind haunted by the deafening echoes of long-past agony that would never be forgotten and was, again, present.

Gold purled around the alchemist and their prey, avid threads coiling rapacious, unfurling the past into the present. It shimmered aureate, that molten lattice, twisting like that vertiginous windstorm only to halt decades ago.

A knoll emerged, woven from golden filaments and shaping into young-Calya. She was curled in on herself, knees pressed into the floor, belly pressed into her knees; her hands shivered, fingers quivering apart, fingernails sinking into her forehead to shield, to shelter, so pointless. Teoda screamed above her before the wind snapped, snapped, snapped in a prelude of pain. It burnt after every scream, searing into her curled back, over and over, shrieking, agony, howling, torture, burning, blazing, branding.

Amok didn't see the matriarch, didn't hear her words—for the memory was fragmented yet woven around the hatred, the shrieking, and the blazing agony. The golden threads holding it whirled further back—into the past of that past, into a dinner and a comment and a ploy perhaps undone.

Burning, blazing, branding, that agony and torture. Entwined into the present through an alive element—a feeling—truthful at that moment: the terror of dying, the nearing of death.

It unspooled, not forgotten but ever-present while the golden threads whirled voracious, spiralling through time, furling deeper into Calya's mind to abolish the present and bring forth another memory.

Dark and small, so dark and small. A closet, wooden and tight, moist and old. The locked door throbbed, throbbed, throbbed while violence leaked through the seamlights in between, rage pounding at little-Calya's door. She tucked herself smaller, so little she was, so flexible, so curled onto herself her chin rested atop her bruised knees.

It hammered, hammered, hammered and red splotched her skin, swallowed as she coughed her own blood again. Her nose was still bleeding, she wiped it on her knees, she pressed her forehead into it—pounding, pounding, pounding until golden light bathed her and little-Calya looked up, up, up to the light eclipsed by the monster bringing death.

Death, death, death and the terror of dying, so certain, so truthful.

That gold marked a halo around Teoda's silhouette, time spinning, revolving volatile, the lattice tightening around Calya and Amok, time unwinding time and time again.

The next fragment was honey-light blurred, diffused by age, but smeared across decades after its origin. The littlest-Calya, caligae pattering over onyx-marble floors, hunger twisting her insides, headache twisting her thoughts. She walked still, the littlest-Calya, patter-patter patter-patter as she looked up. Mama walked ahead, slightly shorter than papa, both whispering with shoulders square, smiles on their faces, rigid, too rigid.

*Mama, papa...* A thought, but it startled the Untamed One as it rolled around, spiralling with golden desire, reeling with longing—enough for it to come again and again and again. *Hug me. Love me.* It had been a need; it was, and remained so. *Please.* So cruelly strong, so demanding, so bare and unmet.

Amok noticed it, wrote it with their glyphs for future use—but the corridor stretched and the golden threads unravelled again, molten light leashing into the present, leaking absolute.

That voice was actual-Calya's, albeit she mumbled, just like she'd done before. "Mother... mother..."

Each word burnished like jewellery, each word coiled back, back, back into the past. Amok followed it, let it carry them albeit it eddied and slung, back and forth, back and forth, from the past into the present and from the present to the past again, flashes golden, glow-woven filaments, glimmering and pulling, folding time. That gleaming path interlaced two memories, too similar, too related.

One, with little-Calya tucked under the bed-sheets, warm and safe, dawn simmering between the fabric's weave, each silver ray feeding her fear, feeding, feeding it because after dawn came mama, and mama terrified her. *I don't want her to come.*

Another, with not-so-little-Calya, neck stretched, chin up, gaze down to read. Half the words she knew, the rest were mere shapes and sketches she couldn't fathom. Not-so-little-Calya pretended to read and read, nodding here and there, there and here because mama did it and so it was good. *If I'm good, mama will love me.*

The searing light returned, washing the memories in golden, amber-glow oscillating around them, tight circles. Near, gone, near, gone—around Calya and Amok, around Amok and Calya.

Teoda's thought-voice clung to those spiralling, closing orbits. '*What a-a waste... to have t-taught h-her... so well...*'

The same cadence, back and forth, back and forth. '*Why... c-couldn't she be... meek and p-pretty...*'

That pendulum endured, its spiral narrowing but still scorching light—around Calya and Amok, around Amok and Calya. Time all around, starlight golden, lattices of amber streams weaving two more memories.

One, young-Calya, watching her own quivering hands, blood dripping between her fingers, blood smearing her palms, blood warming her cheek. Teoda had pressed it into her, the blood of her friend, her murdered friend, the fiend who'd brought agony and pain with her death. There were tears, but they wouldn't wash the pooling blood. There was rage and grief, and they wove together into a rope that became a noose.

Teoda's voice howled then, in and out of the light. '*I should've… killed h-her l-long ago… h-how weak… of me.*'

Two, less-young-Calya and young-Asier, hidden in a forgotten room, their plans never forgotten, their schemes enacted after. It dawned, that memory, and its filigree flung with relief and grief, such a honey-glow, such an amber-like harmony. Relief because power will soon be hers, grief for what had been lost, relief for the new dawn to come, grief for still yearning to be as perfect as Teoda had wanted.

'*I wanted… a tool. Not her.*' Shadows leaked into the golden light, strands weaving darkness into the past's dawn.

*I was wrong.* Calya's thought, a new truth. *I was wrong.*

Amok heard it through her mind, the present piercing the past, rendering it illogical, inconsistent, forever flawed.

It was caustic and it corroded the golden threads, black splotches eroding those glowing filaments, obscuring all senses, the abyss unfolding. Black gnawing the dawn into night, into the abyss of realisation and the cruelty of the present reality. One by one, those threads snapped, that gold diffusing as the past slipped back into oblivion but leaving its echoes in the present.

They fell, Calya and Amok, Amok and Calya—spinning, whirling, into the noir world of the present soul-link.

Three heartbeats after the healer's arrival, three more heartbeats within that golden past. One more heartbeat to fall into the present and be swarmed by the mantle of hollowness woven of shadows, the violence of an ever-present howl billowing somewhere in that breathless blackness.

Black all around, except for the pale blue eyes aflame with hatred.

Black all around, because actual-Calya's *self* was kneeling over her inky-trail while two shadows anchored her down. Each was exquisitely defined, brought into the present from the past, thus threatening to become the present.

Little-Calya, so small and bruised, her chest pressed into actual-Calya's right arm, her little arms wrapping tighter and tighter. She was fear embodied, shame defined, weakness portrayed. *Mama never loved me.* Her thought-speech spiralled, vulnerable, vacant, an anchor that advanced, receded, advanced, receded. *I need mama's love.*

Young-Calya, taller, bonier, more bruised. Her hands clutched Calya's left arm, marking purple-green traces, all tender, all quivering with resentment, all outrage and raging bitterness. *I killed her.* Her thought-whisper purled, so sibilant while exhaling, inhaling, exhaling, inhaling. *I wanted her gone, but not truly gone.*

The Untamed One stepped back and back again, their fraying cloak leaking more glyphs, writing it all. Every alive element, every thought, emotion, pattern, and attitude; every anchor, every past-source, every current-echo, every hope made undone. It was superb, transcending time, that agony of yore brought back by a mind teetering on collapse because pain was what it was because of what it'd been and remained, unyielding, unbroken.

Amidst the looming, lurking maws of nightness the Untamed One's glyphs soared again, whirling around their fraying cloak and weaving inky tendrils—heavy and hollow like Calya's misery, flashing crimson, her desolation unfolding rapidly, too rapidly. The alchemist's eyes narrowed, facetted cerulean gems refracting all possibilities to lock on The Rector's teachings: to dare, to witness the turn of her alive elements, to enable evolution.

Amok craved it, the knowledge, the evolution. They waited, eager to—

"No…" Little-Actual-Calya, shamefully afraid.

In that hallway, the alchemist saw the healers—sitting on their heels, shoulders sagging.

"No!" Young-Actual-Calya, furious, with disbelief, with grief and relief.

In that hallway, the alchemist saw the healers again—shaking their heads, pressing fists into mouths, faces hidden in quivering palms.

"MAMA!!" Actual-Calya, screaming afraid, howling angrily.

She wrestled away from those holding her back and crawled ahead, knees grinding raw against the floor to skitter past Amok's swirling glyphs; they stepped away from her graceless, frantic advance watching as she collapsed into flailing, then flailing to lift her dead mama into her arms.

Calya cried; the three of them cried. Little, young, adult, with loveless fear, with lonely fury, with that pounding, pounding of her heart and the sips, sips, sips of useless air.

The soul-link crumpled at that rhythm. With each bellow of her mouth—narrowing, narrowing, narrowing, that abyss clasping shut, pounding, pounding, that blackness draping with demise, auguring the pressure of unbeing while pounding, closer, pounding narrower, pounding—

"No!" Amok, their glyphs, so hurried, so ruby.

Inky tendrils soared, lashing into the fringes of that folding blackness, holding its falling fringes and reshaping its shade. From those threads a last shape emerged—precursor-Calya, woven from the shadows, black all around, and oppressive like only a truth long known and long ignored can be. Heavy, hollow, so hollow.

She walked to actual-Calya, leant to peer at the dead mother —then tapped the little-one's head. With unwavering sincerity, her thoughts said: *Stop whining; you are weak.* Words, like blades —and they severed little-Calya until that memory became flakes of shadows. Swirling away, away, away.

The precursor turned, scowled at the young with a fury colder than the nothingness beyond the universe. With unshakable firmness, her thoughts said: *You're a fool; a danger to yourself.* More words, more blades—and they mauled young-Calya until that memory became strips of burning paper, charcoal, burnt, branded. Blazing away, away, away.

When the pair remained, Amok circled them both—precursor and actual, the latter kneeling, silent tears tumbling onto Teoda's cheek, the former squeezing her shoulders. With irrefutable truthfulness, she said: *Of course mother didn't love me. I'm unlovable.*

"No..." Actual-Calya, sobbing.

One word: no. It had one meaning for the humans around, a thousand for the alchemist and their prey, locked within that soul-link.

*Unlovable.* Precursor-Calya again, never again, because she blended with actual-Calya. So thoroughly, so deeply, so fully that the next whisper was just Calya's thoughts; hers, only hers. *Not even my own mother could love me.*

That truth bellowed in the abyssal darkness, in the night of reason, at the midnight of desolation when the howls wove reality and each gust clawed perception, stripping reality, peeling emotions until they became logic: factual, analytical, but no longer felt. She couldn't, Calya couldn't, for her symphony of despair etched in the very fabric of existence. Calya couldn't, for her inner war against her *self* was the key to the third turn of her alive elements.

Apathy, unyielding. Reassembling the crystal wall until it became a sphere enclosing Calya, frosted satin blurring the emotional chaos outside, where the storm raged in the nightness of her desperation, and logic—*life*—could not endure.

The Untamed One watched it, driven into stunned stillness, eyes wide open even while that frosted-glass sphere peeled away the soul-link. Strip by strip, dissolving the connection, strip by strip, dismissing Amok's interference, strip by strip while leaking into Calya's self. Drops, drops, drops of frosted glass, expelling the alchemist but not before they saw the most protective embrace a human mind could appeal to.

The rim of absolute stillness.

A semblance of an Integrity Shield protecting Calya's self.

An impossible feat, for a human to craft such protection, for a time-framed being to understand the permanence of identity, to be so acquainted with the fear to cease and the desire to exist. A magnificent outcome, even if shocking.

Shocking.

Shocking.

Like the quiet, hushed tension of that hallway. Desolate even when a dozen guards had arrived, and that handful of healers could only blame age.

The Untamed One watched them, fascinated.

The air thickened, halved by her panting, both cold and warm depending on who moved. The lights were dim, star-silver shimmering from the window, amber-bronze flickering from the lanterns held by too many guards.

*Teoda is gone.* Lady Calya Seve lifted her right hand—*Bleeding? I'll need healers*—then swiped it through the matriarch's eyes, closing that lifeless expanse of pale blue. She took a moment to watch her, then moved the old woman onto the floor and arranged her pale, wrinkled hands atop her breathless chest. Clasped, and pressed down with Calya's own.

There was an echo of pain, the awareness that she should grieve, and the understanding of what her face should enact for everyone to believe her. *Yet still… there is something else.* The Lady clasped a hand onto her chest, the leathers stirring as she did so. Pressure, a vacuum; on her chest, on her stomach, like hollowness eternally black and empty. *Not hunger*, she knew, but something else entirely.

Emptiness. Pure emptiness.

*Amok?* Calya thought that name as clearly as she could, gaze etched in the matriarch. There was no answer and so she sat on her heels, watching the remnants. *Amok?*

Silence, but the alchemist thought-answered at last. *'My Lady.'*

Their voice had that same formal quality it always had, detached and didactic but almost… hesitating. A quaint detail, one Calya noted before thinking, *What are you after, Amok?*

The silence lingered, unfathomable. Long enough for a healer to place a hand on her shoulders, for another to utter meaningless sorrows for her loss. Silence, just silence—and the pretence of grief, the frown that was fatiguing her forehead, the quivery lips she ought to maintain for long enough. Her hands trembled on their own.

*Amok? What are you after?* Calya asked again, when the healers were about to move the matriarch's body.

There was hesitation, but the alchemist's voice rumbled into her mind. *'You. To train you as an alchemist.'*

Calya nodded, to the healers to allow them to move the old woman, and to the alchemist to acknowledge them.

It was a useful revelation, one hint amidst a myriad of others she could leverage, one principle to carve a path forward, one shard of influence wrestled from the absurd. To remain as she'd been—afraid, furious—had invited ruin and abject agony. To remain as she was—ignorant, vulnerable—was to ensure obliteration.

These were just the omens of war, a declaration not to be denied.

To live, to endure, to evolve—it was her only goal. She would survive. No matter the destruction, no matter the pain. She would survive.

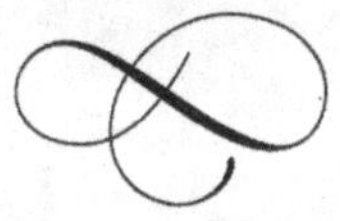

# Author's Notes

Thank you so much for reading *The Omens of War* and for your interest in the Author's Notes.

This is certainly the most complex book that I've written so far, so I wanted to use these Notes to touch upon some of the ideas I leveraged—a brief behind-the-scenes, if you will. It won't be in-depth but I hope you find this interesting!

**PS: There is a freebie at the end.**

## ABOUT THE WORLD-BUILDING...

Something I love about secondary worlds is the ability to imagine political systems that, while somewhat grounded, may not be fully possible in the real world. That is how Firard and Sestel came to be.

Firard is loosely based in the Ancient Roman culture. In particular, I wanted to leverage some Roman-esque values (i.e., honour, service, Rome above all), philosophies (such as Stoicism), and settings (a war-oriented nation) to explore larger concepts, such as the Meridian of Existence. However, given that Firard has prevailed for over 3,000 years, I speculated freely in terms of technology—for example adding steel, and even assuming the adoption of camisias and trousers.

Sestel, on the contrary, is a functionally stratified nobility—

Nobles don't have territories but functions spread across the entire land. Calya explains most of these in Chapter 6, but my goal was to create an equilibrium in which every House is fundamental to the nation and could completely disrupt its functioning.

From there, the understanding of geopolitics and the conditions for war is based on Thucydides—the old historian who documented the Peloponnesian War while also famously asking: *Why do states go to war?* What I took from him is the interplay of interest, fear, and honour, and how everything is done to maintain their equilibrium. Dante makes an explicit reference to this in Chapter 5.

I did use some specific historical moments to inspire book events—such as the Retreat and Calya's return of the misplaced legionnaires. However, I wasn't aiming to copy history, just to somewhat "reproduce" that interplay of fear, honour, and interest in my fantasy setting.

## ABOUT ALCHEMY AND ITS PHILOSOPHY...

Berserk's Meridian of Existence is based on Aristotles' Golden Mean. I was reading his works and asked myself: *What if the alchemists tried to enforce the golden mean onto an entire world?* That's how the concept originated. The answer Calya gives to the librarian (in Chapter 7) could very well be seen as another pathway into it—except it's a realpolitik one.

Does that mean there 'versions' of the Meridian? For sure! Dante still has to propose his approach, so I won't spoil what his answer will be.

We also have Amok and Naturalism... alongside all the so-called adjustments they do to it. If Naturalism comes across as contradictory, I declare myself guilty because it was thoroughly intended. Naturalism is important but, thematically, I want to later explore the things we do to "fit" a reality into a set of principles, and how those principles can become someone's identity.

After all, identity is a fundamental theme in this series, and *The Omens of War* is paving the way for a more in-depth discussion on the evolution of one's identity—as Jean-Paul Sartre said, *existence precedes essence* because we come to life first, and then construct a narrative that defines who we are to give meaning to our actions and existence. Memory, it's malleability, and its impact over time were important here, and will continue to be.

## YET AT THE CORE OF ALL, THIS IS ABOUT DANTE AND CALYA.

Beyond all the philosophy and politics, there was one theme—recurrent in my writing—that I wanted to bring to the forefront: depictions of trauma, and in particular, PTSD (Post Traumatic Stress Disorder) and CPTSD (Complex Post-Traumatic Stress Disorder).

For those who don't know, CPTSD is a condition that develops after prolonged, repeated trauma, often in childhood. It was recognised by the WHO on its International Classification of Diseases (ICD-11), but it's not yet part of the DSM-5—the standard classification of mental disorders used by mental health professionals in the United States. CPTSD has some commonalities with PTSD but one key difference is how each experiences flashbacks. For the former, flashbacks are emotional-driven: the person feels/behaves as they felt/behaved when they were a child... which does not mean they re-experience the situation like it happens during intense PTSD flashbacks.

Allow me to be straightforward: I wrote Calya as a CPTSD survivor, using Schema Therapy to model her maladaptive coping mechanisms—which Amok sees as her 'shadows'. Dante, on the contrary, has both CPTSD and PTSD. I did quite a bit of research into this, but please be aware that while I aimed to work on solid ground, I'm not a psychologist.

That said, my exploration of trauma was just the tip of the iceberg.

Truth be told, I wanted to bring awareness to one point: survivors can appear highly functional—and may even be mistaken for completely healthy adults... and that's only because the brain goes to great lengths to ensure survival. Especially when high-performance is, since childhood, associated with physical safety (as it is hinted it was for Calya and Dante). Yet many coping strategies that emerge under trauma are adaptive in the moment but become maladaptive over time. From the outside, these strategies may look like "mental gymnastics," but in reality, they are developmentally child-like solutions to situations no child should ever have had to face.

In that vein, Calya's quest for power is just her "solution" to not be powerless (because powerlessness implies unsafety), and Dante's search for the Meridian is just a child's attempt to do something big enough that'll finally earn his parents' respect. These 'goals' are not rooted in *adult* logic, because childhood-trauma responses rarely are—they reflect the child's attempt to survive in an overwhelming environment and linger into adulthood.

Food for thought, most certainly.

## WHERE DO WE GO NOW?

*The Omens of War* is just the first book in *The Records of the Orders* series. Hopefully, as you may have noted from this entry, the series brings twisted politics, unusual takes in grey morality, eldritch alchemists obsessed with knowledge, and a deep-dive into psychological horror in a fantasy setting.

If this is up your alley, then I have good news!

There is a prequel novella, *The Genesis of Change* already available. *Genesis* follows Élan and Verve during the mission that led to the events of the Interludes. It's written fully from their point-of-view, and so the humans in that story... well, they are just a means to the alchemists' goals. That novella also visits a place that doesn't really follow the laws of physics: The Towers of The Orders. It's far more philosophical, but it'll give you a good intro to alchemy as a 'magic system.'

Better yet, the ebook of *The Genesis of Change* is free for my newsletter subscribers. I write monthly (or every other month), with something pretty unconventional: thematic secrets of this series, deep-dives into the meaning/imagery, reading lists of non-fiction work I found interesting, and even discussing symbology and clues.

If that piqued your interest, you can **sign up for my news-letter** and get a free copy of *The Genesis of Change* from here:

That said, I honestly hope *The Omens of War* interested you. Thank you so much for reading.

Livia~

# Acknowledgments

I'm deeply thankful to every person who helped, directly or indirectly, shape this book.

To my partner in life and developmental editor, Fernando, for helping me shape not only this book but the universe of The Orders. You're always there to hear me ramble, you give me hope, you give me courage, and you help me polish this through edits. No language is enough to convey how grateful I am.

To my newsletter subscribers and eARC readers. You've been incredibly supportive and encouraging. Being able to share this world I'm writing about with you is a little dream come true.

To all my fellow authors and reviewers who read the ARC, provided blurbs and/or reviews, and made the launch of this book an incredibly exciting moment.

Livia J. Elliot writes dark and thematic fantasy, with an emphasis on character development and meaningful themes—especially struggle, control, identity, self-perception, and bias. She's currently releasing two series: *Records of the Orders* (cosmic horror fantasy) and *Tales of the Bookshelves* (psychological fairy tales for adults).

She is also the lead writer of *Unearthed Stories*, an app publishing interactive fantasy and sci-fi for adult readers. On the side, Livia also hosts the podcast Books Undone, featuring literary analyses of speculative fiction.

If you enjoyed *The Omens of War* and want to learn more about the universe, receive exclusive sneak peeks, and a free prequel novella, then **sign up for Livia's newsletter** using the QR code below, or filling the form at https://liviajelliot.com/newsletter